Also by *New York Times* **bestselling author**

BRENDA JOYCE

and HQN Books

BRENDA JOYCE

Deadly VOWS

HQN™

Recycling programs
for this product may
not exist in your area.

ISBN-13: 978-0-373-77551-4

DEADLY VOWS

For Lucy Childs,
For reading every proposal and every manuscript
(except the paranormals), for all those
words of encouragement and support,
for all the times you played interference,
all the times you calmed me down and, of course,
for being my number one Deadly fan!
Thank you!

Deadly
VOWS

CHAPTER ONE

New York City
Saturday, June 28, 1902
10:00 a.m.

IT WAS HER wedding day.

Francesca Cahill was nearly in disbelief. Three weeks ago, her fiancé had been in prison, under arrest for the murder of the woman who had briefly been his mistress. Three weeks ago, her father had been dead set against Calder Hart in every possible way, and especially against Calder's engagement to his daughter. Three weeks ago, New York society had been thrilled over the apparent downfall of one of its most wealthy and powerful denizens.

Francesca stared at her flushed reflection in the mirror. Hart was notorious, and his reputation had been established long before his mistress was found murdered. He openly flaunted the accepted conventions and mores of the day. His behavior was self-indulgent and often scandalous, his propensity for divorcées and married women was well-known and his art collection was so avant-garde it was shocking to most. He delighted in saying and doing as he damn well pleased; he was so wealthy, he could get away with it.

But that had been three weeks ago, and Hart hadn't fallen. Instead, the city's elites would attend their wedding this afternoon. Soon, they would lift their flutes to toast Hart and herself....

The hypocrisy hardly surprised her. After all, she had been whispered about her entire life. While her older sister, Connie, was properly married to Lord Neil Montrose, Francesca was an eccentric, a highly educated and outspoken bluestocking, an actively radical reformer—and recently, a professional sleuth. In fact, she had helped the police investigate eight shocking crimes since the beginning of the year, and her efforts had been so significant that the police commissioner had admitted that the crimes would not have been solved without her. The press had even begun to cover her activities on a daily basis. She had become one of the city's leading, if infamous, celebrities.

Francesca hardly cared about fame. What she did care about—and had since she was a small child—was helping those far less fortunate than she was. Reform remained as important to her as breathing. Since discovering her innate abilities as a sleuth, she had dedicated herself to helping the innocent victims of dastardly crimes.

Francesca had to pinch herself. She was deeply in love; no woman could resist Hart's dark allure and neither could she. He was the most difficult, unpredictable man she knew. She would gladly help him battle the ghosts of his past—she couldn't wait to marry Hart—but she was also afraid.

Despite his reputation, Calder Hart was wealthy, and that meant he was a catch. Society's reigning matrons had tried their very best to interest Calder in their perfectly groomed, perfectly mannered debutante daughters. He had scoffed openly at their efforts. Then she had begun to investigate the murder of Paul Randall—Hart's biological father. From the moment their paths had crossed, his complicated, dangerously dark nature—coupled with his seductive charisma—had been impossible to resist. He had become a powerful ally, a protector and defender, and even a friend. And while he had never tried to seduce her, very swiftly their friendship had become charged with desire.

Somehow, Calder Hart had come to the conclusion that he wished to marry her, the most eccentric and independent of women. How could she not be afraid that he would eventually change his mind about her?

Calder had been involved with the most beautiful women in the world. She was hardly the kind of sultry seductress he was renowned to associate with. She was romantic, naive and somewhat inexperienced still. Mostly, she was far too clever, far too outspoken and opinionated, and far too ambitious for her gender. Women were not supposed to have high intellect, professional aspirations and vociferous opinions. Nor were they supposed to covet independence, as she did.

Donning a blue skirt and shirtwaist, Francesca turned away from the mirror, shoving all fear aside. The past two weeks had been a frenzy of activity, frantically preparing for a society wedding. Her mother, Julia Van Wyck Cahill—who was not a relation to the crooked former city mayor—would not have it any other way. Julia had railroaded her husband into agreeing to the marriage— Francesca had witnessed moments of the powerful persuasion—and she and Connie had immediately set about the task of organizing the wedding. The ceremony would take place at Fifth Avenue Presbyterian Church and then they would go downtown to the Waldorf Astoria hotel for the reception. Francesca had been shown guest lists, floral arrangements, color schemes, seating plans, dress designs and fabrics. She had simply agreed to whatever her mother and sister thought best. There had been a whirlwind of evening engagements, too, which she had reluctantly attended. Hart had gone to Chicago to take care of as many of his affairs as possible, as he had no wish to attend to business while they were on their honeymoon in Paris, and had only returned a few days ago.

Francesca was pinning up her hair when a knock sounded on her door. She was expecting her sister, who intended to spend the day with her and later help her dress, but it was one of the housemaids. "Who is it, Bette?"

"It is the police commissioner, miss. He says he is sorry to bother you, but he was hoping for a word." The pretty French maid smiled at her.

She was not expecting callers on her wedding day, not even Bragg. Her heart leaped. What had happened?

She hesitated. She had worked closely with Rick Bragg these past months. They had become a formidable team, indeed. He was her dear friend. In fact, before she met Hart—before she had learned that Rick was married, although separated—she had had very strong romantic feelings for him. He had been the first man she had ever kissed.

And he was Calder Hart's half brother.

She refused to think about that ancient romantic attachment now.

Instead, she thought about the fact that a holiday weekend loomed. Many in high society were already gone for the summer, but the city was hardly deserted. While Coney Island and its beaches were a popular destination for merchants and their families, most of New York City would remain occupied over the Fourth. The city's slums were teeming and crime never took a holiday.

Bragg must need her help on another investigation, she thought. But she could hardly help him now!

Francesca stuck another pin into her hair and hurried down the wide, winding carpeted staircase of the Cahill mansion. Bragg was standing in a smaller salon off the large marble-floored reception hall, staring out a window. Bright June sunlight poured into the salon. Outside, beautifully manicured lawns surrounded the house. Francesca could glimpse several hansoms and a small gig on Fifth Avenue, while a few ladies with their parasols strolled on the sidewalk. Across the avenue, dotted with black iron gas lamps, Central Park was clearly visible, the trees behind its dark stone outer walls shady, lush and green. It was a beautiful summer day—the perfect day for a wedding.

For one moment, she had the chance to watch Rick before he saw her, and warmth stole through her. She would always care deeply about him. He was tall, golden and very striking in appearance, but it was so much more than that. He was even more committed to reform than she was; he had spent the past decade in Washington, D.C., as a lawyer, representing the indigent, the mentally incompetent and the poor. He had turned down a partnership in a prestigious law firm to do so. In January, he had been appointed by New York City's new reform mayor, Seth Low, to clean up the police department, which was notoriously corrupt. A recent study estimated that the police took in four million dollars every year from gambling, prostitution and other vices—all from illegal payoffs. Even small merchants like grocers and shoemakers gave their local roundsman a dollar or two a week for protection.

In the six months since Bragg's appointment, he had done his best to break the stranglehold of graft and corruption in the department, mostly by reassigning, demoting and promoting the force's officers. But he was caught between the warring forces of politics and progressivism. Mayor Low had begun to back away from Bragg's reform policies, afraid of losing the next election. The city's progressive elites and clergy had begun to howl for even greater efforts from Bragg. The German Reform Movement, allied with Tammany Hall, kept pushing back. Bragg remained on a terrible seesaw. But he was determined to clean up his police force. Consequently, he'd made far more enemies than friends in a very short time.

She doubted there was a man alive whom she admired and respected more. Except, of course, for her fiancé.

Bragg turned and smiled, coming forward with long strides to greet her. "Francesca, am I intruding?" He kissed her cheek as she took his hand. "I know this is your wedding day."

Releasing his hand, she smiled into his eyes. He hadn't forgotten. "I hope so, as you are on the guest list. I would be crushed if you were not present."

He studied her, his smile fading.

She realized he looked very tired. "You could never intrude. What is wrong?"

"Thank you for meaning that. You seem very happy, Francesca."

She became wary. Bragg had not hidden the fact that he disapproved of Hart entirely. "I'm a bride. Of course I am happy, although I am also nervous." Suddenly she knew why he was there. "You haven't come to share the details of a new case with me, have you?"

"No, I haven't." He was somber.

Her smile vanished and he caught both her hands. "My feelings about this wedding have not changed," he said with urgency. "I am so worried about you."

She tried to tug her hands free and then gave up, as he wouldn't let her go. "I am marrying Calder this afternoon."

"Three weeks ago, Hart was in jail, at the top of our list of suspects."

She pulled free. "No, he was at the top of *your* list. I never doubted his innocence."

"He has you mesmerized."

Hart and Bragg were bitter rivals in every possible way. No two brothers could be more different. They had been raised in the poverty of the city's worst tenements—until Rathe Bragg, Rick's father, had taken them both in. Now, Rick sacrificed the pursuit of the finer things in life in order to help others; his life was dedicated to the reform of society and government. As police commissioner, he lived on a very modest income—and did not care. Hart had taken away an entirely different lesson from his childhood. He was a millionaire, and he displayed his wealth with shocking arrogance. While Hart gave lavishly to several charities and the arts, his ambition had been to acquire power and never suffer poverty and powerlessness again. He had amassed a fortune through hard work and superior intelligence, mostly in shipping, insurance and the railroads. An objective observer would label the one brother the epitome of selfless virtue, the other, selfish and self-serving.

Francesca knew it wasn't true. Hart had his noble side, and she knew that firsthand. With her, he had been nothing but selfless and good. She had come to believe that his arrogance was a facade.

None of that mattered now. She hated the animosity between them. Unfortunately, she knew that a great deal of that rivalry was fueled by her past with Rick and her current relationship with Hart. And that was hardly fair, as Rick had been separated from his wife and since had reconciled with Leigh Anne. "I am far more than mesmerized, Rick. I am in love."

"You have no doubts?"

"I cannot wait to become Hart's wife."

"And that is what worries me so much." Dismay was reflected in his unwavering amber gaze.

"A woman of the world—someone as jaded as Hart—could manage him. But you are as romantic as you are intellectual. And in spite of his courtship, you remain so naive. I shudder when I think of how you trust him, and worse, of your expectations!"

He was echoing the sentiment she had overheard in the past few weeks. "I am hardly going to expect the worst of our marriage. I believe my expectations are fairly realistic," she said. A knock sounded on the open salon door, interrupting them. She gave him a dark look, turning away. Did he have to do this now?

One of the doormen entered, holding a small box wrapped in white paper with a pretty blue ribbon. Francesca knew it was a gift from Hart. She glanced at Bragg.

Rick scowled, shoving his hands in the pockets of his tan trousers as she thanked Jonathon. She went to a desk and unwrapped the gift. The traditional jeweler's velvet box a bride might expect was not within, but she hadn't expected tradition—not from Hart. Instead, she withdrew an antique penknife with a two-inch blade and an ivory handle. The card lying below was scrawled with the initials *CH*.

"My God, he sent you a knife," Bragg said.

"Something old, something new." She laughed. She loved the gift! It was perfect for her. The small knife fit perfectly in the palm of her hand, the better for hiding it when in dire circumstances.

Francesca replaced the knife in the box. This was one of the reasons she loved Hart so. Another man would have sent her jewelry, but not Hart. He understood her so well.

"You are most definitely under his spell."

She nodded. "Yes, I am. And I hope to be under his spell for a long, long time."

He returned quickly, "In the short time you have known him, he has hurt you so much—I have witnessed your pain firsthand."

She wanted to deny it, but she could not. "Please, Rick, not today. Simply wish me well."

But he barreled on. "You must know that Hart is in the newspapers on a nearly daily basis, Francesca. The city's newsmen continue to exploit the details of his sordid affair with Daisy Jones."

She tensed. "I know that gossip still rages about her murder. And I know what they are saying about him— that, regardless of the killer's confession, some in town have decided to believe Hart guilty. These past two weeks, I have been out and about almost every night, at my mother's insistence. I have heard the ugly whispers—as I was meant to. They even say he will tire of me." She managed a shrug, as if she did not care, but she could not smile.

He was silent for a moment, and she knew that he thought, as those matrons did, that Hart would wander, sooner or later. "I was at the Wannamaker affair," he finally said. "You were not. I heard the horrid gossip myself. They want to hang him, Francesca, and by association, they will hang you, too."

She knew Rick was here, causing conflict, because he cared so much about her. "It is payback for all the years he has defied and mocked society and everyone in it."

"He is despised. When they whisper about him, they will also whisper about you."

"I realize that. I grew up in society and I am well aware of how vitriolic it can be. Of course I do not enjoy the gossip. Of course I wish it would end. We will definitely go through a rough patch. It will be some time before society forgets about Daisy's murder. But he is innocent, has been proven innocent, and I will stand by his side steadfastly. That is what a wife does for her husband."

"He broke off his engagement with you when he was accused of Daisy's murder," Bragg said harshly. "And he broke your heart. I know you haven't forgotten. He was selfish then as he is selfish now. Think, Francesca!"

She trembled. "Of course I haven't forgotten. But he was trying to protect me from the scandal—and from himself."

"You have become adept at making excuses for him!" His tone was urgent. "You know, as I know, that he will hurt you again and again, in little ways, if not the biggest possible way. God only knows what demons live within him. He is selfish and cruel. I have seen him deliberately try to hurt you! You deserve someone kind." He took a breath. "I am not asking you to end your engagement. But I am asking you to delay the marriage. I cannot understand this mad rush to the altar."

She trembled, finally tearing her gaze from his. "Why are you doing this?"

He said, "You know why. Because I have never stopped caring about you."

She blinked back sudden tears. Once, long ago, he had been the man of her dreams. And maybe, if his wife had not returned, they would be together now. But she had fallen madly in love with Hart. She hadn't thought it possible to love so deeply, so intensely. And she had made her choice months ago. But his comments hurt now, and she didn't dare analyze why. It was a moment before she could speak. "I can hardly delay now."

"Why not?" he demanded.

She looked up somehow. "He would be terribly hurt if I did so—and I am in love."

His achingly high cheekbones flushed. "And he would

recover, if you batted those blue eyes at him. Right now, you have my brother enthralled."

"I want to marry him today, Rick." There was a warning in her tone.

"Do you? I saw worry and doubt in your eyes—do not try to deny it. I know you too well."

She hugged herself. It was a moment before she spoke. "I admit I am apprehensive. Hart is a difficult man. I fully expect our marriage to have its ups and downs, as most marriages do. My expectations are realistic."

"Ups and downs?" He was incredulous. "When he causes you pain, he does so deliberately—and it is a knife to your heart. I know. I have seen. Francesca, I want to protect you from him!"

She backed away. "Please don't do this today. I am not delaying our wedding. I wouldn't dream of it. In fact, I can't wait to be his wife, no matter that you have upset me."

He grimaced. "I am sorry. I simply care too much. Very well. But I will kill him if he doesn't reform and become the husband you deserve."

She inhaled, relieved. "So you will wish us well? I need your blessing!"

He reached for her, and as inappropriate as it was, she went loosely into his arms. "I wish you well with every breath I take, and I always will. Francesca, you deserve to have all of your dreams come true."

She smiled at him. "Thank you, Rick," she said softly. "So I will see you at four?"

Warmth finally showed in his eyes. "Yes, you will see me at four."

CONNIE SAILED THROUGH the heavily polished front doors of the house. Surprised, she halted midstride as Bragg nodded at her in greeting. As he left, Francesca walked over to her blonde sister and the two of them paused to watch him crank up his black Daimler motorcar in the driveway below the house. A moment later he had put on his goggles and was motoring down the long, graveled driveway toward the open iron gates at its west end.

The doorman closed the front door and Francesca faced her elegant, perfectly groomed sister. Julia had raised her in her own image: Connie was a proper lady, a caring mother and wife, and the perfect hostess. Like Julia, she was an adept socialite. "I see you are already dressed for the wedding," Francesca teased, fully aware that Connie would rush home to change into something even more elegant than the blue pin-striped suit she was wearing.

Connie's eyes widened. "Hardly. Francesca, what was Rick doing here?"

Francesca took her sister's arm and led her back into the salon she and Rick had just vacated. "He came to wish me well," she said a bit too firmly.

Connie gave her a disbelieving look, then walked over to the mahogany doors and closed them. She turned. "You aren't on another case, are you?" It was a mild accusation.

"No, Con, you need not worry on that score."

Connie sighed. "I believe I feel sorry for him."

"Connie, don't!"

"Why not? He was in love with you until his wife materialized out of thin air. And I see the way he looks at you. Everyone does."

She was uncomfortable now. "Con, he loves Leigh Anne."

"Does he? He is certainly fulfilling his duty toward her, and they make a striking couple. But I must say, the few times I have seen them together, I have noticed how tense their relationship is."

Francesca shook her head. "You know that Leigh Anne has suffered a terrible carriage accident. She will never walk again. They are going through a very difficult time. Yes, Bragg is fond of me. I am fond of him." Her heart lurched as she thought about Hart. She bit her lip and looked at her sister. "But, Connie, tonight I am going to be Hart's wife."

Acute desire came suddenly. She had spent hours in his arms—and in his bed. But he had refused to entirely do the deed. For some blasted reason, he insisted on being noble with her.

Connie's smile was knowing. "As your sister, I know you have somehow managed to restrain your passions. I am so excited for you, Fran. Hart is smitten and you are head over heels. God only knows how Mother and I managed to organize this reception in a mere two weeks!"

Francesca laughed, her worries vanishing. All she could think of was Hart watching her with that dark, intense gaze he had as she walked down the aisle. "God only knows how you convinced Father to agree to a wedding in two weeks."

"I think Hart did that," Connie said. "Neil saw them at Delmonico's, having lunch. By the way, he said Father looked apoplectic."

Francesca bit her lip. Hart hadn't said a word about meeting with her father before he'd left town, but clearly he had done just that. She happened to know how adept Hart was at negotiation. Obviously Andrew Cahill, no slouch when it came to business affairs—he had begun his career as a butcher and now ran a meatpacking empire—had been vastly outmaneuvered.

"Have you seen your fiancé since he returned from Chicago?"

"We had a wonderful supper the night before last." She blushed, thinking about it.

"I wish we had been able to organize an affair for last night, but it was difficult enough to prepare the wedding," Connie said. A knock sounded on the closed salon doors and she turned to answer it.

Francesca murmured, "Hart was given a small bachelor's party last night."

Connie blushed and said, "I do not want to know."

"Neither do I," Francesca lied. She couldn't wait to find out where he had been taken and what kind of entertainment he'd been given.

The doorman, Jonathon, was holding an envelope in his hand. "Miss Cahill? This just came. I was told to deliver it directly to you and no one else."

Flowers wouldn't have surprised her, but such a delivery did. Francesca couldn't imagine what the envelope would contain, or why it had been hand delivered. As Jonathon walked past her, Connie glanced at the envelope. She lost some of her coloring.

Francesca saw her reaction and was bemused. She reached for the envelope and froze. It wasn't addressed to her. Instead, a single word in heavy block letters was hand-written upon it: URGENT.

Francesca was assailed with unease. Connie cried sharply, "Fran, do not open it!"

Francesca took the envelope, thanking Jonathon. "That is all," she said. She waited for him to leave and turned it over. The back was blank.

Connie came over to her. "I know you. That must be the beginning of an investigation. It is your wedding day, Fran. Do not open it!"

"I am not going to start an investigation today, Con," Francesca said calmly. She walked away from her sister, ostensibly to stand in the light coming through a window.

In fact, she did not want her sister to see the contents of the envelope until she had done so first.

A printed invitation was inside. It read:

A private preview of the works of Sarah Channing
On Saturday, June 28, 1902
Between the hours of 1:00-4:00 p.m.
At No. 69 Waverly Place

Francesca felt her heart drop as if to the floor. Her knees buckled. She could only stare at the invitation in horror.

"What is it?" Connie cried, rushing forward. "Has someone died?"

Francesca quickly held the card to her bosom so her sister could not see. She looked at Connie, but her mind spun and she did not see her sister at all. Instead, she saw the portrait Sarah had painted of her last April, at Hart's request. In it, she was stark naked, seated on a settee.

Her stolen portrait had surfaced.

Someone had just invited her to view it.

She inhaled. Francesca had no doubt what this terrible invitation was about.

"Fran? Let me get you a glass of water."

Francesca sat down, hard, in the closest chair. Her sister knew that Hart had commissioned her portrait and that it had been stolen, but she did not know that it was a nude. Only a handful of people knew.

Her heart thundered. If that portrait were ever displayed in public, she was ruined. Her family would be more than horrified and shamed—they would be ruined by association with her.

Of all days for the thief to come forward. What did he or she want?

"Con, no, I am fine!" Francesca leaped to her feet. It

was only half past eleven. She could be at 69 Waverly Place in an hour—maybe less, considering a great deal of the city was already gone for the summer. Surely she could be at the church by three, with plenty of time to dress for her wedding.

No one must ever see that portrait!

Connie faced her, her eyes wide. "What is it?"

Francesca managed a smile. "I need a favor, Con, a huge favor—"

"No. Whatever is in that note, it can wait." Connie was frowning. Her mild-mannered sister was becoming angry.

She kept smiling. "I need you to bring my dress, my shoes and my jewelry to the church. I will meet you there at three."

"Absolutely not," Connie cried, horrified.

"Connie, if I do not take care of this—this matter now, I will be in terrible trouble!"

"Take care of this matter *after* you are married."

"Connie, I am going downtown. I will be at the church by three, I swear. Nothing can keep me away!"

CHAPTER TWO

Saturday, June 28, 1902
12:00 p.m.

RICK BRAGG STARED at his Victorian home, the engine of the Daimler idling, but he did not really see the quaint brick house. Instead, the interview he'd just had with Francesca kept replaying in his mind. He was very afraid for her.

He knew Hart would eventually destroy her. His brother had a black, selfish soul. He was cruel and self-involved. From time to time he could rise to the occasion, briefly showing the honorable side of his nature, but in the end, he always reverted to serving only his own interests and ambitions. Francesca was selfless. Hart was selfish. No match could be worse.

But he was hardly an impartial observer. Bragg was afraid to recall the past he had shared with Francesca. He feared that too many old feelings would return. He knew he must not think of the time they had first met, when he had been smitten with her—and she had returned his passionate interest. He must not think about their debates, their discussions, their investigations—or the kisses and caresses they had shared. That was wrong. His wife had returned after leaving him four years ago, and as uneasy as it was, as angry as he had been, they had reconciled. Besides, before Francesca had become charmed by his brother, she had utterly rejected the notion of his ever divorcing. Although he never spoke openly about it, in the most elite political circles it was assumed that one day he would run for office, possibly even for the United States Senate. A divorce would ruin his political prospects.

He had made his own bed, which he now slept in. Leigh Anne had insisted on moving back in with him— and when she had, he had insisted on his marital rights. He had been furious with her for both leaving him and then returning to him. What had begun as an unfriendly reconciliation had turned into a passionate one, but his lust had been fed by his anger.

He had spent half of last night working, the other half thinking about the fact that Francesca was actually going to marry his heartless half brother on the morrow. He did not know where the past few weeks had gone. He had been overwhelmed at headquarters. There had been a series of civilian arrests in the Tenderloin—organized, of course, by the radical reformer Reverend Parkhurst, whose motives were political. Parkhurst vociferously claimed it was his duty as an American citizen to do what the police would not, which was to close the saloons on Sundays, while the press sensationalized every detail of every civilian raid, putting Bragg in the midst of the dispute. The mayor was furious with Parkhurst, but he was also displeased with Bragg. And Leigh Anne had begun to complain of pains in her leg....

And then he had received the damn wedding invitation, only a week ago!

He was certain he could support Francesca's marriage to someone else—someone worthy of her. Hart was not that man. But what could he do? He had tried to persuade her to delay, and she had refused. Now, he would have to stand aside and be ready to pick her up when Hart shattered her into tiny pieces. Bragg had not a doubt that was what his half brother would do.

He realized that the automobile was still running and he turned off the ignition. Reluctantly, he got out of the roadster, placing his goggles on the driver's seat. The holiday weekend loomed. He would take his wife and the two girls fostering with them to the tiny village hamlet of Sag Harbor, on Long Island's north shore. He had spent all of the prior night at his office at police headquarters, taking care of paperwork that only he could manage—the perfect excuse to stay overnight at the office. It wasn't the first time; he had begun keeping a change of clothing there. He was astute enough to realize that he dreaded returning home. He wasn't sure when he had begun to avoid his marriage.

The anger was long gone. It had been replaced by guilt. He had treated Leigh Anne terribly before she was injured. While she did not blame him for the accident, he blamed himself. His cruelty had put her in such a state of distraction that she had been run down.

As for the lust, every time he thought about reaching for her, she would turn away, or feign sleep, or make some excuse that one of the girls was awake, needing her.

He was hardly a fool. Leigh Anne was a passionate woman, but she was also vain and she couldn't stand the changes the accident had wrought in her body.

She had even told him to take a mistress; she had even asked for a divorce. How ironic it was. He had been the one who had wanted a divorce when she suddenly reappeared in his life in February, while she had insisted on reconciliation! He wondered what was left for them, if they didn't have conversation, understanding, affection or sex. He would never turn his back on her now. Even if he knew rationally that the accident wasn't really his fault, she was his wife. If he didn't take care of her, who would?

He walked grimly past a small black gig and gray

horse parked in the driveway. He instantly recognized the vehicle, and his tension increased. Leigh Anne must have summoned Dr. Finney.

He focused on the fact that she must be in more pain—it was preferable to thinking about their volatile and unhappy relationship. He started up the brick path to the small house he had leased, hoping the girls were in the park with their nanny so they would not witness Leigh Anne's distress. He stepped into the house, plastering a smile on his face. Instantly he heard a noise on the stairs. Katie came barreling down the staircase so swiftly he reached for her, afraid she would trip and fall. Her small face was taut with worry. His heart lurched with dismay.

He knelt. "What's wrong?"

"Mrs. Bragg hurts so much," she cried, looking at him as if he might be able to somehow save the day. She was dark haired and seven years old.

Katie was always anxious. When she came to them after her mother's murder, she had refused to speak or eat. Now she spoke, although not frequently, and ate like a little horse. She even smiled from time to time, especially when Leigh Anne was at her best and mothering her. But she worried about her foster mother all the time and he knew it was not healthy for her. He clasped her thin shoulders. "Katie, Mrs. Bragg was badly hurt in that carriage accident. Now and then, she will have some old pain, left over from her injuries."

"Why won't it stop?" she whispered, her dark eyes huge and despairing.

"She has her good days, too. I am going to go upstairs to see what Dr. Finney has to say. Where is Dot?"

"She is having lunch."

"Why don't you join her. Aren't you hungry? Mrs. Flowers is a wonderful cook." He managed a smile.

Katie did not smile back, but she reluctantly turned. He hurried upstairs, his heart racing. Amazingly, he was anxious. He paused on the threshold of their bedroom, wondering how a man could live this way—in dread of going home, to a place without laughter and affection, without sex; in a state of constant apprehension. And then there was the guilt.

Leigh Anne wasn't dressed yet. She wore a modest blue silk wrapper, her jet-black hair piled indifferently atop her head. She had the covers up and a wool throw over her lap, as if she was cold. Finney sat by the bed, speaking with her, patting her hand. His wife remained terribly beautiful, but she appeared as fragile as china.

Leigh Anne saw him and sat up straighter, as if stiffening her spine and squaring her shoulders. He slowly entered the room. "How are you?"

She said, "The pain is worse."

Dr. Finney walked over. The two men shook hands. The doctor spoke softly. "I have given her some laudanum, to dose herself at night. She says she cannot sleep."

"There is nothing wrong with her leg," Bragg said tersely. "Those broken bones have healed."

"Considering there was so much damage, I suspect she will always have some discomfort with her right leg. Try to make sure she does not rely on the laudanum to sleep. She should only dose herself if absolutely necessary."

"I'll see to it," Bragg said. "Let me walk you out."

"I can manage." Finney gripped his shoulder. "See you later, eh? At Hart's wedding?" He shook his head, as if in disbelief, and walked out.

Slowly, Bragg turned.

"I heard every word," Leigh Anne said, her cheeks flushed.

"I am sorry you are in pain," he returned.

"Where are the girls?"

He was aware of how much she had come to love Katie and Dot. He wondered if she was desperately clinging to them. "They are having lunch." He approached, and her eyes widened. As he sat down on the bed by her hip, she tensed visibly, and he wondered if she thought he meant to try to make love to her. In that moment, there was no desire, just a fatigue that felt ancient.

But he knew himself. If she were to reach for him, he would lose himself in lust. He said carefully, "It's after one. Shouldn't you be getting dressed?"

She hesitated. "I do not feel up to the wedding."

He was shocked. Leigh Anne loved society affairs, and although it was late June, this event would be in every single social column from Bar Harbor to Charleston. He thought about the fact that she hadn't gone out in the past few days, not even to be pushed about the block or across the square in her wheelchair. When they had first met, she had been one of Boston's reigning debutantes. Until recently, Leigh Anne had attended almost every luncheon to which she had been invited. She had been at his side at every supper party and charity she had deemed important to his career. He understood that she was melancholy, but it would only become worse if she did not get out.

She grimaced. "Of course I will come. And you're right, I should begin getting dressed. Where is Nanette?"

He had had to hire a lady's maid to help her bathe and dress. As his finances were precarious, he had let the male nurse go. "I will send her up," he said as lightly as possible.

She forced a smile, avoiding his eyes. He went to the door. Then he halted. He hated seeing her so despondent.

But how could he cheer her up? Maybe he should tell her that she did not have to go to the wedding if she truly did not feel well. Bragg turned.

Leigh Anne was pouring brandy from a pint-size bottle into her cup of tea.

FRANCESCA HAD BECOME very familiar with many of the unsavory, crime-ridden lower wards of Manhattan. Still, it was a large city, filled with slums and tenements, factories and saloons, with neighborhoods populated by Germans, Italians and Irish, not to mention Russians, Poles and Jews. In the course of her many adventures, she had even learned that there was a "Little Africa" on the Lower East Side. The various immigrant groups migrating to the city resided in distinct ethnic clusters.

She was proud that she knew the city well, but she did not know it like the back of her hand. In her very first investigation—into the abduction of a neighbor's child—she had met a young, outspoken cutpurse, eleven-year-old Joel Kennedy. He had defended her from a thug, and she had taken him under her wing, not just because he knew so many tricks of the trade, but because she had a secret wish to help him improve his lot in life. When she did not have Joel with her—a rare circumstance indeed—she used a map to navigate Manhattan. Today, Joel was with his mother, Maggie, a wonderful seamstress who had become her friend—and possibly a romantic interest of her brother's. She could imagine the chaos in the Kennedy home just then, as Maggie had been stunned to have been invited to her wedding. Undoubtedly Joel and his siblings were being groomed for the event.

But she did not need her maps. The cabbie she flagged down on the avenue instantly told her that No. 69 Waverly Place was on the north side of Washington Square.

Francesca was relieved. The previewing was but a few

blocks from 300 Mulberry Street—which housed police headquarters.

She was on pins and needles. She had not a doubt in her mind that her portrait was at No. 69 Waverly Place. She had begun to wonder if someone wished to agitate her on her wedding day. If so, that someone had certainly succeeded!

Earlier, she had been relieved to find her father's study empty; perhaps Andrew had been taking his weekend ambulatory in the park. She had made one quick telephone call before leaving the house, and it would have been quicker if the operator, Beatrice, hadn't tried to converse with her about her wedding. But Hart hadn't been home—she couldn't imagine what he was doing on their wedding day—and she had spoken to his butler, Alfred. The butler had asked her if she wished to leave a message, but she had been too frenzied to get downtown to think of anything coherent to say. Before dashing out of the house, Connie had told her that she was a madwoman.

Francesca looked at the small pocket watch she had bought for herself recently; crime-solving was laborious, and she tended to run late. It was half past one. It had taken longer to get downtown than she had thought it would, but she had a good hour yet to explore.

They were on Fifth Avenue, traveling south. Ahead, she saw the green lawns and paved walkways of Washington Square. On both sides of Fifth Avenue she saw old brownstone buildings that were clearly residences, although she also saw a few ground-floor restaurants and taverns. Her hansom turned left onto Waverly Place, which faced the square. More dark brownstones lined the block, shaded by elm trees. Shops were on the lower floors.

She caught the bright sign hanging from one such establishment: Gallery Moore.

"Stop, driver, stop!" Her gaze sought the number above the sign. It was No. 69.

Frantically, Francesca dug into her purse.

"Do you want me to wait, miss?" the cabbie asked. He had a heavy Italian accent.

Francesca quickly looked around. Despite the holiday, the square was full. Women in pretty cotton dresses, some with parasols, were strolling with their children or their gentlemen escorts. Some of the men were in their shirtsleeves, while a few wore suit jackets and top hats. Two cyclists, one a woman in knickers, were on bicycles, weaving precariously along the paths. A few small dogs raced about, while a balloon drifted into the sky. It was a very pleasant, genteel scene.

She looked at the block facing her. Once, the buildings had been fashionable, single-family Georgian homes. There were daffodils growing about the elm trees on the sidewalks, and she saw more flowers in the window boxes. Washington Square was a tired and old neighborhood, but it remained middle-class. Another hansom was passing by and she decided it was safe to let the cabdriver go.

She was in such a rush that she stumbled from the cab. Slamming the door, she turned to face the gallery. Her heart thundered.

Everyone seemed to be in the square; the city block was deserted.

She paused to take her small pistol from her purse. It was loaded. Whoever had stolen her portrait, he or she was, at the least, a thief. And she would certainly not be surprised if that thief was also a blackmailer or an enemy, seeking revenge upon her. She would be a fool to deny her fear.

Her stolen portrait could be inside. She prayed that it was.

There were wide stone steps on her right, leading to the

apartments above the gallery. The gallery itself was on
the basement level, meaning she had to go down several
steps to get to the front door. As she did, the first thing
she saw was the white sign hanging on the door. Its bold
black letters read Closed.

She paused, clutching the small gun. The door was
glass, but set in iron and barred with it. She glanced at
the windows on each side, which were similarly barred.
Most galleries had large windows, to allow in natural
light. She imagined that it was dark and gloomy inside
this space.

A smaller sign was in the right-hand window. She went
closer to read it.

Summer Hours: Monday-Friday, 12:00–5:00 p.m.

The gallery was closed to the public. Francesca felt her
heart leap with relief, but that did not dim her anxiety. A
small doorbell was beside the door, and there was a heavy
iron knocker on it. Francesca reached for the doorknob.

It gave instantly as she turned it, and the front door
swung open.

Clearly, someone was waiting for her.

In that moment, she wished that Hart had been at
home, or that Bragg had still been present when she had
gotten the invitation. She blinked, adjusting her eyes to
the gloom inside. No lights were on, so the gallery was
filled with shadow.

Francesca stepped in and closed the door behind her
very, very quietly. To her satisfaction, she did not hear
even the scrape of iron on the floor.

She could see well enough now and she turned, her
skin beginning to prickle, certain she was not alone. She
almost gasped.

Her portrait faced her.

She trembled. She had forgotten how stunning the painting was—and how provocative. In it, she wore nothing but a pearl choker. Her hair was up and perfectly coiffed. She sat with her back to the viewer, but she was partially turned. Not only were most of her buttocks visible, so was the entire profile of one of her breasts.

There was no mistaking her identity—and to make matters worse, she wore an expression of naked sensuality and raw hunger.

When she had posed for that painting, all she could think about was Hart.

Her instinct was to rush forward and yank the picture from the wall and destroy it. But there would be time for that later. She fought for composure. What did the thief want? Why surface now? Did he or she want money? Did he or she want to ruin her?

Was she being watched?

She felt as if eyes were upon her—and she did not like it, not one damn bit. She had her back to the door. She looked outside through the bars and glass, but the small concrete space beyond the front door was vacant.

Francesca started forward, gun in hand. If the thief was watching her, there was no point in remaining silent. Now she saw the other paintings on the walls. None were Sarah Channing's work. Her style, somewhat classical yet impressionistic, too, was very distinct. "Where are you?" she called out loudly, turning the corner behind the center wall. The area there boasted nothing but blank gray walls. "Who are you? What do you want?"

Her words seemed to echo slightly in this smaller back chamber. She saw an open doorway, but hesitated. "Come out. I know you're here." She swallowed, straining to listen. All she could hear was her own thundering heartbeat and her rapid, shallow breathing.

She was afraid. Why wouldn't she be? Someone had

lured her to that gallery. She needed to take possession of that painting. "I will pay you handsomely for my portrait!" she cried.

There was no answer.

Standing in the back room, facing a dark, open doorway, she knew a moment of despair. What kind of game was this?

She hated releasing her gun, but she tucked it in the waistband of her skirt, only so she could remove matches and a candle from her purse. Months ago, she had learned to carry a large bag in order to keep the necessities of her trade with her. She lit the candle and realized the small doorway belonged to a single room, which consisted of a desk, a chair and file cabinets.

Francesca walked inside and saw nothing but receipts and notes on the desk. She looked carefully at the notes, but they were scribbles. Neither her name nor Hart's jumped out at her. She looked at the saucer, which contained business cards.

Gallery Moore—Fine Arts and Consignments
Owned by Daniel Moore
No. 69 Waverly Place,
New York, NY

She rummaged through the drawers quickly, but there was simply too much paperwork to go through when the clock was ticking. *The time.* She froze, then reached for her purse, which she had laid on the desk. It was almost half past two.

Her temples throbbed. She did not have time to investigate now. But Bragg would be at her wedding and she would tell him everything before the ceremony, and send him downtown to retrieve the painting. But how could she leave the portrait now?

What did the damn thief truly want?

Francesca snuffed out the candle with her fingertips and left it on the desk—she had others in her purse. She took her gun from the waistband of her skirt. Purse in hand, in the darkness, she left the small office.

She thought she heard a small scraping sound coming from the front of the gallery.

She raced through the empty back chamber. "Who is there?"

There was no answer.

Frustration arose. She turned, jamming the gun into her waistband again, reaching with both hands for the oil painting. To her shock, it did not budge.

It wasn't hanging on the wall by a wire; it was nailed.

She jerked on it again. It did not move.

And that was when she heard a lock clicking loudly in the dark.

She whirled to face the front door, expecting to see someone standing there, grinning at her. Instead, she saw a flash of movement outside of the gallery as someone ran up the steps to the sidewalk.

She cried out. Francesca ran to the door and seized it—but it was locked from outside as she had expected.

She cried out again, furiously, and tugged on the door-knob again. It did not budge.

Stunned, she stood there, the knob in her hands, the horror beginning.

She had just been locked in.

How was she going to get out? How was she going to get to her wedding?

CALDER HART STARED OUT of the window of the Fifth Avenue Presbyterian Church's second-floor lounge, feeling very pleased. He was already in his tuxedo, although he had yet to don his tie. Fifth Avenue was deserted. Everyone who was anyone had left town for the summer—except, of course, for those at the uppermost crust of New York society who lived in awe—or fear—of Julia Van Wyck Cahill.

The avenue was terribly attractive this way, in such a state of splendid desolation, with only a single carriage and two black hansoms traversing its paved streets. Stately mansions, elegant townhomes, exclusive shops and clubs lined the thoroughfare. Only three coaches were parked outside the church; it was far too early for guests to arrive. He glanced at a grandfather clock in one corner of the dressing room. It was a few minutes past 3:00 p.m. His gaze wandered back outside. Surely he wasn't looking for his bride—he was not superstitious, but he had no wish to see her before the wedding, just in case. He smiled to himself. He had little doubt that Francesca was already in the church with her sister and mother, frantically applying the finishing touches to her toilette, as if she could possibly be made any more beautiful.

A few months ago, if someone had told him he would be at a wedding as the groom, he would have been very amused—and he would have considered that person an absolute fool. Yet there he was, with a racing heart and a touch of nerves.

"Hey, Calder," Rourke Bragg said, laughter in his quiet tone. "Are you planning a mad dash for the exit yet?"

He took one last look at the quiet avenue. Two roundsmen in blue serge, carrying billy sticks, were standing on the street corner, chatting. Hart suspected they would soon be directing traffic.

He slowly turned to face the young man who had spoken. Rourke took after his father, Rathe Bragg. He was tall and broad-shouldered, with golden hair, amber eyes and a sun-kissed, almost swarthy, complexion. He also had Rathe's inherently sunny, optimistic nature. He was actually Rick's half brother, but having been taken in by the Bragg family at the age of nine, when their mother died, Hart considered him a relation, if not a sibling of sorts.

He also happened to like Rourke, who was in medical school and was devoted to his profession. He had not one hypocritical bone in his body.

Speaking of hypocrites, Rick Bragg had yet to arrive. He had only spent a half an hour last night with them at the private room they had taken in the Sherry Netherland to celebrate the last of Hart's bachelor days. Hart smiled grimly. He rarely bested his perfect brother. He had surely bested him now.

He would never forget that once, months ago, Rick had been smitten with his bride. But Francesca was marrying *him*.

The satisfaction welled. It was savage.

"He must be sweating bullets," Rourke's younger brother, Gregory, said. He was twenty years old to Rourke's twenty-four, and currently clerking in San Francisco for his uncle, Brett D'Archand, a shipping magnate. Upon learning of the wedding, he had taken a train to New York. Hart had asked Rourke, Gregory and their younger brother, Hugh, to stand up with him, along with young Nick D'Archand. Gregory's grin was smug. "My God, Hart, it's all over after today. No more wild women, no more fantastic orgies, just shackles and chains. You must be mad."

Hart slowly smiled. "If you are asking me if I have doubts, the answer is no."

Everyone in the room turned to look at him. The only male in the wedding party who was not present was the father of the bride. Andrew Cahill was downstairs, pacing in the front hall. Hart knew he would meet every single guest personally. "It must be love," Hugh Bragg snickered. He'd arrived from Texas two days earlier.

Hart was adept at ignoring conversations he wished to ignore, and he said, unperturbed, "I am marrying the most interesting woman on this planet. Need I say more?"

Francesca's brother, Evan Cahill, smiled. "Even the mighty fall," he murmured.

"Like I said…" Hugh laughed, reaching for a flute of champagne.

He was only fifteen, and his father adroitly removed the flute before he could take a sip. Scowling, Hugh accepted a root beer from Alfred instead.

Hart meant his every word. He had no doubts. He had realized, within days of meeting Francesca, that she was the most extraordinary of women. She was as brave as she was beautiful. Her intellect was astounding and she had more ambition than most men he knew. She was all that was good, pure and honest in the world, and he worried, because she was so trusting. He had never known anyone more selfless or more generous. She had shown him, time and again, that she could not turn her back on anyone in need.

She was also independent. Most men would hate her refusal to be subservient and obedient; he admired her willful, libertarian nature.

Of course, she was reckless and impulsive; no one had less common sense. But now that he knew how easily she leaped in front of runaway trains, he would be there to restrain her from her poor judgment. She had already caused him to grow a gray hair or two—and they had only known one another for five months.

He had first glimpsed her in Rick's office on January 25, but he hadn't spoken to her until an outrageous party on the rooftop of Madison Square Garden on January 31. By February 23, he had known that she was the one woman in this world who would never bore him. He had looked at her, realizing how much her friendship had come to mean to him, his heart lurching oddly. She had changed his world in a handful of days, and while he thought the human aspiration to acquire happiness incredibly trite, she had warmed his entire life. The decision made in an instant, he had abruptly informed her that he intended to take her to wife. Needless to say, Francesca had been in shock.

She had accepted his suit five days later.

It was almost impossible to believe that they had come this far. But he wanted to marry Francesca Cahill, and he always got what he wanted. No one acquired the wealth and assets that he had, coming from such stark and impoverished beginnings, without sheer will and unholy ambition.

He was even eager for their wedding night, although he tried to feign indifference, even nonchalance. He was so used to casually seducing the beautiful women that crossed his path that it had become a game of sorts. He hadn't wanted to treat her like the others. Francesca, he intended to treat with respect. He had decided that he would not take her innocence until they had said their vows.

He had a moment of hesitation, almost a frisson of fear.

She thought him noble. That was her most astounding feature—her unshakable faith in him. She simply did not understand that he was motivated by self-interest—always. If he were truly noble, he'd tell her to find someone worthy of her—someone like Rick. But he would never do such a thing. She was his first and only friend. His best friend. Of course, he must have her entirely for himself.

She refused to see him as he truly was, and sometimes, that terrified him.

One day, he knew his world would implode—when she realized the truth about him.

And as he had that unhappy thought, the lounge door opened and Rick Bragg walked into the room.

Hart stared at his brother, who had given up all the finer things in life to pursue justice, equality and liberty for all. He despised his virtuous half brother, but he recognized that Rick was as selfless as Hart was selfish, a noble do-gooder. He truly wished to save the world, and it was not a show. Yet Rick was not the perfect gentleman, no matter how he might pretend to be. He had flesh-and-blood needs and dark desires, just like anyone else. Sometimes, Hart could not stand Rick's attempt to cling to his moral code. When it crumbled, Hart thrilled. Unfortunately, those moments were rare. As unfortunately, the world needed men like Rick Bragg, just as it needed women like Francesca. Otherwise, the world would be a living hell.

He just wished that Rick were not his half brother. He was good, Hart was bad. He was loved, Hart was not. Rick was the insider, the wanted one; no matter his wealth and power, Hart was always the outsider.

Mostly, he hated the fact that Rick had seen, courted, kissed and loved Francesca first.

Rick looked grim. Hart did not smile now. Rick was perfect for Francesca. They were exactly alike—two radical, reforming, saintly peas in a pod. He had always thought that they were perfect for one another. But Francesca had chosen him.

He tensed. "Hello, Rick. I really didn't think you would come." He had won this battle. He might as well relish the fact.

Rick did not smile in return. "I debated declining."

He approached, feeling predatory. He was not a hypocrite; he had not asked Rick to stand up with him. "And what, pray tell, changed your mind? Surely you do not wish to celebrate my union with Francesca?"

"I saw Francesca this morning."

Hart started. He did not like being taken by surprise.

"She remains dazzled by you. But then, you know as well as I do that she is trusting and naive."

His fists clenched involuntarily. "She came to see you?" Why would she go to Rick on the morning of their wedding? Oh, he knew why!

Rick stared. Finally, slowly, he smiled. "No, Calder, *I* went to see her. I wanted to persuade her to delay the wedding. I am afraid for her."

He inhaled. For one moment, he had been blinded with jealousy; for one moment, he had thought that Francesca had doubts. "I am going to take care of her—in every possible way." He let the ugly innuendo hang.

Rick flushed. He lowered his voice and said, "And for a while, she will be even more smitten, won't she? But one day, passion will not be enough."

Hart wanted to tell him to get out. But within half an hour, he would be exchanging vows with his bride and he wanted Rick there, suffering through it—as jealous as he himself had just been.

"You know I am right. You broke it off with her after Daisy was murdered, to protect her from yourself. You should do the right thing now. Call off the wedding."

Hart smiled, and it felt ugly. He had broken their engagement when he had been arrested for his mistress's death. He hadn't wanted her ruined by association with him. He would never be able to live with himself if he brought her down that way. "I am not under arrest now. I am not in jail. I am not a suspect in a murder. In fact, what I am is one of the country's wealthiest millionaires."

He couldn't help thinking that Rick was acting as if he still loved the woman Hart was about to marry. His half brother had been detoured by the return of his wife and his lust for her, but lust wasn't love and it did not last for very long. Besides, Rick was no fool. The blinders were clearly coming off. Leigh Anne was as weak and selfish as Francesca was strong and good. Sooner or later, he would realize the mistake he had made—if he hadn't already realized it.

He continued viciously. "I am going to give Francesca the life she deserves—a life of intellectual freedom, with all the power she needs to do as she wishes, when she wishes. Nothing and no one will stop me, and certainly not you. In a few more moments, we will stand before Reverend Cramer and exchange our vows to become man and wife. Tonight I will consummate that union, and no man—not even you, Rick—will be able to come between us. In a few more days, we will be on our way to Paris on our honeymoon. Did you know I bought the vessel that will transport us across the Atlantic?" They would be its only passengers.

Rick flushed. "Lust isn't love. And you don't have a clue as to what the latter is."

"And you do?" Hart mocked. "Is the lovely Leigh Anne downstairs—or upstairs, in your bedroom?"

Rathe came to stand between them. "I cannot believe that the two of you are carrying on the way you did as small boys!" He glared at Hart. "You are provoking him, when you know he has strong feelings for Francesca." He glared at Rick. "You are married, and your wife deserves more. Today is Calder's wedding day—for better or for worse!"

"I am afraid for her," Rick said, not even looking at Rathe. "He will destroy her, either slowly or in one fell swoop." He turned on his heel to leave.

"Rick. Don't bother to attend the ceremony," Hart said softly, furious now. Rick was wrong. He would never hurt Francesca. He just hoped his black past wouldn't ruin them, as it had almost done so recently.

Rick turned back to face him. "I apologize. I gave Francesca my blessings this morning, and I meant it. I want her to be happy. That means I want both of you to have a successful marriage. I am hoping you will be a good and devoted husband." He flushed again. Clearly, the words pained him.

Hart raised his brows, incredulous. "You are giving me your blessings?"

"Unlike you, I prefer taking the high road." Rick stared, his expression hard and tight. "I am trying, no matter how difficult you make it."

Hart had to laugh. "Of course you are—you are so damn noble!"

Rourke shoved a scotch at him. "Drink it. He has apologized, and you should bury the hatchet, at least for the rest of the day."

Hart took the scotch, but did not bother to take a sip. He was utterly amused. Only Rick would sincerely offer him his blessings. He wondered how noble his brother would be later that night, after he and Francesca had gone home to finally and thoroughly make love to one another. He hoped Rick would stay awake, brooding unhappily about it.

A knock sounded on the lounge door and Gregory went to open it. The moment Hart glimpsed Julia's starkly white face, with Connie standing behind her fearfully, his heart turned over with sickening force. He glanced again at the grandfather clock. It was 3:30 p.m.

"Julia?" Rathe hurried forward. Hart saw Rathe's wife, Grace, standing with Julia—her arm around her, as if she might collapse.

"I don't know where she is!" Julia cried. "Francesca isn't here, she isn't at the house, and no one has seen her since noon!"

Hart felt the room still. All conversation ceased. Time stopped.

Francesca wasn't there.

Of course she wasn't. There wasn't going to be a wedding—and he wasn't even truly surprised. She had come to her senses at last.

CHAPTER THREE

Saturday, June 28, 1902
4:00 p.m.

HER THROAT WAS raw from shouting for help. Francesca leaned against the door of the gallery, blinded by a sudden surge of tears. How was she going to get out? She had been crying for help for a very long time, and no one had heard her. What time was it, anyway?

She could barely believe that she remained locked inside. Trembling, she turned to find her purse. She had dropped it on the floor when she had heard the front door being locked. It was on the other side of the central wall where her nude portrait hung. For one moment, Francesca stared through the shadows in the gallery at her own sultry image.

She had been lured to the gallery and now, she was locked inside.

Someone wanted her to miss her own wedding.

There was no other conclusion to draw. She was not going to miss her own wedding! Somehow she was going to get out of this damn basement. She loved Calder Hart— she could not wait to finally be his wife. She would never leave him standing at the altar, in shock, waiting for her!

As she stumbled into the other chamber behind the wall, she wondered who had done this.

She had made many enemies in the course of the past

six months. Every crime that she had solved had involved justice for the perpetrators. The list of those who wished to hurt her was probably long. She would consider it the moment she was out of the gallery and uptown—finally married to Hart.

Her purse lay on the floor, open. Francesca knelt and dug within for her pocket watch. Her heart slammed when she saw that it was a few minutes before four.

By now, her family, friends and three hundred guests were at the church. Everyone—including Hart—must know that she had not arrived.

Surely he was worried about her! She wished she had left a message with Alfred; she wished she had shown Connie the damn note. But she hadn't done either of those things and no one would have any idea where she had gone.

She must have been screaming for help for perhaps an hour, hoping a passerby would hear her. Clearly, the gallery was set too low below the sidewalk, and too far back from it, for anyone passing to hear her. There had to be another way to get out.

Francesca dismissed the notion of trying to escape through the front windows, as they were barred. She ran back into the office, praying that the windows there were not as small as she recalled.

She stared up at the two windows, which were high up on the wall near the ground level, just below the office's ceiling. They were small rectangles that barely allowed any light in. Each was probably eighteen or twenty inches wide. They looked half as tall.

She was a slender woman, but even if she could get up to the windows and break the glass, she feared she would not be able to squeeze through. She shuddered. If it weren't her wedding day, she would continue calling for help—and wait for someone, eventually, to hear her. But she was going to take her vows, even if she was late—which now, obviously, she would be.

Francesca glanced around. She quickly realized she must push the desk to the wall, beneath the window, and stack the file cabinet on the desk, in order to make a ladder. The desk looked small enough, but it was surprisingly heavy, and it was many moments later before she had pushed it across the small space. She cleared the desktop with a determined sweep of her arm. Then she marched to a file cabinet. She pushed it across the floor, then managed to lift it onto the desk. Her back felt broken. Panting, she paused and looked up.

Francesca stared up at the window grimly. If she got stuck in that window, she could hang there all night. The possibility was distinctly dreadful.

But there was no other choice. Determined, she removed her shoes and stockings, the better to gain some traction, and climbed onto the desk. She tested the cabinet for balance by jiggling it. It sat square on the desk and seemed steady enough. Hiking up her skirts, she climbed onto it, clawing the rough wall with her fingers. She paused. She wasn't afraid of heights, but she was now six feet from the floor and she did not think her makeshift ladder all that trustworthy. She sighed. Very slowly, she tried to stand up.

The file cabinet rocked.

She froze, regained her balance and tried again. A short time later, she was standing upright, her fingertips now grasping the shallow concrete ledge of the window, which was about four inches wide. Her face was level with the glass pane, which was thick and dirty. Her heart was thundering, but she was briefly exultant.

Then she grew grim. The window opened onto a grassy patch of backyard, or some such thing. She thought she could fit through it, but wanting to get through it was one thing, actually doing so, another. Once she broke the glass and cleared it away, she was going to have to jump up and try to get her chest onto the ledge, at least. If she failed, she was going to fall to the floor.

Francesca slowly, gingerly reached with one hand into the waistband of her skirt for her gun. The cabinet she stood on teetered slightly, but she felt that it was stable enough for her next move. Raising the gun slowly, she inhaled and slammed it with all her strength into the glass.

It shattered.

She covered her face with her arm, turning away. She felt shards dart against her cheeks anyway.

The rocking cabinet stilled. Her heart was pounding hard, but somehow, she was still standing on the cabinet. She took a few steadying breaths, then used the gun to clear away the remaining glass. The edges of the frame were dangerous—there was no way to make them shard free. But she intended to ignore a few scrapes and cuts. This was her wedding day.

She told herself not to look down. Francesca put the gun through the window and laid it outside on the grass. Then she reached with both hands for the ledge. There was nothing to really grab on to, and she was afraid that she wasn't strong enough to hoist herself up high enough to begin to get out the window.

But she had to try.

She leaped up, pushing with her legs and her arms. For one moment, she thought she had made it. Her breasts hit the concrete and she was briefly suspended there. And then she was falling wildly downward, through the air.

SHE HAD COME TO her senses, realizing the folly of marrying him.

It seemed as if the floor were tilting wildly beneath his

shoes. Then he felt a hand on his shoulder. Rathe, who had clasped his shoulder, said rather inanely, "What do you mean, she isn't here? Where is she?"

He tensed, facing Francesca's frightened mother. Julia was deathly pale. She moaned—a sound she had undoubtedly never before made in public. Behind her, Grace and Connie were almost as ghostly as she was. "She isn't here, Rathe," Julia gasped. "She was last seen at noon, hailing a cab. I do not know where she is!"

A terrible, shocked silence fell. He finally achieved a single coherent thought. Francesca had hailed a cab at noon. A new, darker tension began. Had she run away? He glanced from Julia's white face to her sister's. Lady Montrose seemed very frightened. He turned to look at Rick, who was clearly as surprised as anyone.

She hadn't run away with his half brother, he somehow managed to think, because Rick was right there. But she had run off.

He felt the stares in the room, all leveled at him. He did not look at anyone now. The shock remained, but there was disbelief, as well.

She had run off.

He has been stood up at the altar.

Images flashed of Francesca smiling at him, laughing with him, her eyes filled with warmth and affection, all of it meant for him. He stared through the memories at his half brother, and he wondered how he could have ever thought, even for a moment, that she would actually marry him. He was a fool. She had never wanted him as her husband—it was always Bragg who she had wanted to marry. She had wanted him as her lover.…

She lusted for him, but she loved Bragg.

He was her second choice.

He trembled and realized his fists were clenched. How could he have been such a fool?

"Who was the last to see her?"

Hart started, realizing that Rick had stepped forward to take charge.

Julia said hoarsely, "Connie. Francesca asked her sister to bring her clothing here. She told her she would meet her here at 3:00 p.m."

"I begged her not to go!" Connie cried.

Hart heard, but vaguely, as if from a distance. Something odd was happening inside his chest, but he was determined to ignore it. How could she have done this to him?

More images flashed in his mind of the many moments he has shared with her—over a good scotch whiskey in his library, or inside his coach in the dark of night, or at a supper club by candlelight. There had been debate and discussion, levity and laughter, lust and love. He had committed himself to her completely. He had trusted her completely. Or had he?

He was her second choice and he had always known it; he had never forgotten it.

The odd feeling in his chest intensified, as if something within the muscle and flesh was snapping—no, ripping—apart. He was determined to ignore it. He should not be shocked or surprised. He should have realized how this day would end.

Connie was speaking to him, he realized. "I don't know what the note said. She wouldn't show it to me. I begged her not to go! She swore she would be here at three!"

"Did she leave the note in the salon?" his half brother was asking.

"She had it with her when she ran upstairs to get her purse," Connie said, wringing her hands. "Only Francesca would respond to whatever was in that note on her own wedding day!" She looked pleadingly at Hart.

He stared coldly back. He did not care about any note.

"Did she say anything about the note, anything at all?" Rick asked.

"No," Connie said tearfully. "But she seemed very distressed."

And he almost laughed, bitterly. Francesca had received a note that had distressed her—enough for her to fail to attend her own wedding. He had meant to spend his life with her. He had looked forward to showing her the world, offering her any experience she wished to have, when she wished to have it. He had wanted to open her eyes to the pyramids of Egypt and China's Great Wall, to ancient Greek ruins and the temple of David; he had wanted to share with her the greatest works of art in the world, from the primitive drawings in the caves of Norway, to Stonehenge of Great Britain, and the medieval treasures cloistered in the cellars of the Vatican. How could she have done this to him?

He had taken her friendship to heart. Having never had a friend before Francesca, he had thought her friendship an undying profession of loyalty and affection. How wrong he had been. Friends did not betray one another this way.

He realized Rourke was offering him a drink. He had given her his trust—his friendship—his absolute loyalty—and her desertion was his reward.

In front of three hundred of the city's most outstanding citizens.

"Calder, take the scotch. You clearly need it."

He took the glass, saw that his hand trembled and hated himself for being a weak, romantic fool. He downed the entire contents of the glass, handed it back and walked away from everyone.

Hadn't he expected this? Wasn't that why he had kept staring out the window, waiting for her to arrive? Hadn't he known on some subconscious level that this marriage was not to be?

Of course she didn't want him.

He refused to remember being a small boy, scrawny and thin and always hungry, sharing a bed with Rick, in the one-room slum that was their flat. He did not want to think about their mother, Lily, before she died, standing at the stove, smiling not at him but at his brother, telling Rick how wonderful he was. Nor would he recall her last dying days, when he had been so terrified that she would leave him. It was Rick she was always asking to see, Rick she was always whispering to.

He was an adult now. He knew that she had made Rick swear to take care of his younger brother, but that knowledge didn't change anything. Lily had loved Rick greatly; to this day, he wasn't sure that she had ever wanted him, much less loved him. The more troubling his behavior had been, the more distant she had become, looking at him with sorrow. She had never looked at Rick that way.

"You were a mistake!" his father, Paul Randall, had said.

Hart had been accepted at Princeton University at the age of sixteen. Rathe had been a personal friend of the university's president, but his test scores were superior anyway, allowing his early admittance. Yet instead of going to New Jersey and registering for his first term, he had gone to New York City. Returning to Manhattan as a young man in a suit with a few dollars in his wallet had been strange—and exhilarating. He liked the fact that when he stepped out into the street and raised his hand, a cab instantly pulled up. He liked walking into a fancy restaurant and being called sir. But the trip to the city was hardly impulsive; he had hired an investigator to find his biological father. He had not only found Paul

Randall, he had been shocked to learn that he had a pair of siblings.

Randall had been living in the same house, on Fifty-seventh Street and Lexington Avenue, where he was murdered last February. Hart had succumbed to uncharacteristic nervousness as he approached the brownstone. In spite of having rehearsed a nonchalant introduction, he was speechless and perspiring by the time he reached the front door. He had imagined their first meeting while on the Manhattan-bound train. No optimist, he had nevertheless imagined various scenarios that ended on a happy note.

When he had told Randall who he was, the man had turned deathly white with shock. Instead of inviting him in, he had stepped outside onto the front stoop where Calder stood, closing the door behind them. "Why are you here?" he had cried. "What do you want? My God, my wife must never know."

Instantly understanding that his father did not want him, he had come to his senses. "For some odd reason, I thought it appropriate for us to meet."

"It is not!" Randall had exclaimed. "Please leave— and do not come back." He had shut the front door in his face. Stunned, trying not to feel anything just then, Hart had heard his half siblings behind the door, asking their father who that was.

"Just a boy selling encyclopedias."

Now, Hart stared down at Fifth Avenue, his hands clenched so tightly on the sill that his knuckles were white. Francesca had jilted him. He would always have been the man she had settled for. Except, in the end, she had realized she did not want to settle.

He turned. To his amazement, Rick was still interviewing Connie, as if this were one of his criminal investigations. Well, it was hardly that. As far as he was concerned, the drama was over.

Rick saw him staring and walked over, his strides decisive. "Francesca must be in trouble."

He raised his brows. "Really? Why would you reach that conclusion—when you begged her this morning to postpone our wedding?"

Rick's eyes widened. "Are you blaming me?"

Hart said, scoffing, "Hardly. But don't pretend to care. Don't pretend that you are not delighted by Francesca's sudden change of heart."

Bragg was somber. "I'm not delighted, Calder. I can see you are hurt. But I am worried about Francesca."

He clapped his hands. "Of course you are. And is your white steed outside?"

"Haven't you heard a word Lady Montrose has just said? Francesca meant to be here. She received an urgent summons."

She had received an urgent summons on her wedding day. He laughed coldly. It felt good. "I am hardly hurt, Rick. The truth of the matter is, I am relieved. I have come to my senses. What could I have possibly been thinking? I am not a marrying man."

Everyone was staring at him now. Julia seemed ready to faint. He almost cursed them all, but they hadn't done this—she had done this.

Slowly, Rick shook his head. "Fine. Tell yourself what you will. Do you want my help?"

"No." He did not have to think about it.

"She would never do this on purpose," Julia cried, staggering. Rathe caught her, putting a strong arm around her. "I must sit down!"

Connie took her from Rathe. "Mama, let's go to our lounge." She sent Hart an incredulous, angry look. "Evan, Father is downstairs with the guests. I think he could use your help just now, calming everyone—and averting a full-blown scandal."

"Of course," Evan said, striding forward. He went to their mother and helped Connie guide Julia down the hall.

Hart knew what was coming, now that Francesca's family was gone. He smiled coldly at Rick.

Rick's amber eyes were dark. "You know what? I am glad this has happened. Because we both know that this marriage would have been a disaster. We both know that Francesca deserves far more than you can give her. Maybe she did come to her senses. She was very nervous this morning."

He trembled with anger, but he kept his tone even. "And what will you give her, Rick, now that you are so happily reconciled with your lovely wife? Undying friendship? Unrequited love? Or…a sordid affair?"

"I am her friend," Rick said harshly. "Not that you would understand what that means."

He sent the staggering agony away. "You are so right," he said coldly. "I do not have a clue about what friendship means, nor do I wish to. Enjoy your friendship, Rick." He nodded and stalked past him.

Rourke fell into step beside him as he traversed the hall. "What do you think you are doing?" Hart asked, his tone still cold.

"I am keeping you company. You have had a shock," Rourke said flatly.

"Hardly. I do not need a nanny or nursemaid." He rapidly went downstairs, Rourke remaining abreast of him.

"Then you will have a friend," he said calmly. "Whether you want one or not."

He decided to ignore his near relation. Too late, he realized he was about to descend into the crowd of three hundred tittering, exhilarated wedding guests. He faltered.

The ladies wore ball gowns, the men black tie. Everyone had been speaking, the din hushed yet excited. A terrible silence fell. He saw Andrew Cahill near the church's oversize double doors just as Francesca's father saw him. Cahill seemed incredibly dismayed and distressed. But as their gazes met, he flushed with anger.

"Let's get out of here," Rourke said softly. "If you don't need a drink, I do."

He did not care. Andrew stared at him with accusation—as if this was his fault.

Hart smiled and said pleasantly but loudly, "I am afraid this is your entertainment for the day. The wedding is off and, apparently, I am to blame."

As he stepped onto the ground floor, the crowd parted like the waters of the Red Sea. He refused to focus on any single face, but he knew just about everyone present. He had slept with a dozen of the assembled socialites, with many of the other matrons' daughters shoved his way; he had concluded business with many of the gentlemen. He saw the Countess Bartolla, who was gleeful, and Leigh Anne, who seemed both vacuous and surprised; he saw Sarah Channing, who was in abject concern—for him? for Francesca?—and her mother, who looked shocked.

To hell with them all.

As he stepped outside into the bright sunlight, he heard the crowd erupting behind him into frenzied conversation.

He did not care.

FRANCESCA DIDN'T CARE how bruised she was. For the third time, she climbed unsteadily onto the cabinet on top of the desk. Now, though, tears filled her eyes.

Twice she had tried to leap up onto the window-sill. Both times she had fallen to the floor. It had hurt terribly.

She was losing her strength and her will. She had to make it onto that ledge this time.

Panting, half crying, Hart's image assailing her, she gripped the concrete ledge.

Then she heard a child's cries.

She froze, afraid she was imagining the sound, when she heard a second child's laughter.

There were children outside!

"Help!" she screamed. "Help me! I am locked in the gallery.... Help!"

A moment later a boy's tiny freckled face peered through the window opening. His blue eyes met hers and he gaped.

"Can you help me get out of here? I'm in the Gallery Moore! It has been locked from outside!" Francesca cried frantically.

His eyes popping, he nodded. "I'll get me dad."

Francesca was overcome with relief as he ran off, apparently another child with him. She swallowed hard, praying for help. A moment or two later—which felt like an eternity—a man's face appeared in the window opening. Perhaps in his thirties, he was cleanly shaven, with graying temples. He was incredulous. "I didn't believe Bobby! Are you all right, miss?"

"Not really!" Francesca quickly explained that she was locked in. Remaining calm, the gentleman told her to go to the front door, and that he would find a way to get her out.

Francesca slowly climbed off the cabinet and the desk, every bone in her body aching. She picked up her purse and shoes, aware that her gun was outside, and realized that her nails were broken, her fingers scratched and bleeding slightly. She pulled out the pocket watch. It was half past four.

Frightened, she left the office, hurrying through the gallery. She glanced at her portrait, wishing she had thought to destroy it. She was afraid to leave it behind. The moment she saw Hart, she would tell him what had happened and he would send someone to retrieve it.

At the front door she found the gentleman who had offered to help her with a roundsman, who was busy trying to pick the lock. There were far more shadows inside now. Her portrait was lost in the darkness, one small relief.

The lock clicked about ten minutes later.

Now in her shoes, Francesca rushed outside. "Thank you!"

"Are you all right, miss?" the uniformed policeman asked her, his gaze taking in her untidy appearance.

Francesca imagined that she looked like a bedchamber sneak. She nodded, about to move past him. "I am very late," she began, but he barred her way.

"Are you a relation of Mr. Moore?" the roundsman asked pointedly.

He thought her a burglar or thief! She froze. "No, I am not. Sir, my wedding is today." She flushed, beyond all dismay. "In fact, I was to be married by now. I must go!" Surely Hart would understand. Surely he would be waiting for her.

"The gallery is closed. It says so right there, on the door sign. I'm going to have to take you in, miss, on suspicion of breaking and entering these premises."

Francesca cried out. "I was invited here!"

As if he hadn't heard her—or didn't care—the officer held up her gun. "Is this yours?"

She nodded. "It most certainly is." She dug into her purse and handed him her calling card. It read:

Francesca Cahill
Crime-Solver Extraordinaire
No. 810 Fifth Avenue
New York City
No Crime Too Great or Small

As he read it, his eyes widened. She snapped, "I am Francesca Cahill, sir. Surely you have heard of me. I work very closely with the police commissioner—who happens to be a personal friend of mine."

He looked at her, his eyes still wide. "Yeah, I've heard of you, ma'am." Respect filled his tone now.

"Good. Right now, Rick Bragg is at the Fifth Avenue Presbyterian Church, awaiting my arrival there—along with three hundred other guests." She felt tears well. "Along with my groom, Mr. Calder Hart. You have heard of him, surely?"

"Wasn't he locked up for murdering his mistress?" the gentleman said, standing behind the officer.

She cried, "Hart is innocent—the killer confessed and awaits conviction. Now, I need a cab!"

"I'll get you a cabbie," the roundsman said quickly. "I am sorry, Miss Cahill, for delaying you, but you have to admit it was suspicious, you being inside the closed gallery like that."

"May I have my gun, please?" He handed it to her and she started for the street at a run. She had never been as desperate—and there were no hansoms in sight. Behind her, the cop put his fingers to his mouth and a piercing whistle sounded. Moments later, a black cab turned the corner from Broadway, the gelding in its traces trotting swiftly toward her. Francesca sagged with relief.

Forty minutes later, the tall spires of the church came into sight. Francesca leaned forward, praying.

But the avenue was deserted. Not a single coach was parked outside the church.

She did not have to go inside to know that everyone was gone.

CHAPTER FOUR

Saturday, June 28, 1902
6:00 p.m.

EVAN CAHILL CLOSED the door to his sister's bedroom, Rick Bragg pausing in the corridor with him. They had just thoroughly searched every inch of the bedroom and adjacent boudoir, but had not produced the note Francesca had received that morning.

Evan adored his youngest sister, but he knew her better than almost anyone. Leave it to Fran to help some poor sod in need—and miss her own wedding. While he admired his sister's generosity, intelligence and ambition enormously, this new penchant for sleuthing kept getting her into harm's way. She had been burned, knocked out, locked up and stabbed, all in the past few months. A cat had nine lives. How many did his reckless sister have? His heart filled with dread.

Bragg said, "I would like to use the telephone."

Evan nodded, remembering that he had not turned off the electric lights inside the room. He quickly did so. "It's downstairs, in the library." As they left the bedroom, he said, "I am terribly worried, Rick. Will you begin an official investigation?"

Bragg clasped his shoulder briefly. "Do not worry yet. Your sister is not only intelligent, she is resourceful. She will be fine."

Evan did not think Bragg believed his own words.

A vast concern was reflected in his eyes. He was aware that Rick Bragg had romantic feelings toward his sister. Although he liked Bragg, he did not approve—the man was married. He now thought about the unlucky groom as they went downstairs. "Hart was furious."

"Yes, he was."

Evan knew he would be furious if he were stood up at the altar, as Hart had been. The humiliation would be consuming. He could barely imagine the shock of having one's bride not show up, especially if he were in love. By now, though, Hart must be as worried about Francesca as everyone. Yet he had not come by, demanding to know if they had discovered anything, nor had he called.

As he led Bragg into the library, he could hear his mother's high, distraught tone. Julia was a formidable force and never panicked. She was in a panic now.

He felt his heart lurch as Bragg picked up the heavy black receiver. He was in a bit of a panic himself, he decided. Fran loved Calder Hart. Only something terrible would have kept her from her own wedding.

"Beatrice, it's the police commissioner," Rick Bragg said. "Please connect me to HQ."

Evan jammed his hands into the pockets of his evening trousers. He'd shed his tuxedo jacket the moment they had arrived at the Cahill mansion, about an hour ago. He was a tall, dark, handsome man of twenty-six. Unfortunately, he liked to carouse and was obsessed with gaming, and as a result he had accrued some monstrous debts. Recently he had had a grave falling-out with his father. Andrew Cahill had decided that the time had come to refuse to pay his son's debts—unless Evan married a respectable young lady. Their battle had become terrible and Evan had moved out. Recently, though, he had reconciled with his father, returning to the family business and his own home, adjacent the Cahill mansion.

It should have felt wonderful to be back in the family fold, to be living like a prince and to have a handsome cash flow again. It did not. He hated being ordered about as if he did not have a brain in his head, as if he were a hired—and dim-witted—lackey.

He realized Bragg was asking a desk attendant at police headquarters if Chief Farr was in. He sighed. His own problems could wait—and he did have problems. His mistress claimed she was having his child. He did not want to think of the flamboyant Bartolla Benevente now. He had refused to speak with her at the church.

A moment later, he heard Bragg speaking with an inspector, requesting a police detail. "We will treat this as a missing person's case." Bragg replaced the receiver on the hook.

"What now?" Evan asked grimly.

"We currently have no leads. However, I will let Newman and his team do what they are trained to do—find clues, no matter how small. In the meantime, I suggest you comfort your mother. I am going to make a quick stop at my home and then return to interview your staff at great length."

They left the hall and were about to enter the marble foyer, when Evan saw Maggie Kennedy standing there with her son, Joel.

He halted. They were really only friends, but her blue eyes instantly locked with his. He knew she was there not just because of Francesca, but out of concern for him.

Evan felt himself smile. Tentatively, Maggie smiled back. "Are you all right?" she asked softly.

Evan felt his heart turn over, hard. Recently, he had had to admit that he had become very, very fond of Mrs. Kennedy. He had met her some time ago through Francesca. Maggie was a seamstress, and she had been making gowns for his sister. And then she had become the target of a killer.

Evan had actually been the one to find her in a struggle with Father Culhane, and he had rescued her from the madman. But even before that moment, he had been so admiring of her. Maggie Kennedy was an angel. A widow, she worked tirelessly in order to care for her four children by herself. He had never met a woman as gentle and kind, as solid and determined.

He had begun to visit her and her children, bringing gifts and cookies and cakes, and he had even taken the family on several outings. The very last time he had seen Maggie, he had asked her if he could kiss her, and she had said yes.

He wished he could stop thinking about that single, very chaste kiss, but he could not. He hurried to her. He had seen her and her children at the church, but hadn't had a chance to say hello. Had the wedding gone as planned, he would have danced with her at the reception. Instead, he had been busy with his father, explaining to their guests that Francesca was suddenly ill and that the wedding was postponed. No one had believed them. "Hello."

"Has there been any word?" Maggie asked anxiously. She was a few years older than he was, with very fair skin, a splattering of freckles, vivid blue eyes and shocking red hair. He knew she was wearing her very best Sunday dress.

"I'm afraid not," he said, flinching.

She took his hand. "No one is as resolute as your sister."

He stared into her eyes, feeling the strength of will and purpose in her tiny hand. He raised it to his lips briefly. "I am very worried."

"I know," she said. She glanced past him.

He followed her glance. Bragg was asking Joel if he

had any idea about what had happened to Francesca. Joel was eleven years old, and he knew the underworld far too well. He had been apprehended many times for picking purses. Of course, his cutpurse days seemed to be over, as Francesca paid him a salary for his assistance. Joel shook his head soberly. "Miz Cahill never said a word about any note. She loves Mr. Hart an' only the worst sort of rough could keep her away today."

Bragg tousled his hair, but he did not smile. Evan wondered if his odd expression had more to do with Joel's statement about Francesca's feelings for Hart than it did with her disappearance.

Evan realized he had stepped even closer to Maggie, as if her warmth could comfort him now. "Come inside," he said softly.

"I don't want to intrude. But I am worried about Francesca—and you."

Had the situation not been so dire, he would have thrilled at her words. "You cannot intrude. Mother adores you—as do I." He could barely believe what he had said and he felt himself blush. She blushed as well, and he took her arm and led her into the salon.

Julia sat on the sofa with Andrew and Connie, an alcoholic drink of some sort on the table in front of her. It was obvious she had been weeping; Julia never wept, or not that he had ever seen. It was warm in the room, but someone had thrown a cashmere shawl over her shoulders. She sat up stiffly as they entered the room. "Has there been any word? Any clue? Is she back?"

Bragg was grim. "I am sorry, Julia, but my answer is no to all your questions."

She cried out. Andrew put his arm around her and held her close. "Oh, God! Francesca is reckless and impulsive, but she would never be this irresponsible, Rick! What has happened to her? Where is my daughter?"

"Darling!" Andrew said sharply. "Francesca is fine. She will return at any moment—with some cockamamy explanation for what has occurred today." But he was as pale as his wife.

"Francesca will be fine, Mama," Connie said. "You know Fran. She is unstoppable."

Julia moaned. "And when she does return, then what? Three weeks ago her fiancé was accused of murder! We have hardly gotten over that scandal—and now, there is this! Everyone will be gossiping about Francesca jilting Hart at the altar for months to come."

"Let's worry about the scandal another time," Andrew said firmly.

Evan couldn't agree more.

Bragg stepped forward. "The police will be here shortly. I have to leave, but I will return in two hours."

"In two hours?" Julia gasped in disbelief. "Do you have to leave?"

"I'm afraid so," Bragg said.

Andrew rose and strode to him. "Can I have a private word, Rick?"

Andrew was as much an advocate of reform and as politically active as Rick. They had met years earlier, when Rick's father was in Grover Cleveland's administration. Now they were close friends. The two men stepped into the hall.

For one moment, a heavy silence filled with fear and dread fell over the small salon. Julia seemed frozen. Connie got up and walked into her husband's arms. Montrose was as worried as anyone. Evan tightened his grasp on Maggie, turning to her and lowering his voice. "I will get you a cab." He didn't want her to go, but he imagined she had left her other three children with a neighbor, and surely had to return home.

As they left the salon, Maggie murmured, "I hate leaving you now, in crisis. You have been so helpful to me."

Her concern thrilled him, but he was careful to remain poker-faced. "It's all right. Joel?" he called. He realized Joel had gone outside. "Did he leave?"

"He told me he would help the police tonight. I have never been able to keep him from running around as he pleases," Maggie said with dismay. "I know he wants to find Francesca."

Joel had more courage than most grown men, and shrewd wits. Evan wondered if he had run off to try to find Francesca on his own. At that point, he didn't truly care who found her—as long as she was found.

The doorbell sounded. Evan could not imagine who would call upon them now. As he and Maggie turned, the doorman opened the door, revealing Bartolla Benevente.

His tension knew no bounds.

Maggie flinched.

His ex-mistress strolled into the front hall, holding a pastry box wrapped in ribbon. She was still dressed in a very daring ruby-red ball gown for the reception that had not taken place. She was a stunning, statuesque woman with auburn hair. Once, her face and figure had driven him mad with desire. Now, he found her distastefully obvious.

Bartolla smiled slowly at them. "Hello, Evan." She ignored Maggie, coming forward with the sweeping stride of royalty. In reality, she had no royal blood, although at sixteen she had married a sixty-year-old Italian count. "Has your sister been found?"

"No, she has not. What are you doing here? This is a very difficult time, Bartolla."

"I am aware of that! I must say, I never dreamed Francesca would jilt Hart. I have always thought that he would

be the one to break her foolish heart—sooner than later."
She laughed, clearly amused by the events of the day. "I
do not think Hart will be very happy with your sister
when she returns, Evan."

"You are wrong. He is smitten. Francesca has gotten
herself into trouble, otherwise, there would have been a
wedding today. Once she is found, I am certain they will
plan another wedding day." He realized he had come to
despise her. He did not know how he would manage a
relationship with her after their child was born.

Bartolla laughed again. "I know Hart very well, my
dear, and he loves to hold a grudge. There will never be
a wedding now."

Evan realized she still hadn't looked at Maggie even
once—as if Maggie were not standing there with them. "I
am not going to argue with you. I must get Mrs. Kennedy
a cab."

"Perhaps you should put her on the El, instead."
She smiled. "After all, that is the fare a seamstress can
afford."

He trembled with anger; Maggie touched his hand.
He looked at her and she sent him a silent message with
her eyes. She did not want him upset by the countess. He
inhaled. "Bartolla, this is not the time to call. My family
is very distraught. My mother is not receiving tonight."

"Balderdash. I have brought cakes, Evan. I am so very
fond of Julia and I wished to commiserate with her. Surely
she needs a shoulder to cry on now."

Evan knew she only wished to gloat.

Maggie tugged on his hand, clearly wanting to leave.
Then Bragg appeared, his strides long and brisk. He and
Evan went outside together as Bartolla swept into the
other room in search of Julia.

"What do you really think?" Evan asked him tersely.

Bragg hesitated. "I think Francesca has gotten into some trouble. But I am going to find her, Evan. You may count on that."

SHE WAS AFRAID to get out of the cab.

Hart's home was a huge, neo-gothic mansion, consisting mostly of charcoal-hued stone. Recently built, it was a dozen blocks farther uptown from the Cahill home. He had no neighbors as of yet, and his grounds took up half a city block. Lawns and gardens surrounded the house, while a brick stable, servants' quarters, tennis courts and a large pond were all set farther back on the grounds. A tall, wrought-iron-and-stone fence bounded the entire property.

Francesca did not move as the cabbie got down from the driver's seat. The front gates were closed, although it was only six o'clock in the evening.

She trembled, fighting tears of exhaustion and dismay. She had spent the past thirty minutes traveling uptown, trying to imagine what the scene had been like at the church when the bridal march should have begun. Her mother would have been hysterical, her father grim. She couldn't imagine the reaction of her guests.

Then she had tried to imagine what Hart's mood had been.

The cabbie had opened one of the front gates, wide enough for his cab to go through. He climbed back into the driver's seat, above her closed cubicle. She was filled with dread. She could no longer tell herself that Hart was worried about her. She simply knew him too well.

He had a terrible, explosive temper and a jaded, cynical worldview.

As the gelding trotted forward onto the graveled driveway, she gave in to her overwhelming distress. She always saw the glass as half-full; she always gave everyone the benefit of the doubt. Hart never did either of those things. He trusted no one and nothing.

Except, he had come to trust her, hadn't he?

It didn't matter. She was afraid he was going to be very angry.

But it was even worse than that. She had glimpsed, just once or twice, a terrible vulnerability hiding behind the facade of arrogance and disdain, wealth and power. She hoped she hadn't hurt him. She almost laughed, somewhat hysterically. How many times had she been warned that he would be the one to hurt her?

All relief at escaping the gallery had vanished. She had to explain to Hart what had happened, calm and reassure him, if need be, and then they had to go downtown and retrieve her portrait from the gallery. That last action could not wait! She hadn't said a word to the rounds-man, as she had not wanted him to go inside and look at it. When she had been leaving Waverly Place, she had seen him closing up the gallery, a single, small consola-tion. But now, in hindsight, she wished she had found an object with which to destroy the painting before leaving the gallery.

She paid the driver. The downstairs of the mansion was not lit up. Every now and then, Hart's mood was so black that he dismissed his entire staff, only to wander about his mausoleum of a home by himself, a scotch in hand, admiring his art—and brooding. She would almost believe that he was doing that now, except that she hap-pened to know he had guests. Rathe and Grace Bragg were staying with him indefinitely, as they built a home on the west side of the city. Just then, so was Nicholas D'Archand and two other Bragg siblings.

She had a terrible feeling, and she did not even try to shake it off as she climbed the front steps of the house, passing two huge limestone lions at the top of the staircase. On the roof, far above the front door, was a bronze stag. Before she even lifted the heavy brass knocker, the front door opened. She expected Hart to be standing there, but it was Alfred who let her in.

Francesca hurried inside. "How is he?"

Alfred's eyes widened. "Miss Cahill! Are you all right?"

She knew she was dirty, disheveled and scratched from having to shatter the glass window. "I am not all right, but I do not need a physician—I need to speak with Hart."

"Mr. Hart is in the library, taking care of business affairs."

She started. "Surely you are not telling me that he has taken my failure to arrive at the church in stride?"

"I do not know how he is at the moment, Miss Cahill. He is excessively calm."

She stared, shocked. She lowered her voice. "Is he drinking?" Hart often sought refuge in alcohol when under extreme emotional duress, in an attempt to avoid pain. She found him frightening when drunk, but not because he was inclined toward violence. She knew he would never lift a hand toward her. His mood was always the blackest and he was always the most self-deprecating when he was drinking himself into a state of oblivion.

"No."

She prayed that this was a very good sign—that he wasn't hurt—and that he would be eager to hear her explain what had kept her from their wedding. "Thank you," Francesca said. "I can find the library myself, Alfred."

He hesitated. "You look a sight, Miss Cahill. Do you want to freshen up?"

She shook her head and hurried down the hall, hoping she would not run into any of the family. The house was terribly quiet. It reminded her of a home in mourning. She did not like having such morbid thoughts and she ignored them. She wanted nothing more than to be in Hart's arms.

The heavy rosewood door to his library was closed. Francesca hesitated, her heart racing with unnerving force. Finally she pushed it open.

Hart was seated at his desk, hunched over the papers he was reading. He lifted his head, his gaze slamming onto her.

She managed to smile. "Hello."

The distance of a tennis court was between them. Francesca shut the door and hurried forward, her heart pounding wildly. "Hart, I am so sorry! I have had the most awful day!"

He slowly rose to his full height, which was an inch or two over six feet. There was something controlled about the way he rose to tower over his desk and she faltered. Surely he noticed how untidy and scratched she was. Surely he was worried about her! "I have been locked up," she cried. "And I found my portrait!"

He did not give her his characteristic once-over. Unblinkingly, as if he hadn't heard a word she said, he said calmly, "I see you have had a change of heart, Francesca. I see that you have seen the light."

She was very alarmed. "Didn't you hear me? I was locked in a gallery—that was why I missed our wedding. I am so sorry!" she cried. "I have not had a change of heart!"

He was as still as a statue. She couldn't even tell if he was breathing. "I am well aware that you missed the wedding." He spoke as if they were discussing the summer rain. His calm monotone never changed. "Are you hurt?"

Didn't he care that she had been locked up? "No! Not in the way that you mean!"

"Good." He looked down at the papers on his desk and

reached for one. Francesca was shocked. What was he doing? Wasn't he going to look at her face, her hands, and ask what had happened? Didn't he want to know where the blasted portrait was, so they could retrieve and destroy it?

He glanced at her as if she were a stranger. "Is there something further you wish to say? As you can see, I am quite occupied right now."

"Calder, aren't you listening? I found that damn portrait—that is why I was late." She almost sobbed. "This was to be our wedding night! We must talk about what happened!"

He shuffled the papers, but his gaze was on hers, and it was impossible to know what he was thinking or feeling. His face was carved in stone. "I don't care what happened. We have nothing further to discuss."

She froze. "I beg your pardon?"

He looked down at the papers on his desk again and began to slowly rearrange them.

She ran forward. What was wrong with him? Why wasn't he angry? Why wasn't he shouting at her? "I know you don't mean that. I know you care about what happened to me today." When he did not look at her, she cried urgently, "We must plan another wedding."

He finally set the papers down and stared at her. "There is not going to be another wedding."

She choked, her heart exploding with sickening force in her chest. Only his desk stood between them now. "You can't mean that!"

"But I do." And finally, she heard the twinge of anger in his tone.

It was a moment before she spoke, and it was an effort to control her tone. "You must be very hurt and very angry, even if you are not showing it. I shouldn't have mentioned another wedding, not now."

His gaze black, not even flickering, he did not respond.

"No one stops loving another person in an hour or a day, Calder." She tried reason now. "You cared about me this morning—of course you care now."

Finally, he spoke. "You are assuming that our relationship was founded on love." He stared. "Let me offer some advice—you do not want to have this discussion with me."

No one could miss the warning in his tone. Her heart thundered with more alarm, more fear. "I never meant to stand you up!"

His gaze finally flickered. "It is for the best."

She cried out. "What? I love you. Missing my wedding was not for the best!"

"Good day, Francesca." He sat abruptly down, pulling a folder forward.

She was disbelieving. "Is this your response to what has happened? To pretend you don't care—to refuse to discuss it—to dismiss me as if I am not your fiancée?"

She saw him tremble, but he did not look up.

She had struck a nerve and she meant to strike more. "Have you even looked at me? I have cuts all over my face from broken glass! My nails are torn, my fingers scratched from trying to hold on to a wall while I crawled out of a window!" She was rewarded when he raised his eyes to hers. His expression was dark, like thunderclouds. "I received a strange note this morning, Hart, an invitation to a preview of Sarah's works! The moment I read it, I knew that I was being invited to view my own portrait. Of course I had to investigate!"

His black gaze was unwavering. "Of course."

She rushed on. "When I got to the gallery, the door was open and my portrait was there. But before I could do anything, someone locked me in from the outside. I spent hours and hours trying to get out. Finally—at four o'clock—some small children heard my cries for help." She realized she was trembling incessantly.

Hart steepled his hands and looked down. "You said you were not hurt."

"I'm not!"

When he refused to look up, she cried, "Of all days for the thief to play his hand! Clearly he did not wish for us to marry. I was lured downtown. Can't you see that? Don't you believe me?" She had never been more desperate. Why was he behaving this way?

He finally glanced up at her. "Oh, I believe you. But does it even matter? It is over, Francesca." And he began to read the papers on his desk.

She knew he had chosen to retreat behind this wall of icy calm. Because his behavior was a pretense, wasn't it? A careful and clever facade? Hart was the most volatile man she knew. "Oh, God. I expected you to be angry, but you're not, are you? When you are angry, you explode— and you drink. I have hurt you."

He sat back in his chair, staring at her. "If you are expecting a rage, you will be sorely disappointed. And surely you do not expect tears?"

She did not like that last mocking note which had emerged. She had hurt him, hadn't she? There could not be another alternative. "You have decided to pretend indifference, perhaps even to yourself."

"I have decided that our relationship was a mistake." He was final. "It is over."

She reeled. The one thing she had not expected was this. "I will quote you now. 'It will never be over!'"

"I have never enjoyed clinging women."

She gasped.

He stood up. "Please show yourself to the door."

She did not move. As dazed as she was, a tiny voice in her head screamed at her to leave and come back another time. Men like Calder Hart could not be chased. She spoke unsteadily now. "Hart. I love you."

"Do you know how many times women have declared their love for me?" He was cool.

She cringed. His gaze was scorching and she knew he was in his most ruthless mood. "Don't do this to me."

"Do what? You are the one who did not show up today."

"You have admitted to me that you love me!"

He laughed, the sound mirthless. "You are so unique, Francesca, that I undoubtedly deluded myself for a while, but we both know that I do not believe in love. It was lust, Francesca, and nothing more. You see, I have come to my senses, as well. What was I thinking, to shackle myself to a woman for what might be an entire lifetime? When the lust is gone, all that would remain is the ink on our marriage license."

She inhaled. "I know you don't mean anything you have said tonight."

"I am not interested in what you think—or in attempting to convince you that I have meant my every word."

He could not be serious. "How can you be so cruel to me? How can you dismiss me after all we have shared?"

"And what have we shared, other than some conversation, some danger...and several nights in my bed?"

She felt tears well.

"I cannot stand women who cry," he warned.

She somehow shook her head. "You are trying to make me feel as if I were one of your passing amusements—one of your play toys!"

His stare was filled with innuendo, his silence an affirmative. She was shaken to the core of her being.

"This cannot be happening. We are meant to be, Hart."

He walked out from behind his desk—and past her. "Nothing is meant to be. And darling? I have no intention of being the one to ruin you. My position hasn't changed. Your desires will remain unrequited. Luckily, I'm sure Rick will be more than happy to oblige you on that particular matter."

"Your words are killing me!" she gasped.

"Really? Have no fear. This heartbreak will pass. It always does." He opened the library door and stood there, waiting for her to leave.

She wasn't sure how she approached him. She felt as if she had been cut up into so many tiny, bleeding pieces. "I have hurt you. I am sorry! I love you and I always will— even now, when you are trying to destroy that love."

"Do I appear hurt? I am not. I am relieved."

She choked.

"God, I hate theatrics. Would you mind? This drama has become more than sordid or distasteful, it has become tiring. I have affairs to attend."

She hugged herself. His gaze was as frigid as the Arctic Ocean. "I am not taking off this ring. I am not giving up on us, either."

"Then I feel sorry for you. But you may keep the ring. Use it to buy the portrait, darling."

She could not withstand his cruelty anymore. Francesca ran past him. As she started to stagger down the corridor, blinded by tears, she heard him behind her. She tensed, sensing a final devastating blow.

It came instantly. "Francesca? Do not bother to come back. When I am done, I am truly done. You are no longer welcome here."

CHAPTER FIVE

Saturday, June 28, 1902
7:00 p.m.

FRANCESCA WAS BEYOND shock. Could it truly be over? Had he really meant his cruel words? Hadn't Bragg warned her what she was in for if she tried to go forward with Hart—if she dared to love him?

Oh, God, her heart was breaking apart!

When he had broken their engagement a few weeks ago, it had been entirely different. He had been motivated by the desire to protect her from the scandal of Daisy's murder. He had put her welfare above his love for her. Somehow, their love had emerged even stronger. His feelings had never been in doubt.

But now, he seemed to be completely indifferent to her. As if he had cut her out of his heart—and his life—in one fell, effortless swoop.

"Miss Cahill? Let me help you to a chair."

She realized that she had somehow wandered into the front hall and that she was still crying. Alfred faced her, his dark gaze filled with concern. She struggled for composure, no easy task.

If Hart did not love her—if their relationship had only been based on infatuation and lust—then it was over and there was nothing she could do about it. But if he was as hurt as she suspected, if he had retreated into this pretense to avoid his feelings, if she was really his best friend, then there was hope. She had aroused his passion and love once; she could do so again.

But she could not do anything about their current dilemma now.

And her damn portrait remained downtown in the Gallery Moore.

She wiped her eyes with her fingertips, feeling just slightly better. At least she had a task to accomplish; she desperately needed a new focus. "I am afraid I cannot linger, Alfred. I am on a case."

He started.

"I have had a terrible falling-out with Mr. Hart, but I believe it is only temporary. Tomorrow is another day." She managed a smile. "Hopefully he will be more kindly disposed toward me then."

"I am so sorry, Miss Cahill."

She shuddered. "I was well aware of his occasional moods when I accepted his proposal," she said. She inhaled, finding more resolve. "Can a doorman hail me a cab?" She could not go home. She was not up to facing her mother. Julia would undoubtedly be relieved to see her, but only for a brief moment. Then she would be furious with her for failing to attend her own wedding, never mind the danger she had been in. And she would not be able to tell her parents what had really happened—they could never learn of the portrait.

Worse, Julia would get to the heart of the conversation that had just happened. She was clever and shrewd, and she adored Hart. She would want to know if Francesca had gone to him to explain herself and seek his forgiveness. Julia Cahill was determined to see this marriage come to fruition. Francesca did not want to discuss this new terrible impasse with Hart with her mother.

However, her family needed to know that she was all right. Francesca asked Alfred to send word that she was unharmed, and would be home as soon as possible. The butler assured her he was only too eager to do so. As Alfred sent a doorman out for a hansom, Francesca thanked him and stepped outside into the warm June night. Amazingly, there was a bright crescent moon and a canopy of stars overhead. There was even the whisper of a silken breeze. It had been the perfect night for a wedding. She remained sick at heart from the recent confrontation. She briefly closed her eyes, trying hard to shove the memory away. She had known how cruel Hart could be, but she had never expected him to be that cruel with her.

"Miz Cahill? Are you all right?" a small boy asked worriedly.

Her eyes flew open as Joel Kennedy tugged on her hand. She had never been so pleased to see anyone. She was fond of Joel; he had become a little brother to her. Impulsively she bent and swept him into her arms, hard. "Hart is very angry with me," she whispered before releasing him.

"You stood him up. Of course he's mad, but he loves you and he'll forgive you." His dark eyes were huge in his pale face.

Out of the mouths of babes, she thought, praying he was right.

"You're all scratched an' cut. What happened?"

"We have a case, Joel. Can you help me tonight?"

He nodded, remaining wide-eyed with concern, not surprise. "Do we need the flies? You missed the c'mish. He was here an hour ago—helpin' look fer you."

She smiled just a little, then. "Of course I need Bragg."

In that moment, she had never needed him more.

"PETER," LEIGH ANNE said softly, "would you mind getting me a brandy? I'm afraid my leg is bothering me right now." She wondered if he would refuse her.

But the big manservant, who towered over almost everyone at six foot five or six, did not say a word. If he knew that she had already had a bit of brandy in her tea, she could not tell. His poker face did not change expression as he left the small, dully furnished dining room where Leigh Anne was sharing a light meal with Katie and Dot.

Katie had been eating, but barely. Now, she laid her fork down and looked at her with worry in her dark eyes. Leigh Anne wished she hadn't said anything in front of her. She reached out and covered her hand with hers. "Darling, I am fine, really, it is just a tiny twinge," she lied. She did not know why her right leg—her good leg, the leg with feeling—bothered her so much. But that was nothing compared to the unbearable lump of anguish in her chest, which simply never went away. She woke up with it, lived with it and went to bed with it. She did not know what she would do without the brandy and the laudanum.

The first thing she had done upon returning home from the wedding was to take her tea. It was always liberally laced with brandy.

Leigh Anne did not want to think about the wedding that hadn't taken place. But it was hard to keep the unpleasant recollection from swimming in her mind. She had expected a life of balls and parties—a life of luxury—when she married into the Bragg family. Instead, they had leased a miserable flat while Rick worked night and day to represent indigent clients as a public defender. Feeling betrayed and abandoned, she had gone to Europe. She had thought he might chase her down and beg her forgiveness—but he had not. She had eventually adjusted to the fact that their separation would be permanent. Life on the Continent was glamorous, and she decided to forget her foolish debutante's dreams. She soon moved freely in the best circles, and she was frequently pursued by ambitious financiers and dashing noblemen.

She had only returned to the States upon hearing how ill her father was. When she had learned that Rick was in love with another woman, she had been shocked—and she had given in to the immediate instinct for self-preservation. She had no wish to be humiliated by a love affair, or worse, ruined by divorce. She had immediately left Boston for New York, to claim her husband and her marriage.

At first, he had been furious with her return, but she had been determined. In a way, she had bribed him into the reconciliation. She had told him that if he lived with her as man and wife for six months and still wanted a divorce after that, she would give it to him. She had been very confident of his political aspirations, which a divorce would destroy, and even more certain of her powers of seduction. And she had been right.

But their marriage had been unhappy anyway. He refused to forgive her for the years of separation. And he had changed so much. He was a powerful man now, whom she respected and admired. She had realized that she still loved him. But then she'd been struck down by a runaway coach, and she had permanently lost the use of her legs.

Leigh Anne felt the black despair claim her then. She had been so close to attaining the life she had dreamed of as a young woman. Briefly, she had loved being Rick's wife again, in spite of his rage. She had been certain he would love and admire her in return, in time. He was such a catch now—he came from a good family, he was a gentleman and his political star was on the rise. He received more invitations than he could ever accept. She had loved poring over the cards, deciding whose function to attend—and whose invitation she would reject. She had been shocked to realize the power a single rejection could have. And she had dreamed of the future they would have—they'd adopt the two girls and have more children of their own, while he became a state senator, and then a United States senator. They would move to Washington, the most exciting city in the world, where power and ambition ran riot amongst glamour and wealth...

She wanted to cry. Now, she dreaded his walking in the door. The despair was consuming. She hated being crippled and ugly; she hated her life now!

She had always taken for granted her ability to walk into a room and be the most beautiful woman there. No more. It had been awful entering the church today in her damn wheeled chair. Everyone had looked at her, and she had known what they were all thinking. There had been so much pity in the sidelong glances cast her way, in the whispers behind her back.

What was left for her, other than the two little girls?

Peter placed the glass of brandy before her, his timing perfection.

She inhaled, finding sudden composure, and blinked a tear back. She smiled at him, thanking him the way a lady should. Then she drank the brandy, closing her eyes as it burned its way into her belly, awaiting the release the alcohol would bring her.

The only thing left for her was being a good mother. She looked at the nearly empty glass of brandy. She was afraid to continue with her thoughts. Then she heard the front door. She tensed.

"Mama?" Katie whispered anxiously. "Do you want to read us a story?"

"Story, story!" Dot beamed, clapping her hands. Mrs. Flowers, the nanny, had just wiped them free of apple-sauce.

Before Leigh Anne could agree—she loved reading

bedtime stories to the girls—she heard Rick's footfall approaching. She froze, filled with dread.

He appeared on the threshold of the olive-green-and-gold dining room. He smiled tiredly at her, then went to kiss Katie and Dot on the forehead. He did not approach her, and she was relieved. He was terribly concerned about Francesca's disappearance, she thought. But of course he was. He was loyal to a fault, and he would always care about Francesca. Then she wondered if she truly believed her foolish thoughts. They would always be more to one another than mere friends.

"Did you find her?" Leigh Anne asked. She hadn't decided if she should be thrilled or dismayed that Francesca and Hart hadn't married. Just a few months ago, Rick had been in love with her.

Rick straightened, but as he spoke, his gaze went to her brandy glass. "No. I am very worried. Her disappearance is now an official police matter." He turned to the nanny. "Could you take the girls upstairs and get them ready for bed?"

Katie stood, looking pleadingly at Leigh Anne. Dot cried, "Bed story!" Mrs. Flowers took her out of the high chair and set her down on the floor.

"I will be up in a moment or two," Leigh Anne promised.

Bragg didn't move until the two girls and their nanny had left. She slowly looked at him as he sat down at the table, across from her. "I cannot imagine what could have happened to keep her away from her own wedding. She seemed so happy the last time I saw her. Do you think there is foul play?"

"Yes, I do. The one thing I am sure of is that Francesca did not suddenly decide to jilt Calder." He spoke without emotion. She knew he hated the idea of Francesca marrying Hart. But if he was pleased by this sudden turn of events, she could not tell. "Peter, may I have a scotch, please?"

The Swede nodded and left the dining room.

She looked at her glass, willing herself to have patience. "Chief Farr called. He was looking for you."

"I guess he has heard the news," Rick said grimly.

She wasn't sure what his odd tone meant. "He already knew that Francesca is missing. He said something about how there must have been a commotion today."

Rick looked at her. "What did he say, exactly?"

She started, and finally pulled her drink toward her. "He made a comment about how there must have been a commotion at the church when the bride did not show up. I said it was quite chaotic."

Peter returned and handed Rick a scotch. He took a sip. "Farr doesn't like her."

Leigh Anne finished her brandy. "Surely he doesn't wish her ill, Rick."

Rick grimaced, studying his drink. "I imagine he is pleased that something has befallen her."

"That is a terrible thing to say." He was very concerned, she realized. Carefully, she said, "I hope you are wrong and Francesca had an extreme case of bridal jitters. I hope she is not in jeopardy somewhere."

He stood up abruptly. "I have to call Farr."

"Rick, do not worry about me. I am going to read to the girls and put them to bed. Go find Francesca."

He didn't hesitate. "Are you certain you do not mind?" His gaze strayed to the empty glass on the dining table in front of her.

"I have always liked her." That much was true. Francesca was a pleasant, kind and even admirable woman. "I am worried about her, too."

"Thank you," he said, walking out.

She leaned back in her chair, beyond relief, aware that

she was already forgotten. He wouldn't bother her again that night, and after the girls were asleep, she could dose herself thoroughly with brandy and laudanum.

FRANCESCA HAD SPENT the entire carriage ride filling Joel in on every detail of that day. Joel, of course, already knew that her portrait had been stolen. Two months ago, when she, Hart and Bragg had decided to leave the police out of the investigation—no one wanted anyone to know about the portrait—Joel had wanted to know why everyone was so upset. She had told him that the painting was somewhat compromising.

He hadn't known what the word meant. Francesca had decided not to tell him the absolute truth. She had merely said that she had posed in a manner that society would frown upon. Joel hadn't cared after that. She knew he found the mores of society confusing, irrelevant and at times, just plain stupid, to use his own words.

As No. 11 Madison Square came into view, Francesca felt her heart lurch. The square was deserted at that hour, but the park was beautifully lit from the streetlamps and the moonlight. Bragg's house was a narrow Victorian, on a block filled with similar redbrick homes, just a few doors down from Twenty-third Street. Francesca thought about the time they had walked from his house to Broadway to gaze up at the newly constructed Flatiron Building, which the city's newsmen were calling a "skyscraper." The towering, triangular building remained a stunning testament to the brilliance of mankind.

"He is here," she said, noticing his Daimler parked outside the small carriage house adjacent to the Bragg residence. She paid the driver as she and Joel swiftly stepped down to the sidewalk. Lights were on downstairs and upstairs.

She had regained a great deal of her composure in the

past thirty minutes. Still, she had been badly hurt. A part of her wanted to rush into Bragg's arms, seeking comfort. But another, more mature part of her knew to keep the current state of discord between her and Hart private.

As the cab left, they started up the brick path, toward the house. Francesca knocked on the door, eager to tell Bragg everything that had happened to her.

The door was flung wide open.

Bragg took her arm. "I knew it was you. Are you hurt?"

She came inside, Joel following, so much relief flooding her. Some of her resolve to remain strong and independent crumbled. She smiled tightly. "I have had an awful day."

"I can see that," he said, suddenly releasing her.

In that moment, she knew he wanted to hold her, but he made no move to do so. She did not know if she was relieved or disappointed. Joel broke the silence. "What's wrong with you two? We have a case to solve! Miz Cahill was locked up—someone tried to stop her from marrying Mr. Hart!"

Francesca bit her lip. "Actually, Joel, someone did stop me from marrying Hart." She managed to tear her gaze from Bragg's. Where was Leigh Anne?

"What happened? Why are there scratches and cuts on your face and hands?" He took her arm and guided her into his study, a small dark room with a desk and two chairs. The fireplace was unlit. Joel followed them to the door, but lingered in the hallway.

She allowed herself one final glance over her shoulder, but his wife was not in the parlor at the end of the hall, although the door was open, the lights on. "Am I intruding?"

"Of course not!" he cried. "Everyone is worried about you!"

She tensed. Hart wasn't worried, not at all. Her heart broke all over again, but she decided to ignore it. "I received this by hand this morning, shortly after you left," Francesca said, taking the envelope marked Urgent out of her purse. She handed it to him, the invitation inside.

He quickly read it and paled. "The portrait?"

She nodded, glad to be back on the firm ground of the investigation now. "When I got there, the gallery was closed for summer hours but unlocked. I went in and I saw the portrait. It is nailed to one wall. I felt that I was not alone and I began to explore. Perhaps a half hour later, someone locked me in from outside."

Bragg made a harsh sound—she knew he was angry. "Go on."

She wet her lips. "I called for help, but no one heard me. Then I tried to climb out a very small window in the back office. I had to break the pane. That is how I got cut on my face."

He took her hands in his, not looking down. "How did you hurt your hands?"

"Clawing the wall as I tried to get up to that window."

His expression, already tight, hardened even more.

She couldn't help comparing his reactions to Hart's. Had Calder even noticed her cuts and scratches? "Eventually two children heard me. Their father and a roundsman let me out."

For one more moment he held her hands, and she had the impression that all would be right in the world again. As she thought that, she recalled Hart's cold black gaze, his deliberate cruelty and his words "It is over." She flinched. It could not be over.

Bragg released her, picking up the receiver from the telephone on his desk. Shockingly, he actually had two phones in his house—the other was upstairs in his bedroom. That was truly scandalous, but he claimed it was practical. "It's Bragg. I want Gallery Moore, at No. 69 Waverly Place, cordoned off as the scene of an attempted abduction. No one is to get in or get out, and that includes Moore, the gallery owner. It also includes the police. Let me be clear. You are to cordon off the gallery—I repeat, no one is to go inside. I will be there in thirty minutes." He listened for another moment and hung up. Then he faced her. "You do not have to come downtown, Francesca. I can manage the case now."

Her eyes widened. "Of course I am coming with you!"

He smiled then. "Somehow, I thought you might say that."

She smiled back at him. Very shortly, the gallery would be secured by his men, and no one would be able to get inside to view her portrait. They had to get downtown, but there was less urgency now. She touched his arm briefly. "Have I ruined your evening?"

"No."

His tone was so hard and decisive that she started. Was something wrong? But he then added more quietly, "We agreed to investigate the theft of your portrait privately, but after the events of this day, I do not see how I cannot use the resources at my disposal."

She hesitated. "Hart did not make any headway with his investigators."

"No, he did not—and they visited every single gallery in Manhattan and Brooklyn. No one had seen or heard of your portrait." He said grimly, "Obviously no one can ever see that painting. Let us hope that tonight we recover it, once and for all."

She hugged herself. Hopefully they would recover the portrait within the hour, but that would still leave the thief at large. Why hadn't she gotten more involved? Of course, when the portrait had vanished on April 27 from Sarah's studio, she had still been trying to find the deadly Slasher before he murdered another innocent woman. Then Daisy Jones had been murdered. When Hart had immediately become the prime suspect, her focus had been doing everything possible to clear him. Fortunately, it had taken only four days to solve that case. Marion Gillespie had confessed to the murder of her own daughter on June 6.

"What's wrong?" Bragg asked softly.

"I was just thinking that I wish I had been more involved. But hindsight is useless."

"It is very useless," he agreed. "I understand why Hart chose to thoroughly comb through the city's art world. I expected him to turn up something. But I never expected this, and I am as much to blame as anyone for today's events." He reached for the phone. "Has anyone told your parents that you are safe and sound?"

"You are not to blame!" When he did not respond to that, she knew he did not agree. "Rick," she began.

"Do Julia and Andrew know that you are all right?" he repeated.

"Alfred sent word." She prayed that he would not ask her if she had seen Hart.

He stared, then said, "Still, I feel obligated to call Andrew."

She nodded. "That is fine. I think they would like to be reassured by you, but I cannot face my mother right now."

He gave her an odd look. "Operator, please connect me to Andrew Cahill's home." He laid his hand over the mouthpiece. "Do you wish to speak to your father?"

"Not quite yet. Can you tell them I am fine, that there was some trouble, and I have fallen asleep in your guest room?" she tried.

"Francesca," he objected.

"I am going downtown with you. I have hours to come

up with a plausible reason for having missed my own wedding," she said rather defensively.

He sighed. "Hello, Andrew. I have very good news. I am with Francesca, who has suffered a very trying day.... I am afraid she was lured away from your house deliberately, but she is now fine.... Yes, someone wished to interfere with the wedding.... She has fallen asleep on my sofa.... Yes...I will personally get her home in the next few hours. Good night." He hung up, looking at her.

"I have made you a partner in crime. I am sorry."

"Think nothing of it." Then he softened. "It is hardly the first time, is it? I do not mind telling a white lie for you—and sometimes I enjoy being a partner in crime with you."

She bit her lip, almost thrilling. "It is partly the truth."

He said bluntly, "Have you seen Calder yet?"

She flushed, filled with tension instantly. "Yes. Are you ready to go downtown?"

His gaze was as piercing as a hawk's. She waited, refusing to discuss Hart now. He finally nodded at the door. She started out of the study and he followed, calling for Joel. She said, "Who do you think would want me to miss my wedding?"

Joel came downstairs, apparently having been visiting with the two girls. As they left the house, Joel leading the way, Bragg said, "Hart has enemies, Francesca—hundreds of them, in fact. We agreed two months ago that trying to investigate a list of his enemies was impossible."

"So this thief might want to strike at Calder, not me." They approached the driveway behind the carriage house where Bragg's Daimler was parked.

"It would hardly surprise me." Anger laced his tone. Giving her a dark look, he went to the motorcar and began cranking the engine.

She tensed, watching him. "You can't blame Hart for what happened today—just as you cannot blame yourself. I have made enemies, as well."

"Yes, you have, and Hart and I have actually considered the possibility that someone has decided to seek vengeance against you by stealing the portrait." The engine roared to life and he straightened. He went around to the passenger side and opened her door. Francesca waited for Joel to scramble into the tiny backseat before she got in. As he closed the door, he said, "We have discussed this investigation several times, Francesca."

Her mind raced as he went around to his side of the car and got in. Hart had never mentioned sitting down with Rick to discuss the stolen portrait. "Bragg, I have already made a mental list of the people who might wish for revenge against me. Gordino, Bill Randall, Mary and Henrietta Randall, and Solange Marceaux are the only culprits I can truly think of."

He had put the car in Reverse. He paused and looked at her. She wasn't quite certain what that look meant. "Gordino was incarcerated for running a con in early April. He won't be out on the street till August."

Gordino was a vicious thug whom she had run into several times during her first investigation. "Good. He isn't smart enough to have managed this theft, anyway."

Bragg smiled slightly, now backing the Daimler slowly out of the driveway and onto the still-deserted street. He shifted into Drive. "I agree."

She thought then about Bill Randall—Hart's half brother. They did not really know each other, but they hated one another. Bill had not been able to abide the discovery that his father had sired a son out of wedlock. Hart despised his half sibling as well—a natural enough response, she supposed, to his father's and brother's rejection of him. But there was more to Bill's antipathy. She shivered. "Bill Randall certainly hates me for discovering that his sister murdered their father." She added grimly, "He also hates Hart."

"Bill turned state's evidence on his sister, Francesca."

She already knew that. Bragg was now cruising down Twenty-third Street toward Broadway, where hansoms, drays and an electric trolley were visible. Mary Randall had confessed to murdering Paul Randall, but only after Francesca had nearly exposed her crime. Bill had abducted Francesca to prevent her from going to the police with the facts of the case. Both brother and sister were very dangerous.

Bragg said, "Bill Randall got off scot-free in exchange for his testimony. Mary is at Bellevue. Her lawyers successfully pleaded an insanity defense. She will be locked up for many, many years. However, Bill has an alibi for Saturday night—he was in his dormitory room at the university with both his roommates—and your portrait was taken on Sunday afternoon. It is virtually impossible that he could have arrived in the city the next morning in order to steal the painting. The earliest train from Philadelphia arrived at noon."

Bill was instantly taken off Francesca's list of suspects. No one could arrive at Grand Central Station at noon and make it to the Channing home uptown to steal the painting in less than an hour. Francesca was sorely disappointed. As Bragg turned left onto Fifth Avenue, she asked, "And Henrietta Randall?"

"Their mother was sentenced to one year for her attempt to cover up her daughter's crimes. She remains imprisoned on Blackwell's Island."

"Well, that rules the Randalls out."

"I believe so. However, Solange Marceaux vanished into thin air when we raided her brothel during the investigation into Murphy's child-prostitution ring."

She hadn't thought about the icy blonde madam in months. Francesca had briefly posed as a prostitute in order to get into her establishment. Solange had been furious with the deception—she had even ordered Francesca killed. "She still hasn't been found?" Her nape tingled now. Solange Marceaux was a strong, clever and dangerous woman.

"I'm afraid not," Bragg said, carefully passing the electric trolley, which was devoid of passengers at that hour. The conductor waved at them. "We will find her eventually. I am sure she has set up another brothel somewhere in the city."

Francesca realized they were passing Fourteenth Street, a major crosstown thoroughfare. They would be at the gallery within moments. "Solange was vicious and vengeful, Bragg. She is a truly formidable opponent. But if she is back in business, I cannot imagine her jeopardizing her profits and her liberty by seeking petty revenge against me."

"And just how petty is such revenge? If that portrait is publicly displayed, you will never be welcome in polite society again."

He was right. She glanced at him, trembling. His expression was odd.

"You have given me several long looks tonight. Is something wrong?"

He hesitated, returning his gaze to the street. "You have been calling me Bragg all evening. You haven't called me that since my reconciliation with Leigh Anne."

Her heart seemed to erupt in her chest. She wasn't sure what to say and she thought of Hart, his words cruelly echoing. *It is over.*

As if reading her mind, he said, "Are you going to tell me what happened with Hart tonight?" His tone was terse.

They were already at Eighth Street. Washington Square and Waverly Place were one block down. She saw the shiny police wagons ahead, illuminated by the city's gas lamps, with their bright brass-plated sides and wheels. Three of them were lined up on the street between the park and the gallery. A number of roundsmen were milling around. A slight crowd had gathered, with several children running about, as if it were a carnival. She glanced at Bragg.

He sighed, making a right on to Waverly Place and pulling up behind one of the police wagons. A tall, familiar figure detached itself from the group of policemen. Francesca stiffened in dread.

Bragg let the motor idle as Chief Farr approached. When he stepped into the light spilling from one of the cast-iron streetlamps, Francesca saw that he was smiling. He held a small lantern in one hand.

Farr despised her. And he was not trustworthy—Bragg knew that for a fact. Had he seen her portrait? If he had, she was finished.

"Hello, C'mish. Miz Cahill." He nodded politely at them. "Sorry about the wedding," he added with a half smile, and she knew he wasn't sorry at all.

Her heart was pounding with explosive force. "Thank you. I am sure we will tie the knot another day."

"Sure." He did not sound as if he thought so. He opened her door for her. She got out rigidly, her gaze slamming to the gallery. It was cast in blackness, but she could see wooden barricades on the sidewalk, preventing anyone from going down the steps to the gallery's front door.

Then she took a quick look at the crowd. Thank God the city's carnivorous press corps wasn't present.

Had Farr seen the portrait? she wondered once more. She glanced at Bragg as he came around the front of the motorcar, but his gaze was on the gallery. He said sharply, "Is that door open?"

"I'm afraid so," Farr drawled. "It was open when we got here, C'mish."

Francesca started running, her horror escalating. When she reached the barricade she saw that the front door of the gallery was entirely open. She cried out. Anyone could have walked inside!

"Did you go inside?" Bragg demanded of Farr from behind her.

Francesca did not wait for his answer. She shoved past the barricade and started down the steps, stumbling.

"Didn't have a choice. Clearly, someone broke in. The glass is all busted up."

She realized that the glass on the front door was broken, which made no sense—unless someone had thought to reach in from the outside to unlock the front door. But the front door hadn't been locked when she had left.

"Hand me the lantern and everyone stand back," Bragg ordered. As she pushed open the front door, she felt him behind her. He held up the lantern and light illuminated the gallery.

She froze.

The wall where the portrait had been hanging was empty.

CHAPTER SIX

Saturday, June 28, 1902
Midnight

FRANCESCA SAT IN the passenger seat of Bragg's car as it idled on Fifth Avenue, just outside the open gates of the driveway leading to her family's home. She was finally, truly, exhausted.

Chief Farr had explained that when he had arrived at the gallery with a police detail, the front door had been open—he hadn't touched it. The gallery had been in darkness. He had taken a lantern and gone inside with two men, in case a burglar was present. The gallery had been empty. But it had instantly been obvious that a painting had been ripped from the wall it had been nailed to. Farr had been careful that he and his men hadn't touched anything.

Farr had ordered a search of the premises, the surrounding grounds, and he had sent several officers to speak to the neighbors. No one, according to the chief, had seen or heard anything unusual.

Bragg was putting Inspector Newman on this case. Tomorrow morning Newman and Heinreich would go over the gallery with a fine-tooth comb, looking for clues. They had already dropped Joel at his mother's flat on Tenth Street and Avenue A, and tomorrow he would canvass that neighborhood.

"Are you all right?"

Francesca started at the soft sound of Bragg's voice. She glanced at him. "How can I be all right? Our thief has the portrait again."

"We do not know that it is the same thief," he said quietly.

"No, we do not. But it is probable that it is the same person." She truly doubted some passerby had walked into the gallery and taken her portrait. She stared ahead, through the open iron gates, at her house. Only a few lights were on downstairs.

"Everyone is probably asleep, but that isn't what is bothering you, is it?"

Hart's cold image came to mind. Her reputation remained in dire jeopardy and the man she loved had turned his back on her. Was he even at home? "I was afraid, briefly, that the chief had seen my portrait."

"I know. I was afraid of the same thing. Are we ever going to discuss what is really amiss here?"

She blinked back sudden tears. "I don't know if I should—or if I can."

She tried to stare straight ahead at the limestone mansion. Her hands were on her lap, and suddenly, she felt his large, strong hand covering hers. She stiffened, the heartbreak acute. How could this be happening?

"I am so sorry, Francesca," Bragg said intensely. "I know he was a bastard when you went to see him."

She somehow nodded, feeling all her resolve crumbling.

"And I apologize for prying into a very private matter. It is just…that I care."

She slowly looked at him. "I know you do.… He was horrid, absolutely horrid. He was so cruel.…"

He reached for her. She wasn't sure how it happened, but she laid her face on his broad chest, his arms going around her, and allowed herself a moment to weep. She felt him tense and she told herself that she must stop this nonsense. She fought and managed to turn the tears off. "Do you think he will ever forgive me?"

His hand moved to the nape of her neck beneath her hair, which remained in a haphazard knot. "He is not a forgiving man. Never mind that there is nothing to forgive."

Being in Bragg's arms felt perfectly safe. But she was also reminded of the romantic times they had shared; she was reminded that he was a handsome and virile man. She loved Hart acutely. Francesca pulled away and he let her go. "I am sorry for being a simpering, self-indulgent and silly woman."

"You are none of those things. You are strong and brave, and Hart is a goddamn fool."

She wiped her eyes and gazed at him. "He said it was over. He told me he does not care about what happened today. He told me that he never loved me."

Bragg's eyes widened in shock. "My God! He has no shame! Damn it, he is rotten and selfish to the core, to be so unfeeling—to only care about his own feelings!"

Just then, she did not feel like defending him. "If he doesn't love me—if he has never loved me—then it is over and there is nothing I can do about it."

Bragg's gaze was dark and hard. Francesca expected him to insist that Hart did love her, but he did not. He finally said, "I hate seeing you hurt like this. Francesca, I know you will not believe me, but I also know that you trust me. You will be fine. Maybe not tomorrow or even the day after, but you will get through this."

He was insinuating that she would get over Hart. She turned away. She loved Calder, but if her love was not returned, then she had been in love with an illusion—and she wanted that illusion back. "I had better go in. It is late and we have so much to do tomorrow."

"Yes." He put the motorcar in Drive and it inched forward. "Where will you start your investigation?"

She smiled wanly. "Joel will canvass the neighborhood downtown. He might turn up some interesting witnesses to last night's affair. I think I will start at the very beginning and pay a call on Sarah."

"Perhaps that's a good idea. Why don't you stop by police headquarters when you are done with her, let me know what you have discovered, and we can plan the next step together."

She glanced at him. The police were already involved, and she knew he would stay on top of the investigation in order to protect her. Maybe Newman and Heinreich would have uncovered a new clue by tomorrow. "All right." They had reached the end of the driveway and the wide stone staircase leading to the front door. Francesca hesitated. "Thank you for everything, Rick."

His gaze was sharp. "You don't have to thank me for anything," he said firmly.

She smiled and said good-night and got out of the automobile, hurrying up the steps. She was aware that he waited for her to get safely inside before driving away; in previous investigations she had been accosted both in her driveway and outside her own front door. As she let herself in, she finally heard the car leave.

She thought of Hart as she closed and locked the door, and there was so much heartache and despair. She didn't know how she would have managed without Bragg. He had become a better friend than she had ever dreamed possible. He had always been as solid and dependable as a rock. He would not abandon her now, in her time of need.

A hall light came on.

Francesca jumped, glimpsing her father in his navy blue silk robe, matching pajamas and slippers, standing at the foot of the stairs. He was clearly wide-awake. She bit her lip. "You didn't have to wait up for me, Papa."

Andrew Cahill was a gray-haired man of chubby proportions with huge side-whiskers and a kindly face. He came rushing forward. "What happened today, Francesca? And what happened to your cheeks?"

Francesca smiled tearfully as he took her hands. "I am afraid that someone wants to hurt me, Papa. Someone wanted to prevent my marriage to Calder, and I fell for the bait. I am so sorry!"

He embraced her briefly. "Your mother was hysterical, fearing the very worst. She is asleep now, of course. The moment Rick called and said you were all right, she collapsed."

"I am sorry," Francesca said again, meaning it.

"Who did this? What exactly happened?" Andrew asked, his brown gaze intent.

She trembled. "I was given a note and told that it was urgent that I go downtown. I should have ignored it. I was lured to an art gallery—and locked inside. I never saw the culprit. I tried to get out by breaking a window, but it was very high up and I failed. By the time help arrived, it was well after four o'clock. I am not hurt."

"Thank God," Andrew said grimly.

"I have asked Bragg to help me find and apprehend the person responsible."

Andrew hugged her again, briefly. "I am sure Rick will get to the bottom of this terrible affair. Have you seen Hart yet?"

She tensed.

"Francesca?" Andrew demanded. "Surely you explained yourself to your fiancé!"

She knew she had to tread with care now. Andrew did not like Calder Hart at all. Apparently, he did not think Hart good enough for her. Nor did he trust him to give up his womanizing ways. She procrastinated by taking a deep breath. "Yes, I have seen Calder. He has suffered a shock, as well. It is not every day that a man decides to marry, then ends up jilted at the altar."

"Let me hazard a guess. He doesn't care what you have gone through. He is furious with you." Andrew was cold. People assumed him to be easygoing and benign, yet he was a farm boy from Illinois who had amassed a fortune in the very competitive meatpacking industry through hard work, relentless ambition and razor-sharp intelligence. He was not a man to be dismissed or taken lightly. When necessary, he was formidable.

"Of course he cares," Francesca said, praying it was true. "But he is very upset, and right now, he is not kindly disposed toward having a dialogue with me."

Andrew folded his arms across his chest. "And Rick just dropped you off, after spending the night trying to apprehend this villain with you?"

She did not know where he was leading. "Yes. Papa, I am exhausted. I must go to bed. Can we finish this discussion tomorrow?"

"Of course we can." He softened and kissed the top of her head. "But, Francesca? I wonder if you were about to marry the right man."

MORNING LIGHT POURED through the oversize windows of his Bridge Street office. The office took up an entire corner of the fifth floor. Hart turned to gaze out at New York Harbor as the sun rose even higher in the red dawn sky.

A scotch was in his hand, his fifth or sixth of the evening—he had lost count and he did not care. Except, the evening was now gone.

Hart stood up, staring outside, his head pounding. He could see several cargo ships, a tugboat and a naval

destroyer, all at anchor. From where he stood, he saw the
street almost directly below, which was vacant except for
one lonely-looking carter. Within half an hour, he knew,
the southernmost tip of Manhattan Island would come
alive with frock-coated bankers and scurrying clerks,
city lawyers and ill-suited accountants, rushing to their
various places of business. Vendors would begin to sell
iced oysters and hot chestnuts; cabs and trolleys, all occupied, would crowd the streets.

Holding his glass even more tightly, he cursed. For his
mind was now, finally, made up.

It was definitely over.

She had failed to show up for their wedding. He would
never forgive her such betrayal, but he understood. On
some level, perhaps subconsciously, she had used that note
as an excuse to avoid marrying him. Because she knew
as well as he did that their marriage was a vast mistake.

All he could think of all night and this morning was
their argument, when she begged him for forgiveness and
claimed that she loved him. If she loved him, she would
have never left the house to go downtown; her priority
would have been their wedding. They could have gone
downtown together, after the ceremony. She didn't love
him and she never had. It was so painfully obvious. Rick
was the one she truly loved, deep down. She had loved
him first—she had even said so, not just to Rick but to
Hart. He had remained nothing but her second choice.

Now, he wasn't a choice at all.

But he wondered if she had ever said those three
words—*I love you*—to his brother.

The pain simmered in his chest in spite of the whiskey. It had bubbled there all evening long. Yet he would
never acknowledge it; he much preferred the anger. He
had never been hurt by a woman before, and he did not
intend to start now.

He cursed and threw his glass hard at the wall. There was no satisfaction as it shattered; there was nothing except her tearful image and her protestations that she loved him. Damn her!

He paced to his desk, only to stare down at it unseeingly. He was such a fool. He would not blame anyone for laughing at him now. Maybe, one day, he would be able to laugh at himself.

But now, it felt as if he'd never laugh again. Her betrayal was that vast, that important, and goddamn it, it did hurt.

Francesca was the best thing that had ever happened to him.

It was true, but he didn't care. He was conditioned to reward betrayal with punishment. It was the law of the land, a matter of survival. He would never tolerate such betrayal, not from anyone, and not when he had given her his absolute loyalty. That was why she was no longer welcome in his house. That was why they would never be friends again. That was why he would never trust her again.

The sun suddenly intensified. He looked up at the wall of windows, but instead, he saw her as she had been last night, in tears. He tensed, not wanting to listen to the voice inside his head that told him that Francesca would never deliberately hurt anyone, much less him, and that he was being the fool now....

He cursed and reined in the pain. He refused to entertain all the memories they had made, which threatened to engulf him.

Francesca had been his one and only friend. As he contemplated the future, he felt a moment of fear, when he was never afraid; he felt a moment of intense loneliness, when he was never lonely.

He shrugged the momentary weakness aside.

It was over, and he was relieved. He wondered, though, as betrayed as he felt, if he was even capable of giving up his faith in Francesca. Would a part of him always believe in her? Then he reminded himself that there was no other choice.

Despite himself, he recalled the times she had kept her faith in him. Even at the beginning of their relationship, when they had been strangers, she had refused to see the bad in him. She had fought for him tooth and nail, even when he had been accused of murdering Daisy, when the entire city had been lined up to hang him....

Suddenly her tear-stained image came to mind, her cheeks scratched, her clothes torn.

Hart hadn't wanted to listen to her explanation last night. He had been too furious and too intent on controlling that fury to really listen to her. She had been completely disheveled when she had barged into his library, but she hadn't been hurt. As angry as he had been, he had taken a careful inventory the moment she walked in.

She claimed she'd been lured away from their wedding by the thief who had stolen her portrait.

He would never be able to live with himself if that portrait surfaced publicly.

Remaining calm, he walked back to the window. Below, he saw the streets coming alive. In the end, they had come full circle. The portrait only existed because he had commissioned it. He was a selfish, depraved bastard, and he had insisted the painting be a nude. Had he not done so, the theft wouldn't have mattered—and she wouldn't have gone chasing after it yesterday. She might have used the summons to the gallery as an excuse to avoid marriage, but he was ultimately responsible for her failure to meet him at the church. He hoped that one day he would laugh about that.

Hart became still—the hunter now in pursuit of his prey. He intended to recover the portrait and destroy it. There was no other choice.

Whoever had stolen it in the first place hadn't done so because it was valuable enough to fence. They had meant to use it to blackmail him—or destroy her with it.

And he could not stand by and allow that to happen.

Hart seized his suit jacket, shrugging it on and hurrying from the office. Two minutes later he hailed a cab. She had said the gallery was on Waverly Place. He ordered the driver there, at full speed, offering him a double fare.

The gallery was easy to find. Two police officers were guarding the establishment, which was barricaded from the public. Hart stepped down from the cab, ordering the driver to wait. His senses were warning him now that everything was wrong. But as he took in the neighborhood and the gallery, remarking every detail that might be useful, he could not decide what was bothering him.

As he started forward to investigate, one of the policemen came his way, barring his path abruptly.

Hart didn't even wait for him to speak—he shoved a ten-dollar bill in the man's hand and pushed past him. A moment later he was staring at the empty space where a painting had once hung. He could see from the holes in a section of plywood that it had been ripped from the wall, where it had been nailed.

"Did Commissioner Bragg take that painting down?" he demanded.

"No, sir."

When no more information was forthcoming, Hart turned and gave the officer another bill. The roundsman smiled at him. "I heard the chief talking last night. A painting was stolen, sir."

CHAPTER SEVEN

Sunday, June 29, 1902
9:00 a.m.

FRANCESCA GRIPPED THE banister for support as she started downstairs, expecting the worst. Her mother never left her apartments before noon, but she was certain this morning would be an exception.

The moment she started down the stairs, Julia appeared in the huge hall below.

Francesca inwardly cringed. Julia was already elegantly dressed for the day. The implication of that was dire. "Good morning, Mama."

Julia was unsmiling. "It is hardly a good morning. Your father gave me some jumbled explanation as to why you failed to marry Calder yesterday."

Francesca came down the rest of the stairway. "Someone clearly wished to stop the wedding."

Julia was not sympathetic. "There are reporters on our front lawn, Francesca, a half dozen of them."

Francesca groaned and rushed past her mother, across the spectacular black-and-white marble floors. She peered out the closest window, not far from the front door, where the doorman stood. Julia had not exaggerated—six newsmen were milling about the front lawn. All wore rumpled suit coats. Some wore fedoras. She recognized that cur from the *Sun,* Arthur Kurland, who knew far too much about her private affairs than a newsman should, as well as Isaacson, from the *Tribune*. How would she ever leave the house?

"I hope you are pleased with yourself," Julia said curtly from behind her.

Francesca whirled. Her sister appeared at the far end of the hall, hurrying toward them. "I am not pleased at all! I love Calder, and I wanted nothing more than to wake up this morning as his wife," she said, meaning it.

"Then maybe you should have thought twice about recklessly and impulsively responding to some vague request for help," Julia said flatly.

Francesca cringed again. Connie came up to her, her expression worried. Her sister took her hand and squeezed it, her blue eyes searching. Francesca couldn't smile at her. She had said she would visit Sarah first thing, but she had decided she must speak with Hart before she did anything else. She prayed he had forgiven her. Surely, in the light of a new day, he had realized how much she loved him and that she had been deliberately prevented from attending her own wedding. Surely they would wind up in one another's arms. "I have made a terrible mess of things."

"Yes, you have. Were you really gallivanting about the city last night—sleuthing—with Rick Bragg?" Julia asked incredulously.

"Mama, yesterday I was lured downtown—and locked inside an art gallery. Someone wished for me to miss my wedding. Of course I asked Bragg to help me find and apprehend the person responsible." Francesca looked at Connie for support.

Julia said, "I fail to understand why you weren't with your fiancé last night. Bragg can apprehend that rowdy by himself."

Francesca trembled. She did not want to discuss Hart with Julia.

Connie put her arm around her, finally coming to the rescue. "Mother, Fran did not try to wreck her own wedding. Someone knew her well enough to bait her and destroy it for her. You know that Fran cannot refuse anyone in need—not ever!"

Julia harrumphed. "Andrew said you saw Hart."

Francesca wet her lips. Her head ached. "He is upset with me, but he will come around."

Julia's gaze became intent and searching. "Has he ended it, Francesca?"

She hesitated, and it was answer enough. Julia blanched. "Didn't you explain to him that you were locked up?" she cried.

"Yes, I did. He is very angry right now," she tried, trembling. "But in a day or two, he will calm down, I am certain of it." She did not want to think of his cruelty yesterday.

"This is simply unbearable—one scandal after another. It is all because of your sleuthing! Whatever did I do to deserve such an unconventional daughter? Well, Hart must come around. I won't have you jilted!" With that, her blue eyes flashing, Julia strode for the stairs.

Francesca didn't dare move, not until her mother was out of sight. Nor did she dare beg her not to intervene. She felt as if she had gotten off lightly. Julia was frightening when aroused.

Then she exhaled and faced her sister. "I don't know if Hart will ever come around."

"Well, he might certainly think twice about it if he learns you spent half of last night investigating this incident with his half brother," Connie retorted. She took her arm. "Fran, what really happened? I was here, remember? I saw how terribly upset you were when you received that note. In fact, the more I think about it, the more I am beginning to suspect that you were frightened."

Francesca studied her sister grimly. They had almost no secrets. Connie knew that Hart had commissioned a portrait of her and that the painting had vanished in April. What she did not know was that it was so damn compromising.

Francesca didn't want to worry Connie, but she desperately needed her sister's help now. Not with the missing portrait—now that the thief had surfaced and had begun to reveal his or her hand, she felt certain she and Bragg would soon apprehend him—but she was at a loss where Hart was concerned. She simply could not lose him like this. "The note came from the thief who stole my portrait."

Connie blinked. "I do not understand."

"Connie, my portrait is a nude."

Her sister stared at her. For one moment, her expression did not change. And then, shock and disbelief covered her features. "What!"

"My nude portrait is in the thief's hands, and clearly, he or she intends to use it against me."

Connie cried out, "How could you!"

"Does it matter? I had to recover the portrait before it was publicly displayed," Francesca cried in a rush.

Connie slowly shook her head, as if still dazed. "And Hart blames you for not showing up at the wedding? Is he mad? Doesn't he realize what this means?"

Hart was too clever to not understand the danger she was in. Knowing that, Francesca was frightened—by the fact that he hadn't rushed to her defense. "I think I have hurt him terribly, Con. Otherwise, he would surely be trying to recover the portrait and protect me." She turned and walked back to the window, hiding behind a drapery as she peered out. Her heart was racing. "I am going to Sarah's. It is going to be very unpleasant, trying to get out of the house."

Connie came up behind her. "What about Hart?"

She realized she was so afraid to contact him that day. "I'll telephone first, to see if he is in. If he is, I will call on him and smooth things over."

Connie took her hand. Francesca clung to it.

BUT HART HADN'T been in, so instead, Francesca decided to use the Cahill coach and driver to go across town to the city's rather forsaken west side. Fortunately, Julia was not downstairs when she left. Andrew did not need the carriage until later, and Francesca promised to return it by noon. As for the newsmen, she ignored their questions. Everyone had wanted to know what had happened and if the wedding would be rescheduled.

"Have you changed your mind about marrying Calder Hart? Did you deliberately jilt him?" Arthur Kurland had cried, raising his voice above the din made by his peers.

Francesca had turned to look at him as Jennings closed her carriage door. "No, Mr. Kurland, I did not jilt my fiancé."

"So the wedding is on?" he asked with a sly smile.

She hesitated as Jennings climbed into the carriage's driver's seat. "Of course the wedding is on," she said as the carriage began to rumble away.

The drive through Central Park should have been lovely, with flowers in bloom everywhere and birds singing from the leafy treetops, a few ladies and gentlemen strolling arm in arm, a cyclist pedaling along the carriage path. Francesca hardly noticed. She must not think about those damn newsmen and tomorrow's headlines. She tried to focus on the upcoming interview with her friend, Sarah Channing. Instead, she kept worrying about Hart.

Alfred had finally admitted to her that he hadn't come home last night.

Eventually she arrived at the Channings' gothic mansion. She would concentrate on the matter of the stolen portrait, at least for a few hours. Ignoring the house's abundant turrets and towers, not to mention gargoyles, Francesca went to the front door, where she was greeted by a servant. She had barely asked for Sarah when the young brunette artist came rushing into the front hall. "Francesca! I have been so worried about you!"

Francesca allowed herself to be embraced. She had become fond of Sarah in the past few months. When they had first met, she had assumed Sarah to be a rather unintelligent, very shy and boringly meek young woman. But she had quickly realized just how bohemian Sarah was and how much they had in common. During the course of posing for her portrait, they had become friends. Sarah was as eccentric as Francesca—she lived for her art—it was just not obvious at first sight. "Sarah, I found my portrait yesterday in a gallery off Washington Square."

Sarah gasped. Before she could speak, Francesca clasped her shoulder, pulling her aside toward a huge Venetian mirror. "I was lured there and locked in. That is why I missed the wedding. When Bragg and I returned, several hours later, the portrait was gone."

Sarah paled. "I wish I had never agreed to paint you unclothed."

"Now you are blaming yourself?" Francesca was shocked.

"Francesca, that portrait was stolen from my studio, in my house." Sarah paced, agitated. Her long, curly brown hair was casually pinned up, and chunks of it were falling down. She was simply clad in a shirtwaist and dark skirt, as was Francesca. She had obviously been in her studio, because there was a smudge of charcoal on her cheek. She wore no jewelry. "Because of the damn portrait, you have missed your wedding!" She faced her, dark eyes ablaze.

"I wanted to pose provocatively and you know it." Francesca went over to her. Several trophy heads—a lion, an elephant and an antelope—were above them now. The late Richard Wyeth Channing had been a world-renowned big-game hunter. "Bragg and I have become active in this investigation, Sarah. The thief has surfaced. He or she did not wish for me to marry, clearly. I was hoping to ask you some questions."

"Of course," Sarah said, her gaze attentive. "But, Francesca, do you think the thief a woman?"

"I am not sure, but Solange Marceaux escaped the police when we apprehended Murphy and dismantled his child prostitution ring. I crossed paths with her once, Sarah. She is a dangerous woman—and not particularly fond of me."

Sarah hugged herself. "I recall you telling me all about it. You are lucky to be alive. But I don't think that Solange would care about your wedding, Francesca. If she has the portrait, she means to destroy you with it."

Francesca stared thoughtfully. Preventing her marriage to Hart might have been incidental to the greater motive of destroying her reputation. Sarah was right; Solange wouldn't give a damn if Francesca married Hart. Her interest would be in the kind of vengeance that ruining Francesca could achieve.

"Do you have other suspects?" Sarah asked.

She smiled grimly. "We have a rather attenuated list," she replied, thinking of Bill Randall and his mother. If time allowed, she would try to see Henrietta Randall later in the day. But it was a bit of a trek to Blackwell's Island, where the woman was imprisoned, and she did not think much would come of the trip. She wondered how either of the Randalls would have ever learned of her portrait.

Solange Marceaux's knowledge, if she was their thief, was also a mystery.

"What does Hart think?"

It was hard to meet Sarah's gaze now and she felt herself flush. "I'm not sure."

"Francesca? What does that mean?"

She turned away. "It means that he isn't speaking to me right now."

Sarah cried out, rushing to face her. "Now I feel even worse than before. I should have kept my studio locked—I knew how compromising that portrait was. Oh, he must be so angry, to have been stood up at the altar."

Just then, she didn't have the will to tell Sarah that it wasn't her fault. In a way, every single one of them had had a hand in the portrait's theft. "I am hoping Hart will realize that I never meant to hurt or humiliate him."

Sarah began shaking her head. "At least he truly loves you."

Francesca prayed that was the case.

Sarah seized her hands, as if she sensed Francesca's doubt. "Francesca, he adores you. And rightly so, as you are the most unique of women!"

Pain stabbed through her breast. She would corner him that evening when he came home, as she feared confronting him in his office during business hours. The evening felt as if it was a lifetime from now. "Can we discuss the weekend that the portrait vanished? I have to find that portrait, Sarah, and lock it up."

"Of course we can. But I have already answered dozens of questions. And as much as I hate to admit it, Francesca, the portrait must be destroyed."

Francesca said grimly, "You are undoubtedly right, and that is so generous of you. I know you spoke with Hart's investigators, but I wasn't present. When did you first realize that the portrait was gone?"

Sarah blinked. "Francesca, you were with Bragg at headquarters when I called the police. I discovered the portrait gone on Sunday afternoon, as you know. It was about one o'clock."

The call had come in at 2:00 p.m. "And how did you learn that it was missing? Did you go to your studio and realize it was gone? What was the state of your studio when you went inside? Was anything else taken? Was anything askew? Was the door open or closed—and how did you last leave it?" She knew she must slow down, but her natural enthusiasm had surfaced. She was truly at her best when focused on a case.

Sarah recited patiently, "I always close the door, but it was wide-open. I was instantly alarmed. I only ask for the maids to clean the space perhaps every other month or so. As the studio had been cleaned the week before, I knew immediately that someone had gone inside. The first thing I saw was that the easel with your portrait was empty. I kept it front and center, Francesca, but covered with a cloth. The cloth was on the floor, the easel upright. Everything else seemed untouched."

Francesca had taken a writing tablet from her purse and was making notes. Sarah continued. "Francesca, I have told Hart's investigators and the police all this more than once."

She froze. "You spoke to the police?"

Sarah started. "How could I not speak to the police, when Chief Farr came here personally to investigate?"

Francesca gasped. Bragg had not notified the police of the theft. They had been afraid that a policeman would find and see the portrait, and that word of its existence would come to light. There was simply far too much corruption in the police department.

"Why are you standing there as if shocked?" Sarah asked, bewildered.

She inhaled. For some reason, ever since they had first met, Chief Farr had taken a terrible dislike to her, mostly because she was a woman who dared to investigate crimes both with and without the police. He considered her an intruder in a man's world, and an intruder in police affairs. He had made it clear that his view of women and their place in society was antiquated and traditional; Francesca knew he also judged her relationship with Bragg and condemned it. He certainly disliked her influence upon him. With every passing investigation, his once-veiled hostility had become clearer and more obvious.

"Sarah, what did Farr say when he came here to question you?" How had Farr learned of the theft?

She seemed confused. "He said he was determined to find the portrait and apprehend the thief."

She took Sarah's arm. "Sarah—Bragg never assigned any police officers to this case. We deliberately kept it a very private matter. How did Farr know about it?"

Sarah seemed aghast. "I don't know how he knew that your portrait was stolen. He appeared here the next day, I think, and then twice afterward, all within one week. He was terribly concerned and interested."

Francesca released her, breathless. "Farr came to speak to you three times? He must have known it was my portrait. Did you tell him so?" Otherwise, he wouldn't have given a damn about the theft.

Sarah was pale and silent.

If he had known it was her portrait, Francesca was not surprised that he had questioned Sarah three times. He would want to be involved—and possibly, make trouble for her. She slowly looked at Sarah, horror beginning. "Please tell me that he never learned that the portrait is a nude."

Sarah blanched completely.

"Sarah!"

"I never said it was a nude!" she cried. "But I was so upset and he wanted to know why. I told him that the portrait was terribly compromising and that it must never be displayed in public."

Francesca's horror was complete.

POLICE HEADQUARTERS was not far from the terrible slums of Mulberry Bend. In the warm weather, a very unpleasant odor afflicted the entire neighborhood. As Francesca got out of the Cahill carriage, she held a handkerchief to her nose. Bragg's black Daimler was parked in front of the five-story brownstone building that housed police headquarters. Two roundsmen in their blue serge uniforms and leather helmets were casually guarding the vehicle.

The road car had been a spectacle months ago, when Bragg had first taken up his appointment. Police headquarters was in a terrible neighborhood, and all kinds of lowlife hoods and crooks, cutpurses and muggers, not to mention prostitutes, went about their business on the adjacent streets. Now, no one paid any attention to the car. These days, most of the petty crime took place away from headquarters. Bragg had laid down the law. Mugging and solicitation were not to be tolerated on the department's front steps.

As Francesca left the carriage, telling Jennings to return home—she would cab it for the rest of the day—she wondered if there could ever be a future with a hospitable, crime-free, law-abiding city and citizenry. As long as the tenements were filled to overflowing, the residents living in horrific conditions without adequate light, ventilation or water, with many of the immigrants unable to understand any English, working for mere pennies a day, she thought it impossible. The slums bred desperation, and that encouraged crime.

She glanced briefly at the desk sergeants and the three

complainants in the reception room, noticing two beggars in the holding cell, both of whom were sleeping. The rest of the hall's many wooden chairs and benches were vacant. Apparently it was a very quiet Sunday morning; usually a handful of reporters were present, awaiting a story. She didn't see a single newsman, which was a relief, so she went to the elevator, stepped into the cage and pressed the button for the third floor. A moment later its engine whirred and the iron cage began a slow ascent. Francesca watched the activity below as she went up.

Farr's interest in the case had worried her to no end during the interminable drive downtown. She hurried to Bragg's office and found his door wide open. He stood behind his desk by the window, looking out onto Mulberry Street. He was on the telephone. He nodded when he saw her, his mouth softening, and she smiled in return. Francesca came inside as Bragg hung up the receiver.

"Good morning," he said, his gaze moving slowly over her features. "Did you get any sleep last night?"

He was the one who looked as if he hadn't slept at all, she thought, noticing the dark circles under his eyes. "Actually, I slept like a rock. I was exhausted by the time I crawled into my bed."

"I'm glad. Your timing is impeccable, as always. I just received word from Newman. Apparently he learned last night from a neighbor that Daniel Moore lives a few blocks from the gallery. This morning, they located his home address in that back office." He picked up a pen and scribbled the address on a pad. Francesca came closer to view it: 529 Broadway.

"Perfect," she breathed. "Moore will be my first stop after I leave you."

"We will go together," he said firmly.

She touched his hand. He started and she said tersely, "I have news and it isn't good. Or, I don't think it is."

He studied her. "You are referring to the case, not my brother."

She knew she colored. "I haven't seen Hart since last night."

His brows lifted. "You didn't speak to him this morning?"

She bit her lip. She knew what Rick would think if she told him that Hart hadn't come home. "We are off track! Rick, Chief Farr questioned Sarah about my portrait three times in the week after it was stolen."

His eyes widened in surprise.

"Sarah didn't realize that we were keeping the investigation private," she added. "She mentioned to Farr that the painting is compromising. My God—he has been involved in this case from the beginning!"

Bragg inhaled. His expression was grim, and Francesca knew he was thinking about the last case they had worked on. Farr had withheld information during the investigation into Daisy's murder, but they hadn't called him on it. Instead, Bragg had decided to watch Farr very, very closely. Clearly, he had his own agenda and could not be trusted.

Francesca cried, keeping her voice low, "What if that portrait was still hanging in Gallery Moore last night when Farr and his detail arrived?"

"There is no reason to think that Farr would go to that extent to destroy you, Francesca," Bragg said. "I know he dislikes you, but he works for me and he knows how close we are. Taking that portrait would be a huge gamble, as he could lose his job here if he were ever discovered. Besides, think of the logistics. Farr arrived with his men, Francesca, not in advance of them."

He had already checked Farr's actions. "What are you going to do about this?"

"I am giving him several assignments at once, all of the utmost urgency, to keep him distracted."

"Maybe you should confront him."

His brows lifted. "He will claim he is trying to be a proper civil servant—that he is trying to help us."

Bragg was right, she thought grimly.

"Meanwhile, we have put out word that we are looking for information on Solange Marceaux, and that there is a handsome reward for news of her whereabouts."

"That is a good idea." Francesca had a new thought. "Bragg, I should speak with Rose."

He looked at her. Rose Cooper was an expensive prostitute who had been very close with Daisy Jones. Before Hart had become involved with Francesca, he had solicited her services from time to time. Rose had come to hate Hart; she had been in love with Daisy, and Daisy had fallen for Calder. Still, Rose knew the world of prostitution well. "I spoke with Rose two months ago, Francesca, and she did not have a clue as to where Solange Marceaux was."

"That was then." Francesca smiled determinedly. "And you are not me. I can often persuade Rose to be helpful. And she owes me." Rose had asked her to find Daisy's killer. Francesca would have done so anyway, but she had not only agreed, she had comforted the other woman when she had been grieving. "Perhaps Rose can lead me to Dawn, the prostitute who once worked for Marceaux. Dawn might know where her former employer is, and she was helpful to us when we rescued those children."

"That is an excellent plan," Bragg agreed. He made another note on the same page as previously, and handed it to Francesca. "That is Rose's last-known address."

She glanced at him.

"She was still entertaining the chief, Francesca, in early May."

Francesca inhaled. "I hope the affair continues. It might give me leverage over Farr if I ever need it."

He suddenly walked around his desk and took her arm. "Don't you dare even think to use leverage on the chief. If it is necessary, I will be exerting the pressure," he warned.

He would always be her protector, she thought—not that she needed protection. "Well, then, we will both have leverage, if they are still involved." She smiled at him.

His smile was brief. "I have several calls to make before we call on Daniel Moore. It might take an hour. Can you wait?"

Francesca did not want to wait an hour, but she had seen the fatigue in his smile. She stared closely at him. "Rick, is something bothering you? You were so tired yesterday—and you seem very tired today, as well."

Not looking at her, he sat in the cane-backed chair behind his desk and said, "I worked late last night."

"Did you return to headquarters after you left me last night?" she exclaimed.

He hesitated, reaching for a pencil. He started making notes to avoid eye contact. "Yes."

Francesca stepped forward and placed both hands on his desk, leaning toward him in such a way that he had to look up and meet her gaze. "What is wrong?" She wondered if the white shirt he was wearing was the same one he had worn last night. "Rick, what time did you go home last night?"

He sighed, sitting back in his chair. "I probably got home at four."

Her mind raced. Something was very wrong. She had been so caught up in her wedding—and the events of the past twenty-four hours—that she hadn't paid any attention to all the signs. She took his hand firmly, across the desk.

"What is wrong? What has been going on these past two weeks?"

"I am under pressure, Francesca. That is all." He pulled his hand from hers and looked at his desk. "Low has decided to negotiate with Tammany Hall and the Germans. Parkhurst is leading the elites in a series of media attacks on me. His followers have been raiding brothels and saloons. The newsmen have been eating up the raids. I am in a terrible position."

Her gut told her there was so much more. "How is Leigh Anne?"

He stiffened.

He was having problems with his marriage, she thought, stunned. "Rick?"

He slowly looked up. "Do we have to discuss this?"

"Yes, we do, because…I care, deeply." She was resolved.

He closed his eyes, rubbing his face with his hands. Then he met her unwavering regard. "She hasn't adjusted at all to the paralysis. And the more I try to help her, the more she pushes me away."

"I am sorry," she whispered. When had she last called on his wife? Suddenly she was ashamed. She had called on her once, maybe a month ago, but Leigh Anne had looked well, considering the tragedy that had befallen her. "It will take her time, Rick, to adjust. She loves you."

He stood. "Maybe she loved me once, Francesca. But if there is one thing I am sure of, it is that she doesn't love me now."

She gasped. "You are wrong! She loves you—I have seen it."

"You are a romantic, Francesca. And you are the only reason she returned to our marriage, in case you have forgotten."

She bit her lip and touched his arm. "Maybe so. But

you have reconciled, there are the two little girls, and she is your wife. Rick, I can see that you are anguished. You deserve happiness. I am sure this will pass. Every marriage has its hard times."

He made a harsh sound. "Francesca, I am at a loss these days." He pulled his arm back, and she dropped her hand. Bragg was usually the most decisive, committed man she knew.

He suddenly said, "She complains about pain. She is drinking to mask it. She takes laudanum to sleep." He slowly shook his head. "I think she is escaping far more than physical pain."

"I am so sorry," Francesca whispered, horrified, taking his hand again. She had had no idea of what was happening in the Bragg household.

Bragg looked past her.

Francesca tensed, and she turned.

Calder Hart stood in the doorway, elegant and urbane in his coal-black suit, starched white shirt and dark burgundy tie. He slowly smiled at them. "I can see that I am interrupting, but frankly, I don't give a damn."

CHAPTER EIGHT

Sunday, June 29, 1902
Noon

"WHY AM I not surprised to find the two of you hold-ing hands and whispering in one another's ears?" Hart drawled, entering the office.

Francesca's heart exploded in her chest. How long had he been standing there, eavesdropping? "Hart! We weren't holding hands or whispering. We are discussing the case."

"Ah, yes, the case of the missing portrait. And what clues did you both discover last night?" His dark glance was riveted on her and his mirthless smile was carved in stone. Finally, he looked at his brother. "You move quickly, Rick."

He was so mocking. Francesca was filled with alarm. Someone had told Hart that she had been with Rick last night. "I needed help last night. You were not interested in my dilemma—not that I blame you, as you suffered such a shock. But I could hardly go home, with my portrait hanging in some gallery downtown."

He shrugged. "I don't blame you for trying to protect your reputation, Francesca."

She met his unwavering gaze. She hated it when she could not decide what he was really thinking or feeling. "Well, I am grateful for that. This is hardly the first case we have worked on together, Hart."

"No, but it is the first case you have worked on with

Rick since we ended things." His smile came and went, coldly.

She shuddered, realizing that nothing had changed. He was not interested in reconciliation.

"And, Francesca? I believe my virtuous brother is correct. Love is not lust. His wife doesn't love him, nor has she ever loved him."

She needed to be alone with Hart, she thought, feeling frantic. They had to continue the discussion she had tried to have with him last night. "Why are you talking about Leigh Anne? What does she have to do with..." She trailed off.

"Us?" he supplied helpfully.

She was rigid with dread. "She doesn't have anything to do with our relationship."

"Really?" he asked, his gaze hardening. "In my estimation, my brother is available now."

She had never known such tension. Bragg had nothing to do with their estrangement.

Rick moved between them. "Why are you here, causing discord, when so much is at stake? As if I do not know! You intend to hurt Francesca—to cause her as much pain as possible. As if you did not hurt her enough last night."

Hart smiled. "I was the one who was jilted in front of three hundred guests."

"I was locked up," she tried. "I would never hurt you, not on purpose."

It was as if neither brother had heard her. "I am not available," Bragg retorted. "My wife is an invalid, or have you forgotten?"

"Ah, how could I forget? When you glory in your martyrdom." His smile flitted across his face again, but his hard stare returned to Francesca. "A martyr and a saint. How impossibly perfect."

She bit her lip, wringing her hands. Why did he have to presume that she would find her way back to Rick? "Hart, I wanted to stop by this morning. I desperately wished to talk to you, to tell you again how sorry I am! If I hurt you—"

He cut her off. "You did not. Desperation is not becoming, my dear."

It was a terrible blow. "Can we speak privately? There is no reason for this animosity. I never meant to jilt you, and you must surely know it."

His eyes glittered. "Do you really want to go down that road with me again? Nothing has changed for me, Francesca, since we last spoke."

She trembled. He could not have been clearer. "Then why are you here?" she somehow managed to say. "Have I hurt you so much that you seek to hurt me in return?"

Hart's dark eyes blackened. "No—I am not here to hurt you."

"She is your fiancée," Rick said harshly. Hart simply kept staring at her and she stared helplessly back. "You owe her a private moment."

Hart gave him a bored look. "She *was* my fiancée. I believe I owe her very little at the moment."

Francesca turned. He hadn't softened at all; he was even more set against her now. He might even hate her. She bumped into Bragg, who instantly steadied her. She realized that she was fighting tears. She must not cry now.

I abhor women who cry.

As she fought for self-control, Rick handed her a handkerchief. Hart made a mocking sound.

"I'm fine," Francesca lied, her back to Hart.

"You are not fine." Bragg turned to face his brother. "I don't know why you are here, so state your business and get out—unless you can behave in a civil manner."

Hart shook his head, staring at them. "How fortunate

it is that the two of you are always thrown together by the criminal elements in this city. Can I assume you were crime-solving before my ex-fiancée decided to console you on the matter of your estrangement from your wife?"

Did he really think she would run to Rick now? Less than twenty-four hours ago, they had been on the verge of marriage. The night before that, they'd shared a candlelit supper in his home, and afterward she had been in his arms. "Please stop. You are continuing to hurt me, even if it is not deliberate, and I do not deserve it." His gaze narrowed. She barreled on. "Even if this impasse of ours is permanent—and I refuse to believe that!—I will always undertake criminal investigations. It has become my passion, as well as my profession. One day, Rick will not be police commissioner, but I will still be hard at work, helping victims in need." She inhaled. "Last night, when you dismissed me, I decided to take matters into my own hands. I hardly had a choice! I am not going to allow this thief to ruin me and my family. You chose to turn your back on me when I needed your help, so I turned to Rick." His expression didn't change. "This is not a romantic encounter, Hart. We were discussing the case. I have a lot to lose." She paused before adding, "Rick would never turn his back on me. But you already know that."

He darkened. "Yes," he said. "My brother would never abandon you, no matter the circumstance. He is not merely noble but loyal. I am sure that the two of you will uncover and apprehend the current culprit, sooner than later. You always do." His mouth twisted.

Why was he there if he was still so angry with her? She could only conclude, as she had yesterday, that he was terribly hurt and his cruelty and sarcasm were his means of covering up that anguish.

She did not want to think about what it meant if she was wrong.

Just then, she missed the powerful ally he had once been—the safest harbor she had ever known—a man who would never allow anyone or anything to hurt her. "Can we please manage a private discussion?"

He folded his arms across his chest. The moment he did so, she knew he was acquiescing. "Five minutes," he said. "But I must warn you, I refuse to entertain any entreaties from you. We are done."

Bragg choked. Francesca fought the rush of tears. "I want to speak with you, not beg you for forgiveness. Nor will I grovel."

"Good," he said flatly. "As I am not in a forgiving mood, and groveling is worse than tears."

"I am going down the hall to check on a file," Bragg said. He glanced at Francesca with obvious concern. She wanted to send him a small, reassuring smile but she simply couldn't.

He walked out.

A terrible silence fell.

Francesca walked past Hart to close the office door, acutely aware of his powerful presence. Then, slowly, she turned. "I will always love you."

"Don't."

She bit her lip. "Why can't I profess my feelings? I have already realized that if you never loved me—as you claimed yesterday—then it is truly over. I would never chase you, Hart. I would never beg for your affections. However, even if our past relationship was a lie and if you never loved me and it is over, I will still be your friend."

His eyes widened. Finally, she had an honest reaction from him.

"You see, I can still see the good in you," she said softly.

"Don't you dare!" he exploded, turning dark with anger.

She went still. She watched him flush and instantly rein in his temper. She fought her own wildly racing pulse. He was not immune to her or her feelings, she thought, at once relieved and thrilled. Her faith in him had the ability to arouse him! Very softly, she said, "And if you did love me, then this will pass, and when you come to your senses and realize I was not at fault yesterday, I will receive you with open arms."

His expression tightened. "I have come to my senses. I came to my senses when I realized I was a fool to consider marrying you."

She stared. "Because I am such an eccentric woman? One you lust for but do not love?"

"No, Francesca, because you are genuinely honest, with a heart of gold and enough passion and ambition for a dozen men—because your heart is pure. We never suited, my dear."

"What on earth does that mean? We suit very well!" she cried.

He spoke very softly then. "How often have I said that you deserve Rick, or someone like him? Our estrangement is for the best. Yes, yesterday I was angry. You left me standing at the altar in front of most of New York society. It was rather unpleasant—it was shocking. But I have had time to think about it. I am the wrong man for you."

"I do believe that is my decision!" she cried. "You are the perfect man for me!"

"My decision is final. You can do better, and I have little doubt that you will." His smile was as twisted as earlier.

"My God, are you once again trying to protect me?"

His stare hardened. "I am not being noble, so do not even think it."

"If you are claiming that you are not good enough for me and using yesterday as an excuse to break it off with me on the grounds that I can do better, then I will most certainly think you are being noble!"

He laughed abruptly, mockingly. "I might be using yesterday as an excuse, but you certainly used that note as an excuse to avoid marriage to me, my dear."

She froze. "I beg your pardon?"

"You heard me."

He couldn't possibly believe what he had just said. "I couldn't wait to take our vows! I couldn't wait to walk down that aisle as your bride and then return up the aisle as your wife!"

"You knew deep in your heart that I am your second choice and when the note arrived, you seized the opportunity to race off chasing ghosts, Francesca—avoiding marriage to me."

She cried out. Did he actually think she had subconsciously used that invitation as a means of escaping marriage?

"Have you truly forgotten that, when we first met, you were in love with my brother, and mine was the shoulder you cried upon?" he asked very softly. His black gaze was piercing.

She trembled. Of course she hadn't forgotten, but she would not say so. "I love you,"

One dark brow slashed upward. "I truly believe Rick's marriage is doomed. The two of you are perfectly matched—everyone thinks so. Even I think so."

"Stop it!" she gasped, her heart beating so wildly she felt faint. "Why are you doing this?"

"That note—fate—intervened yesterday, saving you

from a lifetime in my clutches. I am not sorry. And you should not be, either." He was final.

It was a moment before she could find her voice. "I am not in love with Rick, and I had no doubts about marrying you. I did not race off after my portrait because on some secret level, I wanted to avoid marriage to you. I went to save my reputation! I truly meant to arrive at the church in time. But, in case you have forgotten, I was locked inside the gallery, Hart! I was prevented from attending our wedding."

He shook his head, pacing away from her. "It is done, Francesca."

She inhaled. "Only a few weeks ago, you ended our engagement when you were arrested for Daisy's murder, but you loved me then. You said your feelings hadn't changed. Do you still love me?" she cried.

He did not blink. "I am fond of you. Enough to want the best for you."

"Damn it," she cried. "Stop thinking to protect me from yourself!"

He stared for a long moment and said quietly, "But I am the one ruining you now, Francesca. Again."

She tried to grapple with his declaration. "Whoever stole that portrait is hoping to ruin me, Hart, and that person is not you."

His mouth curled. "That portrait only exists in the first place because I commissioned it. Had I been a true gentleman—someone like my brother, perhaps—that portrait would not be as provocative and compromising as it is. I asked you to pose nude. And now, your future is at stake." His smile returned, but it was a simple baring of his white teeth. "Do not tell me that I am not the one responsible for the predicament you are now in."

He blamed himself—of course he did.

He added, "Last time, it was my past that caught up with us. Now, it is my black soul."

She cringed. "Your soul isn't black. It is not defective, not in any way. I not only love you, I admire you—and I always will." But she knew how impossible and unyielding he was in this kind of instance. When Hart decided he must protect her, nothing could dissuade him.

"Then you are a fool." He was angry, she saw. His mouth was hard and tight. Muscles clenched in his jaw.

"Do you want me to see you as some despicable, selfish reprobate?" she cried.

"Yes, goddamn it, I do!" he cried in return, harshly. "Instead of anticipating the day you feel otherwise, it will finally be here!"

She could not understand such gibberish. She stepped forward and touched his strong jaw. "Never."

For one moment, his skin burned, rough and unshaven beneath her hand. In that moment, she wanted to be in the circle of his arms, feeling every inch of his hard body against hers, his powerful heart pounding against her breasts. He pulled away. "Don't."

She wet her lips. "Don't tempt you? Entice you? Why? Because when I touch you, you want me?"

He strode past her, his hands jammed into the pockets of his trousers. He stared outside the office window at Mulberry Street, his face hard and tight. He finally said, "The stirrings of my body are meaningless."

She did not believe it. He was too jaded to become so swiftly aroused. "I miss you," she whispered. "And I need you."

He turned, his hands still in his pockets. "I am here to help you solve the case, as this is, ultimately, my fault."

She began shaking her head. "Blame me, if you are to blame anyone, for being such a fool as to pose nude."

He was silent, but she knew he hadn't stopped blaming himself—and he never would.

At least they were talking. At least he cared enough to want to help her now. She said carefully, "So you are here to help us find the painting?"

He became wary. "I don't want you hurt, Francesca, and I do not want you ruined."

She was very still. "You still care."

His wary expression did not change. "I will always enjoy your company. I will always appreciate your intelligence and wit. I feel as you do—that we will always be friends, unless the day comes where you turn your back on me. So yes, I still care. You are a special woman. I am here as your friend."

Francesca sighed. Had she really thought to maneuver him into some kind of declaration of love? "And after we find the portrait and the thief?"

"I will remain your friend, supporting you in all your endeavors and choices."

It was hard to breathe properly, much less speak. "And if you remain my choice?"

He gave her a warning look. "You cannot pursue me and win."

She trembled. "So we are no longer engaged."

He said quietly, "I am sorry, Francesca. It was a mistake." His gaze moved to the eight-carat diamond she was wearing. "That should be in a safe."

She hugged herself. She wanted Hart back. Of that, there was no doubt. But she had no idea how she should proceed. Just then, honesty seemed the best policy. "I am wearing your ring to my grave."

He shrugged. "I suppose that is your decision."

She looked at the beautiful diamond. It glittered with stunning fire from her finger. Softly, not looking up, she said, "I will not give up on us."

"Yes, you will."

She jerked to meet his speculative gaze.

"You will come to your senses soon enough, Francesca, because my powers of persuasion—and seduction—will no longer be exercised."

He was the most powerful man she knew. Even if he loved her still, she wasn't sure he would change his mind once he had committed to such a strong decision.

Ironically, his reasons were moral, when he claimed to be as amoral as a man could be.

A silence had fallen. He still stood by the window behind Rick's desk. She stood in the middle of the office, not far from the fireplace, no longer at liberty to move close to him, to touch his arm or take his hand or even blurt out whatever was on her mind. A gulf yawned between them—the gulf made by his decision to end things. It felt as vast as an ocean.

The pain of heartbreak stabbed through her again. She was never going to stop loving him, she thought. And even the greatest of oceans could be traversed.

A soft rapping on the door sounded and Rick poked his head in. He glanced at her and then Hart, before stepping back into his own office. "I suppose the lack of fireworks is an indication that some progress has been made?"

Francesca hugged herself rather miserably. She did not know what to say. Clearly, they had arrived at some kind of truce. He meant to aid her in the investigation, which meant they would work closely together. There was hope. It was not over yet.

"I am here to offer my services in this investigation," Hart said, ignoring Rick's flicker of surprise and the concerned glance he cast at Francesca. "By the way, I have fired every one of my investigators. I believe it is time to roll up my shirtsleeves and resolve this matter once and for all."

Rick said, "As much as I'd like to decline your offer, I'll take all the help I can get. No one is better connected than you are to the art world of this city. I imagine that most art dealers would jump at the opportunity to aid you. We were about to interview Daniel Moore. Whatever his story is, Hart, you can certainly verify it."

"I stopped by the gallery this morning."

Francesca looked at him in surprise.

"I had never heard of it. The work there is quite commercial—and inferior. Moore does not know his art. He might be a charlatan, simply out to make a quick dollar."

"That is a leap to make, based simply on his artistic judgment," Rick said.

"Yes, it is. But time will prove whether my leap is correct or not."

"Maybe Moore allowed our thief into his gallery," she said. "Perhaps there was remuneration. In any case, I would welcome a blackmail note."

Rick took her elbow. "Be careful what you wish for."

"I cannot imagine the thief not sending a blackmail note," she said, glancing at Hart. "I feel as if one is impending."

Hart frowned. "If the thief wanted cash, he would have ransomed the portrait long ago, instead of waiting for our wedding day. The thief wishes to toy with you—to torment you."

"Or he or she wishes to torment *you*," Rick said flatly to his half brother.

Hart shrugged. "That remains a distinct possibility. My coach is outside." Hart shoved off the wall he had been leaning against. "I can take Francesca to question Moore."

Her heart leaped wildly, exultantly, again. "Rick, we

could go now and fill you in later." She wanted this time alone with Hart.

He looked carefully at her, warning in his eyes. "I do not mind you interviewing Moore without me, Francesca. But are you sure you wish to do so with Hart, after all that has transpired?"

She looked at Hart, who gazed back at her. "I think the worst is over," she said, truly hoping that was the case. "He has come to help, and we remain friends. And we are agreed on one point—that portrait must be recovered, and quickly."

"That portrait must be destroyed," Hart said.

"Fine," Rick said. "But keep me posted on what you discover."

Francesca could barely believe that she was leaving Bragg's office with Hart. She smiled at Rick, then started out, clutching her purse. Hart fell into step behind her.

It felt odd and yet perfectly familiar. She dared to glance sidelong at him, hoping he would not suspect how nervous she now was.

His gaze was sober. "After you, Francesca," he said, gesturing at the elevator.

She faltered. "You don't have to do this."

"Yes, I do."

He was looking at her directly, without anger, his gaze holding a significance she could not decipher. And in that moment, she knew there was hope. He was on her side, no matter the decision he'd made—and decisions could be changed. She smiled a little and preceded him into the cage.

An awkward silence came between them as they drove downtown.

Uncertain of what to make of their relationship, Francesca forced a smile. "Please, let's not be formal with one another."

"And how is asking for a list of suspects formal?"

"It was your tone." She smiled warmly this time. "I do not think I will be good at this, Hart." When he remained silent, she said, "We are very close, and I can hardly pretend otherwise."

He shrugged, his dark gaze steady.

She sighed. He could be so impossible! "Solange Marceaux is at the top of my list. I am hoping to find the prostitute I met when I was masquerading as one. Dawn might know where Solange is."

"And how will you find Dawn?"

"I will begin by interviewing Rose," Francesca said, glancing intently at him.

He remained calm. "My investigators spoke to her at length, Francesca. She was very hostile to them. I do not trust her, not even now, as there is so much past history between us. She remains hateful of me."

"I don't believe that Rose would go this far to hurt me."

"No, but she might go this far to hurt me." He added, "Rose lives in a brothel off Sixth Avenue. Two months ago, I had Daisy's house thoroughly searched. We found nothing."

Francesca started. "You thought Rose had taken my portrait and hidden it there? How would she have ever known about it?"

"Where else would she hide it if she took it? Under her bed?" His smile was brief. "I commissioned your portrait rather publicly, Francesca—at a ball, in front of guests. The fact that Sarah was painting it was rather common knowledge."

"Yes, but only you, Sarah and I knew it was a nude, Hart. When you first commissioned it, you asked me to pose in my red ball gown."

"I remember." He gave her a significant look that made

her flush. He had been so jealous at the ball. It was the night they had realized that desire charged their relationship. "I admit that I was grasping at straws. In any case, you should talk to her. I am sure you will be at your most persuasive, and if she knows anything, you will discover it."

He had such faith in her abilities, she thought. "Thank you." She smiled, but he turned to glance out his window. She almost sighed. The coach turned onto Broadway. She began to think about the gallery owner, whom she hoped was home. As it was a Sunday afternoon, he might be out and about, strolling in a park, or dining in a restaurant with his wife—if he was married. She leaned forward eagerly, toward Hart, to see which street number they were passing.

"Number 529 is ahead," he said softly.

She brushed his arm with her shoulder, and she simply looked at him, not moving away. The Hart of old would have touched her cheek and removed a tendril of hair there. Instead, he was the one to break eye contact, looking out of his carriage window again.

Francesca settled back in her seat as their coach stopped. She would dwell on her personal life later. Impatient now, she was pleased that Hart did not wait for Raoul. He opened his door, stepping out, then very politely, as any gentleman would, helped her out to the street.

"Thank you." She started forward swiftly as Hart told Raoul to find a convenient space to park the coach. Number 529 was a squat brick building containing two apartments per floor. Daniel Moore's name was on the plaque that read 2A. "He is on the second floor."

Hart reached past her to open the heavy front door, and they entered a pleasant hall with a Persian rug and a brass chandelier. Against one wall, a handsome, if tired, table with gilded claw feet stood, a painting of a house in the snow in a wood frame above it. The oil painting was terrible—Francesca had seen enough art to know the difference between a layman's rendering and that of a genius. "This has come from his gallery, I think," she said.

"I would definitely say so." Hart took her elbow, turning her toward the stairs. She smiled impulsively at him. He dropped his hand and she knew he hadn't thought before touching her in such a familiar way.

She was going to reclaim their love, she thought fiercely, her pulse pounding. Then she turned her attention to the interview about to take place. She hurried up the two flights of stairs, Hart behind her. The moment she knocked on Moore's door, a blonde woman of about thirty answered.

"May I help you?" The woman was plump and well dressed, but she wore only a single cameo pin and ear bobs that Francesca felt certain were glass and paste.

Francesca handed her one of her calling cards. "Hello." She smiled pleasantly. "I am Francesca Cahill and this is my fi—my friend, Calder Hart. I am investigating the theft of a portrait. Are you Mrs. Moore?"

She froze, blanching. Then she began to shut the door in Francesca's face. From behind her, a man called, "Marsha, who is it?"

Hart placed his foot between the woman and the door, preventing her from closing it. He smiled, but not all that politely. "May we come in? We have a few questions. You may answer them now, or later, at police headquarters."

Francesca looked at him. He was angry; she saw it in his eyes. She was very surprised that he would push so hard before the interview had even begun.

Daniel Moore appeared, his expression distraught. "Who are these people and what do they want?"

Marsha wet her lips, stepping back into her parlor, handing him Francesca's card. It was a pleasant room with a round table in its center, a small chandelier overhead. Flowers were on the table. Francesca saw a parlor to her left, with tired furniture and an equally worn piano, music sheets on a stand there. A small dining room was to her right. The table there could only seat four and the sideboard was small and bare of any ornaments. She assumed the bedroom was directly ahead. The couple was, she thought, childless, and struggling to maintain a genteel life.

Francesca followed her inside, as did Hart. He closed the door behind them and said, "Miss Cahill was locked in your gallery yesterday afternoon, Mr. Moore."

Moore had glanced down at her card. He looked up now, still pale, and blinked more furiously. Francesca realized he was hiding something. But it did not appear that he recognized her from her portrait. "Yesterday I received an invitation to preview the works of Sarah Channing. She is a friend of mine, and I was eager to do so. Did you send the invitation, Mr. Moore?"

"No, I did not. I don't know the artist or anything about an invitation," he said, frowning. He was very defensive, Francesca realized, but his answer did not surprise her. She glanced at Marsha, who had backed away and now stood halfway between the center table and the dining room, worrying the folds of her skirts. She looked close to tears.

Marsha knew something, as well, and she would easily break.

Moore continued, "Are you telling me that someone invited you to my gallery—on Saturday—when we are closed?" He was incredulous. "And that you got yourself locked in?"

"Yes, I am. Except—I did not lock myself in—someone

locked me in, Mr. Moore. You knew nothing about it?" Francesca asked with a smile.

"Of course not! I do not know the artist, I have no works of hers and we are closed on the weekends. We keep summer hours."

She glanced at Hart, who nodded at her. Moore was extremely distressed. She said softly, "I am so sorry. I can see how distraught you are. But there was a work of Sarah's in your gallery when I arrived. You haven't seen the portrait?"

He stared at her, scowling. "I don't know anything about it."

Francesca believed he knew nothing of her portrait, but he was hiding something, oh, yes.

"Someone was responsible for locking Miss Cahill in your gallery yesterday," Hart said flatly. "Abduction is a crime—a felony, I believe." Moore blanched impossibly. "And even the slightest involvement is enough to warrant conspiracy charges."

"I know nothing about any invitation, a portrait or her being locked up!" Moore gasped.

"We are not accusing you of any crime, Mr. Moore. We are merely trying to apprehend whoever stole the portrait, which belongs to Mr. Hart. And of course, whoever locked me up must pay the price for such a dastardly deed. The police have already gone through the office at the gallery," Francesca said pleasantly. "Do you have a study here?"

He was whiter now than before. "The police are at my gallery? I will go out of business! I am struggling as it is. I do not have a study in this flat."

"May we look?" Hart asked.

Moore gaped. "No, you may not wander about my home! In fact, I must get to my gallery, and see what is happening there." He turned and ran to a door across the hall. As he rushed inside, Francesca glimpsed a dark bedroom wallpapered in a flocked red floral print.

She said to Marsha, "I am so sorry we are delivering such upsetting news."

Marsha nodded, clearly near tears.

Moore returned, shrugging on his jacket. Hart said, "I can give you a ride. My coach is parked outside."

Moore started, then nodded. "Thank you." The look he gave Francesca was distinctly guilty. He dashed out into the hall, Hart following more slowly. Their gazes met.

She understood that she was to linger with Marsha Moore.

As Hart left, she opened her purse, taking her time. Then she handed the other woman another card. "I missed my own wedding yesterday on account of that strange invitation."

Marsha whispered, "I am sorry."

Marsha meant it, she thought. "So am I. My fiancé is very angry with me, and I love him dearly. I must apprehend the culprit and win my fiancé back."

"I hope you do both," Marsha said.

Francesca made no move to leave. "Are you sure you don't know something that will help me find the villain who locked me inside your husband's gallery?"

She bit her lip, shaking her head no.

Francesca sighed. She would come back another time, because Marsha definitely knew something. "Take care, Mrs. Moore. Good day." She started for the front door.

To her surprise, Marsha rushed after her. "Wait!"

Francesca slowly turned.

Tears fell. "Something bad is happening, Miss Cahill. There is a man…I've seen him loitering outside this building and the gallery, waiting for my husband."

Francesca cried, "How do you know he was waiting for your husband?"

"I know he wished a word because I saw them speaking once. Dan wouldn't tell me who he was or what he wanted."

Francesca took her hand. "When was this?"

"A few days ago, outside the gallery, and last night, here on Broadway."

Would the thief have come here last night after locking her in the gallery? That would be so odd. Could Marsha identify the man? "Please, can you describe him?"

She inhaled. "It was dark, but he was a big man, Miss Cahill, a dangerous man. That's all I can say."

CHAPTER NINE

Sunday, June 29, 1902
2:00 p.m.

THE POLICE BARRICADES remained outside Moore's gallery. Francesca watched Daniel closely as she, Hart and the gallery owner all alighted from his coach. Moore's tense expression never changed, and she felt certain that he was not surprised by the barricades. She wondered if he had already been to the gallery.

An officer standing by a wooden sawhorse started toward them, his hand moving threateningly to his billy stick. "No one is allowed inside, sir," he said to Hart, who was leading the way.

Moore stepped forward, his face pale. "I am Daniel Moore and I own this gallery," he said. "I have just learned what happened here yesterday. I must go in."

"No one can go inside," the officer insisted. He was blond and blue-eyed, no more than twenty years old or so, and he seemed nervous. Before he'd finished speaking, however, Hart handed him a bill. The officer flushed, stuffed it in his pocket and turned his back on the gallery's entrance.

Francesca looked at Hart. "Did you have to do that?"

"Would you rather wait for word from Bragg?"

Moore was already hurrying to the front door. "We had better stay close to him," she murmured.

"Great minds think alike," Hart agreed, taking her elbow.

"We will discuss your strategy of bribing the police later," she said tartly.

He smiled at her.

Her heart leaped and she smiled back. Hart released her with a scowl—clearly having forgotten that they were estranged. She walked past him, her mood brightening. Winning Hart back might not be as difficult as she had thought.

Moore was staring at the central wall, where the bar of plywood remained. "What did they do to my wall? I had a painting hanging here—a wonderful rendering of a circus clown."

"Last night, a portrait was hanging on that wall," Francesca said briskly, turning all her attention to Moore.

Not looking at her, he ran around the gallery, checking the art there. Francesca and Hart followed. Hart said, "Do you not keep the gallery locked, Moore?"

"Of course I lock the gallery. Nothing is missing," Moore said tersely, "except for the oil of the clown."

"How many sets of keys do you have?" Francesca asked.

He stared wide-eyed at her. A long moment passed before he said, "I keep one set of keys with me at all times. The other set, I keep in the office in the back."

Hart gestured, his meaning clear. Moore quickly led the way into the back office. The moment they entered, he cried out. Francesca hadn't paid any attention to the clutter in his office when she had been trying to escape through the window. Now she saw the painting of the clown, leaning against a wall not far from the door, and her suspicion grew.

"How polite and thoughtful our thief is," she said. Sometimes, the smallest clues were the best ones.

Moore turned to look at her. "I beg your pardon?"

"Our art thief not only removed the painting to make room for the stolen portrait, he or she also lugged it to your back office and propped it up on the wall." She smiled pleasantly. "It is a somewhat large painting. I would have simply left it lying on the floor, exactly where I had taken it down, but then, I am a woman, and my arms are not that long."

"Perhaps our thief is obsessed with being tidy," Hart murmured. "Or, perhaps not."

Moore was glancing back and forth rapidly between them. Francesca was fairly certain that Moore was in some kind of cahoots with the thief and that he had either removed the painting himself, or had told the thief to do so. "This is nonsense. Who cares if the thief removed the painting to my office?"

Hart gestured at the desk. "The spare keys, Moore."

Moore went to his desk, flushing, and opened a drawer. He froze, as if very surprised, then began rummaging in it quite busily. He cursed softly and went through the two other drawers at great length, with growing frustration. Francesca glanced at Hart. His gaze told her that he was in agreement with her; this was quite a show.

"I take it the keys have been stolen," Hart said quietly.

"I cannot believe this!" Moore exclaimed. "But now I am beginning to wonder… I had a busy day on Thursday. Two ladies spent quite some time here, and one asked me a few questions about the seascape in the front. She priced it, as well."

"Are you suggesting that her friend stole the set of spare keys while you were preoccupied with the potential buyer?" Francesca asked. She couldn't help imagining Solange Marceaux in the gallery, feigning interest in the ugly seascape in the front of the gallery.

"No, I am not," he snapped defensively. "However, a man came in at the same time, wandering about while I was busy with the ladies."

Moore hadn't told her or Marsha about the big man on the street. Would he mention that man now? "Can you describe him?"

"All I can recall is that he was in a suit." Abruptly Moore sat down at his desk. He laid his face on his arms. Francesca saw that his hands were trembling. "I am afraid I have to ask, Mr. Moore. Where were you Saturday afternoon and evening?"

He paled. "Why are you asking me that?"

"Answer her, if you please." Hart smiled pleasantly.

Moore cried, "I believe we took a walk in the afternoon, and I spent the evening at home with Mrs. Moore, as I always do."

Francesca and Hart shared a glance. He was very upset, she thought.

Hart suddenly clasped her shoulder. "Let's go."

She nodded. "Mr. Moore? If there is anything else you wish to add, or anything you happen to recall that might help us find the thief and the person who locked me in here, I would be terribly appreciative." An idea struck her—and it seemed terribly obvious and long overdue. "Mr. Hart is offering a large reward for the return of his painting."

Moore straightened, turning to them.

Hart cocked a brow at her.

Francesca felt Moore's financial desperation then. She made a mental note that they must look at his bank statements, after speaking to the owner of this building and No. 529 Broadway. "He is offering ten thousand dollars for its return."

Moore paled. "If I remember anything, I will send word."

Francesca thanked him and she and Hart left. Outside, she faced Hart in the bright, June sunlight. "No one would keep their spare gallery keys in the gallery. He would keep them in his flat. I think I should try to find them there, or perhaps let Joel do what he does so well."

"Sending Joel in is a clever idea. And by the way, I have already told the owner and agents of every single gallery in the city that I will pay fifty thousand dollars for the painting's return."

Francesca blinked. "That is a huge sum!"

"Frankly, it pales in comparison to the damage that portrait will do to you."

She trembled. "You care far more than you are letting on."

He gave her a dark look. "What did Mrs. Moore have to say? I could tell from the glimmer in your eyes when you joined us in the coach that she most certainly revealed some clue."

Francesca looked at him. "Calder, she said that a man had been trying to have a word with her husband, and that she had seen him earlier in the week outside the gallery—and last night on the street outside their Broadway flat. Marsha could only describe him as big and dangerous looking."

Hart stared. "That is a poor description."

"Hart, there is more I need to tell you about the case. Chief Farr went to Sarah's three times in the week after the portrait vanished, asking questions. She told him that I was the subject of the portrait—and that it was very compromising."

Hart darkened. "Goddamn it," he said softly, his expression explosive.

This was the Hart of old, she thought, taking his hand.

"We intended to keep the police out of this affair,"

Hart said harshly, pulling away from her. "How did Farr know the portrait was stolen in the first place?"

"We haven't learned that yet. But I imagine a servant overheard the upset the day the portrait was taken. You already mentioned that the commission was not a secret. Servants can be bribed.... And there is more."

He faced her, his eyes hard and intent. "I am afraid to ask."

"When Bragg and I arrived at the gallery last night, Farr was already here. He does not miss a thing that goes on at HQ. Bragg requested a police detail and Farr was apparently the officer on duty. Farr told us that the gallery was open and the portrait gone when he and his men arrived, but when I saw him, I was terrified. My very first thought was that he had seen it when he arrived."

"Are you thinking that Farr did see the painting last night—that he stole it?" Hart was incredulous. "How would he do that in front of a handful of policemen?"

"No. He would have had to come to the gallery before his men. Bragg already checked. Someone in the neighborhood would have seen him remove it—the police have been speaking to everyone. I believe he was telling the truth, that he arrived here to find the portrait stolen. But there is one fact that is very odd. When I left here yesterday to go to the church, I was with a police officer and a neighbor, who had jimmied the lock. But when the police arrived here last night, according to Farr, the door was open and the glass was broken—which I saw myself. It was as if someone had locked the door again and then had to break the glass to reach inside to unlock it."

"Perhaps Moore is lying and he returned and locked the gallery, Francesca," Hart said calmly. "That is a reasonable explanation—even if he is not involved."

"That makes sense," Francesca mused. "Moore

would certainly deny returning, out of fear of being implicated."

He stared back thoughtfully, and said, "We both know Moore is hiding something."

"Yes, we do." She smiled briefly, then sobered. "Well, I have come to one solid conclusion. The chief is not our thief—if he were, he would not have gone to Sarah's three times, unofficially, to investigate."

Hart's expression tightened. "You know, it really doesn't matter how Farr learned about your portrait."

She stared at him. "You are right. We both know that he dislikes me—and that is why he went to Sarah's to question her three times. He intends to find my portrait first! He knows it is somehow compromising and he is going to use this against me."

"No, he won't. I will kill him first."

Francesca inhaled. "Don't even speak that way."

He gave her a dark look. "You know what I am capable of in order to protect those I care about."

She bit her lip. Several months ago, his foster sister, Lucy, had been blackmailed by a felon. He had said then that he would commit murder—to protect those whom he loved.

"Francesca." Hart's harsh tone interrupted her thoughts. "I know what you are thinking—that Farr was the big, dangerous man Marsha saw speaking to Moore last night on Broadway."

"Yes, that is what I am thinking." She trembled. "Farr wants to solve this case, Hart, and we must not let him do so."

His gaze wandered over her features. "Chief Farr is not going to destroy you, Francesca. You may be certain of that. But clearly, we are in a race, and we are going to win."

FRANCESCA'S SPIRITS WERE high as she paused before the dark building just off Sixth Avenue, where Rose apparently lived. Hart would do anything to protect her. She was thrilled. It was so obviously not over between them.

She reined in her delight. Almost twenty-four hours had passed since she had come face-to-face with her portrait in the gallery. It was floating about the city somewhere. She thought about Daniel Moore's statement that two ladies had visited his gallery on Thursday. Could one of the women have been Solange Marceaux?

Couldn't Chief Farr have tracked down Moore on Saturday night, after she had escaped the gallery? He was clever, and it wouldn't have been all that hard to learn where Moore lived. But if that were the case, then who had Marsha seen lingering outside the gallery on an earlier weekday night? Farr wouldn't have even known of the gallery's existence until yesterday. The obvious conclusion was that the big, dangerous man hadn't been Farr after all.

Francesca got out of Hart's coach just as the tracks from the Sixth Avenue El overhead began to rumble and groan. Beneath the elevated railway, it was dark and dismal. Aware that a train was approaching, she tensed. A moment later she heard the roar of the locomotive, and the screaming of its iron wheels. She clapped her hand over her ears as Raoul held the lead carriage horses, until the last cars had passed.

She lowered her hands, coughing from the smoke. Hart had insisted she use his coach for the remainder of the day. He had taken a cab uptown; he had told her he needed to bathe and change his clothes, as he remained in the same garments he'd worn last night. She had so wanted to ask him what he had done last night, and with whom, but she hadn't dared.

The brownstone she now faced was nondescript. It was an unusual location for a bordello, she thought, as the neighborhood was mostly factories, sweatshops and warehouses. The few pedestrians crossing Fourteenth Street under the El were clearly factory workers, the women plainly dressed in simple gingham, the men in dark breeches and cotton shirts. All of the traffic was comprised of wagons and drays, loaded with boxes and barrels. Francesca wondered at the brothel's clientele. She could not imagine Rose entertaining a common laborer.

Hoping that was not the case, Francesca started up the steps and rapped the door knocker loudly several times. Eventually a peephole was revealed, and she met a pair of red-rimmed brown eyes. "We're closed," a woman said, slamming the peephole shut.

Francesca knocked again. "I must speak with Rose Cooper. If you do not let me in, I will return with the police."

The lock clicked a moment later and the door opened. Francesca saw a very tired, plump woman of forty or so, clad in a dressing gown, her hair dyed garishly red. She found herself in a small, barren hallway, a staircase to her left. At the far end of the hall, she glimpsed a dark red parlor.

This establishment was a far cry from the elegant mansion Solange Marceaux had occupied, and it even made Madame Pinke's brothel seem luxurious in comparison. Once, Hart had been one of Rose's clients, although those days had ended with their engagement. She knew he had only frequented the most exclusive brothels. Those establishments had a clientele consisting of the city's elites and powerbrokers. No one from those circles would visit this house of ill repute.

"I don't know any girl named Rose," the woman said. Francesca sighed. It was getting late and she was looking forward to taking off her shoes, sipping a very good scotch while discussing the day with Hart. She wondered if she could finagle that. She was very good at persuasion, as Hart had said.

She opened her purse, took out her gun and pointed it at the woman. The madam paled.

"I am in an unpleasant mood. My reputation hangs by a single thread. I will wait for Rose in the parlor. Tell her it is Francesca Cahill and it is of the utmost urgency, please."

Sending Francesca one last glare, the woman slammed the front door and locked it, then thudded up the stairs, mumbling under her breath. Francesca was certain that she was being accused of being high, mighty and mad. She had to smile.

She glanced around carefully and opened the only other door between her and the parlor. It was a dining room, the walls papered in olive-green, the draperies an equally atrocious shade, a very faded gold rug underfoot. The oval table could seat six or eight. She supposed the room was sometimes requested for supper parties. She backed out slowly.

"Well, hello, Francesca," Rose said, a sneer in her tone.

Francesca turned. The woman stood behind her, hands on her hips. Rose Cooper was a striking woman, with olive skin, green eyes and dark hair. She was quite tall, perhaps five foot eight or nine, with a perfect figure. She was wearing a very simple shirtwaist and a dark skirt; Francesca had never seen her dressed as a shopgirl before. "How are you, Rose?" she asked softly, aware of the belligerence in Rose's eyes.

"Nothing has changed," Rose snapped, breathing hard. "Daisy is dead. I will be alone forever!"

Francesca's heart broke for the other woman. "I am so

sorry. I know how hard this is. I wish I could somehow help."

Rose remained sullen, but grudgingly, she said, "You did help. You found her killer." Tears welled. Abruptly, Rose swatted at them and glared. "What do you want? You are a very unpleasant reminder of a part of the past that I want to forget."

Francesca was not affronted by Rose's rudeness. She was truly sad for her. "I'm sorry I bring back unhappy memories." When Rose simply stared coldly, she said, "I need your help on an investigation, Rose."

"We are even! I don't owe you anything!" she cried.

Francesca touched her arm kindly, but Rose jerked angrily away. "Just leave," she said. "Go away and never come back."

"I can't do that. You see, I am looking for a stolen painting, and time is of the essence. I must find the portrait immediately." As she spoke, she thought about the fact that Hart had believed Rose capable of stealing that portrait, to use it against either her or him. But Rose couldn't have known that the portrait was a nude.

"Does the damn portrait belong to Hart?" Rose cried. "As if I would ever help him in any way!"

Francesca hesitated. She hadn't expected Rose to have softened toward Hart. She thought that Rose would hold a grudge until she died. "Hart did commission the portrait. But I am the one desperate to find it—it is my portrait, actually."

Rose stared. "So paint another one. I don't know anything about a portrait, Francesca."

Francesca hesitated. She did not want Rose to know more than was essential. Rose hated Hart with a vengeance and she always would. But she had more questions for her. Two months ago, Rose had still been entertaining

Chief Farr. She must be thorough now. "Rose, I know you are still grieving. But how are you, otherwise?"

Rose stiffened. "Don't pretend that you care, Francesca."

"I do care. Rose, why are you in this house?"

Rose made a harsh sound. "It is temporary."

Francesca hoped so. "Are you still seeing Chief Farr?"

Rose's eyes widened. "No." Her tone was a bit sharp. "Being as I did not like that cop at all—he is a pig—it is good riddance."

While she didn't like Farr either, she thought that Rose despised men in general. Given her vocation, she could hardly blame her. Still, Francesca was relieved. She decided that Farr hadn't discussed the portrait with Rose. "Do you happen to know where Solange Marceaux is now?"

Rose was incredulous; then she laughed. "If I did, I wouldn't tell you. I know that the police have issued warrants for her arrest. We whores stick together."

She ignored that. "Do you know if Solange is angry enough to seek vengeance against me?"

Rose started. "No, I don't. I was in her brothel, Francesca, but I wasn't there as her friend. She never confided in me."

"I really must locate her," Francesca said.

Rose shrugged. "Well, I can't help."

She fell silent, wondering how to move Rose. If she asked about Dawn now, she felt certain she would get nowhere. Rose said, "What does Solange have to do with the painting?"

"It is complicated." Francesca was not about to reveal the nature of the portrait or that she believed Solange capable of its theft.

Rose made a sound of indifference. "Why not have Hart find her? After all, he must know every decent establishment in the city."

She froze. "That is cruel."

She looked pleased with herself. "Hart is cruel, Francesca. I happen to know."

Her mind raced. It sounded as if Rose didn't know about the wedding. Could she use it to her advantage? "You haven't heard, have you?"

"I haven't heard what?" Rose was wary.

"I was supposed to marry Hart yesterday, but I was lured away—by the painting's thief—and then trapped in an art gallery. I missed my own wedding."

Rose's eyes widened. Then she began to smile. "Oh, my. You missed your wedding. Please tell me you jilted Hart right at the altar."

She sighed. "Not on purpose."

Rose gloated openly. "Hart must have been humiliated. Ha! Is he still in a rage?" She laughed. "Oh, I know he is. He hates being crossed. He can give orders and commands, but he only tolerates absolute obedience. He must be furious with you."

All her sympathy for Rose vanished. "I am glad you are so happy with this turn of events. I love Calder and he has ended things. So, yes, he is very angry, and I am distraught."

Rose sobered slightly. "He hates you now, I am sure of it. You do know, Francesca, that this is really for the best. You are a nice woman. He is a bastard. You'll find someone else."

"We will get through this," Francesca said, and the moment she spoke, she wished she hadn't.

Rose shook her head, amused. "He'll never truly forgive you. If you patch things up, he will always hold this against you."

Francesca held her temper. It was no easy task. "Your glee is terribly unbecoming."

Rose shrugged. "I'm a whore. Who cares?"

"I certainly cared a moment ago, about your grief, and I cared when I sleuthed tirelessly to find Daisy's real killer," she flared.

Rose stared. "You know I am grateful, not that I would have cared if Hart had been bagged for Daisy's murder."

"As far as I am concerned, you owe me now," Francesca said fiercely. "I have always treated you with respect. I have always cared. I solved Daisy's murder. Now I am in some trouble. That portrait must be recovered, Rose." An idea struck her and she said, "It has special relevance for me. Hart commissioned it when we were falling in love. I am truly desperate."

Rose shrugged, unmoved.

"Please, Rose. This is so important! Are you certain you will not tell me where Solange Marceaux has set up shop?"

Rose sighed. "You can be persuasive when you want to be, Francesca. I don't know where Madame Marceaux has gone. And I can't understand what she could have to do with your stolen painting."

"Do you know where Dawn is employed?"

Rose hesitated. "I have heard that Dawn is working on the west side, in the forties, in a bordello run by a pair of gentlemen. I heard it is conveniently located and not far from the El. But I have no idea where, exactly—that is all I know."

Francesca had already taken out her pad, and was making notes. It might take a while, but if Rose was telling the truth, she would find that bawdy house sooner or later. She finished writing and looked up. "Thank you, Rose."

Rose shook her head. "So much fuss over a painting."

FRANCESCA LEANED FORWARD in her carriage seat as Hart's huge home came into view, set back behind stone walls and iron gates. She smiled. Things were going very well, indeed. She had a lead on Dawn—and Dawn might know where Solange Marceaux had relocated. Rose did not know anything about the portrait, but Daniel Moore was definitely hiding something. She wanted to access his bank accounts and learn how dire his finances were. And tomorrow, to make certain that she could definitively cross both Randalls off her list of suspects, she would visit Henrietta in prison. She expected the interview to be routine, but of course, one never knew. Since Philadelphia University was closed for the summer, she would try to learn where Bill was. She would have to speak with him eventually, too.

The coach turned onto the long pale driveway leading to Hart's house. Francesca was aware that she was very nervous, but the beast had gone back to its lair, at least for a while. They were friends, after all, although he might regret having admitted that. She smiled, sighing. Then she pinched herself. Until her portrait was recovered and she and Hart were engaged again, she must not be too content.

A moment later, the coach stopped in front of his house. Francesca alighted and hurried up the front steps.

Alfred greeted her at the door.

He seemed very pleased to see her. "Mr. Hart is in the library, Miss Cahill."

Francesca beamed at him, taking off her gloves. "It has been a very good day, Alfred."

"I can see that. Shall I show you to the library, then?"

"I can show myself in. How is Mr. Hart? Is anyone home?" She knew she would have to face his family eventually.

"He seems to be back to normal, Miss Cahill. There are no dark clouds hanging about him today. And no one else is in just now."

Pleased, she hurried down the hall, wondering if Hart had enjoyed sleuthing with her as much as she had enjoyed sleuthing with him. But she faltered as Hart stepped into the hall.

He was so straight-faced she did not know if he was annoyed, angry or amused. "Have you been defending me to Rathe and Grace?" she tried. Her smile felt anxious.

He did not smile back. "I have told them a portion of the truth."

"Honesty is always the best policy, as is staying as closely as possible to the facts."

"Are you nervous?" he purred.

"Hardly! Hart, I am in need of a good scotch." She was suddenly uncertain and almost intimidated. "May I come in?"

"No."

She inhaled. "Don't be silly, Hart. We are friends now, remember?" She walked past him toward the library, her heart thundering.

He seized her arm, turning her abruptly around to face him. "You have more audacity—and courage—than anyone I know."

"Friends share a good drink with one another." She smiled at him. "You cannot resist me."

And she thought amusement flickered in his eyes. "Do you really think to attempt to manipulate me?"

"You like your scotch as much as I do, if not more, and no one likes to drink alone. And I just saw Rose." She felt rather triumphant. Surely he would take the bait.

But he did not. "Oh, ho! You do think to con me." He released her.

"A drink will hardly hurt either one of us, Hart," she said, teasing.

He folded his arms across his chest and she thought he remained just slightly amused with her antics. "Yesterday you jilted me at the altar—do I have to remind you of that? Today, we searched for clues together, but we are no longer affianced and undoubtedly, your mother has plans for the evening. Those plans might even include some very eligible gentlemen. You should go, Francesca."

She scowled. "Oh, please. We will reconcile shortly and you know it."

"I know no such thing," he said, his mouth firm. "One day, you and I will be able to spend an evening together, but that day is not now."

She was stunned. "You will really send me home?"

"It is suppertime. So, yes, I will."

He wasn't going to invite her in. "Don't you want to hear about Rose?"

A brow lifted. "My darling, I still know you better than you know yourself. If you had a good clue, you would have blurted it out long ago. And, Francesca? You do pout adorably, but I will not change my mind."

She felt like a small, spoiled child, denied a tempting treat. "Fine," she said grouchily. "I will con my sister into a forbidden drink, while you spend the evening alone."

He just looked at her.

She stared back. What were his plans? "You are going to be alone tonight, aren't you?"

He took her arm and guided her back into the spacious

entrance hall. "Is Raoul still outside? Good, I see that he is. He can drive you home."

That afternoon she had been certain that he still loved her. She had been certain enough to dare to call on him—and she had expected to have her way. She hated this impasse. She wanted to curl up on his sofa beside him, and then wind up in his arms. She refused to believe he would escort another woman about town. Surely he had no interest in anyone else. The city was deserted, anyway. The best restaurants were closed.

Alfred had opened the front door. Still holding her arm tightly, he leaned close and whispered in her ear. "Don't ask questions if you fear the answers, Francesca."

CHAPTER TEN

Sunday, June 29, 1902
8:00 p.m.

FRANCESCA THANKED RAOUL, then turned and started for her front door. The bubble of happiness was gone. Clearly, Hart meant to hold to the decision he had made about them. She was, amazingly, more hurt. How was she going to break through his resolve? She had thought herself well on her way toward doing so that afternoon, but clearly, she had been wrong. She refused to dwell on his insinuation that he would not be alone that evening. He would never be unfaithful to her, not like this—not so soon after their failed wedding.

The doorman opened the door for her and Francesca smiled at him. She must call Bragg, she decided, and fill him in on the afternoon's events.

"Lady Montrose is here, Miss Cahill," Francis said.

Even as the doorman spoke, Joel came ambling out of the closest salon, Connie behind him.

Francesca hurried forward, laying her gloves and purse on a side table. "Hello, Connie," she said, hugging her briefly. She decided she desperately needed her worldly sister's advice.

"Where have you been all day?" Connie asked, taking in her rumpled appearance. But she kept her voice down. "Mother keeps asking for you. She is highly suspicious."

Julia must never learn about the portrait. "I will reassure her over supper."

Connie lifted a skeptical brow. "She is demanding details, Francesca, regarding your entrapment on Saturday. She has been interrogating me as if I were some witness in one of your investigations—as if she somehow knows that I know the truth."

Francesca took her hand. "Don't panic," she said softly. Then she turned to Joel. "It is so late for you to be here."

He grinned at her. "A sleuth's work's never done, is it? An' it's no different fer a sidekick. Miz Cahill, Mr. Moore was at his gallery Saturday morning, mebbe at ten or eleven."

"What?" Francesca exclaimed. "Why, if that is true, it confirms his involvement with the thief! Who told you this?"

"Them two children that helped you get out after you got locked in. They were playing with their dog in the yard, and a ball hit the window you tried to get out of. Bobby—that's his name—saw Moore inside when he went to get the ball fer the dog. He was with another fellow, Miz Cahill."

She was excited. "Are you certain Bobby saw Daniel Moore and not someone else? Is he certain? Did you question him thoroughly, Joel?"

"He jist said it was Mr. Moore," Joel replied. "I can ask again tomorrow."

Francesca thought quickly about it. "I am beginning to believe that Moore is involved with our thief, but not the theft. I must not leap to the conclusion that he was at the gallery with the thief on Saturday morning. Joel, do you know of a brothel run by a pair of gentlemen on the west side, in the forties?"

Joel blinked. "Nope. You want me to snoop around?"

"Let me think about it. Raoul has left, but Francis will hail you a hansom to take you home." She retrieved her purse and handed him two silver dollars, although the fare would probably be a half dollar at this hour. "I will pick you up tomorrow morning at half past eight, on my way to police headquarters."

Connie coughed.

Francesca felt an unyielding stare on her back, and she flushed guiltily before turning to face Julia. "Hello, Mama."

"I cannot believe your marriage is hanging by a thread and you are running around town with Rick Bragg on a tawdry investigation!" Before Francesca could respond, she added, "Not to mention that your reputation is hanging by a thread, as well."

"You will be pleased to know that Hart and I ran about the city this afternoon, looking for clues so we might apprehend whomever wished to stop our marriage." Julia started. "Joel, I will see you in the morning."

He thanked her but avoided looking at Julia, whom he was clearly intimidated by, and hurried out with the doorman. Francesca continued, "I hope you offered him a decent meal."

"Of course I did. Don't you dare criticize me and change the subject." Julia's blue eyes seemed moist. "So, does this mean that you and Hart are back on?"

She hesitated. "He still cares about me. He is very concerned. But I am afraid he has gotten it into his head that he must protect me from his past."

Julia flung up her hands. "I am going to speak with him tomorrow. Dinner will be served shortly." There was warning in her tone as she turned and strode out the black-and-white marble entrance hall.

Francesca decided to wait until another time to attempt

to dissuade her from approaching Hart. She looked at her sister. "He is so set against me now," she whispered.

Connie pulled her into the intimate salon, furnished in gold and ivory, which she and Joel had just come out of. "I believe he loves you, Fran, but right now, he is ruled by his male pride."

"I wish you were right. Connie, he has decided that it is in my best interests to marry someone else. We spent the entire afternoon together, searching for clues, and it was so clear that he remains terribly fond of me. But when I went over to his house a moment ago, he would not let me in. We used to share a scotch at this hour and discuss the day, his business affairs and my investigations. He refused to have a drink with me, a simple drink!"

Connie picked up her hand and stared at the magnificent engagement ring Francesca wore. "Maybe you should take that off."

"What?" She was aghast at the notion.

Connie gave her a look. "I think it very encouraging that Hart ran about the city with you today, helping you with this case. But if you already spent the afternoon together, what possessed you to call on him tonight?"

"I love him." Francesca stiffened.

"And he loves you. But he remains humiliated by your so-called jilting of him at the very altar. He probably remains angry. He might even be hurt. I was not making a jest about male pride."

"I hope you are right on all accounts,' Francesca said. "But what am I supposed to do? I love him and I want him back!"

Before Francesca could react, Connie twisted the engagement ring around and removed it. "You must play him, Francesca. And I would begin by locking this in Julia's safe."

Francesca gasped.

"Fran. You can't throw yourself at him. You can't pursue him or beg him to take you back. You must not even attempt to persuade him to see the error of his decision to break things off. He must realize that he is losing you. *He* must be the one to pursue *you*."

Francesca stared at her, almost gaping. Connie was right.

"I am going to lock this up for you," she said sweetly. "And do run about tomorrow with Bragg—the whole world knows Hart is jealous of his brother. If you must have a scotch before supper, do so with Rick. The next time you see Hart, tell him you have realized you have no choice but to accept his decision."

Francesca felt her mind spinning. "You are brilliant, Connie, truly brilliant."

"Men are not that hard to comprehend—some of the time." She smiled. "Do you want to freshen up before supper? I am staying, by the way, to help you survive Julia's assault."

Francesca hugged her again. "I love you. I will be right back." She lifted her skirts and charged across the hall, up the gracefully winding staircase to the second floor, where the family had their bedrooms. She began to exult. She imagined how shocked Hart would be if she told him that she agreed with him, and their breakup was for the best.

Oh, she would give anything to have him pursuing her again.

In her bedroom, she rushed to change into a simple supper gown and redo her hair. The dress she put on was dark green, and she wondered where her emerald teardrop earrings were. She had worn them recently to a supper party with her mother, while Hart was away.

They weren't on her dressing table or on the vanity, nor were they in her jewelry box. She had a terrible habit of taking off her earrings while in motion, and leaving them carelessly about on this piece of furniture or that. Francesca glanced at her bedside table and the occasional table in front of the sofa before the fireplace. Finally, she ran to her antique secretaire. She saw the eardrops instantly, glittering with green fire.

And then she froze.

They were set on an envelope with large, hand-written block letters.

She rushed forward. Only an idiot would fail to recognize those letters.

The envelope was addressed to her. Below her name was the single word URGENT.

She sank into the chair, seizing the envelope, the earrings sliding to the desk and scattering there. She did not notice. Instead, she slit the envelope open with her fingernail. The same weight and color of vellum was inside. She unfolded it, her hands shaking.

If you want the portrait back, be at the bridge in Central Park at 2:00 p.m. tomorrow.
Bring $75,000.

Finally, she was being blackmailed.

She wanted to skip the family supper, but there was no possible way to do so. Instead, she pretended to listen to the dinner conversation, while turning over the fact that she must appropriate seventy-five thousand dollars immediately. As Andrew and Evan chatted about the terrible revolt in Haiti, and Connie and Julia discussed the merits of a new modiste, her mind raced. Did the thief really want money? Why hadn't this blackmail threat come sooner? How was it related to the fact that she had been trapped on the day of her wedding? Something was so very wrong!

How was she to access so much money? Did she dare ask her father for it? She instantly knew she would not—Andrew would never give it to her, and he would ask a hundred questions.

Hart, however, would give her the funds without thinking twice.

She realized that she could count on him, even now.

She was tempted to rush back to Hart's to discuss borrowing the money, but by the time supper was concluded, she knew that nothing was going to be accomplished until the next afternoon. She had begun to consider blackmail suspects. She ruled Moore out—if he had acquired the portrait, she was certain he would have demanded the reward immediately.

Could Chief Farr be involved? He knew her portrait was compromising, and he would certainly stoop to blackmailing her without having it in his possession. But why do that? He would never put his job with the NYPD on the line, not for those funds. Unfortunately, he probably took in that much money from graft and corruption—most police officers did.

She was down to two possible suspects: Solange Marceaux and Bill Randall. She could imagine Solange Marceaux being greedy enough to blackmail her—and she had no doubt that the madam would attempt to take the money and then display the portrait publicly, destroying Francesca anyway.

She had to definitively rule out Bill Randall from any involvement in the theft of her portrait, she thought. She must make certain his alibi hadn't been fabricated. She would interview his mother, Henrietta, in the morning with Bragg, as planned, and then see what the afternoon would bring.

She could depend on Bragg, but he looked like the policeman that he was, and he had been in the news on an almost daily basis. Most of the city could recognize him. If she allowed him to come with her and the blackmailer saw him, she would not recover the portrait.

Francesca knew she could not go to Central Park without backup. Just before finally falling asleep at half past three in the morning, she decided she would see if Hart would let her use Raoul again. And she would bring Joel. As she fell asleep, her last thoughts were that if something went awry, she would instruct Joel to go directly to Bragg. She might even arm him....

Now, banging on Hart's front door the next morning, she thought, nothing was going to go awry. She was determined. By late afternoon, she intended to have her portrait back, and hopefully, she would have identified the thief, as well.

It was very early, but the staff was surely up. Francesca knocked again. As she did, the door swung open and she came face-to-face with Hart. She started with surprise.

He started as well, both brows lifting. "Francesca?"

For one moment, she allowed his powerful presence to wash over her. In that moment, she was tempted to tell him the truth and have him go to Central Park with her. She so wished they were not estranged. "Are you expecting someone?" she asked.

"No. Come in," he said, clearly concluding that something was amiss.

"I am sorry it is so early, but obviously you are up." She managed a smile. "Good morning, by the way." She was almost cheerful!

He did not smile back. He pulled her inside. "What has happened, Francesca?" He closed the front door.

She removed her gloves and avoided eye contact, thrilled by his concern. "I need a private word with you, Hart. It is somewhat urgent—and personal."

She dared to glance up at him. He was staring intensely

and she kept smiling, until his scrutiny made her glance away. "Is anyone else awake?"

"I don't know. I am trying to imagine what has happened between last night and this morning," he said.

She faced him and realized that his gaze had dropped to her left hand. "This is not what you are thinking."

He gave her a slightly amused look. "And what am I thinking?"

She hesitated.

"You are on edge," he said softly. "Otherwise you would not be sending me those falsely cheerful smiles." He took her arm and guided her down the hall. Francesca wished that he was wrong, but he was right—she was nervous. And it wasn't just because of the money she must acquire. Hart often made her nervous, even before their estrangement. But the story she had fabricated, which was plausible but a lie, accounted for her distress.

"I am a bit anxious," she admitted.

"Do not even try to dissemble with me, Francesca." He released her and gestured. Francesca preceded him into the library, very skittishly. Did he sense he was to be played? She needed him to believe her every word.

A small fire crackled in the hearth and she saw papers and newspapers on his desk, a cup of coffee there. She already knew that Hart was very devoted to the management of his business empire. He slept little and worked long hours—he enjoyed negotiations and trades far more than the daily minutiae of running insurance and shipping companies.

He walked swiftly over to a gilded bar cart and poured her a black coffee from a sterling-silver coffee pitcher. He returned to her, handing her the cup. "It is very early, Francesca, even for you."

"Yes, it is." She accepted the cup and wondered if the knots in her stomach would increase if she drank the coffee. It was one thing to investigate someone else's case. With her fate on the line, this felt entirely different.

If she could recover the portrait, they could pursue the thief at leisure. And she could focus most of her efforts on winning Hart back.

Hart was staring at her unadorned left hand again. Francesca felt a brief satisfaction, wondering if he would remark on it so she could be flippant about their circumstances. But he didn't speak. She tried to take a sip of coffee. Her stomach tightened and hurt. She set the cup down. "I hate to ask you for a very large favor, but I must."

"Whatever it is, my answer is yes."

She wanted to hug him; she did not move. "You haven't heard me out yet."

"My answer is yes."

She inhaled, so relieved her knees buckled. He steadied her. She opened her eyes and said softly, with dread and dismay, "I'm afraid I must ask you for a considerable sum of money—when I already owe you so much."

His unblinking gaze never changed. "You owe me nothing, Francesca. I gave you the fifty thousand to aid your brother. How much do you need?"

She cringed. When Andrew had refused to pay any more gambling debts, Evan had been assaulted by some thug. The vicious attack, which had left him bedridden with several broken ribs and a black eye, had been a warning from one of his creditors. Francesca had asked Hart for fifty thousand dollars. Evan owed far more, but they had decided that partial payment would be enough to ward off any further attacks. Hart hadn't hesitated to give them the sum.

He had also insisted on taking it to Evan's creditor himself. Francesca knew he would never accept repayment.

He said softly, "You need never be afraid to ask me for my help."

She inhaled. "I am afraid I need seventy-five thousand dollars," she said grimly.

"I see." A deadly pause ensued. He finally said, "What are the funds for?"

"I would prefer not to say," she said firmly.

"You know I am going to give it to you no matter what it is for."

She couldn't smile. "I am so grateful." This was not the behavior of an ex-fiancé, she thought. This was the behavior of a trusted and loyal partner.

He was studying her far too closely. "You seem exhausted. Did you sleep at all last night?"

"Not really."

"Is the money about recovering the portrait?"

"No."

For one more moment he stared and she could not look him in the eye. "Please trust me," she whispered, but the moment she spoke, she thought about how he had trusted her—and how she had missed their wedding.

But he didn't make a rebuttal. He turned and walked away from her. She watched him take a huge painting down from one wall. The safe was behind it, and he quickly turned the lock. The iron door swung open and Hart began taking stacked bills out. He took them to his desk. "It is not a loan. You could never pay it back, and even if you could, I wouldn't accept repayment. But I do want to know what this sum is for. For you can trust me as well, Francesca."

Francesca walked over to the desk, clutching her purse. "Evan has been gaming again," she lied. She prayed her brother would never hear of her atrocious deception. But she knew he would forgive her, if he understood what was at stake.

Hart sighed. He went back to the safe, closing it, and then replaced the oil on the wall. Francesca suddenly realized that the painting was not the Constable landscape that had been there so recently. It was a dreamy, somewhat abstract cityscape. "You have purchased a new painting."

"I am very impressed with this young artist. His name is Henri Matisse and that is his rendering of Notre-Dame," Hart said, turning. He retrieved her coffee cup and took it to the sideboard. There, he poured a dark liquor into it. He returned to her. "This should ease your nerves."

"It is half past six in the morning."

"You are frightened, Francesca."

"No, I'm not. I am…worried."

He suddenly tilted up her chin with his strong hand. "Do you want to tell me what the funds are really for?"

His hand on her face felt like her undoing. She longed to blurt out the truth. Worse, she so wanted to move into his powerful arms. "I cannot, Hart. Please. Leave it alone."

"I'm not sure that I can." His eyes were dark now, and he glanced at her lips. For an instant, Francesca tensed, thinking he would kiss her.

But he released her. "You have taken up a vocation that is inherently dangerous. You consort, on a daily basis, with the worst criminals, not to mention madmen. I do not like it when you are in jeopardy, Francesca."

"I am not in that kind of jeopardy," she whispered, thrilling at his words. She reached up and touched his hard, clenched jaw.

He caught her hand and said, "Are you being blackmailed?"

She tried very hard not to glance away. She felt her cheeks warm as she whispered, "No."

And for one more moment they stood that way, with

her hand pressed to his face as he held her wrist hard, there. She thought he would take her hand, turn it over and kiss it—as he had so often done. He did not. "I do not believe you."

"Leave it alone, Hart, please," she repeated.

"Does Bragg know that you are here, asking for seventy-five thousand dollars?"

She hesitated. He sighed. "I didn't think so. You will take Raoul today."

She bit her lip, relieved. "Papa is using our carriage today, so thank you very much. I am picking up Joel on my way downtown to police headquarters." She wanted to change the subject. "We will interview Henrietta Randall today. I want to make certain that Bill Randall is not a suspect."

He paced and said, "My damnable half brother was at the university in Philadelphia the weekend your portrait was stolen. There are two witnesses."

"I just want to make certain his alibi is genuine." She knew how much he despised his half brother and his calm demeanor was being eroded by an increasingly dark, angry expression. "Did you speak to Randall?"

"No." He faced her, seeming disgusted. "I left that unpleasant chore to my investigators."

She hurried to him. "He isn't involved in this, Calder. I am merely being thorough."

He caught her wrist before she could caress his cheek. "I cannot believe I commissioned that portrait."

She knew where he was going. "Stop. I chose to pose nude. I enjoyed doing so!"

"Of course you did. You are putty in my hands."

She was taken aback.

"I taint everything—and everyone—I touch, Francesca. You are no exception."

FRANCESCA HAD BEEN TO the notorious Blackwell's Island several times, to do charitable work at its almshouse, but she had never become indifferent to the sight of the prison. As she stood with Bragg in the bow of the ferry that was steaming up the East River from the south—they had embarked from the ferry terminal adjacent to the Brooklyn Bridge—she shivered, and not just because it was cold out on the water.

"You need a shawl," Bragg said softly. Before she could protest, he had shrugged off his suit jacket, placing it over her shoulders.

His masculine scent enveloped her, making her uncomfortably aware of him. It reminded her of a long-ago time, when they had been more than friends. Hart would hardly appreciate this gesture, she thought. "Thank you. Every time I come here, I think about how daunting the penitentiary is."

The prison, built from the island's granite quarries, took up most of the landmass, running from the island's southern tip to its northern end. They were just passing East Forty-second Street on their left, where the traffic was fairly brisk for a late-June day. The steamer had taken less than a half hour to make the short trip from the South Street piers.

"It is certainly a forbidding and imposing structure. In any case, I am glad that Mrs. Randall is in the workhouse, as the conditions in the prison are deplorable." He gave her a long look. "I prefer you do not visit those premises."

She smiled grimly at him. "I already have, Bragg. I am a reformer, remember? I have heard Seth Low rail against the Blackwell's Island Penitentiary for its horrid overcrowding, drug dealing and lack of sanitation for almost a decade. When I came here to do my charity work, I made a point of visiting the prison."

He rolled his eyes. "I cannot imagine how you were allowed inside."

"I have my methods."

"Yes, you do." He sobered. They had had an entire hour to discuss the case. Bragg was up to speed. The only fact he did not know was that she was now the target of a blackmailer. He had apprised her of several new clues, as well: Daniel Moore was deeply in debt and six months behind on his rent for the gallery; he was two months late on his apartment. And a woman had come forward to claim that she had seen two gentlemen leaving the gallery on Saturday. She couldn't recall the exact time of day, but Joel's witness's statement had been corroborated.

Bragg also believed that Moore was involved with Francesca's entrapment on Saturday. Now they meant to look at his bank accounts to see if he had recently received a significant sum of money. In any case, they agreed that it was time to bring Moore down to HQ for some serious questioning.

Francesca had decided to keep Joel in the Washington Square neighborhood, searching for more clues. She had asked Bragg to locate the brothel where Dawn might be working, and he had wired the appropriate precincts. Francesca was hopeful that by the afternoon, she might have located that particular bawdy house. If not, she would at least have a list of the brothels on the west side, in the forties, and in the vicinity of both elevated railroads.

Bragg remained skeptical of Solange Marceaux's involvement.

Their ferry was now steaming up the west side of the island. They would alight from the piers there. "So why are you so ragged this morning? I thought you and my brother were mending fences."

She looked at him carefully. The moment she had arrived at his office, he had noticed that she was not wearing her ring, but he hadn't said a word. "I thought so, too. But he is resolved to be noble now. He believes it is in my best interests that we do not resume our engagement."

Bragg stared, his expression not moving. To his credit, he did not look at her left hand.

"I know you are pleased."

"I am very pleased, but I prefer not to evince my pleasure, not when you are suffering such heartache, Francesca." His gaze was searching.

"I remain optimistic," she said.

He half smiled, their gazes holding. "You are the eternal optimist."

She smiled back, but briefly. She sensed he wished to ask her about her engagement ring and that he was restraining himself. She bit her lip. Wasn't he her closest friend—after Connie? "I took off my engagement ring, as you can see. It is tucked safely away in Julia's safe."

"I noticed. However, I suspect you have hardly given up on my brother."

She hesitated. "Connie told me to take the ring off."

His eyes widened with instant comprehension. "Do not think to manipulate Hart!"

She winced. "Connie is far more experienced than I am. She gave me sage advice, Bragg."

"To do what? To play him, by pretending you are in agreement with him that things are off now? He will see through that con immediately."

She was suddenly afraid that he was right, but her course was set now. She decided to change the subject. "How are things with you? We are always discussing my affairs, when I care as much about your problems as you do mine. Have you made any progress with Leigh Anne? Is she feeling any better?"

He started, then spoke carefully. "With the holiday

weekend looming, I have been entirely wrapped up in police affairs, Francesca."

"Well, surely you have had a conversation or two with your wife." She was joking.

He didn't smile. "I have barely been home for more than an hour or two at a time. Nothing has changed."

She was now, finally, very concerned. Surely this was a slight bump in the road of their marriage, wasn't it? "Rick, you must make time for your family. You cannot live at police headquarters or hide from Leigh Anne in your work."

He was cool. "I am not hiding from anyone or anything, Francesca. I remain a very busy man."

She made up her mind. She must call on Leigh Anne before the Braggs left town for the July Fourth weekend. If she could help somehow, she would.

Bragg suddenly took her arm and as he did, the bow of the ferry struck the pier. Francesca stumbled and he caught her in such a manner that she was in his arms. Instantly, their gazes met.

It was just a bit too familiar, she thought, her heart lurching. She gently dislodged herself as lines were cast ashore, and she wondered if he was reluctant to let her go. The ferry captain was approaching. "Hope it was a good voyage, C'missioner." He was ruddy cheeked and portly, with huge white whiskers.

"It was a very fine trip," Bragg said. "Francesca?"

She handed him his jacket and thanked the ferry captain as he shrugged it back on. She glanced past him. The front hall of the penitentiary almost appeared gothic with its high sloping roof, and it jutted out from the rest of the building at a right angle. She knew that the prison's eight hundred cells were to the left, the workhouse, penitentiary hospital and the asylum all to the right. At the most northern end of the island was the almshouse, where she had often gone to visit the city's poorest widows and orphans.

"I hope the conditions in the workhouse are far better than those in the prison, Rick. Henrietta is hardly a felon. I cannot even believe she was convicted for her knowledge of what Mary had done."

"She did not come forward when we interviewed her, and while keeping her silence is not a crime, the jury obviously did not like her degree of involvement." They traversed the walkway to the reception hall's front doors. A group of prisoners was tending the gardens in front of the hall under the supervision of an armed guard. "But hers is a very minor offense, and that is why she is in the workhouse, rather than in the prison with hardened criminals." He opened one of the pair of heavy wooden doors for her, then paused. "I will worry constantly about you if you think to play my brother."

She couldn't help being touched, and perhaps even thrilled. "Just as I am worried about you and Leigh Anne," she said softly.

His expression hardened. "Let's go, Francesca."

They went inside. The hall was very much like the lobby of a shabby, fifth-rate hotel. It was dark and gloomy, with a seating area for visitors, a reception desk and an area for registry. The space was old, but not dirty, and she had no doubt that various prisoners kept it clean. Bragg had wired ahead, and he hadn't even reached the clerk at the reception desk when a large man came out of an adjacent hall, beaming. "Commissioner Bragg! It is a pleasure to meet you, sir."

The director of the Blackwell's Island Penitentiary shook Bragg's hand, then beamed at Francesca. "It is even a greater pleasure to meet you, Miss Cahill. I have been following your sensational investigations in the newspaper. You are even more famous than the commissioner, I believe—and so much prettier." He winked.

"I hope I am not more famous, but I hardly mind being a bit more attractive," Francesca said, smiling. She had never met Richard Coakley before. He seemed a very pleasant, good-humored sort; his character was incongruous with his task of overseeing the various institutions on the island.

They followed him down a long, dank hall. Francesca shivered. There was scum in the corners of the floors, which were cracked. She glanced out the windows, which were hard to see through, as they were quite dirty. The grounds were kept up, as was the front hall. But that was all—it even smelled oddly in the corridor.

Large signs appeared overhead, alerting visitors that the penitentiary hospital was on their right. He said, "I checked into Mrs. Randall's file. She is doing very well. She has been given cooking duties, which she performs without mishap, and she does not cause trouble at all. She never complains and has kept mostly to herself. She is, in fact, a model inmate."

"I am glad to hear that," Bragg said.

"She is serving six months, is she not?" Francesca asked. Formidable signs ahead read Blackwell's Island Workhouse.

"Yes, and her release date is October 22." Coakley pushed through the iron doors. "The dormitories are upstairs. We have over three dozen different workrooms, as you can see."

They continued briskly down the dark corridor. The only sounds now were the humming and whirring of the machinery the various inmates were using in the nearby workplaces. Francesca glanced into one workroom and saw several dozen women busily pushing garments through sewing machines. Everyone wore a gray prison uniform and no one spoke. "This way," Coakley said with vast cheer.

He pushed open a pair of doors. They found themselves in a large, institutional kitchen, where the din of pots and pans was terrific. Three dozen people milled about. There were probably a dozen stoves and half a dozen ovens. "This kitchen feeds everyone on this island except for the felons in the penitentiary—the pen has its own kitchens," he said loudly.

Francesca saw a mouse scurrying under a table. That was, she thought, better than a cockroach. She had barely had that thought when she thought she saw one of the insects vanishing into the wall.

A guard had approached and was conferring with Coakley. Francesca scanned the many workers in the kitchen. She suddenly saw Henrietta, pushing a huge tray into an oven. "There she is," she said to Bragg, already starting forward. "Henrietta!"

The older woman closed the oven and turned. Her eyes widened.

Francesca came forward, hating the fact that Henrietta was in the workhouse. Once, Henrietta had been plump. Now she was thin. She had aged a decade in the past few months. Her hair, once blond, was entirely gray. Instead of being stylishly curled, it was severely pulled back into a simple ponytail. "How are you, Henrietta?"

The woman looked past her at Bragg, who was clearly instructing Coakley to leave them. "How do you think?" She trembled. "Mary is locked up in Bellevue. Thank God my boy was not arrested for a crime he did not commit! And I am here, in this horrid place!"

"I am very sorry you were convicted and incarcerated," Francesca said, meaning it.

"You hate my family—you hate all of us!"

"No, I don't," she said earnestly as Bragg joined them.

"I feel very sorry for Mary, in fact, but even sorrier for you. And…I understand why Bill did what he did. He was only protecting his sister."

"You can't mean it," Henrietta cried. "You are with that rotten cur, Calder Hart!"

Francesca stiffened. Bragg said, "Francesca and Hart were engaged, but if you have not seen the papers, I will tell you that the wedding is off. Francesca is not marrying Hart."

Henrietta seemed surprised. "We only get the papers once in a while—and only if we pay triple the newsstand price. I cannot afford a newspaper."

"I will make sure you get a daily, Henrietta, and it will not cost you a cent." Francesca was outraged, but she understood how prisons worked. The guards would pocket the costs. "Do you like to read? Should I send you books?"

Henrietta stared. "Why are you here? Why are you being nice? What do you want?"

"We were hoping to speak with Bill. As the university is closed for the summer, we thought you might know where he is staying."

She paled. "What do you want with my boy? He is a good boy! He has done nothing wrong! Is he in trouble?"

"He isn't in trouble, Henrietta," Francesca soothed. "But we are on an investigation, and he could be helpful to us. That is the only reason we wish to speak with him."

"I haven't seen him in months. I do not know where he is! He is such a good boy—he is studying to be a lawyer. One day, I know he will free Mary."

Francesca hesitated. Mary was mentally ill, and she knew Henrietta knew it. She decided there was no point in saying that Bellevue Hospital was the best place for her. "When was the last time you saw Bill?"

"I don't know—months ago—he was at my trial." She laughed bitterly.

Francesca caught her hand. "I know how horrid this place is. I am so sorry you are here. I am going to send you books. And you will be out in October—you will be free in October, Henrietta."

The other woman started to cry. "I don't want your kindness. I miss Mary. I miss Bill. I miss our home, our family.... She is good, Miss Cahill, and she never meant to hurt her father! Never!"

"We know she did not mean it, and of course you miss your home, your son." Francesca clasped her shoulder. She didn't dare look at Bragg now.

"He is such a good boy. No woman could have a better son! He has visited me every single weekend—" She stopped, her eyes wide with fear.

Francesca started. "Bill visits you every weekend?"

"No, no, I only wish he would do so!" she cried.

"Was Bill here this weekend, Mrs. Randall?" Bragg demanded. "Tell us the truth. If you do not, we will merely check the visitors' log. No one can visit without registering with the prison."

She was pale, her hands fluttering now. "He visits me almost every weekend—only an examination keeps him away."

My God, Francesca thought, looking at Bragg. He said sharply, "Was he here this weekend?"

"Yes," she whispered. "He was here—he was here Saturday morning."

Bill Randall was now Francesca's number-one suspect.

CHAPTER ELEVEN

Monday, June 30, 1902
Noon

MAGGIE KENNEDY HESITATED, holding a garment bag to her bosom. She was walking past the elegant circular driveway on the eastern side of the Metropolitan Club. As she stared through the open iron gates and across the pale limestone, she saw a trio of beautifully and expensively dressed ladies alighting from a hansom. Liveried doormen in crimson and gold had leaped to open the cab doors for them. The women had not even noticed. More doormen rushed to open the club's glass doors. Laughing and chatting, the trio vanished inside the marble building, undoubtedly on their way to the Ladies' Restaurant.

Maggie could barely breathe. Evan frequented the Metropolitan Club. So did most of the city's millionaires. The ladies who dined there were their wives, their sisters and their daughters. Francesca had probably eaten there often. Surely the countess Bartolla Benevente had, as well.

What was she doing?

She, Maggie Kennedy, would never dine in that club!

She wouldn't even be allowed to walk up that grand circular driveway.

Maggie had left her Tenth Avenue flat almost an hour ago. She had taken the Third Avenue El uptown to Fifty-ninth Street. She would never hire a hansom—the fares were too outrageous and she worked too hard for every penny earned—so she had walked across town to Fifth Avenue, browsing the storefronts. At the Grand Army Plaza, she had turned uptown.

Staring at the pale marble building, Maggie bit her lip, debating turning around and going home. She was on a fool's errand, surely. Bringing Francesca's new custom shirtwaist to the Cahill home was just an excuse to see Evan, and she knew it.

Are ye fallin' in love, my silly girl?

One little kiss and he has yer whole heart?

She didn't want to think about her beloved husband now. He had died many years ago, when Joel was just a small boy, but she had loved him with all her heart and she still did. She would never stop missing him, and hearing him in her head was so comforting. She knew he would be worried about her now. And while he was half in jest, she also knew that Josh was dead serious—and that he was also right.

He's not for ye, no matter what he says. All men can turn a pretty word fer a pretty girl!

Maggie wished Evan had never kissed her. She wished, desperately, that he hadn't confided in her. She even wished that anyone but Evan Cahill had saved her from the Slasher, just a month ago.

But he had kissed her—and she had let him. And it had been glorious. She hadn't thought she would ever want to be kissed by a man again, but she had been so very wrong. In his arms, her entire body had awoken, as had all the wild yearning in her heart. Being in his arms had felt safe, perfect and so right.

He had confided in her about his gambling, his debts, his estrangement from his family and the subsequent reconciliation, and the child the countess carried. The countess was having his child.

Maggie trembled. She didn't hate the countess; she feared her. Bartolla had called on her several weeks ago. At first, Maggie had hoped that she wished to order new gowns. Instead, the other woman had mocked Maggie for her feelings for Evan, and she had made it very clear that Maggie must stay away from her lover. Bartolla had been cruel, condescending and vicious. She had even threatened Maggie's children.

Maggie had been shocked by her rudeness and her threats. When she had first seen Evan and Bartolla together, they had seemed like a magical, fairy-tale couple. Now it was so clear that the countess was mean and hateful. She could not bear the idea of Evan being trapped in such a loveless marriage.

She wanted to help him in every possible way—her nature was caring. Initially, she had encouraged him to marry Bartolla and give his bastard the family he or she deserved. But Evan had looked into her eyes and shocked her by telling her that he did not even like the countess. He had declared that he simply couldn't marry Bartolla, but he would, of course, provide for her and the child.

Maggie realized she was crossing Sixty-first Street now. She had been relieved when he had told her that he wouldn't marry the countess. In fact, she wasn't certain when she had ever known such relief.

Yer such a foolish girl!

He should marry the countess and ye know it. He certainly won't marry you.

Josh was right. She was being terribly foolish, as if she had lost the wisdom of her many years. Maggie prided herself on her common sense, but where Evan Cahill was concerned, it had gone flying out the door. The only thing she knew for certain was that she would stand by him, no matter what, and that he would never be happy with an evil woman like Bartolla Benevente.

The Cahill mansion was ahead. Maggie was breathless. She hadn't seen the Cahills since Saturday night, when the house had been in chaos due to Francesca's disappearance. She happened to like Francesca deeply, and she had been as worried as anyone. The newspapers claimed that the wedding was off. Maggie hoped that was not the case, and Joel had assured her that Mr. Hart and Francesca remained as enamored of one another as ever. They were having, he had said, a bit of a spat.

Maggie slowly walked up the driveway, instantly remarking the Cahill coach in front of the house. Joel was with Francesca, working on this new case. Her son was making a handsome salary as Francesca's assistant, but most of all, he was no longer cutting purses. Francesca was a wonderful influence on him.

Maggie had just reached the house's front steps when the front door opened and Andrew Cahill came out, clad in an elegant suit and a dark bowler, swinging a very handsome ivory-handled walking stick. He smiled pleasantly at her. "Good day, Mrs. Kennedy." He added, "Francesca went out at the crack of dawn today."

Mr. Cahill was as kind as his daughter. Maggie flushed and returned the greeting, wondering what he would think if he knew of her feelings for his only son. As he got into the waiting carriage she turned away, hoping he would never learn of her romantic foolishness. She smiled at the doorman, Jonathon, as she walked into the front hall. As always, she was overwhelmed.

She would never get used to the grandeur and glamour of the rich. She was just a simple Irishwoman who sewed clothes for a living. Whenever she came uptown, she was overcome by the differences between her kind and their kind. She lived in a tiny, one-bedroom, windowless flat with four children; they lived in the lap of luxury in palatial homes filled with fancy furniture, fine paintings and marble floors. Her walls were rotting; theirs were covered in fabrics and wallpapers. Her floors were cracked and threadbare; their floors were marble or gleaming parquet, covered with rugs from all over the world.

Recently, she had begun to read the society pages. Not a day went by that Julia Van Wyck Cahill, Lord or Lady Montrose, Francesca, Evan or Mr. Cahill weren't mentioned, dining at some famous establishment or attending some elegant affair. Reading those pages almost made her feel as if she were a family member.

But she was not an insider, and she would never be one, Maggie thought. Facts were facts—she must simply remember them.

The doorman had barely closed the front door when Julia appeared at the other end of the hall, surprised but smiling. "Good day, Maggie. Is that Francesca's shirtwaist?"

Julia's stare seemed sharper than usual—as if there was suspicion just behind her welcoming smile. "Yes, it is. I thought she might wish it for the weekend."

"That is very kind of you," Julia said briskly, taking the garment bag. As always, she was the epitome of elegance and sophistication, in a fitted pale blue dress and aquamarines. "Bette, please hang this in Francesca's room," she told a passing maid. With the garment gone, she faced Maggie, her gaze intent. "Francesca isn't here."

Maggie felt herself flush. "I know. I saw Mr. Cahill as I came in." She added in a rush, "I would like to say that I am so relieved that nothing terrible happened to her on Saturday."

Julia softened. "I know you are. You are a good woman, Maggie."

"I am sure Francesca and Mr. Hart will make new plans soon," Maggie said quickly, her gaze straying past Julia. They hadn't discussed it, but she assumed Evan would soon leave the city for the rest of the summer, as the entire upper class did. The wedding had kept him in town—much to her relief. She knew that Evan often had breakfast at the Cahill mansion with his parents and she wondered if there was a way to ask for a word with him.

"Can I help you with anything else?" Julia's tone had tightened.

She knows, Maggie thought, her insides curdling. She somehow smiled. "No, I just wanted to make sure Francesca had her new shirtwaist for the holiday. She has taken Joel about today on her new investigation. Joel is the happiest when with Miss Cahill." How odd that comment sounded.

"That is my daughter—a crime-solver extraordinaire."

Maggie's gaze returned to Julia. Francesca's mother was angry. Before she could comment on what a gift Francesca had—she had solved so many ghastly crimes—she heard footsteps on the stairs. Her gaze met Evan's.

His eyes widened as he hurried down the stairs. "Maggie! Is everything all right?" he cried.

Her heart was thundering.

Yer smitten, Josh accused.

Yes, I am! she told him helplessly.

"Everything is fine," Maggie managed to say. He was the handsomest man she had ever laid eyes on—and the kindest. He adored her children and was always bringing gifts and treats. He would make a wonderful father.

Aye, to Bartolla's bastard!

Evan visibly relaxed. He smiled at Julia. "Good morning, Mother."

Julia's blue gaze had turned to ice. "Maggie has brought Francesca her new shirtwaist and she is just leaving."

Evan seemed taken aback by her firm tone. Maggie

cringed. What was she thinking? Doing? Evan would one day find true love with a beautiful, elegant young lady—someone from his own class. He might be fond of her now, and fond of her children, but he was the Cahill heir. Even the newsmen of the city called him that.

"Maggie has a long way to go to get back to her home." He turned to Maggie and smiled. "Are you hungry? I am going to take a late breakfast. Would you care to join me?"

He had the most beautiful smile in the world, one of sunshine and laughter—one that reflected his innately good nature. "I've already eaten," she lied.

"Then eat again." His blue eyes twinkled. "Because I am having pancakes, eggs and sausage. With loads of butter and maple syrup from Vermont."

She felt her stomach growl. Breakfast at home consisted of Irish grits. They could not afford eggs or sausages, much less butter or maple syrup.

"I insist," Evan murmured, taking her arm. He glanced at Julia. "Will you join us?"

Julia frowned. "I have a luncheon at the Hotel Essex," Julia said. She smiled politely. "Thank you for bringing the shirtwaist, Maggie." Giving Evan what might have been a reproving glance, she went out.

The moment Julia had gone out the front door, he laughed. The sound was as warm as his smile. "She is so transparent. She is dismayed because I am so pleased to see you." And he took her hand and squeezed it.

She melted. "Well, our friendship is hardly usual."

He gave her an odd look and she wondered if he was thinking that this was far more than friendship. He said, "I am very glad you have come by and that you are going to dine with me. I have a better idea. Let's walk down to the Metropolitan Club. Of course, we will have to forgo pancakes for a luncheon fare."

She froze. "I can't go in there."

"Of course you can."

Was he mad? They would never let her in!

He said softly, as if reading her mind, "I am a member, Maggie. I can bring any guest I choose."

She wet her lips and lied. "The pancakes and sausage sound so good."

He slowly smiled. "You do know your wish is my command."

She knew he was flirting, but her heart flipped wildly. Feeling as shy as a thirteen-year-old girl, she said, "I wasn't sure you would still be in town."

"I am to spend July and August on Fire Island with friends. I was supposed to be there already, but Fran's latest adventure has delayed me."

She wondered where Fire Island was, and who his friends were. "How is Francesca?"

He became grim. "I hardly ever see her. She is on some grand new case, trying to apprehend whoever lured her from her own wedding. Meanwhile, she and Hart are estranged. At first, I did not blame him, but now I am growing annoyed that he doesn't see reason. He must forgive her—she loves him terribly."

"I am sure they will work this out, Evan," she said softly.

He suddenly took both her hands in his. "Maggie, I would never leave for the entire summer without saying goodbye."

She bit her lip. "I am glad," she managed to say. What she wanted to do was tell him how much she would miss him. Two months seemed like an eternity.

He began to smile. "I have an idea. Let's take the children to Coney Island for an entire day's outing."

She hadn't ever been to Coney Island. They could not afford it, no matter that she knew her children would love the rides and amusements and they so dearly needed an outing. "You want to take us to Coney Island?"

"Yes, I do. It's a beautiful day—why not go?" He grinned.

She inhaled, wanting to go so badly it hurt. But she said, "Evan, you know I can't afford it and I can't possibly let you take us on such an expensive outing." She meant to be firm, but all she could think of was how much her children deserved a day at the amusement park.

"I know you can't afford it, but I can. I intend to take you and the children and show you the best time you have ever had!"

Maggie knew she was about to cry. She was so moved she couldn't even speak.

"Hey." He caught her face in his hand. "Why are you crying?"

And she gave up. She didn't even try to reply.

"Maggie," Evan murmured, and pulled her into his arms.

Maggie held on, hard.

FRANCESCA STARED OUT the carriage window as Hart's coach continued west on Seventy-second Street, entering Central Park. They were nearly at the bridge spanning the lake. Within moments, she would be confronting her blackmailer. Very grimly, she faced Joel, but it was Bill Randall she was thinking about.

The last time she had encountered Randall, he had been vicious and cruel. He had locked her in his sister's bedroom, tying her ruthlessly to the bed there. She had managed to escape. When he had realized that, a violent encounter had ensued. Fortunately she'd had the winning hand—she'd struck him over the head with a fry pan.

He'd been hateful before she had exposed his sister as a murderess. With Mary incarcerated at Bellevue, his

mother serving a sentence at Blackwell's Island, she imagined he was even more hateful now. And she feared she
was about to meet him on the bridge.

She tamped down her fear. She was going to get her
portrait back!

She inhaled, opened her purse and stared at the two
small pistols there. She took the one she had recently
purchased and looked at Joel.

He started. "Is that a new gun?"

"It is. I realized some time ago that I had better have
a substitute. And today, you will carry this one."

His mouth dropped wide open. "I ain't never shot
nuthin' or no one."

"Don't worry—it isn't loaded." It had seemed terribly
irresponsible to give Joel a loaded gun. "But you are going
to be my protection. I am assuming we are about to come
face-to-face with Bill Randall—and he has never seen
you. You can hide this under your shirt. Do not reveal it
unless I am in trouble. He won't know the chambers are
empty."

He smiled at her. "I can strap it to my waist with my
belt and pull my shirt over it," he said, clearly excited.

She wondered if she should have told Hart the truth.
He wouldn't be very pleased with her right now, either.
But she had overcome Randall once before. Surely she
could do so again.

She also had to consider that the blackmailer might
not even be Randall. She might come face-to-face with
Solange—whom she considered an even more dangerous
adversary. "I am going to wait on the bridge with the
valise for the blackmailer. But you will precede me, Joel.
I want you to take that ball and play with it, about halfway
across the bridge. When you see me make contact with
our thief, pretend not to notice, but watch us with care. If

all goes well, I will exchange the valise for the portrait. If things go awry, come running with that gun."

"Don't worry, Miz Cahill," Joel said with arrogance. "We been in worse times before. We'll get the painting—and the buzzer."

Francesca certainly hoped so. She turned to gaze out the window. The bridge was beautiful, pale gray stone spanning the lake, with a few pedestrians and carriages crossing it. Ducks and swans floated on the water, as did one small toy sailboat. She noticed two boys on the lake's edge on this side of the bridge—apparently they had launched the miniature sailboat.

Overhead, puffy cotton-candy clouds floated in an azure sky, the sun shining brightly. It was a perfect summer day.

With any luck, the nightmare of her missing portrait would be solved in a few more minutes.

She knocked on the ceiling of the coach and told Raoul to park. A moment later she and Joel alighted. The hansom that had been behind them now passed. Raoul waited for his instructions. "You can stay here," Francesca told him. "I won't go more than halfway across the bridge. I do not know if the thug I am meeting will cause trouble or not."

Raoul grunted. He was a big, dark man of Spanish descent who had served with Teddy Roosevelt in the Rough Riders in the war for Cuban independence. Francesca had not a doubt that Hart had already instructed him to keep a close eye on her. Before they had even become engaged, Hart had decided that Raoul would be a bodyguard of sorts for her.

She warmed in her chest, just a little. Hopefully, later that night, she and Hart would share a scotch together as she recounted the events of that afternoon. Hopefully, they would be celebrating the outcome.

She turned off her thoughts, glancing at the bridge. A single couple was crossing it now, as were two hansoms. She wondered if Randall—or Solange Marceaux—was in one of those cabs. She nodded at Joel.

He had his shirt out over the gun. A ball in his hand, Joel walked jauntily across the bridge, whistling. He began tossing the ball at the railing, and catching it as it bounced back.

One of the hansoms had stopped, quite near the midpoint of the bridge. Francesca's heart thundered. She picked up the heavy valise and smiled grimly at Raoul. He was expressionless. It occurred to her that she had never heard him say a single word.

She marched to the bridge and started up it. The couple glanced at her as they passed her, somewhat curiously. After all, she did not carry a parasol, wasn't wearing gloves and was toting a man's leather attaché case. She carried her purse—with her pistol—in her other hand.

Francesca paused not far from the hansom, glancing at it as she set the valise down. Joel was now some ten feet head of her, playing ball vigorously. He was truly a wonderful assistant.

She suddenly noticed that they were the only ones on the bridge. It was very odd. As she had that disturbing thought, the hansom door opened.

Francesca froze. But a pretty young woman got out and hurried to the railing, crying out in delight. She turned and said something in German, and another, older woman got out to join her.

Francesca's disappointment was acute. They were foreigners, clearly visiting the city and admiring the view.

She glanced around, but she and Joel remained the only ones on the bridge, other than the German tourists and the cabdriver. She turned to stare suspiciously at him, but he was curled up in his seat, reading a news journal. Where was the blackmailer?

She was incredulous and frustrated, all at once. The two ladies returned to the cab, climbed in, and it drove off. Another carriage approached the bridge, along with a bicyclist. Francesca tensed, but a moment later, the carriage passed by her, unoccupied. She turned to stare intently at the oncoming bicycle.

A man was riding it. As the bicycle came closer, she saw that the rider was a man about Bill's age, but it wasn't Bill or anyone else that she knew. He looked like a laborer in his dark tweed trousers and cotton shirt. He even had a lunch pail strapped to the handlebars.

She sagged in disappointment. Francesca opened her purse and glanced at her pocket watch. She had been on the bridge for over twenty minutes. And as she wondered if the blackmail note had been a ruse, she looked up—the cyclist was veering toward her!

He meant to run her down.

Too late she realized she was about to be rammed. But instead, just as the front tire brushed her skirts, he jerked the handlebars and something was shoved into her hand. The impact was forceful enough to send her stumbling backward. She recovered her balance, her heart exploding, and glanced at the piece of paper she had reflexively grasped. Francesca opened it—and saw a rough charcoal sketch of her in the nude, clearly an imitation of her portrait.

She cried out, stuffing the paper in her purse, as Joel reached her side. "Are ye hurt?" he demanded. "He ran ye over on purpose!"

"We must get him!" she cried, about to chase after the cyclist, who had turned abruptly around and was pedaling as fast as he could back the way he had come. Then she saw the valise. She could hardly leave it.

"I'll get him," Joel said and he broke into a run. But the cyclist was already a speck on the street ahead, on the west side of the bridge. Joel would never catch him now.

"Joel!" Francesca called. "Come back!"

Joel faltered and slowed. He halted, shaking his fist as the cyclist vanished from sight. Francesca felt like shaking her fist, too. Worse, she almost felt like crying.

"Goddamn it," she said softly.

She felt Raoul come up behind her and she turned. "Can you take the valise for me?"

But Hart was standing behind her, not Raoul.

His expression was hard and grim. "Did you really think I would let you meet a blackmailer by yourself?"

She cried out incoherently.

He cupped her jaw. "Are you hurt?"

"No." She began to tremble.

"Let me see the note."

"You followed us?" She was incredulous, but she opened her purse and handed him the note.

"I followed you in a hansom, Francesca. Had you not been so preoccupied, you undoubtedly would have noticed." She recalled a cab passing their coach when they had halted before the bridge.

"That was you?" she gasped.

"It most certainly was." He looked at the sketch and darkened. "He is toying with you, Francesca. This is not about money, at least, not yet."

"What does the thief want?" she cried in frustration. "Does he or she mean to torture me before destroying me?"

"It certainly seems that way." He took her arm, signaling Joel, and guided her back to the coach. When they were all inside, Hart looked at Francesca. "May I assume that there is a blackmail note?"

Francesca hesitated. He was angry with her. And she hadn't told Hart about the visit to Blackwell's Island, either. Her tension escalated. "Yes, you may." She bit her lip. "Why did you follow me today, Calder?"

He eyed her. "You made it clear that you were not going to tell Rick about the blackmail threat. I would never let you meet a dangerous rough by yourself."

She'd had Raoul as protection, but she decided not to remark on that. "I am glad you cared enough to follow me, but as you can see, it was all for naught." She trembled, opened her purse and handed him the blackmail note. "I am so very disappointed."

"You were almost run over by the cyclist," he said sharply. He stared at the envelope with the word URGENT written on it in bold block letters. "We will give this to that fellow at headquarters, the one who is so brilliant at crime analysis."

"Heinreich," she supplied.

"What aren't you telling me?" He handed the note back to her.

She wished she did not have to tell him that their number-one suspect was his half brother. "As planned, Rick and I went to see Henrietta Randall today." He became very still and watchful. She said, "Bill Randall was in the city on Saturday. He visited his mother at the Blackwell's Workhouse at ten in the morning. Henrietta let that slip and we confirmed that he signed in the visitors' log."

Hart finally said, "So my damn brother is behind the theft of the portrait."

"Perhaps. We have requested the logs for April. They are in storage."

"The university is closed for the summer. If his roommates are not traveling, we shall certainly find them, in order to interview them another time."

He sat facing her in the rear-facing seat. She reached

out to touch his knee. "There is a chance his alibi is the truth, and his being here on Saturday is a mere coincidence."

"You do not believe that."

"No, I do not."

They exchanged a long look. Very softly, Hart said, "If Bill stole that portrait—if he is the one who has put us through hell, if he is the one who thinks to destroy us—I am going to kill him."

Francesca cringed and looked at Joel, who sat beside her, listening raptly to their every word. "You do not mean that!" She faced Joel. "He was speaking figuratively, Joel, not literally. He did not mean it."

"He meant it," Joel said. "But that's okay. My lips are sealed."

Francesca groaned as Hart called to Raoul, "Fifty-seventh and Lexington, Raoul—the old Randall residence!" He gave her a black look.

"Do not even think of blaming yourself for any of this," she cried.

"And who should I blame? Sarah, for painting the portrait? You, for agreeing to it? Mrs. Channing, for failing to lock all her doors?"

"Yes and yes and yes!" she cried.

He suddenly reached across the small space separating them and seized her hand. Their knees bumped. "I despise it when you place yourself in danger. And I am even unhappier when I place you in danger." He released her, his eyes ablaze.

How would they ever get through his belief that he was at fault for all that had happened? It might have been different—easier—if he hadn't come to this conclusion on so many previous occasions. She said somewhat lamely, "We are getting closer to the thief."

"No, he is getting closer to us."

She turned to look out the window, realizing that the day wasn't going to have the happy ending she had so hoped for. Then she glanced at Hart, acutely aware of his presence in the back of the coach. He filled up the large space, making it seem small and tight. He would turn her away that night, too, she thought dismally. It was as if the thief wanted to permanently estrange them—and was succeeding.

She looked at Hart directly. "We should speak to Daniel Moore after we search the Randall home. Joel has learned that he was at the gallery Saturday morning with another man. And someone did lock it up after I left Saturday afternoon—unless breaking that glass was a ruse."

"And the plot thickens."

"Moore is involved in my entrapment."

"Obviously, but he isn't our thief—and he isn't our blackmailer. If he knew where the portrait was, we would have it by now. He is desperate for funds, in spite of the deposit he recently made into his savings at the East River Savings Bank."

Francesca sat up straighter.

"I checked out his finances. He is behind on both leases, to the gallery and his Broadway flat. But he deposited a thousand dollars into that savings account on this last Thursday."

"A payoff from our thief—to use his gallery?"

"I would assume so," Hart said. They were on Lexington now. The traffic was always heavy on that avenue, where huge wagons laden with retail merchandise and industrial supplies vied for the right-of-way with electric trolleys and mostly empty cabs. Theirs was the only private coach in sight.

Moore knew who they were pursuing. It was time to drag him downtown and make him break.

"We're here," Hart said abruptly. As they all alighted, he clasped Joel by the shoulder. "By the way," he said to the small boy, "I am proud of how you tried to protect Francesca from that cyclist."

Joel beamed at him. "I saw him change direction and knew he meant to run her over."

"You have good instincts, Joel, and more importantly, you are terribly brave. Francesca is fortunate to have you at her side."

Joel flushed with more pleasure. Francesca hid a smile and said, "We are looking for any clues relating to the blackmail note, the theft of my portrait or Bill Randall having been in the city. Joel, why don't you take the up-stairs. Hart and I will nose around the ground floor."

They started for the redbrick home, which was just off Lexington Avenue. A large For Sale sign was posted on the iron gate. Hart unlatched it and they walked inside. "Did you know the house was for sale?" Francesca asked.

"No, I did not," Hart said.

He sounded so grim. Francesca imagined that his memories of this house, which he had been to only a few times, were not pleasant. She hated the fact that his own father had rejected him. Impulsively she reached for his hand.

For one moment, he let her take it, before he slipped his palm free. "I don't care about Paul Randall," he said flatly.

She grimaced, wondering if he truly believed that, while trying the front doorknob. Of course it was locked.

Several moments followed, with Joel attempting to pick the lock. Hart went to walk around the house, hoping for an open window. Francesca tried to pretend that nothing was amiss, but several shopgirls looked at them oddly as they passed, as did the street vendor on the corner of Fifty-seventh Street. He was selling candles, but he gave that task up, instead watching with interest as Joel kept jimmying the lock.

Hart appeared from inside the house, opening the front door for them. "The back door is unlocked."

They hurried inside. "That street vendor might rouse up a roundsman."

Hart shrugged. "I got in through the parlor. Francesca, come look."

He took her arm and they walked into the small parlor where she had interviewed various members of the family after Paul Randall's murder in February. Joel ran upstairs. Francesca hesitated, a memory of poor Henrietta coming to mind as she had been while the matriarch of this small house, and as she now was, at the Blackwell's Island Workhouse. She had lost her husband, her family and her life.

The parlor remained dark and dreary, as if in mourning, with wine-colored draperies and wine-and-cream-striped walls. She glanced past the sideboard, with its bric-a-brac and photographs, ignoring those of Bill, past the candelabra and small painting on the mantel of the fireplace, to the main seating area. A moss-green sofa faced two red chairs. There was an empty drinking glass on one side table, some newspapers on the occasional table in front of the sofa. The glass, of course, could have been left there months ago—or by one of the family's real estate agents. Francesca rushed to the low table and picked up the topmost newspaper, which was the *New York Times:* Walkout Order Goes into Effect Today. She gasped, wondering if this article was in reference to the much-anticipated strike at Union Pacific in Omaha. She glanced at the date on the paper. Monday, June 30. "It is today's paper."

Hart's brows lifted.

She looked at the two other papers. They were both from Sunday. Hart said mildly, "Bill is the only one capable of trying to sell this house. But anyone could have been here today—an agent, a buyer, anyone."

"Yes—and Bill might have been here today," she exclaimed. She hurried into the kitchen and he followed her. She could feel his mood softening. But now, she hesitated—this was where she had encountered Bill after escaping, and where she had knocked him out with a cast-iron pan. She turned and saw a plate with some bread crumbs on it on the small kitchen table. A knife and fork were on the plate. She went forward and touched a crumb—it had been left recently, she was certain. Then she went to the sink and saw several dirty dishes. "No agent would leave such a mess behind."

Before Hart could respond, Joel ran into the kitchen. "Someone's sleeping in the bed upstairs in the man's bedroom!"

Francesca turned to Hart. His eyes were dark with anticipation. She was fairly certain that Bill Randall was staying in the family home. As much as she wanted to apprehend him, she truly hoped he would not walk in the door. She did not trust Hart just then.

"An' someone's staying in the other bedroom, too," Joel added, his eyes alight with excitement.

Francesca started. "Are you certain?"

"Follow me!" He grinned.

They trooped up the narrow staircase and Joel led them to Mary's small, spartan bedroom. It was unchanged from when Francesca had been imprisoned in it. But the bed was not made, the blankets were tossed back, the pillow was dented as if recently slept in. And the room's single window was open.

She glanced at Hart. He murmured, "Someone is most definitely using this room."

She was uneasy. "Joel, where is the man's bedroom?"

He led them across the hall. The bed was made, but toiletries were on the adjacent table, as was a two-week-old issue of *Harper's*. As she approached the bed, she smelled a man's cologne. Her stomach churned—she thought she recognized the scent. In any case, it reminded her of Randall.

"I have no doubt that Bill is in residence, with an accomplice," Hart said, staring at her. "It's getting late. Let's take Joel home and then I am taking you home. You have been up since dawn."

He cared enough to want her to get home and rest? Hiding a smile, she said, "Bragg needs to have this house under surveillance."

"I'll call him when we get home."

She wondered if his words were a slip of the tongue. "Maybe we should make a brief detour to Bellevue and speak with Mary. If Bill has a habit of visiting his mother, I would wager he calls on his sister, as well."

"I'd rather not," Hart said flatly.

As they returned downstairs, Francesca realized she was exhausted. The last person she wished to spar with was Mary Randall. She had never met an angrier or more bitter woman. "It has been a very long day," she said, angling for some sympathy.

She gave him a sidelong look, which he pretended not to see. They locked the front door and left the house through the parlor. When Hart didn't comment, she added, "Not only was I up at dawn, I barely slept at all last night."

Had Hart's mouth quirked? He looked at her, taking her elbow and guiding her from the small yard to Fifty-seventh Street, Joel following behind them. "What is it you want, Francesca?"

She smiled at him. "I would love nothing more than a good stiff drink."

CHAPTER TWELVE

Monday, June 30, 1902
6:00 p.m.

SHE STARED AT the clothing scattered across her bed. She had dresses for every occasion—for teas and luncheons, for a stroll down the Ladies' Mile, for shopping at B. Altman's or the Lord & Taylor store, for charity lunches and supper balls. Leigh Anne stared helplessly at the pile of gowns, Katie hovering anxiously by her right side. The new maid, Nanette, waited expectantly.

Why couldn't she choose which dresses to pack for their holiday weekend? She couldn't imagine the upcoming weekend with Rick and the girls in that little cottage on the beach, much less summon up a decision about her clothing. Her brain felt befuddled and fogged. She couldn't even decide whether or not to take the girls out for a stroll.

"You should take the pale blue, the dark pink and the one with green stripes," Katie whispered.

Leigh Anne glanced at the child, whose mouth was curved down, her dark eyes filled with anxiety. She somehow reached for and found her hand. "What a lovely choice," she said, smiling as brightly as she could. But the anguish was burying her alive.

She needed new clothes, she thought dully. She needed gray and beige dresses, or even black—sober colors more suited to a crippled matron in a wheelchair. Her right leg ached. Where was her tea? It was laced very liberally with brandy.

"I will pack these pretty dresses right up," Nanette said cheerfully. "Is there anything else you wish to bring for your holiday? It might be cool on the beach, Mrs. Bragg."

The Frenchwoman was always smiling. Why was she always so happy? Didn't she know that tragedy could strike in a single heartbeat, forever changing one's life?

Katie suddenly brought her teacup. As she handed it to her, Leigh Anne flushed, afraid to look the child in the eyes. "Thank you," she said softly. Katie had seen her pouring brandy in her tea.

Leigh Anne knew she had become a terrible mother. How had that happened, when she so loved the girls? Of course, they had Rick, whom they could always depend upon. Except, he was never home now.

He claimed he was working late hours in order to be ready to leave the city for their holiday on Thursday. She had reassured him that she understood his preoccupation, his schedule and the rigorous demands of his job. But she also knew he was spending a great deal of time with Francesca, investigating. She didn't care—did she?

"Can we go downstairs?" Katie whispered.

Leigh Anne focused. "We certainly can." She managed to smile as Peter was called. She hated being carried downstairs, more so now than ever. This day was worse than most—some days were so dark, there simply was no hope.

A few moments later, the children were in the dining room, beginning their supper. The doorbell sounded. Leigh Anne couldn't imagine who would be calling at the supper hour, as none of her acquaintances ever visited now. It was as if she had conveniently left town—or as if she no longer existed. She was still reeling from how awkward it had been to attend Francesca's wedding.

The fact of the matter was that Leigh Anne no longer existed—a stranger had taken her place.

She nodded at Peter to get the door, even though she had no desire to entertain. "Dot," she told the rambunctious two-year-old. "Don't you like the meat loaf? It is not meant to be toyed with—it is meant to be eaten."

"I'll help her," Nanette said quickly, taking her fork from her.

Leigh Anne recalled a time when she had helped Dot finish her food without allowing a mess to be made. Hearing footsteps, she tensed. A woman's high heels accompanied Peter's heavier footfall.

"Hello, Leigh Anne. My, what a charming family scene! All that is missing is the police commissioner." Bartolla Benevente beamed.

Leigh Anne's heart sank. What did the other woman want? She no longer considered Bartolla a friend. It had been clear from the first that the countess delighted in Leigh Anne's new predicament. Once, they had dined and shopped together in Europe, frequenting the same supper parties and balls. Leigh Anne had never allowed the other woman's petty malice to bother her. And why would she? Bartolla had always been jealous of the attention she received. Now she struggled to find her dignity and indifference. No one was as catty as the countess. "Hello. This is a surprise, Bartolla. The children are dining, as you can see."

Bartolla was a striking woman, and she was gorgeous in her royal-blue ensemble. "I forgot how early children dine. I wanted to call before I left for the Catskills. Darling, are you ill?" Her auburn brows lifted.

Leigh Anne knew that she was referring, inelegantly, to her poor, pale looks. "I have been having some slight pains," she said, too late realizing she shouldn't discuss this in front of the children. Katie had stopped eating to listen to her every word. "Finish up, darlings. I will entertain the countess in the parlor."

Peter was already behind her and wheeling her chair out the dining room, down the short hall and into the parlor. Leigh Anne said, "Why don't you bring us two sherries."

"I am so sorry you aren't well," Bartolla exclaimed as he went to the bar cart. "Leigh Anne, you have lost so much weight."

She did not know what to say to that. "Who are you visiting in the mountains? I have heard the Catskills are lovely at this time of year."

Bartolla sat on the sofa, accepting her sherry. "I have been invited down by the Rutherfords. Dear, I must be atrociously bold. That dress no longer suits you."

Leigh Anne took a very large sip of sherry as Peter left. "I must call in a modiste." She took another calming sip of sherry and stared at Bartolla. She knew all about her failed affair with Evan Cahill. "I think I will try that Irishwoman, Maggie Kennedy. She has done such wonderful dresses for Francesca."

Bartolla put her glass down, her eyes gleaming hatefully. "I cannot believe you would give her your business!"

"And why wouldn't I?"

Bartolla stood. "She is a harlot, Leigh Anne. She has been carrying on with Evan right under my very nose."

"Really? She seemed like a fine and decent woman to me."

Bartolla spat. "I cannot believe he is sleeping with her! He will realize, sooner or later, that it is his fortune she is after."

"As he did with you?"

Bartolla stiffened. "My, my, you still have claws. I have never liked rivals, my dear, as you may remember." The innuendo did not escape Leigh Anne. They had been rivals once, but never again. Then Bartolla smiled. "How is Rick, darling?"

"He has so many burdens, as you know."

"Yes, I see that the newsmen in this city write about him every day. You will lose him, Leigh Anne, if you keep on this way."

Leigh Anne stiffened. She did not want to discuss Rick Bragg—or her marriage—with this hateful woman.

"You are still pretty. I am sure if you wore some rouge and a different dress you could attract his interest as you used to."

"My husband is devoted to me," she said tersely.

"I have heard that he is running all over town with Francesca, now that her engagement to Hart is off." Bartolla laughed. "Did you see Hart's face at the church? He finally got his comeuppance. It was priceless, that moment of humiliation."

"I have always liked Calder."

"Hmm, I suppose that is because you are the only woman he hasn't slept with." Bartolla blinked with feigned innocence. "For that would have ended your relationship with Rick—once and for all."

Leigh Anne wished she had another drink. "They get along better now," she finally said.

"Ha! They hate one another. Francesca has always been deeply in love with Bragg. She did love him first, before you returned to claim your marriage. I know. I was here." She gloated. "Don't you see what is about to happen? Rick will turn to her if you continue this way, as a despondent cripple."

Leigh Anne had no response to make. Bartolla was right.

"I do not want you to lose him," Bartolla said, taking the seat closest to her chair. "You must fix yourself up."

Leigh Anne wished she could get up and walk out of the room. A part of her didn't want to lose him either, she realized. But she hated the woman she had become. Francesca Cahill was perfect for him. If Rick left her for the sleuth, it would be best for everyone—except, of course, for poor Calder Hart. "Would you pour me another sherry?"

Bartolla leaped up to do so. "You don't seem very distressed at the idea of Rick leaving you, Leigh Anne."

"I am too tired to be upset."

Bartolla shook her head, perplexed. "You have lost more than the use of your legs. I feel sorry for you. Francesca will walk off with Rick very shortly, if I do not miss my guess."

Leigh Anne wondered if Bartolla was right. She wondered if she cared. She wondered if she could live alone with the girls. She needed her laudanum, she thought. Either that, or she would take the morphine her former male nurse had managed to procure for her. It was so much better than the laudanum.

"Of course, Francesca might wind up very much alone," Bartolla said suddenly. "Sarah is so upset these days. She has been in a frenzy, really, all because of that stolen portrait."

Leigh Anne could barely follow Bartolla.

"You do know that Hart commissioned a portrait of Francesca, and that it was stolen several months ago." She laughed. "My God, what an uproar that has caused."

Leigh Anne finished the sherry. "Yes, I vaguely recall Rick mentioning it."

"And did he mention that if that portrait is ever displayed in public, Francesca will be ruined?"

Leigh Anne stared. "No, he did not."

"Ah, of course he didn't tell you—he is protecting her."

"I think you should go," Leigh Anne said. She simply couldn't withstand these tactics any longer. She was tired. She wanted relief. She wanted to become mindless, to float through the rest of the evening.

Bartolla leaned over her. "The portrait is a nude, Leigh Anne. I saw it myself, in Sarah's studio. If it ever surfaces, she will never be able to set foot in polite society again."

Leigh Anne was shocked.

"I can see you had no clue." Gaily, Bartolla kissed her. "If I don't see you, have a wonderful Fourth."

Rather stupefied, Leigh Anne watched her swagger to the door. There, she paused. "And do put on some rouge—unless you truly wish to send your husband into another woman's arms."

Leigh Anne decided not to bother to try to form a reply. Bartolla was leaving. Everything would be all right. She simply needed to dose herself. Before she knew it, she would be floating in a world where there was no pain, no despair and no regrets.

FRANCESCA WAS ACUTELY aware of Hart. His masculine appeal, his power and sensuality, were impossible to ignore when they sat together alone in his coach, sharing the backseat. Joel had been taken to his flat a half hour ago. Only a hand's span separated them.

He glanced sidelong at her.

She felt her heart beating slowly. Francesca pretended not to notice his regard. Outside, the night was postcard perfect. A million stars glittered in the city's inky sky. They were traveling up Fourth Avenue, alongside the excavations for the railroad tunnel, and most of the buildings along the street were dark and unlit. There was no traffic, and their pace was brisk. Francesca stole a glance at his hard, handsome profile. She knew exactly how she wished for this day to end.

She turned back to her open carriage window. Had she not gone downtown to Moore's gallery on Saturday, they would now be man and wife. They would be aboard a cruise ship, dancing every night away, sharing fine wines and champagne, on their way to France.

They would be making love till dawn.

His gaze strayed to hers, a flicker in his eyes. She smiled slightly, somehow biting back the words that so wanted to arise. She did not want to go home. She did not want to spend the rest of the evening alone, or worse, in her parents' company. She wanted to spend the rest of the evening with him—debating the merits of this new case before making love. It was so hard to hold her tongue. But she was going to follow Connie's advice.

His glance dropped to her hands. She hoped he would ask her why she wasn't wearing her ring so she could offer up the flippant, casual reply she had prepared, but he said, "Why aren't you wearing gloves?"

She smiled, facing him more squarely as the coach turned west on Fifty-ninth Street. They were passing the Plaza Hotel. She would be home in mere moments. "I thought I might need to use my gun when I confronted the blackmailer, and gloves would make the chore more difficult."

He shook his head once. "Yes, I doubt you could effectively shoot a man while wearing gloves."

Was he angry? "You know I carry a weapon with which to protect myself."

"You know I have never approved of your doing so."

She hoped they would spar. "It has come in handy."

"One day, you will shoot off your big toe."

She thought his mouth curved. "I hope not!"

He studied her, his mouth softer now. "I don't think Mrs. Kennedy will appreciate your having given Joel a weapon."

"It wasn't loaded." She hesitated. "That was wrong of me."

"Yes, Francesca, it was."

Their gazes held. She was well aware that they were almost abreast of the Metropolitan Club, as they had passed the Grand Army Plaza, which she had seen through Hart's window. Francesca thought he meant to remain silent. Her heart had picked up its beat. Her entire body had become languid. But he suddenly said softly, "What am I to do with you?"

She stared breathlessly, wanting to ask him if he would invite her to his house so they could continue the evening. Somehow she said, "In the end, while no progress was made, no harm was suffered, either."

He eyed her and she flushed. Her tone had been throaty and they both knew what that meant. "You are like a cat with nine lives. I haven't decided how many you have left."

There was tension in his tone. She couldn't decide why. She hoped he was feeling the pull of the magic between them, as well. She hoped, very much, that he hadn't meant a word he had said to her on Saturday night, and that he not only loved her, but desired her as he did no other. Ahead, she saw her front gates. She held her tongue, clasping her hands in her lap. "I'll call Rick when I get in," she began.

He caught her left hand. He said softly, "You could have been hurt today."

"But I wasn't."

"Do you have to throw yourself in front of speeding locomotives?"

"There wasn't a train in sight. I was simply meeting a blackmailer."

He hadn't released her hand. His grasp tightened. "I think I need a drink, as well."

She went still. That heavy anticipation permeated her every pore. "Are you suggesting we share a very old, very fine scotch?"

"Will I rue the day?" And his mouth softened, along with his eyes.

"We can discuss the case and what we must do tomorrow," she cried, smiling. Other far more romantic ideas danced in her mind. Then, recalling her sister's advice, she said, "Or we can discuss the case tomorrow, over breakfast."

His gaze narrowed with speculation. "So you prefer breakfast tomorrow?"

"I hardly said that. You know how fond I have become of a good scotch."

When he simply stared, she added, "I do not want you to think I have any ulterior motives, that's all."

His brows lifted. "Do you?"

"Of course not," she said quickly, smiling. Why hadn't he asked her about the ring? "What I am trying to say is that I have done a great deal of thinking—about our relationship." She waited for him to respond, and when he did not, she said, "I am not going to chase you, Calder."

His stare remained impossible to read and he still did not take the bait. She sighed. "I am beginning to comprehend your rationale. I am even beginning to think that you are right."

He finally said very calmly, "Are you trying to tell me that you have changed your mind…about us?"

She swallowed. Deceit was not her forte. But Connie was so much more vastly experienced than she was. "I treasure our friendship. It means everything to me." That was the truth. "I cannot imagine my life without you in it."

"Please, do go on."

"Our friendship remains more important to me than the desire we have shared." She smiled firmly, amazed at how well she was lying. "As you have made up your mind about us, I began to realize that my pride would never allow me to chase or pursue you. Then I began to wonder if you are right. I mean, we get on famously as friends. But as lovers, we always seem to fight." There, that had sounded simply perfect.

His gaze was watchful and steady upon her. Never removing it, he said to Raoul, "We will go directly home." Then, "Are you playing me, Francesca?"

She bit her lip. "I doubt that any woman could ever play you."

"So that is why you aren't wearing my ring? You have agreed that we are off."

She inhaled. "We are two very different individuals, are we not?"

"Yes, we are two very different individuals."

He was not being helpful, she thought. "My sister advised me to take it off—as did you. Aren't you pleased with my rationale, Calder?"

His stare remained enigmatic. "So for once in your entire life, you have decided to take the advice of others, instead of following your own inclinations? For once in your life, you have decided to adapt to circumstance, instead of remaining infuriatingly stubborn?"

"And how do you know what my inclinations are now?" She sat back, still anxious about her deception. "And I can see reason, Calder. In fact, I pride myself on it."

"You told me," he said dryly, "that you would never

take my ring off, that you would wear it to the grave. And you were very passionate about it."

She hesitated. She must not cave and blurt out how madly in love with him she was. "That was then and this is now. Connie gave me an earful. As did you. And even I can see how different we are from one another, now that I am calmer. Our engagement was made in haste—and perhaps it was made without logic."

He looked at her as if she had just suggested they take a trip to the moon. "You have never been logical, not about our relationship."

Her pulse pounded. She moved in for the final blow, hoping he would be convinced. "We are meant to be friends—good friends—eternal friends. But I am no longer sure that we are meant to be anything more." She managed a firm smile.

"Really?" His brows lifted, as if he was mildly disbelieving.

"Really." She smiled again. She had won that round, hadn't she? She decided to deliver a last jab. "For isn't a good marriage built on common interests and common goals?"

"Probably."

She smiled widely now. She had won. He believed her.

"Are you gloating?" he asked very, very softly.

She hid her smile. Very innocently, she said, "I much prefer our relationship like this—as one of equals. It was not very pretty of me to be reduced to tears the other day, much less to grovel."

"You have never groveled," he said as calmly. "And you are a bald-faced liar."

She blinked at him. "Did you just call me a liar?"

He smiled slowly, suggestively at her. "I beg your pardon. That was terribly rude. On the other hand, you have just spent the past five minutes delivering a carefully rehearsed speech, when you are the most impulsive and spontaneous woman I know."

He didn't believe her? "Are you becoming angry, Calder?" she asked carefully.

"Why would I be angry? I have been jilted at the altar, in front of most of society, and the woman I meant to take as a wife is now in dire jeopardy due to my depraved nature. My recent bride-to-be is now eager to be my dear friend. In fact, she is so eager to be my friend that she has forgotten our rather unique history. Oh, and did I mention that my brother is probably responsible for all this? If not for dear Bill, we would be on a ship, bound for France, with a wedding ring on your finger. Except, of course, for the fact that ultimately I brought this house of cards down." He lapsed into a brooding silence.

Francesca hated having pretended that she was fine with their estrangement. She could not decide if he believed her or not. Was he hurt? Angry? He didn't seem upset. Hurting Calder was the last thing she wished to do. She hated following Connie's advice, but she wanted him back, and begging would hardly achieve that end. Then she realized he was staring. His scrutiny was unnerving. She must never underestimate Hart. "I am not going to fight your decision," she said simply. "And it is a matter of both logic and pride."

"I am glad you have seen the same light that I have," he said softly.

His tone was so sensual that she shivered, tingling from the tips of her toes to the nape of her neck. He smiled at her.

A few minutes later they were walking into the library, a delighted Alfred rushing off to ask the cook to prepare a light meal for them. "Is anyone else home?" Francesca asked. Hart walked past her and brushed her as he did.

She trembled, ready to leap into his arms. He turned on two lights, apparently unaware of the contact.

"I have no idea." He walked over to the bar that was built into one floor-to-ceiling bookcase. "But Rathe and Grace are leaving for Newport Beach on Wednesday, taking Colin and Gregory with them. Nick is going back to San Francisco tomorrow, until the fall semester begins. I believe Rourke intends to mope about the city—and moon over Sarah Channing." He turned and handed her a scotch.

Francesca smiled happily at him, her nerves stretched taut within her body. "I do hope a romance is brewing for Sarah and Rourke." She walked over to the sofa and sat down, aware of Hart watching her. She was certain his mind had gone in the same direction as hers, never mind her declaration of friendship. She took a sip of scotch, sighed with pleasure, then unbuttoned and removed her kitten-heeled, black-patent shoes.

He still stood by the bar, a drink in hand. She did not turn around to look at him. Images flashed. She had wound up naked on that sofa several times. She would love to wind up naked on it now.

He had such a powerful effect on her. Surely he felt the same way about her.

"I can feel your thoughts," he said, having come to stand behind the sofa where she sat.

She arched to look up at him, over her shoulder. "Really? So there is gypsy in your blood?"

His eyes were definitely warmer. "Hardly. But I know you very well, now, don't I? Better than anyone—even better than Rick."

"Don't," she said, the sexy moment on the verge of vanishing. "But it is true. No one knows me as well as you."

He sipped his drink thoughtfully. Then he reached

past her and set it down on one of the sofa's end tables. A moment later he laid a hand on each side of her shoulders. "So you now wish for us to be friends. Will that really satisfy you, Francesca?"

He was leaning over her from behind. She sank back into the couch, staring up at him. His face was inches from hers. She tore her gaze from his mouth to his eyes. "We are already great friends—so I hardly need to wish for that."

"You didn't answer my question," he murmured.

She looked at his mouth. "Of course it won't satisfy me."

His eyes gleamed. "You are so transparent."

She gave in to the urge to touch him and reached up to caress his jaw. "Then you must know what I am yearning for right now."

"But we must hold to logic, darling. We must be mere friends," he murmured. But he turned his face slightly and kissed the center of her palm. "You can only play me if I let you."

Her entire body was on fire. "Then let me," she said, and she reached up and caught his face and arched upward, pressing her lips to the corner of his mouth.

He did not move, braced above her, his knuckles white as he grasped the sofa, one hand on each side of her. Francesca strained higher, managing to brush his mouth with hers, softly, gently, several times. "Calder, I have missed you," she whispered. "And I am rather desperate now."

He was breathing harder. He pulled his head back slightly and their gazes met, his eyes black with desire. "When will you admit that you lied to me in the coach?"

She was taken aback, finding it hard to think clearly. "Not now, Calder."

"Oh, yes," he said softly. "Now."

His mouth curved and he lowered his face, briefly brushing her cheek with his. Then his mouth moved over her exposed throat. She sighed in raw pleasure. Fire fanned within her, dancing through the entire core of her body, tightening her, swelling her. His mouth moved lower, down the column of her neck, and lower still, until he nuzzled her cleavage. "Admit that you baldly lied."

Francesca moaned, reached up, finding his tie. She tugged on it. "I lied. Come to the sofa and kiss me properly."

She felt his mouth curve with satisfaction. "Sit up," he ordered against her ear.

She was dazed with desire and absolutely breathless, but she straightened. His hands went to the back of her dress. Her heart thundered as he undid the buttons, deftly and skillfully. Francesca stood up, her skin tingling, and slowly stepped out of her dress, letting it pool around her feet on the floor. She turned and looked at Hart.

His eyes were black with desire. Her chemise was sheer, her corset ivory. She stepped out of her petticoats. Her drawers matched her corset, coming to midthigh. Garters held up her stockings.

"You are wearing new underwear," he said calmly.

She turned and walked around the sofa, reaching for his tie. "I am so glad you noticed."

He caught her wrists, his grasp unyielding. "No." And for one moment, they stood that way, his dark eyes smoldering. Francesca knew he was not going to allow her to be in control, and she did not care.

"Tell me what you really want—tell me the truth," he said harshly.

"I want you."

Hart moved. He wrapped her in his arms and their mouths fused. Kissing her deeply, his hands on her buttocks, he moved her back around the sofa. He pushed her back, coming down on top of her. Francesca gasped with pleasure and need as she came into contact with his huge arousal.

"So we will be friends—and lovers?" he murmured with laughter, ripping apart her chemise. He nuzzled her bare breasts, spreading her thighs. "I have missed you, too."

"Hurry up," she demanded as his hand snaked between her thighs. And because it had been so long—a matter of days—the moment he touched her, she started weeping, the explosion immediate.

Francesca gave herself up to the series of climaxes, vaguely aware of his removing her drawers and settling his face against her. His tongue began probing. She wept again.

And when she was back in his arms, recovering from a series of explosive orgasms, she began to think about his need and his pleasure. He caught her hair, which was now loose, with his hand. "Francesca."

She managed to open her eyes. "Calder," she breathed, loving him impossibly—so much so that it continued to hurt. She kissed him again and again, now fumbling with his trousers.

"Do you really wish to remain mere friends?" he asked harshly.

She caught his beautiful face in both her hands. "Of course not! I love you."

He slowly smiled and she had the disturbing notion that she shouldn't have admitted the truth. But she would worry about her confession later. Francesca reached down and yanked his fly open.

He inhaled harshly as he sprang into her hand. Francesca stroked him and smiled, guided him carefully between her thighs and looked at him. His eyes were tightly closed, his face glazed with passion and strained with self-restraint. Immediately, he looked back at her. "You cannot tempt me."

"I want to be lovers—real lovers," she whispered.

"Absolutely not."

They had had this same argument a thousand times. This time, she meant to win it. She started to move her calf over his back, but he caught her leg and stilled it. "You cannot win this battle," he said.

"Damn it, Hart! My victory is overdue. No one will ever know!"

"I will know."

They stared. She was not really surprised. For some odd reason, he thought that they should not consummate their affair until they were actually married. But her frustration hadn't changed.

"My poor darling." His mouth curled with amusement. "Do not play the desperate card now. I am the one suffering."

Before she could respond, he caught the hair at her nape, leashed it and kissed her deeply, his mouth hard and unyielding. Francesca forgot about making a protest. He knew exactly how to touch her and move against her, and she tightened impossibly. And because she remained aware of his shocking arousal, she sat up, pushed him down and bent over him. When he allowed himself a moan, she felt a moment of triumph.

He was as still as a statue now, except for his heavy breathing. Francesca nuzzled his great length. She slipped her tongue over the tip. Suddenly he pushed her down on her back, reared over her and began rubbing his arousal over her breasts and neck. She gasped with more pleasure. She wanted him to experience the same fireworks she had.

He suddenly turned from her. Francesca pulled him

back. Smiling, she bent over him. Hart inhaled—and he cried out.

Sometime later—Francesca did not know how much later, as Hart had been ruthlessly determined to give her more satisfaction than ever before—she floated back to earth. She sighed, draped over his body, as the sofa was too small for them both. They were both fully unclothed now.

Being with Hart was perfect, she thought. The satisfaction was so vast, so consuming, and she felt that she had never been happier. She smiled when he kissed the top of her forehead. Then she turned over to lie atop him, and their gazes met.

He gave her a lazy, sensual, rather arrogant and very satisfied smile.

And then she recalled her confession. She wished she hadn't made it. Did confessing under sexual duress even count? But surely they were now reconciled—or well on their way to reconciliation? "There is nothing," she said softly, "like a good, stiff drink."

"I have so thoroughly corrupted you." But his smile faded. "Are you hungry?"

"I will have to think about it," she said. She nipped his jaw.

He sat up, causing her to do so as well, and gave her an unfathomable look. Francesca hoped he would not bring up any unpleasant subjects. "Actually, I am famished," she said, reaching for her underclothes. She did not want to discuss anything of consequence—she did not want to ruin the rest of the evening.

He took a sip of his scotch, watching her pull the short pants on. Francesca retrieved her petticoats and corset, wondering what he was thinking. She decided to forgo the corset due to the late hour, but she slipped on the torn shift. Hart was usually quiet after lovemaking, but she glanced at him carefully. His gaze was hooded. She smiled at him. "You have ruined my beautiful chemise, Hart."

He smiled back. "I will buy you another one."

She picked up her dress, pleased that she had made him smile. "I believe I have heard that line before."

"Yes, I believe you are right. I owe you several garments." His mouth firmed as he stood up. She pulled on the dress and gave him her back, holding up the mass of her hair. He quickly did up the buttons. How often had they done this? she wondered. But instead of kissing her nape, as he usually did, Hart simply released her.

Francesca turned to stare. Weren't they well on their way to reconciliation? What else could their lovemaking mean?

He said, "You are an impossible temptress. But you know that, don't you?"

Why was his tone so serious? "Do not be absurd. I am an unfashionable bluestocking, but somehow, I have ensnared you anyway."

He walked away and stepped into his trousers. As he zipped them up, he said, "An impossible temptress—and a very bad liar."

"Let's call Alfred," she said quickly, not wanting to begin the subject she feared he was about to broach.

He caught her arm before she could go to the door. His gaze was frighteningly somber now. "I do not want to lead you on, Francesca."

She was alarmed. "Why would you even suggest such a thing?"

"Your sister obviously encouraged you to attempt to manipulate me, did she not? Let me guess—she advised you not to chase or pursue me in any manner."

Francesca stared uneasily. "I do not like being less than honest with you," she finally said.

He touched her face. "I cannot tell you how many women have pursued me, either before or after an affair. But you are not those other women."

"What are you saying?" She was uneasy. She had the uncanny feeling she would not like whatever was on his mind.

"I am saying that I appreciate your candor, your honesty, your impossibly impetuous and open nature. I appreciate the woman you truly are. I despise your resorting to the kinds of games other women play. You do not have a scheming bone in your body."

She bit her lip. She hadn't really liked such a pretense, and not when it was aimed at Hart. "I don't think crying—and begging you to take me back—was a very effective tactic."

"But you do want me back."

Her heart raced. Now what? "Can't we just return naturally back into our relationship?"

His eyes darkened. "I know that you would not allow my lovemaking if we were mere friends, Francesca. You are a woman of logic—when it comes to investigations. But when it comes to love, you are a woman of passion."

She hesitated. "What are you trying to say? I trust you, Calder. I trust you with my heart—with my life. And you are right—I would not have leaped into your arms tonight if my feelings were casual."

He was grim. "I am fond of you. Very fond, in fact, but nothing has changed."

"What does that mean?" she cried, bewildered. Hart would never use a tepid word like *fond* when declaring himself. His cruelty Saturday night returned full force to her mind. But she no longer believed him. Of course he loved her, otherwise the past two hours would not have happened. "You are *fond* of me? What on earth are you trying to say?"

"Yes, I am fond of you," he said, flushing.

She was overcome with confusion. "We just nearly made love!"

"I should have controlled my desire for you tonight. I let you play me, Francesca, and well." He picked up his drink and drained it. "I did not care for your declaration of casual indifference, not one bit. But I am glad you have taken off my ring. It belongs in the safe."

She inhaled, shocked. "Are you telling me that we are not reconciled?"

"We are not reconciled," he said flatly.

She felt the room still. No, the world stilled. Why would he continue to do this?

"This is my fault entirely," he said. "Playing games of manipulation with me is never a good idea."

Hurt began. "This is impossible."

His face was hard. "I am holding firm to my decision of Saturday night. I can't—I will not—marry you, Francesca."

She choked. A long, terrible moment passed, in which she could hardly think. "Have you just used me?"

He started. "I would never use you."

"I want more than your kisses, Hart. I am not one of your divorcées!"

His eyes flickered. "I am aware of that. But I have just shown my true colors, haven't I?" He sounded disgusted now.

"Are you telling me you behaved like a cad with me? Because I refuse to believe it."

"You tried to manipulate me with that silly speech. I don't like being manipulated, Francesca. Two can play that game."

She now recalled her confession, made in the heat of the moment. "So you just manipulated me?"

He hesitated. "Sex can be a weapon."

"Against me?"

"Even against you."

She trembled. "I do not seem to be thinking clearly after the passion we just shared. In fact, I am confused. If we have not reconciled, then what just happened a moment ago?"

"I wanted you to admit that you spewed nonsense in my carriage—that you are not indifferent to me."

She stared. Sometimes, she thought Hart incredibly vulnerable—that he hid behind a facade of arrogance, conceit and power. But he did not look vulnerable now. "So you have apparently gotten what you wanted."

"Yes, I have gotten what I wanted." He paced away from her.

It was very hard to think clearly, as shock, hurt and confusion mingled. "This is incomprehensible! How could you make love to me if you did not mean to reconcile?"

"I am a selfish bastard, remember?"

"But you have never treated me the way you have treated other women!" She choked. "I assumed that if we made love, you would come to your senses and realize that we are meant to be together."

He shoved his hands in his trouser pockets. "That is very romantic."

She trembled, hugging herself. "My assumptions were wrong."

"Have you forgotten that I am not a romantic man?"

He had been terribly romantic toward her, but just then, she could not speak.

He wet his lips. "The last thing I ever wish to do is hurt you," he said. "When I tell you that I care deeply, you may believe my word. Francesca, I care enough to truly want to make your every wish come true! I truly want to give you the world on a silver platter. And as your friend, I hope to do just that. In fact, you might come to think of me as an odd benefactor, a champion of your dreams and desires. But I am not the right man for you. And once this infatuation passes, you will see the fact as clearly as I do."

"You are the perfect man for me," she heard herself somehow say.

"No, Rick is perfect for you."

She closed her eyes in despair. "Please don't start on Bragg. This is about us."

"His marriage will soon be over, Francesca, in case you haven't noticed. He is miserably unhappy."

She started. "I hope you are wrong. But I am not discussing Rick now!"

"You're right. This is about us. I told you once and I will tell you again—I am not going to be your downfall."

She stared at him. "So you are being noble now? You will sacrifice yourself for my sake? Instead of blaming me for jilting you, you have now taken up your old position that I deserve someone better?"

"Precisely. My mind is made up," he warned.

"We had this same argument three weeks ago!"

"Three weeks ago, I was accused of murder. By association, you were about to be ruined."

"And you have been proven innocent. So this is about the portrait?"

"You know me so well," he said softly.

She trembled. "It is not your fault!"

"Your future is at stake—and it is entirely my fault."

Francesca was in disbelief. How would she ever get him to change his mind?

"I am very sorry I took advantage of you a moment ago."

She bristled. "Your apology is not accepted!"

"I hope that one day we will look back on our ill-fated romance and laugh about it."

They were spiraling downward now, at breakneck speed, she somehow thought. "While I am married to another?"

"Yes."

It was impossible to decide how to proceed, when she was so upset. She looked around for her purse. All she felt like doing was retiring to her bed and shamelessly crying. She felt terribly used. Was this how those divorcées had felt? she wondered. Maybe it was truly over.

She found the purse on a chair and retrieved it. "I am not marrying anyone else." She refused to look at him now. "I think I will pass on supper."

He strode to her. "I will take you home."

"I prefer to ride home alone."

He started. Then, carefully, "I will always be your friend, Francesca. I will always be on your side—I will always champion your causes. You need only ask."

She finally looked at him. His stare was dark and intense. "Friends do not make love to one another, Hart."

"No, they don't." He hesitated. "I don't want to lose your friendship. I refuse to do so."

It crossed her mind that she had one last card to play. She hesitated, uncertain if she was willing to use the threat of withdrawing her friendship. Because it would be an even worse lie than her previous one of indifference. Hart needed her; she would never abandon him, no matter how angry she was. "We will always be friends."

He stared sharply. "You don't sound convinced."

"I am not feeling particularly friendly now."

"I see. Have I just destroyed our friendship?"

She trembled. She thought of what had just happened— and her expectation that they would be affianced anew afterward. "We are on very shaky ground, I think." She somehow found her pride. "I believe I will investigate on my own tomorrow."

He was very still. "I don't think that is a good idea."

The extent of his rejection was hitting her. "Then I will ask Bragg to play escort and bodyguard."

Did he flinch? "Good."

She fought not to hug herself. She felt terribly used, and it was a horrible feeling. She had trusted Hart completely. If he was merely a friend, then it was truly over. She would never leap into his arms again or walk down that aisle with him. If he was a friend, she had lost the greatest, and only, love of her life.

In silence, he walked her from the library and down the hall to the front door. As they waited for Raoul, he looked at her. She stared back. How could they be even more estranged now than they had been on Saturday night?

"Francesca." He suddenly took her arm.

She met his dark, unhappy gaze.

He made a sound and released her. "I am sorry—very sorry."

Her heart pounded and she heard herself ask very calmly, "Do you love me at all?"

A terrible pause ensued. She heard the carriage approaching. And Francesca was afraid of his reply.

He said, clearing his throat, "Raoul is here."

Francesca did not say good-night.

CHAPTER THIRTEEN

Tuesday, July 1, 1902
10:00 a.m.

BELLEVUE HOSPITAL WAS on the East River. Once, its reputation had been notorious, boasting a patient-mortality rate that was one of the highest in the country. But that had been decades ago. Since the middle of the nineteenth century, huge efforts had been made to turn Bellevue into a premier medical and teaching facility, removing most of its inmates to other facilities. The insane ward was a tenth its original size, with most of its patients incarcerated at the asylum on Blackwell Island; only select cases remained. Serious renovation of the entire facility had begun in 1891, and many of the pavilions were so modern, well-equipped and well-staffed now that there was a waiting list to get appointments with its medical faculty. The entire complex took three city blocks, from Twenty-third to Twenty-sixth streets.

Francesca had agreed to meet Bragg in the main lobby at ten in the morning. There was no point in driving all the way downtown to police headquarters to pick him up. She was walking toward the front doors of the Pavilion for Internal Medicine and Obstetrics when she heard him call her name from behind her.

It was a pleasant summer day, with birds singing from the tops of the trees that had been planted about the pavilion, the sun bright and shining overhead. Francesca rearranged her expression as she turned. He knew her far too well, and she did not want to discuss Hart with him. But it was almost impossible to think about the case.

"Perfect timing," Bragg said, smiling, as he left his car double-parked on the street.

For one moment, she recalled Hart insisting that Bragg was perfect for her. He strode toward her, a tall, handsome, golden man with the same inner moral compass that she had. As his smile faded, she thought about how they shared the same hopes and dreams for the world. But she loved Hart. She wasn't sure she had ever been so worried, and she felt sick and used.

Could Hart really walk away from the future they had planned?

Bragg reached her and took her arm, his gaze searching. "What's wrong?"

"I meant to call you last night to tell you that Bill Randall and a guest are undoubtedly staying at the old Randall residence."

His gaze moved over her features. "That is good news. It is hard to believe that you didn't call. Let me guess—you were sidetracked."

"Yes."

He took her arm. "You are very distressed."

She trembled. His touch was, as always, reassuring. "You should send a detail over. I am sure you will be able to pick him up sooner or later." She smiled at last. "Hopefully, he will know where the portrait is."

"What has he done?"

She hesitated, aware that he referred to Hart, not Randall.

He took both her hands in his. "You look utterly ravaged, Francesca. Damn it. My brother has once again twisted you into knots. Or is your heart somehow broken all over again?"

She inhaled, meeting his angry gaze. But she saw a deep concern, as well. "I always knew that Hart was different from everyone else. Not because of his wealth and power, but because he is so dark inside. I knew he was difficult…that his smile, his indifference, his mockery hid so much more. I was never deluded, Rick. I knew that life with him would be a wild ride. And I was so astonished, truly, when he made his feelings clear. I mean, why on earth would Calder Hart choose me, of all women, to seriously pursue?"

"You outshine every other woman in this city, and he is hardly blind."

Francesca knew that Bragg was not referring to her appearance. She suddenly recalled the very first moment she had laid eyes on Hart. He had been in Rick's office. She had walked in on them, and the tension had been huge. Their discussion—or argument—had ended, and Hart had turned and left. His glance at her had been brief but direct as he walked out.

She had been falling in love with Bragg at the time. But she had turned to watch Hart go. His charisma, even then, had been irresistible.

"You've always thought—and still think—that he couldn't help wanting me because of you."

Bragg's gaze darkened. "I believe, at first, he flirted with you simply to annoy me."

"He flirted with me because it is second nature to him," she said, and recalling the time she had found him terribly inebriated in his library, she smiled. He had just learned of his natural father's death. Francesca had known that he would never admit he cared. She had worried about him, wanting to rescue him from his dark despair. She had left him that day realizing he was the most fascinating man she had ever met.

"What has he done now? I take it you have not patched things up."

She shoved the memories away. "I really thought he was softening—I really thought that we would slide back into our relationship. We spent the afternoon on the case. It was so easy to do."

"I happen to believe that my brother, as rotten as he can be, is not entirely rotten. You bring out the best side of him, Francesca. The only problem is, a leopard cannot change its spots."

"I know he cares about me. He has even said so. But caring is a far cry from love. I am in love with him, Bragg," Francesca said softly. "And I believed that he loved me back as deeply, as irrevocably, as I love him."

Bragg inhaled.

"Do you think he loves me?" she heard herself say roughly. "Do you think he ever really loved me? Or was I just some passing amusement?" There, she had said it.

"You shouldn't do this to yourself."

She felt tears rise. Just a few days ago she had been so certain that he loved her the way that she loved him. But she wasn't certain of anything now. "I am so inexperienced. I believed that because he asked me to marry him, because we shared several heated moments, because I loved him, that he loved me. But that isn't necessarily the case, is it?"

Rick put his strong arm around her. "No, it is not. I feel like pounding some sense into him. He must have said something terribly cruel to cause so much doubt."

She trembled in his arms. "We have not reconciled. And he has been quite explicit."

"I suspected as much."

"I don't know what to do! Connie told me to take off his ring and pretend indifference—it backfired."

"Don't play games with my brother, Francesca. As clever as you are, he is a world-class player."

"Yes, he will always win, for that is inherent in his nature, too."

"He has proven that he cares about you. I would have never dreamed that Calder would ever really give a damn about anybody, but I was wrong. Still, caring for someone, desiring someone, is a far cry from wanting a future with them."

"I am starting to realize that," she said. It still hurt so much. "My instinct is to pursue him. My instinct is to never give up."

Bragg sounded alarmed. "That will certainly backfire, too. Until now, Hart has been the one on the hunt. Trust me—you will wind up even more hurt if you reduce yourself to chasing him."

"I know that," she said. "I really do. God, he is such a difficult man!"

Bragg didn't say a word, but she knew he was thinking "I told you so."

"I thought he was coming around." She felt ill, thinking about how their lovemaking had ended. "But Hart has not changed his mind at all. We are, apparently, done. Apparently, he can live without me. And if he can, then I have been making a series of very wrong assumptions." But even as she spoke, she recalled his passionate outburst.

I will always be your friend.... I will always be on your side.... You need only ask....

I want to give you the world on a silver platter.... As your friend, I will do just that....

Have I just destroyed our friendship?

Bragg was silent. She glanced at him. "The one thing I am sure of is that my friendship means the world to him."

He finally said, "You are an angel and a saint,

Francesca. You never turn your back on those in need. Of course Hart needs you. You are the only person in the city—and perhaps the country—who thinks highly of him. You are the only one who sees any good in him. I have even heard you call him noble. Of course he will wish to keep you as a friend."

"Hart is good, Bragg, and he has his noble moments."

"You still defend him?" He was incredulous.

She stared. If she didn't defend Calder Hart, who would? "He is actually being noble. He is back to his old tune—that he is not good enough for me—so by jilting me, he is doing me a vast favor."

"Yes, he is being noble in this single act, and that amazes me—so if it is any consolation, he clearly cares for you. Otherwise he'd barrel on into this marriage, enjoy your favors and then cast you aside when it suited him."

She stared, stricken. Bragg had just verbalized her most secret fear. She had always wondered if, even after they were man and wife, he would one day tire of her and go to another woman.

"He has admitted that he cares for me," she said shakily. "That is not quite the declaration a woman wishes to hear, but I am glad he is capable of making it."

"I do not think Hart capable of loving anyone, not genuinely."

She trembled. "You are wrong."

"Francesca, he can't even live with himself."

She tensed. She knew Hart fought demons in the dark of every day and every night. And that was why he needed her.

Bragg slid his hand over her shoulder. "I hate seeing you like this. Maybe you should start to carefully consider that a man like Hart can only make you unhappy. Life with Hart would be a series of peaks and valleys. I am not sure the lows would be worth it."

She met his searching gaze. "We have been very happy...mostly."

"It has only been a few months, Francesca. Good relationships don't materialize out of thin air. They are built upon firm foundations of mutual interest, shared ambition and compromise. I have never thought that you and Calder had very much in common."

She pulled away. What did they have in common?

"A few weeks ago he ended things with you and your heart was broken. The cycle clearly continues."

She could only, silently, agree. "Why would he even think to marry me if he did not truly love me?"

His eyes widened. "I know you have believed for some time that Hart has fallen in love with you. Why do you doubt that now?"

"I don't know what to think, Rick," she said. "And I wish I did." Was it possible he had been smitten, but those feelings were already fading? If so, wasn't she fortunate to learn that now, before it was too late?

When he had ended their engagement during the investigation into Daisy's murder, he had told her that he loved her too much to drag her down into ruin with him. She had believed him. Their love hadn't been in question. If anything, the bond between them had grown stronger.

Hadn't he mentioned last night that he refused to be her downfall? The difference was, he wasn't declaring his undying love and devotion. He now insisted the engagement had been a mistake.

"You won't give up on him."

She met Bragg's golden gaze. It was searching and serious. The thought had never crossed her mind. "Even if our love affair is over, even if we must become mere friends, I will never give up on him. He has a friend in me for life, whether he truly wishes it or not." She added, "As do you."

Bragg frowned. "He does not deserve you, not in any way," he said, and when she was about to protest, he added, "But I am glad he has you in his corner. No man should be an island."

She froze. Hart was exactly that—a man alone in this vast world—an island in icy oceans. He was the most complicated man she knew and she would never love anyone more. So there was one thing to cling to—her love.

She must stand by Hart no matter what, even if they never reconciled.

"You are right," she said, suddenly feeling so much better. Yes, she was hurt and dismayed—even frightened—but Hart cared. He had said so. Well, she loved him in return. And if he really didn't love her now, he would just have to manage that. There were, it seemed, strings attached to her friendship.

She smiled.

Bragg's brows rose. "You are feeling better?"

"You always make me feel better," she said.

"Dare you flirt with me now?" But he was smiling.

She hesitated. "I probably should not. Thank you. Thank you for listening—and thank you for caring."

"I will always care." He flushed and glanced away.

For an instant, she studied him, recalling Hart's insistence that Bragg's marriage was in trouble. "You know, I am so preoccupied with my dramas that I have given no attention to yours."

"I detest drama," he said, but his tone was wry. "Where is Joel?"

"He has gone to Coney Island for the day with the entire Kennedy clan." She caught his arm before he could start for the pavilion. "Is Leigh Anne better?"

A long moment passed as he stared at her. "I wouldn't really know. I have hardly been home all week, Francesca.

Police business occupies most of my time," he said before she could protest. "Shall we?"

He did not want to discuss his personal life, even if she had bared her soul to him. Francesca sighed. She so wanted to help. "There's one more thing before we go inside," she said quickly, her mind shooting with gunfire speed back to the case. "Please don't be angry, but I received this on Sunday night." She took the blackmail note from her purse and handed it to Rick.

His gaze widened. And then he was incredulous. "When were you going to tell me? Please do not tell me you went to meet the blackmailer alone."

"I went with Joel. But I had borrowed the money from Hart, and he actually tailed me. In any case, no one showed up." She proceeded to tell him about the rendering of her portrait and the cyclist.

"If you receive another note or instructions to meet, I expect to be the first to know," Bragg said angrily. "Not the last! Francesca, blackmail is a crime. It is police business. And did you really think you would hand over seventy-five thousand dollars and receive your portrait in return?"

"I had certainly hoped to."

He gave her a dark look, took her arm and guided her toward the pavilion. "I am glad Hart followed you. And I am very angry with you."

She winced. "I wanted to tell you, but I was afraid that if you were present, the blackmailer would see you and flee. Not only do you look like a spot, you are very famous now. Your likeness and photograph is in every day's newspaper."

"That is a pitiful excuse. Once again, you overestimated your own capabilities. You are giving me gray hair."

She looked at him as they walked inside the pavilion. That was exactly what Hart often said.

"By the way, I also have news." Bragg paused just inside the front doors. The lobby was pale and spacious, with granite arches and stone floors. "We have found the bordello where Dawn might be working."

"That is wonderful news—I will go speak with her the moment we are through with Mary. And what about Bill Randall?" She regretted not calling Bragg last night. She had been too upset, but if she had spoken to him, Randall might already be in custody.

"I'll have the house put under surveillance. I am thinking we should tail him, Francesca, not arrest him, as we do not have a solid case against him. Instead, we'll see where he leads us—hopefully, it will be to your portrait."

They walked over to the long reception desk, where he checked them in as visitors, and the clerk went to fetch his superior. Bragg smiled at Francesca and she smiled back, glad to be firmly back in the midst of an investigation—and glad that she had reached a decision about Hart.

A tall man came out of the back corridor, wearing a doctor's white overcoat. "Commissioner? I'm Dr. Jones. This is very unexpected."

Bragg shook his hand. "This is Miss Cahill, Doctor. Is something wrong?"

"Yes, there is. The patient you wish to see has apparently vanished."

"MR. HART, Mrs. Andrew Cahill is in reception. She doesn't have an appointment," his clerk said.

Hart had been reading a contract that would bring a midsize Danish shipping firm under the control of his global shipping empire. While he had lawyers to do just about everything necessary to execute his many enterprises, he preferred to read every correspondence pertaining to his business affairs, and all legal documents, himself. He often went through the invoices of his various companies. His mind was razor sharp. He'd caught employees stealing, cheating and embezzling a hundred times. He hated disloyalty, but he knew it festered and could not imagine another way of managing his business empire. There was no one he could trust.

It crossed his mind now that it would be pleasant to have an associate whom he could trust.

He thought of Francesca, his heart lurching. It was amazing how hurt and anguish could coexist with so many other emotions. Her image brought instantaneous delight to his heart and a smile to his face, and there was no denying the warmth that stole through him. Yes, he cared deeply. Yes, he loved her. She was the most extraordinary, the most original, the most intriguing person he had ever met. But he had done the right thing. Of that, he had no doubt.

However, he was very, very angry with himself for hurting her. He was a selfish and depraved bastard. But what did she expect, especially when she had tried to play him? It would have been amusing, if the sight of her unadorned left hand hadn't been so shocking.

The urge to overpower her—to make her admit that she wanted and loved him—had been impossible to resist. He was accustomed to using sexual persuasion to gain his ends. He hadn't even thought about using her attraction to him to get her to declare her true feelings.

He hated the fact that she had put his engagement ring in the safe, but his decision remained. They were no longer affianced. There would be no wedding. Now he was managing the facts: the engagement was off. Francesca and he would be friends—forever, if he had any choice, and he usually did. He would, somehow, encourage her to turn to someone else. If she chose his brother, he would find a way to live with it.

He had been out of sorts and he knew damn well why—he was secretly as distressed as she was. But he refused to admit to himself that he was upset—or worse, consider why there was a painful bubble in his chest. He was not good enough for her. She deserved better. He would not be her downfall. He could not live with himself if that happened.

Those four statements had become his mantra.

And should he be tempted to forget the reasons behind his decision to end their relationship, he had only to remind himself of the most recent developments. Not only was he responsible for the existence of the portrait in the first place, it now seemed that his dear brother Bill was the one trying to ruin her! How perfect was that irony?

Why couldn't she see how bad he was for her?

And now Julia was here to lobby on behalf of her daughter. This, he supposed, was just what he needed—for he loved a good challenge. Now he had to charm Francesca's mother without revealing that the wedding was off. For good.

For he meant to keep Julia on his side. She was a formidable force in Francesca's life. He had meant it when he had told Francesca that he intended to be her friend and ally, her champion and defender. She wouldn't become his wife—or his lover—but he intended to remain entirely in Julia's good graces.

"Show Mrs. Cahill in," he said pleasantly. He rolled down his shirtsleeves and put on his suit jacket, retying his tie. A few minutes later Julia strolled into his office, beautifully dressed in a pale blue watered-silk jacket and skirt, diamonds and aquamarines at her throat and ears. No one would ever mistake her for anything less than what she was—one of the city's most powerful and elegant women.

"This is a pleasant surprise," Hart said, coming across the spacious office to greet her. He took both her hands warmly and kissed her cheek.

"I inquired at the house, and I was very surprised to learn that you were at your offices today." Julia was smiling, but her gaze was sharp. "Calder, it is July the first."

Hart slowly smiled. "I can always find business matters to attend to, even on July the first."

"I imagine that you can. But it is simply a shame that you are here today, when you and Francesca were scheduled to be steaming across the ocean to France."

"May I offer you some refreshments?" he asked smoothly.

"Oh, Calder, I hardly need tea. What happened Saturday was a terrible tragedy, and we haven't had a chance to discuss it."

"A tragedy was averted," he said, smiling, "as Francesca escaped her captor. By the way, you may tell Andrew that I will take care of the costs of the failed wedding."

Julia studied him. "I doubt he will let you do so. Francesca is being very closemouthed about what actually happened. And she has the police involved." He didn't react, so she continued, "You don't seem angry with her."

He said truthfully, "I doubt I could ever remain angry with Francesca for very long. I care too much about her."

Julia beamed. "I am so relieved! Most men would be furious—they would call the wedding off."

"I am not most men. I was certainly angry on Saturday, before I learned of the facts. Now I am relieved that no real harm was done, and I look forward to apprehending the perpetrator of the misdeed."

Julia blinked. "I am so very fond of you, truly. You are an exceptional young man."

"Thank you," Hart said, inclining his head.

"So what will we do now about the wedding? Everyone has left town, so we can hardly have an affair till the fall. Andrew is champing at the bit to get out of town, anyway. We are going up to Saratoga Springs tomorrow, but I wanted to talk with you first. Should we plan a fete for September?"

"I am glad that you have come to me, Julia, although I would have happily met you uptown if you had sent word. Why don't you let Francesca and I sort this out? But certainly, you must leave town for the rest of the summer. Saratoga is exceedingly pleasant at this time of year."

"Well, nothing can be arranged at this moment. Connie has lingered in town as well, and I think that is because she is worried about her sister. But clearly, she need not worry, need she?"

"Perhaps if you remind Connie of how deeply I care for Francesca she will cease fretting." He smiled. "Please tell her I am not angry, not at all—I am simply looking out for Francesca's best interests."

"I will do that. But I am loath to leave town with Francesca on this investigation of hers. I know her, and she will not join us until the case is solved. She has involved Rick Bragg, you know."

Hart murmured, "He is an excellent police commissioner."

Julia blinked. "You do not mind? I do not care for them keeping all hours of the night!"

He did not move his smile. "I prefer she investigate with an escort, Julia, whether that be Bragg, myself or my driver, Raoul."

"Well, if you will remain in the city with her, I suppose

I could manage that. Francesca needs guidance, Calder. I do not trust her if she is left to her own devices."

"No one needs guidance more," he said, meaning it. "She would climb a telephone pole in the rain to rescue a stray cat."

Julia laughed, taking his hands. "Yes, she would. You know her so well, and clearly you love her deeply. I am so relieved! This was not the audience I expected."

"I am glad you are pleased. I suggest you enjoy your summer holiday, and I will keep an eye on Francesca, to make certain she does not climb any telephone poles."

"Very well." Julia squeezed his hand. As she left, she called, "And do write us when you have decided on a new date."

Hart smiled as she left. Then his smile faded. He didn't want to think about Francesca running about the city with Rick, but the image was now engraved in his mind. Well, at least she was safe. And didn't he want to encourage the liaison?

Even if it killed him?

"HELLO, DAWN," Francesca said.

The brunette had just come down the stairs of the Georgian mansion, which was between Madison and Fifth Avenues, where the brothel was housed. A tall, pretty young woman, she faltered, her gaze widening. "Emerald?"

Francesca had come alone. Joel was with his family at Coney Island and she doubted she would get any information from Dawn if Bragg or another police officer was present. He hadn't been all that pleased about her interviewing the prostitute alone, but Francesca had pointed out that it was early afternoon; the brothel would most likely be closed to customers, and very little could go wrong in the light of day. She had compromised by agreeing that a pair of roundsmen would lurk as discreetly as possible outside. Meanwhile, Inspector Newman was bringing Daniel Moore in for further questioning.

Francesca remained astonished over the discovery that Mary Randall had somehow "vanished" from Bellevue. Apparently the staff, including the doctors treating her, were in a state of utter confusion. One nurse thought that she had been transferred to the asylum at Blackwell's Island. Dr. Jones, who hadn't treated Mary in weeks, finally found a note to that effect in her file. But the paperwork ordering such a transfer had not yet been found. Meanwhile, other staff seemed to think she had been released—an impossibility, of course. In fact, no one seemed to know exactly when she had been transferred—or if she had simply disappeared—or escaped.

Bragg meant to check it out immediately. As calm as always, he had reminded her that, in all likelihood, she was at Blackwell's Island. Francesca genuinely hoped he was right.

"It is Francesca, remember?" She smiled at Dawn, handing her one of her calling cards. She had used the alias of Emerald while posing as a prostitute in the spring, during their investigation into a child prostitution ring. She couldn't help recalling Hart's shock and disbelief when he had found her in that establishment, after he had decided to do some sleuthing on his own. He had been so very angry with her.

She let the warm remembrance go. "A maid let me in, Dawn. I expected it to be harder to get inside to see you."

Dawn looked at her card, still surprised. "I didn't think I would ever see you again, Em—Francesca. And they are not strict here, not as long as we mind our manners—and our customers—after the doors open to the public at six."

"I didn't imagine our paths would cross again, either. However, I am on a new investigation."

Dawn began to smile. "How are those little girls we rescued?"

"They are all doing very well, thank you." Francesca smiled back. "I don't think I ever thanked you enough for helping us round up that horrid gang."

"You thanked me. And it was the right thing to do." She hesitated. "I believe in Jesus, Francesca, in spite of what I do for a living. But what investigation would bring you here?"

Francesca hesitated. "It is actually personal. I am in some trouble, frankly."

"Oh, no!"

"I am being blackmailed. Someone has the ability to ruin me, Dawn. I was wondering if you could help me at all?"

"I don't know what you are talking about. How could I possibly help?" Dawn seemed genuinely perplexed.

"For starters, it would be a vast help if you knew where Solange Marceaux is."

The warmth in her eyes vanished. "What does she have to do with this?" she asked.

"Perhaps nothing. But I would like to speak with her."

Dawn shook her head. "That is not a good idea. She hates you. And how do I know that you wouldn't call the flies? She would be arrested, wouldn't she? She was trafficking those children!"

"I am not interested in arresting Solange, not at this time," Francesca said. It was partly the truth. Eventually, she would love to see the other woman behind bars. But that was not her priority. While it certainly appeared that Bill Randall was their man, Solange must be ruled out.

"I need to talk to her. I want to make certain she isn't involved in the blackmail."

Dawn stared. Francesca could tell she was thinking madly. She finally said, "I don't know where she is. But you should stay away from her." Then she added, "I am very sorry that you are being blackmailed. You are a nice lady."

"How would you know that Solange hates me, Dawn?" Francesca asked softly.

Dawn started. "I was there during the bust! Her hatred was all over her face. Because of you, her beautiful establishment was destroyed. Of course she hates you, with a vengeance! She is a strong and cold woman, Francesca."

Francesca believed that Dawn had spoken with Solange since the raid on the brothel. How else would she be so certain of the madam's feelings for Francesca? "Could she hate me enough to want to destroy me?"

Dawn's eyes popped. "I don't know. Maybe."

Francesca took twenty dollars from her purse and handed it to the other woman. "Are you certain you don't know where she is?"

"I haven't seen her since the bust." Dawn shoved the bills in her bodice, flushing. "Francesca, stay away from her. Please. For your sake, not mine."

Francesca hesitated. Dawn had most definitely been in touch with the madam—or even remained in touch with her now. "Thank you for your help. If you recall anything else, could you send a note? You can send it to the commissioner at police headquarters, if that is more convenient than sending it to me."

"I won't recall anything," Dawn said.

CHAPTER FOURTEEN

Tuesday, July 1, 1902
5:00 p.m.

MAGGIE SLOWLY CLOSED the door to her one-bedroom flat. She was ready to pinch herself to make certain that she was not dreaming. She watched Evan and Joel carry groceries into the kitchen area of her apartment. Although small, it was neat, basically furnished and clean. The boys slept in the back of the parlor—she had sewn yellow-and-green-floral curtains to partition their sleeping quarters off from the rest of the room. There was a small vase with three daisies on the table in front of the sofa; a rug with red roses, rescued from the common garbage, covered the worn wooden floors. There were pansies on the windowsill outside the kitchen, petunias in the single box outside the parlor window. She kept a sunflower-yellow cloth on the kitchen table, and she had made seat covers for the chairs in a pretty yellow gingham. Still, the apartment was shabby and dark. The contrast with Evan's Fifth Avenue home was glaring.

"My vote is that we fry the steaks, what do you say?" Evan asked, grinning at Joel. He removed his suit jacket and glanced at Maggie, smiling, as he began rolling up his shirtsleeves.

"Yum!" Paddy cried, careening over. "Fried steaks! Can I help cook 'em?"

No one was hungry—they had gorged on frankfurters,

sauerkraut, pickles, ice-cream soda, root beer, sarsaparilla and popped corn while exhausting the children on ride after ride. Still, Evan had insisted that he was famished, and on their way home, they had stopped at the farmer's market not far from the ferry terminal, and then at her local butcher. He had bought far more groceries than they could ever use in a single meal, including staples she simply couldn't afford. She knew what he was doing—he meant to buy enough groceries to feed her and the children for a week.

And he had held her close to his side on Coney Island's most infamous ride—the frightening roller coaster.

She stared at his bare forearms, recalling the thrill of the ride—and the even greater thrill of being pressed against his body. Why did he have to be so kind?

Joel and Evan were rattling pots and pans, discussing how they planned to fry the sirloin steaks Evan had purchased. Paddy and Matt were chasing one another about the apartment, pretending they were still aboard the roller coaster. Lizzie tried to join them, but they ignored her. Maggie bit her lip, watching as Evan turned to unpack the groceries. When would he realize that she was just a simple Irishwoman who sewed for a living, who could barely support her large family, while he was the Cahill heir, destined for someone far more beautiful, accomplished and well-bred than she was?

He glanced up at her, his smile gone. This was not the first time he had looked at her very seriously.

Desire erupted in her breast. This was an infatuation, she reminded herself. Not a romance.

But for one moment, their stares locked, and all she could think of was that she wanted his kiss. She reminded herself that he was leaving for the summer. He would join his wealthy friends on Fire Island. There, he would soon forget her. He would meet someone else, someone far more appropriate than she was.

He turned to Joel. "I need someone to peel the potatoes."

Joel wrinkled up his nose. "We can skip potatoes. I thought we were having a loaf of bread."

"We are. But we are also having potatoes. I'm going to fry them up with the steaks, Joel. Fried potatoes are very, very good—I promise you." Evan grinned, clearly aware that half their diet consisted of potatoes.

Maggie wondered if he had any idea of how to make a meal—she doubted it. She shook herself free of her longing—and fears—and came forward. "Joel, take the boys outside and peel the potatoes."

Joel looked at her and then he looked at Evan. Slowly, he grinned. "Sure, Ma."

She was afraid he sensed the attraction between them. She did not want him to get his hopes up. She knew how fond of Evan he was. She would have to speak seriously with him tomorrow, and explain that their relationship was one of friendship—that it was not a romance. As Joel rounded up his brothers, Lizzie rushing to join them, she turned to look at Evan, her heart simply rioting. She thought she was flushing, too. "This is too much, Evan."

"It is hardly too much." He watched the children trooping out of the flat. "Joel, make certain no one runs off. It will be dark soon," he called.

He would make such a wonderful father! She sobered. He was going to be a father—to his own child—not to her children.

"You are spoiling us so."

"Good." He faced her squarely. He was a tall, lean man, and when they were alone like this, she felt tiny and petite, although she was of average height for a woman.

"The children had such a wonderful time today. I doubt they will ever forget it."

Very softly, he reached out and cupped her jaw. She trembled, almost swaying against him. "What I want to know is, did *you* have a wonderful time?"

She slowly nodded. "Yes."

He stared. Finally, he said, "I want to do so much more, Maggie. You deserve so much more."

"You don't have to do anything else," she managed to say, trembling. He continued to cup her cheek. She pulled away, when she wanted to move closer to him.

"Don't," he said, taking her hand. "Don't run from me."

She inhaled. "This isn't right."

"Why not?"

"You're a gentleman. I'm a seamstress."

"I don't care." His gaze widened. "You know me well enough by now to realize I would never toy with you."

She wet her lips, well aware that Evan had been quite a ladies' man. "I think you would never deliberately pursue me with the wrong intentions."

He hesitated. "What does that mean?"

"It means you are mistaking your interest in me, surely!" she cried, about to pull away. But his grasp on her hand tightened.

"The only thing I know is that I have never met a woman as kind and generous as you. I have never known anyone with such a heart. And you are so beautiful," he exclaimed roughly.

She was a faded redhead, worn beyond her years, and she knew it. "This isn't real," she whispered. "It can't be."

"Why not?" His eyes blazed. And the moment they did, Maggie knew what he meant to do and she gasped.

But his arms were already around her and he was bending toward her. "Why the hell not, Maggie?"

She so desperately wanted this moment to be real—to be based on love, not lust; on friendship, not gratitude. She knew she should protest, just as she knew she would not. His mouth gently covered hers. Maggie closed her eyes and gave herself over to the sensation of being in Evan's arms, his mouth plying hers.

She had never been in a man's arms before like this. He was strong and powerful—and he was the kindest, most considerate man she had ever known. As she opened her mouth to take in more of his kiss, she suddenly realized that no haven could be as safe as that offered by Evan Cahill. And she realized that she more than loved him—she trusted him, too.

"Are you all right?" he asked huskily, his mouth still on hers.

She somehow nodded, tears arising, joy bursting through her heart. She lifted her face and kissed him wildly, passion erupting inside her.

He cried out, his embrace tightening, and then he kissed her back as deeply. But she sensed his restraint. A moment later he broke the kiss, his chest rising and falling swiftly against hers.

She didn't want him to stop. But she buried her face against his silky cotton shirt. "What is it? What is wrong?"

"Nothing is wrong," he said roughly. Then, "I am falling in love with you."

She froze. Had she really heard him say that?

He made a harsh, self-deprecatory sound and stepped back so he could look down at her. She stared up at him, amazed. "I wish you could see yourself the way that I do," he said.

She was speechless. Vaguely, she heard one of the

children racing up the stairs outside her apartment. It was Paddy, she thought. She knew the sound of each of her children's footsteps.

Evan smiled at her. Did she dare tell him that she was already in love with him?

"Ma!" Paddy screamed.

Maggie leaped out of Evan's arms in alarm. "Paddy? What's wrong?" she cried, fear engulfing her.

"Lizzie's gone! Some thug took her!"

FRANCESCA HURRIED INTO the reception hall at police headquarters, hoping that Bragg hadn't begun his interrogation of Daniel Moore without her. Because of the hour, she hadn't seen any newsmen in the building across the street, where they often sipped coffee and conversed while waiting for a scoop. Everyone, she thought, was keeping summer hours. And that was just fine with her.

She beelined for the elevator, thinking about Dawn, who clearly was in contact with Solange Marceaux. Her mind turning over all the facts and clues discovered thus far, she reached for the door to the cage. But before she could grasp the lever, someone caught her arm from behind. She tensed, turning, and came face-to-face with Arthur Kurland of the *Sun*.

She sighed impatiently, while anxiety began. "And to think that I thought myself reprieved when I saw that your newsroom across the street was vacant."

Kurland grinned. "This is my lucky day. I was about to leave and catch a bite to eat. Ever been to Joe's Fish House? It's on Broadway. I'm happy to treat, Miss Cahill."

"I am very busy, Mr. Kurland," she said coolly.

"Oh, yeah, I forgot. What are you and the c'mish working on? Heard you went to see someone on Blackwell's Island yesterday. Everyone is being so closemouthed."

Francesca stared coldly. Undoubtedly Kurland had bribed an officer and knew far more than he was letting on. "If we wished for you to know something, there would be a news conference. Good day."

She turned away, but he leaped between her and the elevator. "What happened at Gallery Moore? Why is Daniel Moore upstairs? An' how come I heard this gossip that you missed your wedding because of Moore?" He grinned then. "I also heard that Calder Hart isn't in a forgiving mood. Guess the wedding's off, huh?"

She stared unhappily at him. She wondered if any of Hart's staff would dare to speak to a newsman.

"I even heard you're not a welcome guest over there," he said.

Sometimes, the truth was the best policy. This was not one of those times. "Then you have heard wrong. Now, if you will excuse me?"

Kurland stepped aside and Francesca hurried into the elevator. She hit the button for the third floor, trying to appear indifferent and even nonchalant. As the elevator began its ascent, Kurland grinned at her. "You should really try Joe's," he said. "Dinner's on me. Anytime."

Francesca ignored him, but she felt flushed. He was an annoying man. She hoped she hadn't made a mistake by insinuating that she and Hart remained closer than they actually were.

A moment later she stepped out of the cage and saw Bragg standing in the corridor, speaking with Chief Farr. Her tension was instantaneous. She had no reason to suspect Farr of any foul play, even if he had been investigating the theft of her portrait when the police had not known about it. But it still bothered her that he had been on the scene with his men before she and Bragg had arrived at the gallery Saturday night. Once again, she couldn't help thinking that he was such a big, striking man.

Then she shook herself free of any suspicion. She believed that the thief had removed the portrait shortly after her escape from the gallery—before she had seen Bragg and revealed all that had happened.

Both men fell silent as she approached. Farr nodded politely. Francesca tried not to bristle and managed a smile in return. She was very glad that Rose was not seeing this man as a client. "Is Mr. Moore here?"

"He is in the conference room. Mrs. Moore is in my office," Bragg said.

Francesca was surprised that Moore's wife had been brought downtown, but Farr said, "She insisted on coming with him."

Francesca hesitated. She wished a word with Bragg alone. He glanced at the chief and said, "We'll be right in, Chief."

Farr grunted and walked off toward the conference room, which was just down the hall. "Well?" Bragg asked.

"Did Marsha Moore recognize the chief?" she asked.

"No, Francesca, she did not even blink upon first seeing him."

She turned to him. Farr was now out of sight. "Marsha Moore said that a big, dark man was loitering outside their flat that night, waiting for Daniel. She also saw him at the gallery a few days before. Farr isn't dark, although he is big. But it was not Farr, as Marsha did not recognize him. However, Bill Randall is tall and he is dark."

"You are slipping," Bragg said, smiling warmly now. "She described the loiterer as big and dangerous."

She had slipped. "It wasn't Farr. But I don't trust him at all. I don't like his involvement in this case."

"Neither do I, but it is too late to get him off the case. Let's hope that Randall is the one who paid off Moore to use his gallery on Saturday, and let's assume he returned for the stolen portrait after you escaped." He took her arm, lowering his voice. "There has been no activity at the Randall home this afternoon, Francesca. I have asked the detail that is watching the house to gather up the family photographs."

That was an excellent idea, she thought. "We can show his photograph to Mrs. Moore."

"Yes, we can."

How she hoped there would be a positive identification! Then Francesca quickly told him about her conversation with Dawn. Bragg said, "Finding Marceaux might be moot, Francesca. Hopefully, Randall is our man and we will soon apprehend him. I look forward to receiving the visitors' logs from Warden Coakley."

"So do I," Francesca said.

Bragg guided her to the conference room door, which was ajar, but paused once more outside it. "There is news. It isn't good. I just got a wire from the warden of the Blackwell's Island Asylum. Mary wasn't transferred there."

Francesca halted in her tracks. Mary had escaped. "So Mary vanished from Bellevue Hospital into thin air?"

"I doubt she vanished. And I think we both know who helped her escape."

They stared at each other. Mary could not be their thief. She had been in custody in April, when the portrait was stolen. "If only we knew when she escaped," Francesca said in a whisper.

And Bragg, of course, was reading her mind. "Mary is a small woman, but I believe she could have taken that portrait down from the wall with sheer adrenaline."

If Bill Randall had stolen it, he had gained an accomplice, but how recently? Francesca wondered. Bill would have stolen the portrait from Sarah's studio, acting alone.

But had Mary helped him lock Francesca in the gallery and retrieve the portrait on Saturday? She was chilled. Mary was deranged and that made her even more frightening than her brother.

Bragg gestured. Hating the idea that Mary was on the loose, Francesca stepped into the conference room.

A long table dominated it. Inside, the light was pale and yellow. Daniel Moore was clad as if for a holiday in a darker sack coat and pale trousers. He was seated as they walked in, Farr standing nearby, Inspector Newman seated across from him. Newman, a rotund man, was doodling on a notepad. A uniformed officer stood by the door in case he might think to escape. Moore leaped to his feet.

Francesca smiled. "Hello, Mr. Moore."

"I am outraged," he said. "I have done nothing wrong!"

Bragg walked over to him and pushed him back into his seat. "Really? Lying to the police—even mere obfuscation—is a felony, sir."

Moore blanched. "I haven't lied!"

"Not only do we have your financial records, we have witnesses who saw you at the gallery last Saturday morning. Yet you told me on Saturday night that you had not been to the gallery since you closed it on Friday for summer hours," Bragg said.

"You have witnesses?" Moore was incredulous.

Francesca knew that the children's testimony would never hold up in a court of law, but the woman's surely would. "Apparently you were not alone, Mr. Moore. Would you mind explaining this discrepancy?"

Moore stood again. "Very well. I went to my gallery that morning, but only because there was a leak in the bathroom faucet! A plumber was with me. That is not a crime!"

Francesca glanced at Bragg, who said, "And who is this plumber, Moore? Obviously he will have to corroborate your story."

"My story? But I have done nothing wrong. Someone broke into my gallery and imprisoned Miss Cahill there. I had nothing to do with her abduction or the stolen portrait!"

Francesca glanced at Farr. He smiled at her. She turned quickly away. "Would you mind explaining why a deposit of one thousand dollars was made last Thursday into your East River Savings Bank account?"

He gasped. "That was from the sale of a painting!"

Francesca realized that was an entirely credible answer. Bragg said, "Then you will show us the receipt?"

Moore said, "Of course."

Bragg nodded at Newman, who lumbered to his feet. "Escort Mr. Moore to his gallery, please. Bring back his receipts—all of them."

Farr's eyes glittered.

Francesca turned. "Don't we need a warrant?"

"I will arrange for one immediately," Bragg said.

"And what about my wife?" Moore asked, shoving his hands in the pockets of his jacket.

"You can wait for her in the lobby," Bragg said.

Moore cried out. "What do you want with Marsha?"

"We have a few questions for her, that is all," Francesca said. He was as nervous as a very guilty man.

She preceded Bragg from the conference room. Before opening the door to his office, she said, "Do you really think to get a warrant after the fact?"

He smiled. "There won't be any receipts, Francesca. I feel certain that he was paid off by Randall, or whoever originally stole that painting, for the use of his gallery. I don't believe him a thief, just an accessory to the theft and your abduction. I can smell the guilt on him."

"I happen to think you are right," she said.

He reached past her to open the door. It did not occur to her to move out of his way, and his arm brushed her. Instead of stepping back, she smiled at him. He smiled back, then pushed open the door for her. About to walk past him and inside, Francesca hesitated.

Farr was coming down the hall. If he had noticed anything, he gave no sign. He stared at the floor as he passed them.

She felt as if they had been caught in a compromising position. Of course, Bragg had only opened the door for her. However, they were so obviously close. Neither one stood on propriety.

"Are you all right?" Bragg asked, his gaze searching.

She met his warm amber regard. She wanted to tell him that she was becoming worried because she hadn't spoken with Hart since last night. "I am fine." She cleared her throat and walked into his office. He followed, closing the door behind them.

Marsha Moore was sitting before his desk, clutching a handkerchief. Her eyes were red from crying.

She leaped up. "He is a good man, really."

"What aren't you telling us?" Francesca asked in her kindest manner. She clasped the woman's shoulder.

"He hasn't done anything wrong!"

"Mr. Moore is allowed to lease out his space to whomever he chooses, Mrs. Moore, so you are right about that. It is also true that he is not responsible for the fact that someone lured me to his gallery and trapped me inside."

"Then why are we here?" she cried fearfully.

"If he knew what was about to happen and was paid for his participation, then he is an accessory to my abduction," Francesca said, rather exaggerating the facts. A good defense attorney would argue that she hadn't actually been abducted.

"And he might even be accused of fencing stolen goods," Bragg said. They both knew that mere knowledge of a crime was not a criminal offense.

"Of course he didn't know that you were locked up, and he would never deal in stolen paintings!" she cried, ghastly white. "We already have so many problems. Dear Lord, we hardly need any more!"

"Then why are you so frightened?" Francesca asked.

"We are trying so hard to make ends meet. It isn't easy these days. But you wouldn't know about that, would you, Miss Cahill?"

"Who approached your husband and asked to lease the gallery for a single day?" Bragg asked firmly.

She looked frantically at him. "I don't know! He doesn't tell me anything. He keeps me in the dark, he does. It wasn't always that way." She covered her face with her hands and started to cry.

Francesca felt sorry for her. "Mrs. Moore, I am certain that your husband had no idea what would happen when he leased out his space. I am also convinced that he is being threatened not to reveal the name of the man who paid him to use his gallery on Saturday. If he will simply tell us the truth, there will not be any charges. I will make certain of it."

Marsha stared tearfully at her now.

Bragg came up to them. "I won't press charges, Mrs. Moore, nor will the D.A., if your husband is an innocent victim of this thief, as Miss Cahill is."

"He never tells me anything," Marsha breathed.

There was a knock on the door and Bragg went to get it. Francesca didn't move. "I know how worried you are. Are you certain he didn't tell you that he meant to lease his space out for a single day?" she tried.

Before Marsha could respond, Bragg returned. He was holding a framed photograph in his hand, and he gave it to Marsha. Francesca instantly recognized Bill Randall, standing arm in arm with his small, pale sister and mother. "Is this the man you saw outside the gallery and outside your flat?"

She stared. "No. That is not him."

Francesca started. But that was impossible!

Bragg was as incredulous.

"Are you sure?" Francesca cried.

"I am certain. I have never seen that man before."

FRANCESCA WAS SUDDENLY aware of just how tired she was. It had been a very long day, but she had yet to manage an investigation where the hours weren't exhausting. Pausing on the threshold of the front hall, she asked, "Is anyone home, Francis?" She wouldn't mind having the house to herself. She could curl up in her father's study with a hot meal and a glass of wine, and make notes about the case.

Of course, what she really wanted to do was freshen up and call on Hart. Shouldn't he be told that Bill Randall might not be the thief? That Mary had escaped? She trembled, imagining Hart's reaction to that bit of news. Maybe he would cease blaming himself for their current predicament.

In that moment, she decided she would rush upstairs, wash her face, apply rouge and perfume, and go over to Hart's. Sometimes, one must simply take the bull by the horns. "Mr. and Mrs. Cahill have gone out to supper. They will be at the Metropolitan Club, if you wish to join them," Francis said dutifully. "But, Miss Cahill, you have a caller. She has been waiting here for the past hour."

Francesca was dismayed. "Is Sarah Channing here?" She turned toward the salon on her left as Francis closed the front door. Then she froze as a woman got up from the gold brocade sofa where she had been seated.

Rose Cooper hurried forward. "We have to talk—and I don't have much time before I have to get back."

"I'll send you downtown in a cab," Francesca said quickly, surprised. Taking her arm, she guided Rose back into the blue-and-gold salon. Recovering from her surprise, she closed the door and faced her. "I am so surprised that you would come all this way to see me, Rose." She saw that Rose had been served tea and biscuits. "What is wrong? You seem worried."

"I *am* worried!" Rose said, her green eyes flashing. "Francesca, this is about your portrait."

Francesca went still.

Rose paced, casting an odd, sidelong look at her. "I lied to you. And I am so sorry. You helped me so much when Daisy was murdered. Last night I dreamed about her. She was so beautiful!" Tears filled Rose's eyes. "When I awoke, it was as if we had really visited. I knew she would be angry at me for lying to you, when you are always so damn kind."

"What did you lie about?"

Rose hesitated. "I knew about your portrait. Daisy told me about it."

Her thoughts raced wildly. How had Daisy known about the portrait? "Daisy told you about my portrait?"

"Yes."

Francesca stared closely at her. Had Rose seen it? Did she know it was a nude? What did she want, really? Was she the thief? Was she cleverly toying with her? "I didn't even know that Daisy knew Hart had commissioned my portrait. He stopped seeing Daisy after I accepted his proposal on February 28. So he must have told her about it before that, when she was his mistress."

"I don't know when Hart told her, or if he did. I only

know that Daisy told me about it. She was jealous of you, once it became clear that Hart was so enamored." Rose looked away.

Francesca tried to sort this out. Hart wouldn't have mentioned the portrait after Francesca had agreed to marry him, she was certain. That meant that Daisy had known about the portrait in mid-February, shortly after he had made her his mistress. She hadn't been asked to pose nude until the end of March. Hart would have never mentioned that to anyone, much less Daisy. "Do you know where my portrait is?"

Rose's eyes widened. "No!" She seemed fearful. "You are one of the kindest people I have ever met and it didn't seem right, to have lied to you. You help people, Francesca, all the time, and you helped me. I don't want to see you hurt." She finally looked directly at Francesca.

Francesca felt her heart racing. "What else do you wish to say, Rose?"

Rose bit her lip. "Nothing." Francesca waited. "I wish I knew where your portrait was. I'd help you if I could."

Francesca felt taken aback. Why did her words seem rehearsed?

She focused. "Who else knows, Rose?"

"I don't understand."

"Did you tell Farr?"

Rose stiffened. "I don't recall discussing you or your portrait with Chief Farr. That pig has one thing on his mind when he is with me."

She let that unpleasant fact go.

Rose and Farr had been lovers, and lovers spilled their deepest, darkest secrets. That bothered her terribly, still. "I appreciate your honesty," she finally said. "Because if that portrait is ever displayed in this city, I would be destroyed."

Rose's expression remained controlled. "I hope you

find it," she finally said. "I imagine you have made a lot of enemies, doing what you do."

Francesca smiled grimly. She had thought Bill Randall to be their man, but the mystery had deepened, and there were many pieces of the puzzle to examine. Still, something was nagging at her. Something was very wrong with Rose coming forward like this.

Was she an enemy or a friend?

A knock sounded on the front door. Francesca opened her purse and handed Rose cab fare. "I appreciate your coming here to tell me the truth. And I hope we are friends, Rose, because I wish you well." She meant it. But the other woman flushed and glanced away. "Please, use this to hail a hansom."

"Thank you," Rose said, starting out of the salon.

Francesca fell into step with her, almost certain that she was hiding something. She hoped Rose was not the thief. But now, she had another reason to speak with Hart. She would do so immediately.

Joel was in the front hall, his face stark white except for an agitated flush. She instantly knew something was amiss. Rushing past Rose, she cried, "Joel? What is it?"

Joel ran toward Francesca. "Someone stole Lizzie!"

CHAPTER FIFTEEN

Tuesday, July 1, 1902
8:00 p.m.

THEY WERE MERE moments from Maggie's flat. Avenue A was ghostly, with no traffic at all. A few pedestrians were about, mostly leaving the ward's various pubs and saloons in a rather inebriated state. Because of the hour, they had made good time getting downtown.

Francesca had never seen Joel as upset. He had told her every detail of what had happened. While the children played outside on Tenth Street, a thug had grabbed Lizzie and thrown her in the back of a wagon. The man had leaped in after her, and someone else was driving. The facts were stunning—and senseless. Francesca held his hand. He let her, a sign of how scared he was. Sometimes, she forgot just how young Joel was, only a little boy of eleven.

Ahead, Francesca saw a police wagon, shining brightly beneath a streetlamp, one big brown horse in the traces. Several officers were milling about it, mostly with their hands on their billy sticks. A crowd of neighbors, all gawking, had gathered. She scanned the crowd for Bragg and saw him instantly.

Her heart leaped with relief. The first thing she had done was call Bragg, who had still been at police headquarters.

"The c'mish is already here," Joel cried, leaning eagerly forward. "Mebbe they already found Liz!"

Bragg was conversing with Maggie, his expression professional and restrained. They were standing directly under a gas lamp and she could make them out clearly. Maggie looked terrified and had been crying. She was so clearly trying not to cry now. Paddy was clinging to her skirts. Matthew stood with them, hovering anxiously. Surely they would find Lizzie alive and well!

Evan was nowhere in sight.

"They ain't found her yet," Joel said, seeing his mother. He cursed, enough so to make her blush. "Why didn't I watch her like I was told to?"

She reached for him. "Joel, this is not your fault. Surely you do not think you are to blame?"

"Who else is to blame? Mr. Cahill told me to watch the boys an' Lizzie," he said with anguish. "I knew he wanted to kiss me mom, so I took 'em all outside! An' I took my eyes off her so I could chat with Tom O'Leary an' his sister! Damn it!"

The Cahill coach halted. Joel was already rushing out the door before she could try to reassure him. Francesca followed more slowly. Bragg had seen them and he was striding toward her as she got out. He was very grim.

"There is no news?" she asked.

He shook his head. "We do not even have a lead. A 'big' man simply seized the child and tossed her in the back of a waiting wagon. He climbed in with her as the driver took off."

Real fear began. "Why would anyone abduct Maggie Kennedy's child? She can hardly afford a ransom."

"But Evan can," Bragg said seriously. "And so can you. This abduction was planned carefully and for a reason."

She was briefly surprised and she mulled that thesis over.

"Francesca, you have an unusual friendship with Maggie. I am sure it has aroused speculation and interest—just as I am certain that Evan's interest in her has been the talk of the town."

"You don't think this is related to my stolen portrait, do you?" She lowered her voice. "Surely whoever thinks to torture and destroy me isn't now lashing out at my friends and family?"

"I hope not."

Their gazes met. He was uncertain, and more dismay crested. "How will we find Lizzie?"

"My men are interviewing everyone, but I believe we will shortly receive a ransom demand."

She glanced past him at Maggie, who remained in tears. "Maggie is distraught. Where on earth is Evan?"

"Apparently he took off on his own search the moment the first police detail arrived." Bragg hesitated. "Evan isn't gaming again, is he?"

She instantly recalled the deception she'd undertaken with Hart, accusing Evan of doing exactly that so he might lend her money for the blackmailer. "Not that I know of." She knew Bragg was considering every angle—including one of Evan's creditors seizing Lizzie as leverage against him.

"Should we make certain we are on the same ground?" she asked briskly.

He smiled slightly at her. "Please do."

"Joel said he was watching the children while peeling potatoes on the street, but then he was distracted by a friend, Tom O'Leary, and his sister. Before he knew it, Lizzie was by the street, where a large male stranger simply seized her, put her in a wagon and drove off, another rough at the reins."

"That is exactly what Paddy and Matthew have said. And we have three other witnesses—two fellows who were leaving the bar across the street and a neighbor, Mrs. Hannity."

She looked toward Maggie, who was in the arms of an older woman. She could not believe that Evan wasn't there to comfort her. "Did my brother say specifically where he was going?"

"No, he did not. But Evan dotes on Maggie and he would never leave her now like this unless he had an inkling of where to go to find Lizzie."

A new tension began. She prayed Evan was not gaming again, and this incident had everything to do with her. She saw two men in their twenties, in plaid shirts and trousers, behind the couple. A heavyset woman sat on a chair by the front stoop of Maggie's building. "Are they our witnesses?"

"Yes."

"Do we have a description of the thugs?"

"Only a generic one—he has been described as gray-haired and tall, with a portly or muscular build. And he was wearing a darker gray cap. The driver wore a red shirt and was much smaller."

Francesca nodded and said, "Are your men canvassing the neighborhood?"

"Yes, they are, but without a ransom note, this feels very much like a dead end." He was grim. "I think I will ask your brother for a list of his creditors—when I can find him."

She nodded worriedly, not ready to make that leap. Bragg touched her arm. "Maybe Maggie knows what lead Evan thinks he is following."

Francesca glanced at him. For a moment, their gazes held and she thought about how solid he was in a crisis, and how superb they were as an investigative team. In the next moment, she wondered where Hart was that evening. He was a powerful ally, always, and incredibly astute.

And sometimes, his jaded experience brought very interesting insights into their work.

The older woman released Maggie, who faced her, wiping her red eyes with one of Evan's embroidered handkerchiefs. "Who would take Lizzie?" she cried. "Oh, Francesca, you must find her!"

Francesca embraced the red-haired woman. "We will find Lizzie. Trust me, Maggie, please." She stroked her hair.

Maggie nodded fearfully at her. "Why would someone take my daughter? I am a pauper, Francesca, not a princess like you."

She hesitated. "I don't know. But we are friends—and you are friends with my brother. We can certainly meet a ransom." She had no intention of discussing the myriad possibilities of what this abduction might truly mean and frighten her even more.

Maggie gasped. "You think someone will ask you or Evan for a ransom? That's mad!"

Francesca held her hand. "Yes, I think there will be a ransom demand, sooner rather than later." She meant to be reassuring. Maggie was attentive now, as was Joel, who stood protectively with her and his younger brothers. "Maggie, where on earth is Evan?"

Her eyes welled. "He swore he would find Lizzie. The moment the police arrived, he rushed off."

"Do you have any idea where he was going?" Bragg asked.

"No, I don't," Maggie cried. "But…it was almost as if he had an idea of what had really happened to Lizzie."

Francesca exchanged a look with Bragg. Was this about Evan's gambling after all?

Bragg said, "Maggie, I hate to ask, but I must. Is Evan back at the tables?"

She paled impossibly. "No. He is a good man, Commissioner! And he has sworn off gaming."

She believed her every word, Francesca thought. She so hoped that Maggie was right. "Can you think very hard about where Evan went? Surely he said something that might give us a clue."

"He didn't say anything," she said miserably. She suddenly turned and hugged each of her sons, hard. "We will find Lizzie. She will be home very soon!" Then she looked fearfully at them.

Francesca stared closely. "What is it?"

She trembled. "I am sure it is nothing. Except I keep thinking about it."

She stiffened. "If you have some inkling, you must share it with us."

Maggie inhaled. Then she turned to Joel. "Take your brothers upstairs, Joel. It is getting late."

He began to protest.

"No, I am telling you to help them get ready for bed. I will be up shortly."

Very unhappy at being dismissed, Joel took Paddy and Matthew and returned to the building. Only when he was gone did Maggie face them. "I know I am making a mountain out of a molehill," she said. "But I was threatened two weeks ago—I mean—the children were threatened."

Francesca could not believe she was only telling them this now. "By whom and for what reason?" she cried.

Flushing, Maggie whispered, "The countess called. At first, I thought she wanted to become a new customer. But she was cruel and condescending."

"Are you speaking of Bartolla Benevente, whom Evan used to see?" Bragg asked calmly.

She nodded. "She told me to stay away from Evan. She said she would hurt the children if I did not."

A woman scorned, Francesca thought grimly. And

Bartolla Benevente was no average woman—she was dangerously manipulative. But the question remained, was she also vindictive? "Well, we have a lead, at last."

EVAN'S FURY KNEW no bounds as he strode up the walk to the Channings' front door. The night was eerily quiet, with most of the west side deserted in anticipation of the holiday weekend. His cab had been the only vehicle crossing the park. Now, Evan could barely breathe as he thought of Maggie's distress, or worse, what little Lizzie must be going through. He loved the little girl as if she were his own daughter. She must be terrified. He prayed that she wasn't harmed.

He'd taken a hansom uptown, leaving Maggie the moment the police had arrived. Now he used both the heavy brass door knocker and the bell, ringing again and again while pounding on the door. Surely Bartolla wasn't so amoral as to do something as despicable as abducting a child

A manservant appeared. "I am sorry, sir. Mrs. and Miss Channing are not available this evening."

He rudely shoved past the manservant, who gaped at him in shock. "Is the countess Benevente in tonight? If not, I will wait." His smile felt like a snarl. He was fairly certain she hadn't left town yet.

"She is in her rooms and has explicitly said she is not to be disturbed."

His fury roiled. "Really?" But the single mocking word had barely erupted when he heard the swish of skirts. Someone was coming down the hall from the back of the house. He turned expectantly—viciously—but disappointment arose. Sarah entered the hall, wide-eyed.

"Evan? What is wrong? I heard all that banging and ringing. What has happened?" she cried.

Once, long ago, Sarah and Evan had been engaged,

the result of her mother's meddling. He had dismissed her then as a uselessly meek and mousy sort of woman, a woman he would never have been interested in. But he knew her a bit better now. Sarah was surprisingly clever and strong, and just a bit like his sister. "I am sorry to rouse you, Sarah, but this is an emergency. I must speak with Bartolla."

Sarah's hands were smudged with charcoal. There was a smudge on her chin as well, and her shirtwaist was half tucked in and half pulled out of her slim navy blue skirt. Her gaze was wide. "I hope everyone is all right. You are so distraught!" She turned. "Would you please ask my cousin to come downstairs, Barnes?"

When the manservant had started up the stairs, she looked at him. "Do you wish for a drink? What has happened?"

He exploded. "Someone has kidnapped Lizzie Kennedy!"

Sarah stiffened. "You mean Maggie Kennedy's little girl?"

When he nodded and cursed, she cried, "But why?"

He looked at Sarah and realized that she actually cared. "God only knows," he began, "but Maggie is beside herself." As he spoke, he heard Bartolla's footsteps on the stairs.

Sarah took his hand. "I am sorry, Evan," she said, meaning it.

For one moment, he looked into her eyes, and was ashamed that he had judged her so swiftly and unfairly. Then he pulled free and turned.

Bartolla was gliding down the stairs in a green silk dressing gown, her long red hair down. Crystals sparkled on her black velvet slippers as the robe parted over her ankles. He could tell she wore little or nothing beneath the robe and thought she had been expecting him. "I am afraid you have caught me in a state of dishabille." She smiled, clearly unashamed. "I am leaving for the Catskills tomorrow, and I have stayed in tonight to finish my packing." She reached him and kissed his cheek.

He jerked away, thinking she still did not look pregnant. Sarah said, "Bartolla, we would have waited for you to change into something more befitting a caller." But her tone was calm, not shocked.

"Oh, please. You know as well as I do that Evan was my lover until very recently. Why stand on formality when he has seen me in my robe many times?" She peered more closely at him. "Are you upset, darling? Shall we all share a drink?" She stroked his cheek.

He caught her wrist far too tightly for the gesture to be pleasant. She went still as he said, "Lizzie has been abducted, Bartolla."

Her eyes widened. "Who?"

He jerked on her as Sarah made a sound of protest. "Don't play games now! Lizzie Kennedy has been abducted. Are you involved?"

Bartolla gasped and jerked her wrist free. "How dare you?" she said. "What is wrong with you? You must be speaking of one of those brats that belong to your seamstress. How dare you accuse me of…involvement."

A terrible silence fell. Sarah stepped forward as Evan scrutinized his former mistress, trying to decide if she knew anything at all. "Evan, what are you saying? Surely you do not think Bartolla knows something about that poor child?"

He stared at his ex-mistress and she stared back. Her eyes gleamed with amusement—and he did not know what to think. She did not care about the child, much less Maggie. Of course not. Bartolla only cared about herself. "Did you take Lizzie? Do you know where she is?"

Bartolla's brows lifted and she laughed. "My God,

have you lost your wits? Are you accusing me of abducting that child? Why on earth would I do such a thing?" She laughed again. "Dear God, where would I even put a child?"

He tried desperately to read her mind. Sarah said, "Evan, Bartolla is hardly a criminal. She would never abduct someone's child!"

But she was a fortune-hunting bitch and a very angry woman. She hated Maggie.

Bartolla walked over to him and clasped his cheek. "Darling, I am many things, but I would never hurt a small child. I especially wouldn't hurt a child you are fond of... I remain in love with you."

He drew back. "I pray you are telling me the truth. Because if you are behind this, Bartolla, you will be very, very sorry."

Bartolla was mildly amused. She lowered her voice. "Are you threatening me? What will you do—leave me and our child out on the streets, to beg and to starve?"

He could barely breathe. He had been so certain that Bartolla had abducted Lizzie. "If you are behind this, God help me, you will pay."

Bartolla stopped smiling.

And that was when Evan heard the doorbell ring behind them.

BRAGG'S MOTORCAR WAS idling. They had just arrived at the gothic Channing mansion. The downstairs lights remained on, but otherwise, the grounds were eerily dark. Only two gas lamps graced the street in front of the house. Francesca and Bragg made no move to get out of the car. Instead, they stared at one another.

The drive uptown had taken twenty minutes, and she had just told him about her conversation with Rose that afternoon.

"So Rose does not recall discussing your portrait with the chief," Bragg finally said, sighing.

"The more I think about it, the more I find it likely that she lashed out at me and Hart by doing so," Francesca said. "That might explain Farr's knowledge of the theft. Once she told him about my portrait, he probably started snooping about the Channing home. But I just can't come to grips with Rose being our thief. What would she have to gain by coming to see me today and making a partial confession as she just did? And we don't even know if she knows that it's a nude portrait. I don't know how she would have ever found that out."

"The thief is toying with you, remember? If this were about money, we would have the portrait in our possession," Bragg said.

"If Rose stole the portrait and paid Moore to gain the use of his gallery, then she hates me as much as she hates Hart." How disturbing that notion was!

Bragg reached across the space between them and covered her lightly clad shoulder with his large, gloved hand. "As with all mysteries, there won't be any clear answers, not until the case is solved."

His touch always brought back memories she preferred to avoid. "It is so late," she finally said, shifting her body so his hand fell from her shoulder. "It must be half past nine at least—I doubt you will be home until midnight."

His stare remained steady. "I doubt it is that late. But you are probably right."

"Bragg, avoiding your wife will hardly solve matters."

"Are you now an expert on domestic relationships?" He spoke quietly, without censure, but his words hurt.

"Obviously not. We always discuss the case and my problems, but I remain worried about you."

His expression softened. "Don't you have enough on your plate now, with my damn brother?"

"You are changing the subject," she said flatly. She did not want to think about Hart now, but she did. Where was he, at that hour, while they were at Sarah's?

His mouth curled. "Yes, I am."

"We are only allowed to discuss my problems?"

He hesitated. "I have a confession to make. I dread going home, Francesca."

She was shocked.

He pulled off his gloves and opened his door, alighting from the roadster. Francesca did not move. "Surely you do not dread being with Leigh Anne!"

He walked around the front of the automobile and opened her door for her. She stared, still stunned, as he pulled her to her feet. "Hopefully Evan is still here, as I wish a word with him as well as with Bartolla."

She came to her senses. As they started up the walk, she said, "May I call on Leigh Anne tomorrow?"

"Absolutely not."

She stumbled and he caught her arm, steadying her. "Are you in jest?"

"I am deadly serious, Francesca, I know your intentions are as good as gold, but sometimes your desire to help backfires." They paused at the front door and he rang the doorbell.

"I am forbidden from calling on your wife?" she gasped.

He turned to face her, very seriously. "I would hardly forbid you anything. But, Francesca, I am asking you not to interfere in whatever is left of my private life. Please," he added.

Her heart broke for him. She had heard the desperation in his tone and it was shocking. Rick Bragg was the calmest and most rational man she knew. Yet he was undone by his marital problems now. She had to help.

To her surprise, Sarah opened the front door. Instantly, Francesca saw that she was agitated. She looked into the grand entrance hall, where Evan and Bartolla stood. Her brother was grim, but Bartolla seemed very amused. Suddenly Francesca didn't know why she had ever liked the other woman.

"Thank God, the police are here," Evan said harshly. He approached them with long strides. "Have you found Lizzie?"

"I am sorry, Evan, we have not," Bragg said soberly.

Anguish distorted his features. "Have you seen Maggie? How is she?"

Francesca put her arm around him. "She is managing. She needs you."

More anguish flickered. "I know. I wanted to speak with Bartolla, Fran. I wanted to make certain she is not behind this."

Francesca glanced at Bragg, who nodded. She pulled him aside, murmuring, "Excuse us." They paused before the open doors of a small salon as Bragg began speaking to Bartolla and Sarah. "She is very distraught, of course. Bragg and I were at the scene, covering every possible angle and searching for clues."

"What did you find?" he cried.

"Thus far, not very much, although we have three witnesses to the abduction." Evan ran his hand through his hair, his expression ravaged. He loves Maggie so much, Francesca thought. It was terribly obvious. "Evan, I must ask. Could this be about the remainder of your gaming debts?"

His eyes widened. "My God, I hope not!"

"Evan, no one would take Lizzie in the hope of gaining a ransom from Maggie. But the abduction might have been made to gain a ransom from you."

"I had already wondered if I would be approached for a ransom," he said tersely. "But if this is about my debts, then they will threaten to hurt Lizzie!"

She took his arm. "We don't know that this is about your gambling."

He trembled. "If it is, we are over."

It was serious, Francesca thought, no longer surprised. Her rakehell brother had met his match in a simple, honest and hardworking Irishwoman. It crossed her mind that he would be in for a terrible battle with Julia one day. She dismissed the thought for now. "Evan, I must ask. Are you gambling again?"

He was horrified. "No. There was one relapse, Fran, just after Bartolla told me she was having my child, when I realized—" He stopped.

She knew what he had meant to say and she touched his arm. "When you realized she would be in your life, always?"

He nodded. "Clearly, my involvement with her was another mistake."

"Don't do this to yourself now. And I still wonder at the convenience of her pregnancy." She shrugged.

"Sometimes I wonder, as well. And if she is pregnant, I wonder if I am the father." He lowered his tone, not that they could be overheard.

"There is more," Francesca said. "Whoever is behind this, he or she might think to send me a ransom note."

"You?" His eyes widened.

"Maggie and I are friends. She was a guest at my failed wedding." She inhaled. "You might as well know." She lowered her voice now, too. "I am embroiled right now in a case where I am the victim."

Evan started. "What? I know you were supposedly

lured off from your wedding to help some poor soul in need, but this is the first I have heard of anything else. Please, do not tell me that you are in trouble!"

Francesca didn't hesitate. She knew she could trust her brother. "The portrait stolen from Sarah's studio was a nude, Evan." He simply stared in confusion, so she said, "I posed nude for the portrait. On my wedding day, I received an odd invitation to preview Sarah's works. I instantly knew that my portrait had surfaced."

He began to turn red. "You did what? Have you lost your mind? My God, where is the portrait now?"

"We have been racing time to find the painting before it is ever publicly displayed. It was at the gallery where I was invited, but when Bragg and I returned to retrieve it later Saturday night, it was gone."

Her brother's flush deepened. "Did Calder ask you to do this? If so, your fiancé is a madman. Your reputation hangs by a thread, Fran!"

She took his arm. "Apparently we both like to live dangerously."

At her reference to his gambling obsession, he became quiet. "Touché. I will not judge either of you."

"The point I am making is that someone wishes to hurt me—I was prevented from attending my own wedding. That person might even wish to destroy me. I cannot rule out the possibility that Lizzie's abduction is just another cruel twist in a sadist's game."

He blanched. "What am I to tell Maggie?"

"Nothing, at least for now. But if Lizzie's abduction is related to either one of us, there is a strong chance that we will be asked for a ransom, and right now, that would be good news."

Evan stared thoughtfully at her. She finally said, "And that brings us to a third possible motive—romantic revenge."

He tensed visibly. "Bartolla called on Maggie two weeks ago. She explicitly threatened the children if Maggie did not stay away from me."

"Maggie already told us. And Bartolla strikes me as a very vindictive woman. What did she say to you?"

"She claims she would never do such a thing." He spoke with heated anger. "She is very vindictive, Fran, and she is furious that I am seeing Maggie and that our wedding is off."

Francesca glanced across the room. Bragg and Bartolla were still speaking, and she turned her gaze back to her brother. "I don't trust her," she said, "but abducting a child is beyond vengeful—it is criminal and sociopathic."

He folded his arms, glaring at his ex-mistress. "She is leaving for the Catskills tomorrow."

"I doubt that," Francesca said quickly. She started toward the countess and Bragg. "Am I intruding?" She was deliberately polite.

Bragg smiled at her. "We are done and it is late."

Did he mean to imply that he had had a change of heart and would go home to his wife and family? She certainly hoped so. She managed to smile at Bartolla. "I hear you are leaving for vacation tomorrow. Where are you off to?" she asked pleasantly.

"I have been invited to stay with friends at a hotel in the Catskills," the countess said.

"I beg your pardon," Bragg interrupted, as Francesca had known he would. "I am sorry, Bartolla, but you will have to delay your departure."

She was shocked speechless.

"Until Lizzie Kennedy is returned, you will have to remain in town."

Bartolla's eyes flashed. "You can't forbid my leaving!"

"I most certainly can. And I have no issue with

approaching Judge Harris for a court order to that effect, Countess." He was at his most authoritative now. "Do not leave the city, and do not change your residence until otherwise notified. This is an official police matter, and I will undoubtedly have more questions for you."

Bartolla flushed with fury. She turned her glare upon Evan. "You did this, didn't you? First you think to destroy our future—my future—and now to deny me my freedom."

Evan was taken aback. Sarah stepped between them, taking Bartolla's arm. "Bartolla, stop. This is serious. Don't say another word."

Bartolla breathed hard as Bragg said, "Sarah is right. You might need a lawyer, Countess." He smiled at Francesca. "Shall we? Evan, I can give you a ride, as well. Good night, ladies."

Sarah murmured, "Good night." She was ashen. Bartolla did not speak, her gaze shooting daggers at them.

They started for the door, Evan behind them. It wasn't until they were outside and walking toward the Daimler that Francesca spoke. "What do you think?"

"I think she is capable of committing many dastardly deeds, but I am not sure she is foolish enough to have committed this abduction," he said.

Francesca glanced back at her brother, but he was clearly lost in thought. "I think she might have lost all judgment when she lost my brother to Maggie."

"That is a good point," he said quietly, pausing by his car.

She took his hand. "You shocked me earlier."

He instantly understood. "Don't."

"Please, call it a night."

His regard wandered over her face. "I cannot. Lizzie is missing. So is your portrait."

"So, you will avoid her now? And what will that solve?

Speak to her, Rick, the way you speak to me, with candor and honesty."

Sorrow filled his eyes. "We have never been able to communicate, Francesca. Not the way that you and I do." He removed his hand from hers.

CHAPTER SIXTEEN

Wednesday, July 2, 1902
9:00 a.m.

SHE WAS IN Hart's arms, and his smile was filled with warmth and affection. Francesca sighed, realizing that everything would be all right—that Hart had changed his mind, that he still loved her. She was so happy, and she did not want to ever leave his embrace. But she heard the insistent knocking on her door.

"Francesca Cahill, I must have a word with you," Julia said sternly, standing over her bed.

Wide-awake and terribly disappointed that she had only been dreaming, Francesca blinked up at her mother. A maid pulled open her draperies, letting bright morning sunlight into the bedroom. As the last remnants of her dream faded, she immediately remembered that little Lizzie Kennedy had been abducted. "I have overslept," she cried, sitting up. She threw the covers aside. She had so much to do!

Julia had both hands on her hips. She was already dressed in a striped pink ensemble, meaning it must be terribly late. "If you think you are rushing off to meet Rick Bragg, you are wrong."

She had one bare foot on the floor, and she glanced at the gilded clock on her bedside table. It was only nine. Relief began. It wasn't as late as she had thought. Clearly, she had been exhausted, to sleep so long. "I know you must want to talk to me," she said, standing. "I mean, you are supposed to be in Saratoga Springs, yet here we are, still in the hot city." She tried a warm smile on her mother.

Julia scowled. "You are, as usual, rushing about the city on some madcap criminal investigation and neither your father nor I know all the details about what really happened on Saturday. Do you ever intend to tell me?"

"Mama, you know I cannot reveal the details of an ongoing criminal investigation, but hopefully, we are close to solving the case." She then added, no longer smiling, "Did you hear that Maggie's little girl was abducted yesterday evening?"

Julia paled. "No, I did not. Poor Maggie!"

Francesca was grim. "Time is always of the essence in any investigation, Mama. As the trail gets colder the longer it takes to solve a case. We need a good lead now."

"We?" Her brows rose and her tone was cutting. "When did you last see your fiancé, Francesca?"

She bit her lip. "Could we have this conversation after I finish dressing?"

"No, we are going to have it right now. I saw Calder yesterday."

Francesca felt her heart lurch with dread. Yet while Julia was angry, she was not livid or in hysterics. Wouldn't the ending of their engagement cause fury or a huge drama? Francesca knew she would genuinely be undone by their estrangement. "I believe I mentioned that he is somewhat angry with me." Why was she bothering to hedge? After talking to Hart, her mother had to know everything.

"He adores you—even after being stood up at the altar."

Francesca straightened her spine, disbelieving. "He said that?"

"I was terribly relieved. I expected him to end the engagement. But how much can a man put up with? No gentleman would care for his intended to run around with another man, Francesca. I want you to turn this investigation over to the police, entirely, and then you and Calder can join Andrew and I in the Springs."

She was astonished. What had Hart said to Julia? Why hadn't he told her mother that they were through? Had he been protecting her from Julia's wrath or did he truly intend for them to reconcile at some point?

She came to her senses. He had meant his every word when he had told her that the engagement was off and it was best for them both. He had meant his every word when he had said she deserved someone as virtuous and morally upstanding as Rick Bragg. But no one was as charming as Hart; no one could play a game as well. Why would he wish to antagonize her mother, when he meant for their friendship to endure? Carefully, she said, "Did you invite Calder to the Springs?"

"Actually, I have just sent him a note, in spite of your father's displeasure." Julia was grim. "You know how hard it's been to manage Andrew, Francesca. There is no doubt in my mind that he is relieved that your marriage did not take place. You and Hart need to reschedule the nuptials for the fall, immediately, before Andrew is lost to our cause with even more conviction."

Francesca simply stared, a smile plastered on her face. It had always amazed her that Andrew had come around. He disapproved of Hart entirely.

Finally, Julia smiled and took her hand. "Do not misunderstand. I remain appalled by your behavior. I have done nothing but think about how to put an immediate end to this scandal—and you may be sure, it is a scandal.

Everyone is talking about your jilting Hart. However, I am thrilled that Hart remains smitten with you. But, Francesca, you must come to your senses. Even Hart will only put up with so much. I am a wise woman, and you really must consider what I am saying." Julia kissed her cheek and marched for the door. There, she turned. "We will stay in the city until you and Hart have made your summer plans. Hopefully you will join us and we can all plan another wedding together." She frowned. "Rick Bragg called."

Her heart slammed. What had happened? She prayed Lizzie had been found. Then she prayed that they had had a major break in the case of her stolen portrait. "Is he at police headquarters?" As she rushed to pull on a wrapper, she wondered why she had bothered to ask. He dreaded going home.

"Has anything I have said made any sense at all?" Julia barred her way. "Are you going downstairs to speak on the telephone dressed in your nightclothes?" She was incredulous.

Francesca flushed. "Mama, no one can see me when I am on the telephone. What if Lizzie has been found? Don't you want to know? This could be the break we have been waiting for!" Francesca had already darted around her mother and was racing into the hall.

"You don't even have your slippers on," Julia cried. "Only Hart could be smitten with such behavior!"

Francesca raced downstairs, ignoring her mother's last remarks. Jonathon was on duty at the front door, and he did not bat an eye as she flew through the front hall and into the corridor. Her father was in the study, on the sofa with the *Sun*. He smiled warmly at her.

She kissed his cheek. "Good morning."

"I am glad to see that you have slept in. I cannot recall when you last did so."

"I was tired," she confessed. "Papa, I have to call Rick."

"I am aware of that." He rattled his newspaper and returned to reading it.

Unlike Julia, he did not mind her racing about town with Bragg. She was afraid that meant he was turning against Calder again. She sighed, going to the telephone and lifting the heavy receiver. She would worry about her father and Hart later. Francesca asked the operator to connect her to police headquarters, chatting pleasantly with her for a moment about the weather, never mind that Beatrice kept asking about her fiancé.

"Francesca?"

"Bragg! Have we had a break?" she cried hopefully. She was aware of Andrew glancing at her over his newspaper. "Please, has Lizzie been found?"

"I'm afraid not, but there has been a major break in the case of your stolen portrait," Bragg said. "I received the visitors' logs from Blackwell's Island this morning. Bill Randall paid Henrietta a visit on Saturday, April 26, at a quarter past one."

Francesca inhaled. Bill Randall had been in the city on the day her portrait had last been seen by Sarah, which might have been the day it was stolen. He had been in the city this past Saturday, when her portrait had resurfaced. "But Marsha Moore didn't recognize him. Perhaps the man waiting for Daniel Moore wasn't the thief."

"I wonder how clearly Mrs. Moore was able to see that night," Bragg said. "Randall was on the train from Philadelphia, arriving here at noon. He would have arrived at Grand Central Station and gone directly to the pen. He also went to great lengths to fabricate an alibi for that evening."

"True. That is incriminating, obviously." Francesca

wished they could apprehend Randall and speak with him at length.

"Moore has also produced a receipt for the sale of a thousand-dollar painting on the Thursday prior to your wedding day. Apparently I was wrong to believe that the funds came from the thief."

She was dismayed. "We must speak with Randall. I'd even like to speak with Moore again—and Rose. I would like to know where she was on Saturday evening."

"Yes, I agree with you. I have issued a warrant for Bill Randall's arrest. But he didn't return to the old Randall residence last night."

"He is onto us," Francesca said grimly. Randall was in hiding, which made him seem even guiltier. "Will we meet at Maggie's? Or are you otherwise preoccupied today?"

"Finding Lizzie is my main concern right now. I will see you shortly at Maggie's," Bragg said.

Francesca smiled to herself and hung up—only to find both her parents staring at her.

BRAGG WAS STANDING on the sidewalk in front of Maggie's brownstone when Francesca arrived. He was speaking to the corner grocer, and Joel was at his side. Francesca's heart broke as she got out of the cab. Joel was pale and his expression was anguished. Maggie must also be frantic and devastated, she thought.

She paid the driver, thanking him, and hurried over. Bragg smiled at her, his gaze sliding over her trim shirtwaist and dark gray skirt. She smiled back. "Any news?"

"Mr. Schmidt saw the children last night as he was closing up, Francesca. And he says his last customer was a big fellow with gray hair and a gray cap."

Francesca cried out. "Did he by any chance give his name?"

The grocer, a lumbering fellow with reddish hair, shook his head. "He bought chewing tobacco, Miss Cahill, that is all."

Francesca was familiar with the grocer. His daughter had been an important witness in a previous investigation. Bragg said, "He had a wad of cash—what seemed like an excessive amount for a simple laborer."

Of course, the thugs were hired. Bragg thanked Schmidt as Francesca put her arm around Joel. "We will find Lizzie," she murmured.

"Yeah, we will," he cried furiously. "An' I'll kill the sod who took her!"

"Joel!" Francesca was aghast, because Joel had meant his words.

"I'm gonna go sleuth on my own," he said, shrugging her off.

Francesca and Bragg watched him stride off, his hands in the pockets of his knickers. She turned, noting that Bragg seemed as tired as ever. "Maybe Joel will turn up a clue. How is Maggie?"

"I haven't been up yet," Bragg said. He gestured and Francesca preceded him up the grayish red stone steps of the brownstone and into the small dark foyer.

She paused as he shut the heavy wooden door behind them. It was terribly dark in the tiny hall. "I overslept this morning."

He smiled slightly. "That must be a first."

"I was exhausted," she said, not moving to the stairs. "Did you catch any sleep at all last night? I am very worried about you." Rick could not go on like this.

He sighed. "You know me well. No, Francesca, I hardly slept at all. I got home very late and I tossed and turned most of the night, worrying about Lizzie—and you."

"I will be fine. We will either break Daniel Moore and learn who leased his gallery, or we will apprehend Randall at any moment. Hopefully, he is our man."

"I pray we will recover that damn portrait—but even so, will you be fine?"

How adeptly he had turned their conversation onto her problems, she thought. "Hart didn't tell Julia that we are off, Bragg."

His face hardened. "Have you reconciled?"

She inhaled. "I haven't seen him since Monday night. I have little doubt that he remains set against me—against us. But he is fond of my mother and he probably wishes to remain on good terms with her."

"I know you don't want to hear it, but it is for the best."

She decided not to tell him how worried she was. The silence was becoming ominous. Then he took her hand and said, "No matter how much you think you love him, there will only be more pain if you do reconcile."

"Are you speaking from personal experience?"

He dropped her hand. "You are a ferret sometimes."

"I worry about you as much as you worry about me. I assume you got home after Leigh Anne was asleep, and you did not speak with her."

He hesitated. "I am thinking about letting her take the girls to Sag Harbor by herself, and staying on here in town to finish up police matters."

She gasped. "You cannot do such a thing!"

"I have no intention of leaving town if we have not found Lizzie and recovered the portrait. The time to apprehend the thief is now. And Lizzie must be discovered while we have a trail to follow."

She was aghast. "Of course we must find Lizzie immediately, well before Friday!" She could not imagine the child being missing for much longer. "But you are using this case as an excuse to avoid the weekend with your wife. You need the holiday."

"I need to solve this case and the case of your stolen portrait." He started past her, but she seized his arm before he reached the narrow stairwell.

"Rick, maybe it will be a wonderful weekend. You will never know if you don't go."

He met her gaze. "I cannot imagine sharing that small cottage with her."

She wanted to cry for him.

"And I don't imagine you will be running off for the weekend, either, not if Lizzie isn't home. Not if your portrait is still at large," he said.

"We will find Lizzie very shortly." She was firm. They had to find the little girl. "But if we haven't found the portrait, you're right. I couldn't possibly leave the city."

He suddenly took her hand. "If you stay in the city this weekend, have dinner with me."

She was stunned.

And then he flushed. He released her and gestured at the stairs. "We have a child to locate."

An image of the two of them dining in an empty restaurant came to mind. Shaken, she started past him. "Yes, we do." And she faltered, as her way up the staircase was barred.

"Hello, Francesca," Hart said, his tone mocking.

Her heart raced. "What are you doing here?" she cried. His expression was as dark as thunderclouds.

He stared and she began to realize that he might have been standing above them on the stairs for some time. Tension began. Had he heard their conversation? Had he overheard Bragg asking her out? Did it matter? Why hadn't he stopped by or sent her a note—it had been a day and a half!

Hadn't he missed her at all?

"Sarah Channing called this morning and mentioned that Maggie's daughter had been abducted." His cold gaze moved over her from head to toe, then fixated on Bragg. "Hello, Rick. I can see that the two of you are busy sleuthing away."

Clearly annoyed, Bragg did not answer. Instead, he stepped past Francesca, no easy task as the stairwell was so narrow. She shrank against the wall to allow him to move up the stairs. As she did, Hart shrugged past her as well, going down. Francesca did not move, shaken by the sexual look Hart had given her. It had been dismissive. Bragg gave her a grim look before continuing up to the third floor, where Maggie's flat was. Below, the front door slammed. Francesca turned and raced down the stairs after Hart.

"Wait," she cried, rushing outside.

He turned and stared, his expression cool. "I hope you enjoy your weekend with my brother. As a matter of fact, I hope you enjoy spending this day with him, as well." But he did not turn to go. His eyes were black upon hers.

Her heart lurched with dread. "That isn't fair. We are friends and we are on a case."

He made a disparaging sound.

"I haven't heard from you since Monday night." She tensed. Too well, she recalled their boundlessly passionate lovemaking—and his rejection of her. Being there with him reminded her of how much she loved him and how much she had missed him. His powerful presence was consuming. "I have been worried," she added.

"We are estranged," he said flatly.

"But we are friends," she said pointedly.

His stare never wavered. Finally, almost upon a sigh, he said, "Yes, Francesca, we are friends."

She smiled nervously. "Have you come to help find Lizzie?"

"Yes. I am fond of Joel, Francesca." He was grim. "I am fond of Mrs. Kennedy."

She bit her lip. "And you happen to know how fond I am of them both." His expression did not alter. "You do not have to be angry, Hart. Bragg and I are investigating, that is all. My feelings haven't changed."

He folded his arms. Had his expression softened ever so slightly? "I am hardly angry. I have expected a reversal from you all along. I want you to run about town with my brother. In fact, you should accept his supper invitation."

"You cannot mean that."

"I never say what I don't mean, Francesca, damn it."

"If we dine together, it will be as friends. But that is the last thing on my mind."

"Really? Because your heart is breaking for him, of course. He is in anguish, and your shoulder will be the one he cries upon." He shrugged as if he did not care, but his gaze was blacker than before.

"I will always be there for Rick—and I will always be there for you—and anyone else I care about who needs me," she cried.

Suddenly he touched her cheek. "And that is your allure, is it not?"

His caress vibrated through every inch of her body.

Hart's fingertips slipped down her neck. "He is pursuing you, Francesca," he said softly and seductively.

She inhaled as he dropped his hand, desire slamming through her. He had aroused her on purpose—but why? To prove he could? "He is doing no such thing. We are friends. He is married. Even you have remarked how moral he is. What we are doing is desperately trying to find Lizzie!"

He jammed his hands in his trouser pockets. "Even

someone as virtuous as my brother must sometimes give in to temptation."

She choked. "Stop throwing me at him!"

"I'll think about it. Has there been a ransom note?"

She was startled by his abrupt change of topic. "No, there has not. Evan swears he has not been gaming again, and I believe him."

"I hope he is telling the truth. If our thief has done this, there might never be a ransom, Francesca."

She hadn't reached such a horrific conclusion. "Please don't tell me you think that our thief continues to torture me by striking at those I love."

"Our thief is very clever and very ruthless. I am worried about Lizzie."

She reached for his hand. For one moment, he allowed her to grip it. "So am I."

He withdrew his palm from hers. "I remain worried about you, Francesca."

She was relieved. "I have been surprised that you did not call, to find out if we have turned up any new leads."

He was wry. "I did call—just not you. I already know that Randall was in town the weekend the portrait was stolen and that Rick has a warrant out for his arrest."

She gaped.

"I have a telephone, Francesca, not to mention a coach and driver, and I am hardly shy about demanding details from my brother." His gaze held hers. "I spoke with Rick twice yesterday, at some length."

Rick hadn't said a word. "Then you also know about Rose? That she knew about the portrait? Daisy told her."

"It is such a small world," he mocked. "I did not trust Rose in April, and I do not trust her now. You and Rick should speak with her again." A tinge of anger was in his tone. "Isn't it fortunate that fate continues to throw you and my brother together?"

"I want you, not Rick," she said immediately, without thinking.

A terrible pause ensued. Then he said slowly, "I did not hear you turn him down, Francesca."

She felt her heart thudding. "He is one of my dearest friends. That is all."

"Do you really believe that?"

That image flashed, of her and Bragg dining together in some deserted establishment. No, she did not believe that—the affection between them was simply too strong.

"I thought so," he said harshly. He started past her.

She ran after him. "Please wait. I will admit how fond I am of him. But damn it, Hart, you are the man of my dreams."

He whirled. "No, I am not, and I have never been the man of your dreams! You rescued me—as you do everyone. And I used all of my charm and appeal to seduce you."

She seized his arm. "And I am glad!"

His eyes blazed and she realized he was absolutely furious, just as she also realized he was an instant from sweeping her into his arms and kissing her. She went still, her heart thundering, as he stared at her mouth. "Goddamn my black soul."

She cried out. "Don't you say that this is all your fault!"

"But it is. Have you ever considered that if you had not posed nude for that portrait, you and I would now be man and wife?"

He was right. "Damn that portrait!" she cried.

"Ah, so finally, you admit the portrait is a damnable thing." He pulled away from her. "I am not leaving the city either, Francesca, until we have recovered the damn portrait and thrown the thief in jail."

She inhaled. "You would never abandon me in my time of need. I had no doubt."

"No, I would never walk away, not at a time like this."

She touched his jaw. "Then we can dine together this weekend. After all, you are my champion and my defender—you have said so yourself. I need you, Calder."

"That is not possible, Francesca," he warned. He caught her hand, but did not remove it. "Do not think to seduce or manipulate me."

"I miss you terribly," she breathed. "I miss our evenings. I miss being in your arms—you know it. And I believe you miss me, too."

Grimly, he removed her hand from his face. "There will be no such confession."

Francesca did not hesitate. "Yet."

And for an instant, the dark light in his eyes softened.

She smiled. "You are here, Hart. And you called Rick."

He made a sound. "I have an inherent instinct to protect you, Francesca. I will freely admit it. And I doubt that will ever change." But before she could become thrilled, he continued. "Even though the writing is on the wall."

"There is no writing on the wall."

"We will see."

They stared at one another. Hart finally said, "Are you going up?"

Francesca didn't pause to think. "Will you come with me? I could use your help, and I am being sincere."

He hesitated, then abruptly nodded.

CHAPTER SEVENTEEN

Wednesday, July 2, 1902
11:00 a.m.

SHE HAD WON this round, Francesca thought, acutely aware of Hart as they started toward the brownstone where Maggie lived.

"Don't gloat," he said. She felt his breath on her ear and the warmth of his body behind hers.

She smiled to herself. "I am not gloating, Hart. You happen to bring very useful insights into an investigation, jaded as you are."

"Should I be insulted?"

"No. I need a good dose of healthy cynicism now and then."

"Yes, you do. And you are gloating, Francesca, I can feel it. I have never denied that we are friends or that I wish to aid you in your various endeavors, nor will—" He stopped before finishing his sentence.

Francesca turned. Hart was looking toward the street in sharp surprise. She followed his glance and saw a burly fellow in a plaid shirt climbing from a wagon, carrying a package in his arms. Except the package was squirming....

"Lizzie!" she screamed.

Hart was already rushing toward the ruffian. The grayhaired man dropped Lizzie, who fell on her hands and knees and started to howl in a toddler's shrieking rage.

The stranger was reaching for the back of the wagon to jump in; another smaller fellow was in the driver's seat. As Francesca rushed toward Lizzie, she saw the rough grab the back of the wagon bed with both hands, hauling himself into it. As the driver yelled, "Giddap," to the horse, Hart seized the man by one shoulder. The wagon began to move. Hart pulled the man off the cart, throwing him down into the street.

"Lizzie!" Francesca cried, kneeling and sweeping the crying child into her arms. "It's all right," she soothed, but she was watching Hart as he descended upon Lizzie's abductor. And instantly, she knew he was a man bent on vengeance. "Hart! No!"

If he heard, he gave no sign. He reached down, hauled the man to his feet and slammed his fist into his face. Francesca heard a bone crack. "Hart!" she screamed.

Hart held the rough up and drove him across the sidewalk into the building. He hit him in the face again. "I despise bullies and cowards," he said coolly.

Francesca held Lizzie tightly as a crowd gathered. She saw the big German grocer amongst the gawkers. "Mr. Schmidt! Please—get Bragg. He is at Maggie's!"

"Is that the bastard who took Lizzie?" a young man exclaimed angrily.

"That's the crook who stole Maggie's girl!" a boy about Joel's age cried, holding a baseball bat and a glove.

The thug was surrounded now, his nose and eye bleeding. Francesca knew he was frantically looking for a possible means of escape. She bent and kissed Lizzie's soft blond hair. "It is all right. Your mother will be here shortly."

Lizzie looked up at her, her face tear-stained, and smiled angelically. "I have a new doll," she said, showing Francesca a tiny porcelain figurine with blond hair.

Tears welled. If Lizzie had been given a toy, then she

hadn't been mistreated, and she certainly did not look upset now. In fact, she looked clean and happy. "Are you hurt, sweetheart?" Francesca asked, cuddling her.

"Mama," Lizzie said fiercely. "I want Mama to see Fran."

It took Francesca a moment to realize that Lizzie wanted to show the doll to her mother—and that she had named it after Francesca. Francesca straightened, holding the little girl tightly. Hart glanced at her. She shivered, because the look in his eyes was frightening.

Hart said to the thug, "Don't even think it. I should love to break open your skull."

"I ain't done nuthin' except follow orders," the man cried, wiping blood from his face.

"Whose orders?" Hart calmly asked.

Francesca knew he was going to hit him again. She knew he should not. She didn't speak—neither did the thug. Francesca quickly covered Lizzie's eyes. Hart slammed his fist back into the man's nose. Bones broke. The man screamed.

"String him up!" someone cried. "Hang him for stealing Lizzie!"

"Whose orders?" Hart asked again.

The thug was panting. Hart did not look away from him, but he said, "Boy, give me your baseball bat. I need to borrow it."

Francesca cringed as the boy rushed forward to hand Hart his bat. Before she could tell him to stop, the door to Maggie's building flew open, and Bragg, Maggie, Joel and his brothers, and Evan came rushing out. Maggie saw Lizzie in Francesca's arms immediately. She ran forward to take her daughter, crying out.

Keeping one eye on Hart and the thug as Bragg quickly strode through the crowd, she said to Maggie, "I don't think she was hurt."

"No one is getting hanged today," Bragg told the crowd, which roared in protest. He looked at Hart. "In this city, judges in courts dispense justice."

Hart looked at the gray-haired fellow, who was cringing against the wall of the building. "Ignore him—he is the virtuous one. I am the son of a bitch who is going to break your kneecaps with this baseball bat. Whose orders?"

"She calls herself Countess!" he cried. "She's one of them rich snobs over on the west side!"

Hart smiled at Bragg, triumphant. "You can thank me later."

"You should ice that hand," Bragg said tersely. "And you can thank me for not pressing assault charges, Calder. This is a civil society."

Hart rolled his eyes and strode past Bragg. The crowd parted for him. Their gazes instantly met. Hart handed the bat back to the boy, never looking away from her. And in spite of knowing better, in spite of the values she treasured, her heart swelled.

Her pulse raced as she left Lizzie and Maggie in one another's embrace. She slowly walked forward. "Your hand is bleeding, Hart."

"It's his blood, not mine."

She doubted that. "Hart," she began, about to reprove him.

"Don't. It will only remind me that you and Rick are perfectly suited."

She bit back what she wished to say—that he shouldn't have taken the law into his own hands. Then she smiled. "Thank you."

"For what?"

"For seizing that crook and—"

"And beating him until he identified Bartolla?" He brushed a tendril of hair out of her eyes. The gesture was so impossibly tender that she went still. "You know, Francesca, where you live, it is a 'civil' society. We should all aspire to the rule of law. But this is a vast city—and an even vaster world. There are times when clinging to the law is sheer insanity. At times, might makes right—and an iron fist is all that separates good from evil."

She hated admitting that he was right. Then the reality of Lizzie's kidnapping struck her, hard. Bartolla had paid that thug to abduct Lizzie. "It is suddenly sinking in." She reached for his hand and he winced. "I cannot believe that Bartolla would do such a thing."

"I can," Hart said flatly. "And I'm not the only one."

He wasn't looking at her. Francesca turned. And the expression on her brother's face was frightening.

As FRANCESCA GOT OUT of her cab at 529 Broadway, she smiled to herself. Lizzie was just fine. It had taken her about an hour to tell her story, and it sounded as if she had spent the night in a hotel room with a young woman who might have been a housemaid. She had been well fed, read to and given the toy. She had been told that she was on a holiday.

Bragg had sent men to the Channing residence to bring Bartolla downtown for questioning. The thug who had abducted Lizzie had gone silent after being taken into custody. There wouldn't be any charges until a case could be proven in court. Bragg had had a meeting with the city council, so he had left Francesca to her own devices.

She still couldn't believe that Bartolla would stoop so low. Maggie was furious—she wanted Bartolla behind bars. Francesca did not blame her.

She trembled with ballooning joy. She had taken Hart over to the grocery, sat him down on a big barrel and provided him with an ice pack. As she had hovered over him, trying to hold the ice for him, he had looked at her with the dangerously sensual gaze he so often had. It had been impossible keeping her hands to herself.

What are you doing?

I am icing your hand.

I am an adult, Francesca, I can hold the ice myself.

Her hands had fluttered over his shoulders. He had given her an intense look.

What are you doing?

There is dust on your jacket—no, dirt.

Can't keep your hands to yourself?

No, Hart, I can't.

For one moment, she had thought he would take her in his arms or upon his lap. Instead, he had stood, tossing the ice pack aside and thanking Schmidt for it. Then he had told her he had business matters he wanted to pursue. And he had put her into a cab....

Now she faced the front door of the building where the Moores lived. He was thawing. Desire still raged between them. She loved him and she felt certain he loved her. He hadn't meant a word of what he had said to her on Saturday evening, after she had failed to show up for their wedding.

She was almost certain.

The only thing he had meant was that he wasn't good enough for her. She sighed. He might think that till the end of his days, but she did not believe it, not for a single second. But hadn't she known, going into the marriage, that Hart was complicated and dark and that their journey wouldn't be easy?

Today had proven to her just how powerful an ally he could be.

Francesca pinched herself, reminding herself that she was on a case, and she went up to the Moores' residence. It was early enough that she expected Marsha to be at home. The gallery was still the scene of a criminal investigation, so she did not know if Daniel would be in or not.

His wife answered the door directly after her first knock. She appeared stricken to see Francesca, who smiled. "I am so sorry to call without advance notice. May I please come inside and speak with you, Mrs. Moore?"

Marsha was pale. "Miss Cahill, I have nothing more to say." She began to close the door.

Francesca stepped forward, so the door struck her hip, and she winced. "If your husband is innocent, as I believe he is, don't you want to help prove it?"

Tears arose in Marsha Moore's eyes. "I am so tired of this! What have I done to deserve so much unhappiness?"

Francesca did not care for self-pity, but she felt sorry for Marsha. "You have already been a huge help. Don't you believe your husband is innocent of any wrongdoing?"

A moment passed. Then she opened the door, allowing Francesca inside. "Yes, I do. But—" She stopped.

"But what?" Francesca asked gently.

"These are hard, difficult times. It wasn't always this way."

Her compassion escalated. Marsha seemed like a kind, solid woman. "I am sorry for all your troubles," Francesca said, meaning it. "You do not deserve any of this."

"Thank you."

"Mrs. Moore, on Saturday night, when you saw a man on the street outside this building, waiting for your husband, was it dark out? The street is well lit at night."

"It was late, so it was dark. When I looked out the window and saw Daniel below, speaking to that strange man, they stood by one of the oak trees. Daniel was entirely visible, but the other man was harder to see."

"So you didn't see his face?"

She hesitated. "He was in the shadows, Miss Cahill, but not so much so that he didn't upset me. I recognized him from earlier in the week, and as I said, he looks like a dangerous man."

"Was it also dark when you saw him outside the gallery?"

"No, it was only five or six, but he loitered by some trees then as well—he did not want to be seen." She was firm.

Francesca decided that Bragg had been right. Marsha could not possibly identify the loiterer with certainty. It could have been Bill Randall outside the apartment and the gallery. "I am sorry for intruding and taking up your time." She smiled. "If you remember anything else that has happened that you think odd, which might help us find the culprit who locked me in the gallery and stole the portrait, please do contact me or the police."

Marsha Moore didn't move.

Francesca became alert. "Is there something else, Mrs. Moore? Something you have yet to reveal?"

She hesitated. "Maybe...I don't know."

"Please, I will gladly take any clue."

She inhaled. "There was a woman in his gallery earlier in the week."

Francesca thought of Rose and stiffened. "Go on."

"I do the books there every week. Daniel told me she was shopping for an oil, but...I didn't believe him."

"Why not? Can you describe this woman?" Francesca cried.

"Because I heard them arguing. She was so angry. I peeked out from the back office just for a moment. She was dark haired, Miss Cahill. That's all I know. When they saw me, they became silent—as if hiding something. I went back to the books, and apparently, she left."

Rose was dark; Rose was volatile and angry; and Rose

had known about the portrait. Had she been at the gallery, negotiating for its lease? Was she the thief, after all? Francesca thought her heart might explode with excitement over this new clue. "Would you recognize this woman again?"

"I think so," Marsha Moore said.

GRAND CENTRAL STATION was in chaos. Dozens of passengers were alighting from private coaches, public taxis and the occasional motorcar before the Lexington Avenue entrance. Luggage was piled up on the sidewalk and in the street and adjacent portico. Porters were helping passengers navigate their way into the terminal with their bags. Evan shoved a dollar bill at his cabdriver and leaped from the cab.

Bartolla had not been home when the police had arrived at the Channing mansion to detain her. He had left Maggie happily ensconced in her flat, with milk and cookies for all her children, the moment he had heard the thug confess. She had rushed after him. "Leave Bartolla to the police!" she had cried, so in tune with him that she knew exactly what he was doing. He had smiled grimly at her, kissed her on the mouth and told her not to worry.

He had arrived at the Channings' before the police, and the butler had told him that he had just missed the countess. She was taking a 3:15 train to Kingston, New York.

It was 2:50 now. Evan strode through the crowd, his gaze on a pair of policemen who were also intent on getting into the station. He cursed inwardly. If he did not miss his guess, a plainclothes officer was with them. Had Bragg sent them?

He had never been as enraged. He struggled to remind himself that Bartolla was carrying his child. Or was she?

Now Evan entered the vast, granite-floored lobby, his gaze veering to the huge information boards overhead. It took him a moment to locate her train: Syracuse: Track 10 A; Departing 3:15. On Time.

Evan broke into a run, shoving past the men and women milling around the terminal. From the corner of his eye, he saw the navy blue uniforms of the police. They were following him, obviously intent on locating the same track. He lengthened his stride, outdistancing them.

It seemed to take an eternity to cross the lobby and find track 10. The train hadn't arrived yet, but a hundred passengers stood beside the rails, with their larger bags and carry-on valises. Evan hesitated, then saw a glint of red about halfway down the track.

Fury consumed him. There she was, in a navy blue ensemble, a tiny blue hat barely covering her red hair. He started viciously forward.

She had meant to hurt Maggie.

She was selfish, vindictive and evil.

And it was his fault, because once he had lusted for her.

Bartolla saw him and froze.

He slowly smiled at her, lifting a hand.

She blanched but smiled. "Darling! Have you come to wish me bon voyage?"

Evan reached her side. "Why else would I come?" He took her arm in his as an approaching locomotive sounded, its engines roaring.

She seemed nervous. "That must be my train, darling. I am going to miss you…. I heard they found that poor child."

"Yes, they found Lizzie." He felt as if he had somehow stepped outside of himself, like a madman. He wasn't sure if he could control his need to destroy her for what she had done. He tried to remind himself that she was carrying his child—or so she claimed.

"What is wrong?" She tried to tug free of him and failed. "You look so strange. That child is all right, isn't it?"

The train was coming closer and its whistle sounded again. The noise was almost deafening and he had to raise his voice to speak. "That child has a name."

Bartolla seemed terribly frightened now. "Yes, I know—her name is Lizzie! You are holding me so tightly! That is my train, look!"

He glanced at the huge, black locomotive. One push was all it would take.

"Ow," she gasped. "What is wrong with you?"

His grasp had tightened. It was now or never—the train was almost upon them. But as much as he hated her for what she had done, he was not a killer—and she might be carrying his child. He did not release her. "Are you pleased with yourself? You drove Maggie insane with fear."

"Let me go, Evan," she cried as the train roared past them. Her body shuddered against his from the force of the locomotive. "I don't know what you are talking about!"

He did not release her, the train now slowing. "Hart apprehended one of your thugs," he said.

Her pale expression did not change. "You are speaking gibberish."

"Am I? Because he confessed to your involvement."

Her eyes locked with his.

"You are about to be arrested," he said softly—with relish.

"How can you let them arrest me in my condition?"

And he could take it no longer. "Is there a condition? There are no signs! If there is a child, is the child even mine?" He realized that he was shouting, that passersby were turning to gawk at them.

"Of course it's yours," she gasped. "You're hurting me!"

He stared, refusing to let her go, and she stared back. He loathed her, but he would never abandon his own child, not if the child proved to be his. But first, he must learn if she was even pregnant. There was one way to provoke her, he decided grimly.

He leaned close. "I can't do this, Bartolla. I do not want anything to do with you. I don't care if you are carrying my child. I suggest you find another means of support. There will not be any more monthly allowances."

She choked, shocked. "You are cutting me off now?"

"My generosity is over. In fact, I intend to marry Maggie as soon as she will have me. Father will probably disown me all over again, so even if I wanted to, I will never be able to support you when I go back to clerking. You will have to find another means of support."

She was breathing hard, her eyes still wide with disbelief. "Are you insane? You would marry that tramp—that slut—that little fortune hunter?"

He wanted to strike her, but he somehow kept his free hand at his side. "I'd be careful, if I were you, about calling the kettle black."

She struck him hard and viciously across the face. "What did I ever see in you?" she screamed. "You are a weakling and a fool! Thank God I was not foolish enough to become pregnant, Evan. You are right—there is no child! And I am glad!"

His knees buckled with relief. She had lied. For one more moment, their stares locked and he saw the vindictive look in her eyes. "You will never come near Maggie or her children again," he warned.

She spat at him.

He turned, still holding her, his burning cheek now damp, and faced the two approaching policemen. "I believe you are looking for this woman," he said. Then he smiled at Bartolla. "There has been a change of plans, Bartolla. I know you have been looking forward to a view of the mountains. I hope you enjoy a view of concrete walls through iron bars."

ROSE HAD TO BE the thief.

Surely she was the dark, angry woman whom Marsha Moore had seen! She had argued with Daniel Moore at his gallery just a few days before Francesca had discovered the stolen portrait there. How could it be a coincidence?

Could Rose hate her that much? Francesca hugged herself as her cab approached the driveway of her house. Rose hated Hart with a vengeance. Apparently she felt the same way about Francesca.

But how had she discovered the true nature of the portrait? Hart would have never told Daisy.

And if Rose was the thief, the man who had loitered outside the gallery and the flat could be insignificant. He did not have to be related to the case at all.

There was one problem with her newly drawn conclusion: Randall had been in the city on both Saturdays. Randall hated her and he hated Hart—he was just as vengeful as Rose. Francesca realized she had to determine if he truly came to visit Henrietta every weekend. If so, Randall's presence in the city might be unrelated, after all. But then why had he bothered with such an elaborate alibi?

Francesca had debated stopping at headquarters on her way uptown, but she had decided to rush home to change her clothes so she could call on Hart. They were making headway, and she meant to press on. She had visions of spending the evening in his arms. She had never been more determined. There would be reconciliation sooner or later. Now she couldn't wait to tell him about this latest clue.

But she would call Bragg the moment she got home to apprise him of the latest developments. Rose should be brought downtown immediately for further questioning.

They had almost reached the Cahill front gates. As the cab turned into the driveway, Francesca noticed a black hansom parked just inside the front gates, quite a distance from the house. It was very odd. "Driver, please stop beside that cab," she said. As she spoke, she realized Dawn was in the other hansom.

Brakes screeched and the horse whinnied as it was pulled up far too quickly in the traces. "I'll be but one moment." She opened her door and Dawn got out of her cab. Francesca could not imagine what she wanted. She saw that the woman was agitated and unsmiling. "Dawn! Are you waiting for me? Is everything all right?"

Dawn hurried forward, clutching an envelope, her expression terse. "Yes, Francesca, I am. I have a note for you—I was asked to deliver it myself." Dawn shoved the white envelope at her.

The front was pristine. Francesca turned it over, but the word Urgent was not printed on the envelope. She looked up. Dawn was hurrying back to her taxi. "Who gave you this?" she cried.

Dawn climbed into her hansom, closing the door and calling, "You must be very careful, Francesca. Very careful!"

"Please don't go," Francesca tried, but the hansom was already moving past her, the gelding in the traces trotting briskly toward the house, where it would circle back out of the driveway and onto Fifth Avenue. Her heart hammering, Francesca slit the envelope with her nail and extracted a piece of stationery. A woman's script greeted her. "Meet me at The Fountain at 4 pm today—SM."

She inhaled. Solange Marceaux had finally surfaced.

But why now? Solange was no longer even on her list of suspects, was she?

Of course she would meet her. Solange was still wanted for her participation in child abduction and prostitution. But she was going to have to rush. It would take twenty minutes to get downtown to the vast department store Siegel-Cooper, where the famed water fountain was. The fountain was a very popular meeting spot for the ladies, and Francesca did not doubt that was what the note referred to. She would not be able to dress up for her evening with Hart, she realized.

Francesca paid the driver, tipping him generously, and hurried to the house, dwelling upon the possibilities the note brought. She could not get over the timing of when she had received it.

Francis was on duty when she went inside. Still holding the note, she paused. "Is anyone at home? The house seems vacant." The last thing she needed was to be delayed by her mother.

"Most of the staff has left for Saratoga to get the house ready for the family," Francis said. "Your mother has decided that she and Mr. Cahill will leave tomorrow afternoon. I believe Mrs. Cahill is around the block with your sister, Miss Cahill. Your father is at the club."

"Thank you," she said, surprised that Julia had decided to leave the next day. She knew she would be pressured to do so as well, with Hart. But that was impossible. They were closing in on her portrait and the thief. She couldn't go anywhere, July Fourth or not.

Briefly worried, she rushed down the hall to Andrew's

library. Julia was formidable when her mind was made up. They would have a rousing battle over her staying behind in the city.

Hart's image was engraved on her mind, and Bragg's flashed there, as well. She wasn't so foolish as to contemplate meeting the madam alone. She picked up the receiver and asked for Mr. Hart's residence, her pulse beginning to pound. Although he had told her he was going downtown to his Bridge Street offices, she prayed he was home by now. When Alfred answered, her heart sank. "Alfred, where is Hart?" she cried. "He said he had business matters to attend, but I thought he'd be home by now!"

"I don't know, Miss Cahill. He might still be at his offices, or he might be dining somewhere. Mr. Hart rarely leaves me with an explicit schedule."

"Alfred, this is of the utmost urgency. Locate Calder and tell him he must meet me at The Fountain at four! But he must hide—we are on a case, and if he is recognized our quarry will flee. Tell him I am meeting Solange Marceaux." She made a mental calculation in her head. "And send someone to his offices, please, in case he is still there." If Hart was downtown on Bridge Street, it would take a servant forty-five minutes to reach him, even without traffic.

She prayed he would walk through his front door at any moment. What if he was traveling uptown, even now, while Alfred sent her message downtown?

She thanked Alfred and hung up, beginning to perspire. When she reached the operator at police headquarters and asked for Bragg, she was told he had stepped out.

She groaned. Now what?

"Miss Cahill, can I be of any help?"

She froze at the sound of Chief Farr's voice. "Hello, Chief," she managed to say. Her mind raced. There were warrants outstanding for Solange Marceaux's arrest. She could use the help of the police. But she wanted a word with the madam alone first. Yet even if she lied to Farr and told him to arrive at a later time, she feared he would arrive earlier to hide his men. She inhaled. "I'm afraid not. When you see the commissioner, would you ask him to meet me for a coffee at Siegel-Cooper, perhaps at a quarter past four? I have some new leads I'd like to discuss with him, but I must buy my niece a birthday present first."

"Sure," Farr said amiably. "I'll do just that."

Sweating, Francesca hung up. Well, if she had to confront the madam alone, she would. But she was hoping that either Hart or Bragg would get her messages and show up.

She heard the floorboards creak as someone paused on the threshold of the library.

They were a man's heavier footsteps. She turned, expecting to see her father standing there. Her heart dropped with sickening force.

"Hello," Bill Randall said pleasantly, closing the library doors behind him. He locked them. "I heard you are looking for me."

Shock gave way to fear. She had left her purse with her pistol in the front hall. She was defenseless—almost. What did he want? "Hello, Bill. Yes, we are looking for you."

His gaze was almost black, but he did not remind her of Hart, not at all. Something was wrong with this man, although it wasn't as obvious as with his sister. She tensed as he started toward her. "I haven't committed any crime, Francesca. In fact, I turned state's evidence on my poor sister. So why are the police looking for me? I can't even go home."

His intensity was frightening. "I am very, very sorry about Mary and your mother."

His odd smile vanished. "Like hell you are. Because of you, my sister was locked up at Bellevue...because of you, my poor mother is in the workhouse."

Francesca stepped back against the desk, groping for a paperweight. "Your sister murdered your father, Bill. I merely solved the crime!"

"You have destroyed my family," he said. "I intend to destroy you and my brother now!"

"Did you steal the painting? It was you, wasn't it?" she cried.

He slowly smiled at her. "Now you accuse me of being a thief? Why would I steal a painting, Francesca?"

Was he as insane as his sister? "Hart and I are over. It's in all the newspapers."

He laughed. "You are only over because someone locked you up on your wedding day. I wonder who that could be. I wish I had been there to see Hart jilted in front of three hundred guests."

"It was you, wasn't it? You locked me up—you stole the portrait. Where is it?" she cried desperately. How else would he know that she had been locked up? Or had he bribed a police officer to learn the fact?

He approached. She cringed against the desk, crowded there by him. His body pressed against hers, making her want to retch. He cupped her jaw, then slid his hand around her neck. "One snap is all it would take," he murmured roughly. "I would love to come to the funeral and watch Hart crying over your coffin."

He was going to kill her. She managed to close her right hand over the paperweight. "Where is the portrait?"

"I don't know." He smiled viciously at her. "For my sister, Francesca, and my poor, dear mother."

As his hand slowly tightened on her neck, she raised

the weight and slammed it at his temple. He saw it coming and dodged the blow, releasing her to do so. Francesca screamed at the top of her lungs. "Help!"

For one moment, Randall crouched before her, clearly debating murdering her anyway. Then he ran for the closed doors, unlocking them. They flew open. The doorman and a maid stood there. He shoved past them, vanishing down the hall. Francesca felt her knees give way. Francis and Bette would never be able to stop that madman.

"Miss Cahill! Are you all right?" Francis reached her first.

She was already recovering and reaching for the phone. By the time Bette had brought her a scotch whiskey, Farr was on the line. "Bill Randall just left my home."

"I'll get right on it."

CHAPTER EIGHTEEN

Wednesday, July 2, 1902
4:15 p.m.

SIEGEL-COOPER AND COMPANY took up an entire block on Sixth Avenue, between Eighteenth and Nineteenth streets. When Chicago-based Siegel-Cooper had first arrived in New York City, it set an entirely new standard for department stores in the city. Every competitor had imitated the great emporium, taking up vast retail spaces and filling them entirely with merchandise. The fountain was in the exact center of the store, a replica of the French sculpture *The Republic* in its center. It had become a popular meeting place for ladies on their way to have lunch, tea, shop or go to the afternoon theater. The refrain "Meet me at The Fountain" was often heard.

Francesca stood rigidly by the edge of the fountain, able to see the main Sixth Avenue entrance, as well as the entrances from the side streets. The store would close for the evening at five, but it was still relatively busy with customers, all of them women. Everyone seemed to be in a rush that afternoon, and she supposed a great deal of the present company would be outward bound on the morrow. She began to fidget, her tension high. It was fifteen minutes past four. Where was Solange Marceaux?

She clutched the small penknife Hart had given her as a wedding gift in the palm of her right hand. Her pistol was tucked in the waistband of her skirt, beneath her jacket, instead of in her purse. Of course, she was not wearing gloves, the better to handle either weapon. She supposed she was very nervous.

And why wouldn't she be? She had just had a frightening encounter with Bill Randall. He was clearly mentally unstable.

Francesca knew she must forget about the terrible encounter. She had to remain on guard. She was about to confront a very ruthless woman, who despised her just as much as Randall.

Francesca stared at the glass doors that opened onto Sixth Avenue. No one came in. She inhaled. From her past experience with the madam, she felt certain that Solange would not think twice about murdering her on the spot. Or, she would bring her thugs with her and order her dumped in the East River, with shackles on her wrists and ankles.

With her ungloved left hand, she wiped a trickle of sweat from her brow. Her anxiety increased. She hadn't seen a glimpse of Hart or Bragg, so she assumed she was working alone. But she was armed. She was ready. Whatever Solange intended, she would be on her toes, anticipating her every move.

A beautifully dressed woman in royal blue was coming up the aisle from the Eighteenth Street entrance. Francesca tensed, for she had Solange's proportions and pale hair, but as she came closer, she finally saw her face. Her heart sank. It was not Solange.

Someone tapped her shoulder from behind…a woman's soft touch.

Francesca whirled, her heart exploding in fright.

"Hello, Francesca." Mary Randall smiled at her. "Fancy meeting you here."

For one moment, Francesca glanced wildly past Mary for Bill. But her brother was not present. Mary laughed with real delight. She was a thin, dark-haired woman. Malice danced in her eyes. "He's not here. It's just you and me—you bitch." And Mary pointed a tiny derringer at her heart.

Francesca did not move, shocked.

"Have I stunned you into speechlessness?" Mary laughed again.

Francesca recovered. She considered a way to escape. There were customers moving about the fountain and the store's various aisles, but if she screamed, she had no doubt that Mary would shoot her in the heart. Mary's wide grin spoke volumes, as did the fervor in her eyes. Somehow, when she spoke, she kept her tone calm. "Mary, I would like to talk to you. But you must put the gun away. We will attract attention."

Mary was mocking. "I may be mad, but I am very, very clever, Francesca. I am not putting the gun away. We will certainly attract attention when I kill you, you lying, scheming, immoral bitch. You know I am capable of it."

Francesca knew that she must not discuss their past. Mary had been put behind bars because of Francesca's success in solving Paul Randall's murder. Fighting for calm, she said, "How on earth did you know to reach me with such a ruse?"

"I have learned to be adept at bribery, Francesca. How do you think I got out of Bellevue? You have destroyed my family, but Bill still has means—and he would never leave me to rot in an asylum!"

"He loves you very much," she said. Her heart was hammering with terrific force. Perspiration trickled from her temple, but she did not attempt to wipe it away.

"Oh, stop patronizing me! You have been pursuing Bill. Apparently you have also been after Solange Marceaux. We can sleuth just as you do, Francesca." Her eyes held a brilliant, fanatical light. She added softly, with a grin, "I think you have met your match."

Francesca wet her lips. "I have just seen your brother. He is very angry, and I don't blame him. But more violence doesn't solve anything. I am very sorry about your mother, but you do know she will be released in the fall?"

"Shut up!" Mary jammed the gun into her breast and Francesca heard the trigger click. Her heart stopped—but no shot sounded.

Francesca thought she might faint. Sweat poured down her body.

"It's called Russian roulette, Francesca. Even I don't know which chamber my bullet is in." She laughed. "You should see your face!"

She was dizzy and ready to faint. Mary only had one bullet, but was it in the next chamber? It was clear she didn't care if she killed Francesca. "Mary! The police will be here at any moment. Put the gun away!"

"I don't believe you—and if they show up, so what? I will simply pull the trigger—and pull the trigger—and pull the trigger—until you are dead." She spat.

The spittle struck on Francesca's cheek, but she didn't dare wipe it. She clutched the penknife more tightly, yet how could she go up against this madwoman, who had a pistol pressed into her heart? "Why do you hate me so?" she cried unthinkingly.

"Because of you, I have no family! And you love that bastard who destroyed my mother! The two of you deserve one another."

She knew that pleading with an insane woman was a lost cause. But she said, "Hart is your brother. Nothing that has happened is his fault!"

"Hart is a bastard!" Mary screamed, flushing red.

A movement caught her eye and her gaze went from Mary's rabid grin to Hart's fierce expression.

Hart had come! Her relief was consuming, but it vanished as instantly as it had come. He stood several feet behind Mary, near some potted palms. He had obviously seen Mary pull the trigger—he was as white as a ghost. She felt certain he had also overheard them. He shook his head immediately at her. His warning was clear—engaging Mary was a mistake. She could not be reasoned with.

Francesca looked back at Mary, so she would not comprehend what was happening, but not before she thought she saw Hart produce his own gun.

If Hart shot Mary from behind, Mary would shoot her, because Francesca felt certain her finger was on the trigger, unless his aim was perfect, killing her instantly. She doubted he was such a marksman—he had never mentioned being adept as a sniper. "Why don't you take your finger off the trigger, Mary?" Francesca asked loudly. It was so hard to breathe.

She didn't dare look Hart's way again. She prayed he had heard her.

"Because I want to watch you at my feet, bleeding to death and begging for mercy!" Mary's eyes bulged. "You have destroyed my entire life! Because of you, I am locked up and called insane! You are the insane one, Francesca, to pose naked for a painting, for the entire world to see!"

Mary knew about the nude portrait. In that moment, she didn't care. She only wanted to get away from the barrel of Mary's gun, which continued to press into her breast. "I never meant to hurt anyone," she said desperately. "Your father was dead. I wanted to help!"

"You wanted to help Hart!" Mary accused.

Mary was right. Francesca just stood there, sweating and panting.

Then Mary smiled slyly. "I must admit, you are a very beautiful woman, Francesca."

Francesca licked her lips. Mary had seen the portrait. She and Bill had to be the thieves. "Where is the portrait?"

"As if I'd tell you!" she crowed.

"You locked me in the gallery, Mary, didn't you? You and your brother lured me there on my wedding day."

"Oh, poor Francesca, she missed her wedding!" Mary laughed. Then she jammed the gun deeper into Francesca's bosom. "Let's go. If I have to, I'll kill you here, but I prefer to do so in an alley. I don't like Bellevue, Francesca. I am not going back. I'd rather die."

"If you murder me, you will never be free again," Francesca tried desperately.

"But you will be dead and I will be overjoyed. And I am not going back to jail. Let's go. Turn around, bitch. And if you scream, I will shoot you."

Francesca looked into her wild eyes and knew there was no reasoning with her. As she turned, Mary kept the gun pressed against the side of her breast. How was she going to get away?

She glimpsed Bragg on the fountain's other side, crouched down by a counter, a gun in his hand. He nodded his head once, hard.

He wanted her to leave the emporium, or at least move forward.

Did he have officers outside? Or did he intend to take a shot at Mary once he had a better angle?

She wanted to glance backward over her shoulder at Hart to see what he wanted her to do, but she didn't dare.

"Move!" Mary screamed.

Francesca's heart lurched with dread as several women with shopping bags turned to glance at them. A pair of shopgirls was passing by, as well. One turned to look at them. "Are you all right, miss?" the dark-haired girl asked with concern.

"Mind your own business," Mary spat. "Move, Francesca, now!"

Francesca saw the dark-haired girl pale; she thought she had seen the gun. "I am fine," she tried.

Both shopgirls ran away from the fountain, and Francesca heard one scream, "She has a gun! The lady has a gun!"

And suddenly, she heard a gunshot from her right. Women ran past the fountain and through the aisles, some screaming. Shopping bags went flying. Instantly Francesca realized that Bragg had fired his gun to create pandemonium. Mary hesitated, her eyes wide with surprise. Francesca saw Hart standing ten or twelve feet behind them. He was aiming his revolver at the back of Mary's head.

His expression was twisted, and she knew why. If he missed Mary, he could hit her.

It was time to do something. Francesca still held the penknife in her right hand. She clicked it open and jammed it upward into Mary's ribs, then tried to twist away from Mary and the gun she was holding.

Mary's eyes widened as she was stabbed and she cried out, "Bitch!"

Two shots sounded. Francesca felt the impact and she stumbled, going to her knees. The burning pain was along the side of her shoulder. Mary gasped and her gun clattered to the floor. She took off at a run.

Francesca tried to hold herself up on her hands and knees, but it was too painful and she fell onto the floor.

"Francesca!"

Hart steadied her, pulling her against his chest. She cried out, his touch on her right arm causing so much pain. "You will be all right," he said roughly.

She somehow opened her eyes to look up at him, wanting to smile and tell him she was fine. But his image was hazy, swimming oddly, and she couldn't seem to smile at all. "Mary?"

Bragg appeared in her distorted line of vision. His expression was incredibly concerned as he ripped her sleeve open. She fought not to weep. "It's a graze, Francesca." To Hart, he said, "Put pressure on it. I'm going after Mary." He leaped up and ran off.

The burning was unbearable. She wanted to whimper; she refused. Somehow, she looked up at Hart.

"I shot you," he said, his eyes stark.

But Bragg had said it was a graze. She thought she told him that. She wanted to reassure him. But he was spinning now, far more rapidly than before, and she knew she was about to faint. She tried to tell him, but there was only darkness.

"You will hardly realize you have a wound in a couple of days." Rourke Bragg smiled cheerfully at her.

Francesca lay on the sofa in Hart's most intimate salon, a lavish red-and-gold affair that his extended family tended to gather in. She had been propped up with pillows, and he'd given her a scotch the moment they'd arrived at his home. There was little pain now—just a dull throbbing. She smiled at Rourke, who had cleaned, disinfected and bandaged the wound. As Bragg had said, it was a mere graze. But it was Hart who consumed her attention.

He stood behind Rourke, having shed both his jacket and vest, his sleeves rolled up, his shirt unbuttoned at the neck. His tie was gone. He held an untouched drink, and she thought it his second. He looked very grim. When she had first glanced at him upon awakening from her faint in Siegel-Cooper, his expression had been ravaged with worry and concern. There was one obvious conclusion to draw—he had been terrified for her.

He loved her still.

Francesca smiled at him.

He did not smile back. He said to Rourke, "Thank God you were home."

Hart had taken her into his arms the moment she had awoken and carried her to his coach outside. He hadn't asked her where she wished to go; he had directed Raoul to his mansion, using his tie to bandage her bleeding wound. She understood. If Rourke were home, she would be treated far more swiftly than if they went to a public emergency room at a nearby hospital. But what truly pleased her was that he hadn't considered sending her to her home, not for an instant.

Rourke snapped closed his satchel and stood. "Francesca would have been fine even if you had treated the wound yourself. Now, would you mind telling me what happened?"

Before she could open her mouth, Hart said, "As always, Francesca rushed off to save the world by herself without a thought of the danger."

He was angry with her. She hid a smile and wriggled her toes. "My feet hurt," she said. "Would you?" She gave Hart a sweet look.

A cashmere throw was over the lower half of her body. Hart set his drink down somewhat forcefully, and took a single stride to her side. He removed each of her shoes as if it were a huge task, his face very, very grim.

He still loves me, she thought happily. She realized Rourke was staring and she smiled at him.

He smiled back. "Feeling better?"

"It must be the whiskey."

"It must be." He winked at her.

"I can't imagine what you both find so amusing." Hart was cold. "I arrived at an emporium to find Francesca with a gun to her chest and my damn half sister about to kill her."

Rourke's good humor vanished. "I thought Mary Randall was incarcerated in an asylum."

"She escaped," Hart said tersely, "with my brother's help."

"Half brother," Francesca corrected. "And we are assuming Bill helped her escape. We do not yet know that for a fact."

Hart's look of annoyance increased.

Rourke glanced at Francesca. She decided now was not the time to mention that Bill had paid her a call—in her very own home. She'd save that for later in the evening. She smiled yet again.

"You are in exceedingly high spirits, considering that I shot you," Hart exclaimed angrily.

"You shot her?" Rourke asked.

"There were two shots—Bragg might have been the one to graze my shoulder," Francesca said instantly.

"No, Francesca." Hart was adamant—and furious. "For once, your intellect is deserting you. Bragg was standing on your right, at an almost ninety-degree angle. I was standing behind you. I moved slightly left when the chaos began, hoping for a better shot. There is no possible way that Rick shot you in the left shoulder."

He was right, she thought. Realizing how upset he was, her heart melted. "It was an accident. Mary wanted to kill me. You had to try to stop her."

He picked up his drink and slammed a third of it down.

Rourke pulled an ottoman over and sat beside her.

"I am very sorry, Francesca, for what you have gone through."

"Thank you." She glanced from Rourke to Hart. "They must be the thieves. Did you hear our conversation?"

"I caught bits and pieces of it."

"Mary has seen the portrait. She was bragging about it—and gloating."

Hart gave her a dangerous look, but did not move.

"You cannot possibly blame yourself!" she cried.

"Why not? We are back to square one. I commissioned the damn portrait. You could have died." He was final.

She became uneasy. He loved her. Surely they would reconcile!

Rourke laid his comforting palm on her good shoulder. "Where is Mary? Did Rick apprehend her?"

Hart turned away, so Francesca said, "He was chasing after her, Rourke, when I fainted. I don't know what happened afterward."

"I'll give HQ a call. If he is not there, I'll call him at home."

"He won't be home, not at this hour," Francesca said.

Both men looked at her, Rourke with interest, Hart with moody speculation. Hart said, "Rick is either at headquarters or he is on his way here, to check up on Francesca. You may trust me on that."

"I'll call him right now to let him know that she is all right." Rourke paused. "Is there anything else that you need, Francesca?"

"I am fine."

"That wound is like a minor burn. Do you want laudanum to help you to sleep?"

She shook her head. Rourke smiled and left.

And they were alone.

Hart was staring. Francesca stared back, wishing he

wouldn't blame himself for her having been shot—and for everything else. "I am fine, Hart, really."

"I can't tolerate your running about town, chasing madwomen and criminals with no one at your side!" he exploded. "I nearly had a stroke when Alfred gave me your message."

She tried to get up. "I thought I was meeting Solange, but it was a ruse, obviously. I am so glad Alfred found you."

He strode to her and took Rourke's place on the ottoman. "Don't you dare. You could faint." His hand closed over her right arm as he pushed her back onto the couch. "You rushed off to meet Solange, fully aware of how dangerous she is—while not knowing if I would even receive your message."

For once in her life, she had no interest in debating the merits of the case. "I think I knew, in my heart, that you would come."

"Really?" He made a hard sound and slid his fingers to her neck. "How could you go to meet her alone? Why couldn't you have waited to locate me? Why do you have to be so impulsive, so impervious to danger? Francesca, you are mortal!"

"You are so worried about me, Hart," she breathed, acutely aware of his large, strong hand as it moved to her nape.

"Damn it, Francesca," he breathed. "It is not amusing. Mary almost murdered you tonight—right in front of me—while I watched."

She went still. As distraught as he was, his eyes were smoldering. She lifted her hand and clasped his rough jaw. "I love how worried you are. I love how much you care."

His gaze moved to her mouth. "Of course you do."

"Hart?" she asked softly.

Slowly, with effort, his gaze lifted to hers.

She rubbed his jaw, and then slid her hand down his strong throat and into the open V of his shirt. "You will never give me up. You can't give me up. And I won't let you, anyway. You are stuck with me—forever."

ROURKE PAUSED IN THE lobby of police headquarters. As Francesca had suspected, Rick had been at police headquarters when he had called, approximately an hour ago. But Rick hadn't given him more than thirty seconds on the telephone. His only interest had been in knowing if Francesca was all right. Then he had told Rourke he had police affairs to attend and that a long night lay ahead. Before Rourke could even ask about Mary, he had told him to wish Francesca well and hung up.

Rourke loved both his older brothers. He considered Hart a sibling, even if they did not share blood or a name. He was very fond of Francesca, but like everyone in the family, the love triangle that had developed worried him immensely. Because Rick was married, and Hart so shockingly alone, he had concluded that he must root for Hart and Francesca. When he had learned what had happened at the Siegel-Cooper emporium, he had been instantly concerned.

Tonight had proven one thing: Hart was still, obviously, head over heels for Francesca. He felt certain that, in time, they would work their relationship out. He knew no one as determined and tenacious as Francesca. Not that her work wasn't cut out for her. Hart was infuriatingly stubborn.

It was Rick he was concerned about now.

He held a paper sack that contained a bottle of scotch. It was time to sit down with his brother and have a very long conversation—whether Rick was amenable or not. He had never been to police headquarters, much less Mulberry Street, and he was curious as he glanced around.

Several civilians stood at the reception desk, arguing with the officers there. One woman was clearly a prostitute. Two men were in the holding cell, both passed out from an overconsumption of alcohol. He did not know where Rick's office was, but he doubted it was on the ground floor. There was an elevator and a staircase on his right.

"C'mish?"

Rourke turned and realized the officer who had approached had mistaken him for his brother. That was not an infrequent occurrence. "I am the commissioner's brother, Rourke Bragg. Is his office upstairs?"

When he was directed to the third floor, he proceeded to the stairs, forgoing the elevator. Rourke took the steps two at a time. Rick's door was open, his office vacant, but he knew he was in the right place. Family photographs covered the mantel over the small fireplace. There was only one photograph of Leigh Anne—a bridal portrait. There were no pictures of Rick and Leigh Anne together and he wondered what the absence meant. It worried him. How could it not? He was aware of his brother's unhappiness.

Then he heard voices coming from another room. Recognizing Rick's calm tones, Rourke didn't hesitate. He walked over to a closed door with an opaque glass window. A woman was screaming shrilly from within.

He heard his brother say, "This is a one-time offer, Mary. I will not make it again. Tell me where the portrait is and I will make certain you are housed like a princess when you return to Bellevue."

"Go to hell!" she shouted. "Even if I knew where it was, I wouldn't tell you, you bastard!"

He heard a glass crash and he winced. Bragg said, "I am not done with her. Find her a chair, put her in a corner and cuff her. Maybe a night without sleep will do wonders for her temper." The door to the interrogation room swung open.

Rourke smiled as he came face-to-face with his brother. "Sometimes, it is prudent for Mohammed to go to the mountain."

Rick blinked. "I am very busy."

"You are always busy. It is a tiresome excuse."

Rick flushed. "I suppose I can spare you a few moments."

Rourke glanced past him and saw Mary Randall standing with a policeman and Chief Farr, her white face blotched red, her eyes ablaze with anger. She was a tiny, shrewish-looking woman, too small to hurt anyone—or at least one would think so. She was so clearly unbalanced that he shivered. He saw a broken drinking glass on the floor.

"She claims she doesn't know where the portrait is," Rick said, leading Rourke into his office.

Rourke closed the door and took a bottle of very fine, very old scotch whiskey from the paper sack. "Do you believe her?"

"Unfortunately, I do." Bragg sat down, sighing, but he looked with interest at the bottle of scotch.

Rourke could feel how tired his brother was. "Is it worth it?" He uncapped the scotch, took a swig and handed the bottle to his brother.

Rick took a long draft, like a very thirsty man. "Is what worth it?"

"This job." Rick carried the burdens of law enforcement for an entire city upon his shoulders. It might as well have been the burdens of an entire planet.

Rick made a harsh, mirthless sound. "Someone has to fight crime and corruption."

"Yes, someone does. So is it worth it?"

Rick got up, walked to a small bureau and returned

with two glasses. Rourke poured. Rick said, "There are good days and bad days. There are days of victory—and days of immense frustration and defeat. Even worse, there are days of terrible tragedy." He stared, pausing. "You heard Mary. What did you think?"

Rourke sipped the scotch, thinking about how heroic his older brother was. "She is insane, Rick. She might very well believe her own lies—or she might be telling the truth."

He absorbed that. "How is Francesca?"

That hadn't taken very long, Rourke thought. "She suffered a graze. It is truly nothing."

Not looking at him, Rick drank from his scotch, asking quietly, "Is she at Hart's or at her home?"

"She is at Hart's."

There was silence. Rick finished his scotch swiftly and Rourke refilled it. Rourke said, "They will probably reconcile sooner or later. Hart is beside himself with worry for her. He remains in love with her."

Rick looked up coldly. "He is destroying her bit by bit, piece by piece, day by day."

"That is unfair. I happen to think that she is the best thing to have ever happened to him."

Rick drank and said harshly, "I agree." He stared down at one of his yellow pads darkly.

Rourke said quietly, "Are you still in love with her?"

Rick slowly looked up, his expression unhappy. "I am a married man, in case you have forgotten."

"Married men are quite capable of falling in love with other women."

"I have a duty toward my wife—my invalid wife."

"Rick."

"Fine! I care deeply—and I always will. There is no one I respect or admire more than Francesca." He did not look at Rourke, sipping his scotch and clearly lost in a great many dark thoughts.

Rourke grimaced. This was exactly as he had suspected. "Once upon a time, you admired and loved your wife."

Rick looked up. "I was a boy, and I was infatuated as only a boy can be." Then he added, refilling his glass, "Why are you doing this? I don't want to have this discussion."

"I am doing this because I am your brother and you are so terribly unhappy." Rourke cradled his glass and stared. "I want to help—I just don't know how."

Rick met his gaze unflinchingly. He spoke thoughtfully, after a pause. "You're a doctor, so maybe you can help. Leigh Anne is unhappy, Rourke. She is filled with melancholy. I am worried. This accident has changed her entirely. She is drinking, and dosing herself with laudanum. I don't know what to do. She refuses to discuss anything with me—in fact, she does her best to avoid me."

Rourke said gently, "It might take some time for her to adjust to losing the ability to walk. Or she might never adjust. Unfortunately, some people rebound from tragedy, others do not."

Rick leaned back in his chair. He made a harsh sound. "I already know she will not recover. Do not tell me to think otherwise, to have hope. She isn't a very strong woman…she has never fought for anything. And the truth is, I am doing my best to avoid her, as well." He suddenly covered his face with his hands.

His brother was crushed, not by the burdens of law enforcement, but by the burden of his marriage, and possibly, the loss of Francesca Cahill. "Why do you feel that you must avoid her? She is your wife."

"She has made it very clear that I am intruding

whenever I set a foot in my own home." Rick looked up and stared. "In truth, I have never forgiven her for leaving me and I couldn't forgive her for returning to me! Did you know that she bribed me into reconciliation?"

"No, I did not." Rourke was surprised. "I do not know Leigh Anne well. She did walk out on you shortly after you were married. No one can blame you for your anger. But she did return, and she returned to fight Francesca for you."

Rick stared. "That is unfortunate."

Rourke said gently, "What are you going to do?"

"I don't know." Rick drained the rest of his glass and set it down hard on his desk. "Do you want to know the worst part?"

"Yes, I do," Rourke said seriously.

"Sometimes, when I look at her, I feel nothing but guilt."

"Why on earth would you feel guilty?"

It was a long moment before he spoke. "I was furious that she had returned. I was cruel. I tried to chase her away. I knew exactly what I was doing. In a way, I am responsible for her accident."

Rourke gasped. "She was run over by a coach! You were hardly involved, much less responsible. My God, you are the most rational man I know, yet logic has completely escaped you."

"Has it?" Rick turned away. A long silence fell.

Rourke's mind raced. How could this impasse be solved? If Rick was right, Leigh Anne would remain a changed woman, for the worse. He was afraid she did not have the strength to fight for her marriage now. He was even more afraid of where that left his brother.

"None of it matters, though, does it?" Rick interrupted his thoughts. "I am her husband, until death do us part, whether I hate her, love her, desire her or dread looking at her...it doesn't matter. I have to take care of her. If I don't, who will?"

Rourke was grim. "Could I suggest a stay in a sanitarium or hospital? If Leigh Anne is becoming dependent on alcohol and laudanum, she needs medical attention. And she can hardly be a proper mother under such circumstances."

Rick started. "I could never do such a thing."

"Hospitalization might be in her best interests," Rourke tried, meaning it. "And I suggest that you seriously consider it, at least as an option."

Abruptly Rick stood. "I could never live with such a decision."

Rourke was grim. "Then you are stuck."

"Yes, I am."

Rourke wanted to tell him that no man could live this way, in such a state of distress and conflict. But he knew his brother would not listen. His brother's next words confirmed it.

"There is no point in dwelling on what might have been. There is no point in bemoaning the present. We are married, and she isn't well. We are fostering two little girls. I have a family to provide for, and I intend to do just that."

FRANCESCA FELT HART's heart pounding beneath her hand, its beat becoming more rapid. He finally said, "Forever is a long time."

"Yes, it is."

His heated gaze held hers. A pulse throbbed in his throat. "You are very sure of yourself tonight."

She smiled, briefly. "Yes, I am."

"I openly confess that I was terrified for you."

"I know," she whispered, thrilling. She slid her hand

across the rock-hard slabs of his chest, across his taut nipples.

He seized her wrist. "I should send you home."

Although he held her hand still, she rubbed her thumb across his warm skin. "Why?"

He inhaled. "Because Julia will murder me, Francesca. Because…we are estranged."

"No, she won't. She adores you, and she will be thrilled if we spend the evening together." She added, "And are we truly estranged?"

His face hardened. "Did it ever cross your mind that you might die tonight?"

"Of course it did. I was terribly frightened—and I was so relieved when I saw you behind Mary." She meant her every word. "I am not a foolish woman, Hart. I am well aware of my mortality."

"Damn it," he whispered, leaning closer to her. "You are so damn reckless!"

Inches separated their lips. Francesca lifted her face and feathered his hard mouth with her softer one. He did not move. "I almost died tonight," she whispered, aware of exactly what she was doing.

"Now you play me?" He was incredulous, but his tone was thick and he did not move away.

"But you love me," she said. "So, yes, I dare to play you a bit."

He stared, breathing hard. "Yes, Francesca, if it makes you happy to hear my ultimate confession, I do love you. But that doesn't mean we are suited—"

Even though it hurt to use her left hand, she caught his face with both her hands and kissed him deeply. He opened immediately, kissing her back while pushing her down on the sofa. His huge body settled atop her as their mouths fused. He was already aroused; she thrilled. And then he broke the kiss.

"Am I hurting you?" he demanded.

She caught his nape. "You can't hurt me, not like this. I want you, Hart."

For one moment he stared, desire searing his eyes, but she saw despair and anguish, too. He had been so afraid for her! And she saw the moment the internal battle was won. Hart claimed her mouth, hard.

The possession was absolute—and it told her everything she needed to know. But his urgency stunned her. Francesca opened and their tongues mated greedily. She reached for his shirt; he reached for hers. And as he rained hot, wet kisses and bites down her bare breasts and torso, she lay back, writhing and incoherent now, her nails raking his back. One thing was clear: Hart wanted her as never before.

On the floor now, he reared up over her. Their gazes met. Francesca reached up to touch his face. She desperately wanted him to say those three magical words again.

"Don't speak," he said harshly. "I am never giving you up."

CHAPTER NINETEEN

Thursday, July 3, 1902
5:30 a.m.

THE MOMENT HE stepped inside the small, dark front hall of his home, he knew that the children were asleep. The Victorian house was achingly silent. Or was it his heart that ached?

Rick Bragg walked quietly inside, shutting the front door, as some birds began their morning songs outside. He had actually caught a few hours of sleep in his office, in his desk chair. He supposed that, if his marital situation did not improve, he should get a sofa for his office.

He felt old beyond his years as he slowly went upstairs, trying not to awaken anyone, feeling like an intruder. Who was he fooling? He and Leigh Anne were at an impasse. She did not want to fight for their marriage, and he was losing interest in waging the battle by himself.

But he had meant his every word when he had shared that bottle of scotch with Rourke last night. He would never abandon Leigh Anne, not in any way. He wouldn't give her a divorce, and he would never send her to an institution. This was her home.

No, he corrected silently, it was their home. And his heart ached even more strongly.

The door to their bedroom was on his left; he ignored it. The door to the girls' room was on his right. It was open, and he paused on the threshold there.

He stared at the sleeping children, his heart swelling with affection. He had become so fond of them, and they deserved a good home.

Leigh Anne was desperate to adopt the girls. He was grim. How could they go forward and adopt the girls when their marriage was in such a shambles? Katie and Dot deserved a mother who was not stricken with self-pity and prone to taking brandy in her morning tea. They needed a mother capable of nurturing them in every possible way. Every time he saw Katie, she was filled with anxiety and tension. She worried day in and day out about Leigh Anne. No child should have to bear such a burden.

But his wife's intentions were the very best. She doted on the girls and she needed them.

He would never send them to another foster home. But it didn't seem right to continue with the adoption. He stared at the girls, simply not knowing what to do, feeling utterly helpless—the way he felt about his wife.

He walked into the bedroom then. He kissed Dot, who was smiling in her sleep. He hoped she was dreaming about fat ponies, happy clowns and red-and-white candy canes. Katie was moving about restlessly, her small face set in frown lines. He sighed and kissed her, too, stroking her dark hair. Instantly, her eyes opened and she was wide-awake.

"Everything will be all right," he said in his most reassuring voice.

She smiled sleepily at him.

Katie was fond of him now, too, and she loved Leigh Anne. At least he could put a roof over their heads, food on the table and some security into their lives. "Go back to sleep," he whispered.

Her eyes drifted closed, and he saw that the frown was gone from her expression. Maybe he could somehow make the girls comfortable, secure and happy, in spite of the discord in his marriage. Maybe it was best that he was absent from the house as much as possible, since that satisfied Leigh Anne.

Tension stiffened every fiber of his being as he entered the master suite. He tried not to look at Leigh Anne as he walked past her as she slept, taking off his shirt as he did so. But twisted images flashed, mocking him—haunting him. Would he always remember the first time they had met—when she was so breathtakingly beautiful? Did he have to remember the first time they had danced—the first time they had kissed? Did he have to recall his most wild, youthful yearnings? She had destroyed far more than their marriage when she had fled to Europe; she had destroyed his hopes and dreams.

More memories came, recent ones—of their intense, fiercely sexual battles, and then her withdrawal, her drinking, her sorrow.

He looked at her. The woman he had fallen in love with had never existed. What had existed were his hopes and dreams and the utter naiveté of a young, optimistic man.

Sex had been the foundation of their reconciliation. There had never been love, affection, shared interests and values. So when tragedy finally struck, it meant that they were left with nothing.

And in that instant, he realized that nothing could heal their marriage, because she had already decided that it was over. And why was he at all surprised? She had left them when they were newlyweds. Selfishly, she had walked out, making the decision to end things without even a discussion. As selfishly, she had decided now that she would not participate in their marriage anymore.

He felt as if he was having an epiphany as he stood there. It was over—in fact, his marriage had never even begun.

He had never loved her; she had never loved him.

There was only one woman he loved, and she was hell-bent on marrying his brother.

He strode to a bureau and undressed, feeling vicious now. He was strong, he would manage—he would do what was best for everyone—care for everyone—provide for everyone—whether Leigh Anne wanted it or not.

His bedside telephone rang.

Naked, he leaped into his drawers as it rang again. The sound was a loud jangle, yet Leigh Anne never stirred, and he wondered how much laudanum she had taken. When he reached the phone, she hadn't moved. It was the chief.

"We got him, boss," Farr said, his tone smug. "My boys got Randall as he was trying to get into his house about an hour ago."

"Perfect," Bragg said, feeling savage. "I'll be right down." He hung up, wanting to call Francesca. But it was only six in the morning. Still, servants would be up. He'd leave a message.

Andrew Cahill picked up the phone.

"I'm sorry to bother you at this hour, Andrew," Bragg said. "But I have news, and I think Francesca will be very pleased to hear it."

"She isn't here, Rick. Because of her injury, she stayed at Hart's last night."

Of course she had. It felt as if someone was twisting an ice pick in his chest. "Thank you, Andrew. And again, I am sorry to have bothered you." He hung up and saw Leigh Anne watching him.

"I have to go," he said. "It is police business."

"You had a telephone call, Francesca."

Hart's breath feathered her cheek. Francesca slowly awoke, deliciously sated. As she stretched beneath the covers, catlike, she recalled Hart making love to her numerous times. Eventually she had been put to bed in a guest room. Had he actually pulled the covers up? She grinned, aware that she was deliciously naked.

He was fully dressed in his shirt and trousers, the sleeves uncuffed. As he leaned over her, his expression was wry. "Good morning, Francesca."

She reached for his jaw, desire causing her to shiver. As she did, she thought about the fact that she had not gone home last night. "I am ruined, Hart." He'd have to marry her now!

"You're a virgin," he said calmly. "And a very pleased one, at that."

She rolled her eyes. "Barely."

"Barely is enough." He sat down by her hip, pulled her into his arms and kissed her, very, very thoroughly. Francesca was so surprised by the open display of affection that when he ended the kiss, she blinked speechlessly at him. They were surely reconciled, she thought breathlessly.

"Do not ask," he said flatly, standing. "Bragg called. Randall is in custody."

Her mind sprang to life. "I have to go."

"You had better stop at home first, and soothe your parents. Andrew just called, as well."

In the act of leaping naked from the bed, she froze.

He smiled rather appreciatively. "I called them last night and explained that your wound made it inconvenient for you to go home. But your father is not very happy with me."

She threw herself at him and hugged him hard, then kissed him quickly on the lips. "I do love you!" She dived into her drawers. "Mary has seen the portrait—Bill must be the thief." She found her chemise and shrugged it on.

"Please leave so I can get dressed. Will you meet me downtown? Surely you want to hear Bill confess."

"If you tell me how long you will be, I will chauffeur you downtown, Francesca."

She wanted to tell him five minutes, but she sighed. "An hour. I am sure I will be thoroughly grilled by both Andrew and Julia."

"I'll pick you up then," Hart said. He touched her chin, his gaze impossibly warm. "Good luck."

IT TOOK ANDREW only thirty seconds to confront her. Francesca had barely walked through the front door when her father appeared in the entrance hall. He instantly faltered, his gaze going wide at the sight of her bloodstained shirtwaist. Knowing she looked awful in the bloody shirt, and intending to use her brush with danger to her full advantage, Francesca sailed forward and hugged him. "It was only a graze, Papa, but it did hurt, terribly! That must have been the reason I fell asleep on Hart's couch after Rourke treated the wound."

Andrew's gaze lifted and he said grimly, "It was half past eleven when Hart called me, Francesca. Can you imagine how worried your mother and I were?"

She heard her mother's heels rapidly clicking as she approached from the hallway. Lowering his voice, Andrew said, "I did not tell her you were shot. She would have never slept a wink. I said there was an incident that prevented you from coming home, a brush with another criminal element, and that you were unhurt."

He whirled as Julia appeared. "Julia, I confess to a vast deception last night, but it is only a graze. Francesca is unharmed, so do not worry yourself."

Julia stumbled, caught herself on the banister and turned white. "I do not believe what I am seeing!" she gasped. "Oh, I cannot abide this sleuthing of yours!"

Francesca rushed forward. "Mama, I will admit that I was shot at, but Hart was there—he rescued me."

"Frankly, I do not want to know the details, as long as you are safe. Francesca, we are off to the Springs at noon. Your bags have been packed and sent on ahead, dear."

There was no time to relish having successfully diverted Julia from an attack on her profession. Francesca prepared for battle. "I cannot go to the Springs today, Mama, but I will come very shortly. Our number-one suspect is in custody and I am on my way downtown with Hart."

Julia's hands fisted on her hips, but before she could speak, Andrew stepped between them. Francesca tensed, because he was very angry. "Papa? Surely you understand that I must go to headquarters today."

"Oh, I understand. I understand that you are twenty-one years old, and madly in love. Or so you believe! But you are a lady, Francesca. No matter how hurt, you cannot spend the night with a gentleman, let alone a disreputable rake like Calder Hart."

"Andrew," Julia began, but he cut her off.

"Francesca cannot run about this city as if she is an amoral socialite."

Francesca felt color flooding her face. Andrew was never so critical of her! "We are affianced," she tried to reassure him. "And I was hurt." She didn't dare try to tell him that they had done nothing wrong.

"Really?" His tone was cold. "I do not see his ring on your finger. Not that that matters! I have come to my final conclusion, Francesca, and that is that your having jilted him at the altar on Saturday was for the best."

She cried out. "Papa," she began in horrified protest.

But Julia interrupted. "Andrew, we must prepare to leave the city. Hart is going to join us in the Springs!"

"No." He did not look at his wife. "I have had enough.

Hart is an unconscionable man. I have never liked him and I have never trusted him—and that will never change. You belong with someone like Rick Bragg. You are a woman of virtue, Francesca, and you deserve a man of great morality! Against my better judgment, I was forced into accepting this marriage. Well, I rule this roost. You are my daughter, Francesca, and while you might think me cruel now, I am looking after your best interests. You are not marrying Hart, not now, not ever."

Francesca was struck speechless.

Julia said harshly, "And you do not intend to discuss such a monumental decision with me?"

"Hart has played you for a fool," Andrew said. Then he turned to Francesca. "I suggest you go upstairs and refresh yourself. We are leaving this house at eleven." He strode down the hall, vanishing into the corridor.

A terrible silence fell.

Julia cried, "You should have come home last night."

Guilt assailed her. "Mama—I love him."

Tears filled Julia's eyes. "I know you do, but Francesca…!"

"I am going to marry him eventually. What are we going to do about Papa?" she asked with real concern. She was certain that this was no passing fancy. Andrew had made up his mind and he would not change it, no matter what happened next. But nothing would stop her from marrying Hart, not even her beloved father.

"We have all summer to work on your father. Leave him to me," Julia said firmly.

Francesca was not relieved, but she nodded. "Mama, don't you want to see the culprit responsible for luring me away from my wedding brought to justice?"

"You know that I do."

"Hart certainly does. He said he will not leave town until that culprit is in police custody. I can't come to the

Springs today. But as soon as Hart and I attain a confession and the police apprehend everyone involved, we will join you there, for the rest of the summer." Hart would murder her, she thought. But Julia would certainly give over.

And Julia took the bait. "It might not hurt for your father to see Hart attending you, Francesca, for then, he will surely see what I have seen—that he is smitten with you. Very well. Come as soon as you possibly can. I will leave town, knowing you are in good hands." She gave her a conspiratorial look.

Francesca kissed her cheek. "I am late. I must change. I will wire you when we know which day we are coming." And she flew up the stairs. "I love you!"

THE MOMENT SHE got into his coach, Francesca saw that Hart was brooding. Raoul closed the door and leaped into the driver's seat above them. She looked at him and said, "What is wrong?"

He eyed her. "Is your father prepared to murder me?"

Her eyes widened, afraid he was having doubts about their reconciliation. "He would like nothing more, Calder."

Hart looked grim. As the coach began to speed down Fifth Avenue, he stared out his window. Francesca said reluctantly, "I suppose I should have gone home last night."

"You fell asleep." He turned his black gaze on her. "You were exhausted, and not just from my lovemaking."

She colored slightly. "It was a difficult day." She thought about her confrontation with Bill Randall, which she hadn't mentioned yet. She was fairly certain Hart's dark mood had little to do with her father and everything to do with his brother's involvement in the theft of her portrait. He was surely still excoriating himself for his role in the portrait's theft.

"Why are you wincing?" he asked.

He did not miss a trick. She managed a light smile. "I told Julia that we would come to the Springs as soon as possible, and spend the summer with them."

Impossibly, his eyes darkened. "I am not spending the summer in Saratoga with your parents." He was final. "You're still wincing."

She bit her lip. "There is one small thing that I have failed to tell you."

His eyes widened and he shifted in his seat, to sit up straighter. "Oh ho. This will be arousing."

She inhaled. "Well, we are on our way to get a confession out of Bill."

"What haven't you told me, Francesca?" His tone was dangerous.

"When I got home yesterday afternoon, before I went to Siegel-Cooper, Bill confronted me in Papa's library." She kept her tone very calm.

He choked. "What happened?"

She reached for his hand but he pulled away. Grimly, she said, "He didn't admit anything." Actually, he had admitted to intending to destroy her and Hart, but she wasn't going to tell him that. "But he did know that I had been locked up."

"So do most of the newsmen in the city, as unsavory gossip spreads swiftly." Hart stared. "What aren't you telling me, Francesca?"

His words suddenly echoed. *You have destroyed my family.... Why would I steal a painting?*

"What happened?" Hart demanded.

"He assaulted me," she said quickly. "But I called for help and the staff heard, so in the end no harm was done."

Hart cursed.

"This is not your fault!" She seized his hand.

He flung her off. "He wants revenge against me, not you!"

"He wants revenge against us both!" she cried in return. Then she wished she hadn't spoken.

"Ah, so now we get to the truth." He stared out his window as they crossed town on Fourteenth Street. There was no traffic to speak of, except for one empty trolley. Francesca settled against the luxurious squabs grimly. "Francesca?"

She sighed. "Yes, he admitted that he wants to hurt us both."

Hart made a harsh sound.

When he did not speak, she finally said, "He must be our thief. Mary knew the portrait was a nude, so she has seen it. Mary must have been at the gallery earlier in the week, arguing with Moore—Marsha mentioned seeing a dark, angry woman there. He must be the thief, Calder."

Hart finally looked at her. "What about Rose? I do not believe in coincidence, not in a circumstance like this one."

"What is your point?"

"They are all involved." He was firm. "We simply do not have all the facts."

Was he right? Was Rose somehow involved? "It is odd that Rose knew about the portrait—although I don't think she knows it was a nude."

"Farr obviously told her about it, after it was stolen in April."

"No, Daisy told her that you had commissioned my portrait," Francesca corrected. "In February."

Hart straightened. "And how would Daisy know such a thing?"

They had turned onto Mulberry Street, which was almost as quiet as crosstown. Francesca stared. "You didn't tell Daisy that you had asked Sarah to paint my portrait?"

"I would never discuss such a thing with Daisy. Our affair was very brief and ended with my engagement to you."

Her gaze was riveted to his now. "The commission was common knowledge," she began.

"Daisy does not run in those circles. She would have never heard about the portrait."

As Raoul halted the carriage behind Bragg's black Daimler, Francesca and Hart stared at one another. "What are you saying?"

"For whatever reason, Rose is lying. Daisy did not tell her about the portrait because Daisy did not know about it—I am certain."

Francesca was aware that a clue was staring her in the face and she was missing it. "Rose has lied quite a bit," she said thoughtfully.

"Yes, she has," Hart said flatly. "We're here." But he did not move to get out of the coach.

He was deeply and quietly angry, she thought, but not with her—with himself. Would he always torture himself this way? "Hart," she murmured. She moved closer and kissed his cheek. "I love you so much. You are not to blame for your half brother's insanity."

His gaze met hers. "I suppose I must accept your faith."

"Yes, that is exactly what you must do."

His mouth softened. "You are a handful, Francesca."

She smiled a little, glad he was thawing. "The better to keep you on your toes," she teased.

He grudgingly smiled.

Raoul had opened the coach door and was waiting

there. As they alighted, Francesca glanced over her shoulder at the brownstone across the street. Sure enough, several newsmen were gathered there, never mind the holiday weekend. Kurland waved at her. She turned her back on him.

Hart guided her inside the lobby, muttering, "He needs to be taken care of, sooner rather than later."

"He is harmless," Francesca said.

"Really? So is paying him off."

They entered the cage. As it began to ascend, Francesca decided to argue the morality of bribery another time. She said, "We still don't know how Bill learned about my portrait."

"I am sure we are about to find out."

They lapsed into silence, each thinking their own thoughts. The cage settled with a bump against the third floor. Hart pulled open the iron door and they left the elevator and strode down the hall, past Bragg's office. Francesca hoped they hadn't missed Randall's confession, and her strides increased. Hart knocked once on the closed door to the interrogation room, and she stole a quick glance at him. He was simmering with anger now. Worry began. "We should let Bragg handle this," she whispered.

He gave her an incredulous look.

Bragg opened the door, stepping out of the room. He allowed them a glimpse inside before he closed the door behind him. Randall was seated at the long wooden table, his shirtsleeves rolled up, his appearance ravaged. Farr was present, standing, his expression rather smug. Inspector Newman and a roundsman completed the assembly.

"How is your arm?" Bragg asked her.

"Sore. Has he confessed?" Francesca asked quickly.

"No. He has a single refrain—that he does not know where the portrait is." Bragg stared at her before glancing briefly at Hart. "I brought Mary in yesterday afternoon after she tried to shoot you. She has said the same thing—neither will admit to stealing the portrait."

Francesca was in disbelief. "Well, has either one explained how Mary knew it was a nude? I do believe she has seen it!"

Bragg touched her arm to calm her. "We will get to the truth, Francesca."

"There are other charges we can press," she began, about to tell him about Bill's assault.

Hart interrupted. "Leave me alone with him."

"Absolutely not," Bragg said.

"You are a fool, a virtuous fool." Hart shoved open the door and strode in. Alarmed, Francesca followed with Bragg.

"Hello, little brother," Hart said coolly, approaching.

Randall leaped to his feet, his chair falling over. "Go to hell—and take her with you."

Hart never broke stride. "When I do, I am sure I'll meet you there."

"Hart, no," Francesca tried.

But she was too late. Hart slammed his fist into Bill's nose. Blood spurted. And neither Farr, Newman nor the police officer moved a muscle. Worried, Francesca glanced at Bragg. Although a muscle ticked in his jaw, he did not say a word.

Hart smiled coldly at Randall. "Did you take the portrait from Sarah's studio?"

Bill spit at him. "Don't you want to know!"

Hart took something out of his pocket. Francesca choked in horror at the sight of the derringer in Hart's hand. "Yes, I do."

Bill cried out as he was struck across the face with the gun.

Before Francesca could protest, Bragg had reached

Hart and Randall. But he didn't order Hart to cease. Bragg said, "You might want to reconsider, Randall. I have patience, but my brother does not."

Randall was breathing hard. "I told you—I do not know where the portrait is."

Hart seized his shoulder and pressed the tiny gun to his right temple. "You son of a bitch. Do you know your sister played Russian roulette with Francesca?" And he pulled the trigger.

Francesca almost screamed as a loud click sounded. Randall turned white, his knees buckling, but Bragg caught him, holding him up. Francesca was in disbelief. Bragg meant to aid Hart in torturing Randall for answers!

She glanced at Farr, who did not seem upset with the method of interrogation.

Hart smiled cruelly, the derringer still pressed into Randall's temple. "How does it feel to be on the verge of death?"

Randall cried out incoherently.

Sweat poured down Francesca's body. Hart was not a killer—or was he? He did know which chamber that bullet was in, didn't he?

I would kill to protect those I love.

He had been speaking about his foster sister, Lucy, at the time, but she would never forget his words—or the moment when he had spoken them. They had both known he had meant it. He was capable of murder if he had to protect a loved one.

Francesca glanced wildly at Bragg, hoping he would stop Hart. Bragg shook his head slightly at her. Did Bragg know Hart better than she did? He would never let Hart murder Bill Randall.

"Isn't this amusing?" Hart purred. "I would prefer everyone to leave the room, Rick. So there are no witnesses…just in case." He shoved his mouth against Bill's ear. "I want to kill you, you bastard. Give me the excuse."

Bill cried out, "Fuck you! I took the damn portrait—there—I have confessed! We have been planning revenge on you and that bitch ever since our father was murdered! I stole the portrait from Sarah Channing's studio! It was so easy to snoop around—I followed Francesca one day and discovered her posing nude." He laughed then, hard and wildly.

Hart pulled the trigger, Francesca screamed. But only a loud click sounded.

Sweat poured down Randall's face. "I watched, you fucker, I watched her posing, yes, I did!"

Francesca now realized that everyone in the room knew the truth about her portrait. She glanced at Farr wildly. Calmly, he returned her gaze. If he hadn't guessed the truth about her portrait, he knew it now. But he did not seem surprised.

Hart lifted the gun.

"Hart, stop!" Francesca screamed.

Instead of pulling the trigger, he struck Randall across the face with the barrel of the small gun. Randall crashed to the floor. Hart got on top of him and hit him again. "Where is it?"

"I don't know," Randall shouted, sobbing. "Someone else took it from the gallery Saturday night! But if I had it, I'd put it on display—after taking you for all the money I could!"

Hart jammed the gun into his ear. Francesca screamed, "Please don't! Hart!"

Hart growled, "Did you send Francesca that invitation, you bastard, to preview Sarah's works? Did you and Mary lock her in the gallery? Did you?" He jammed the gun harder into his ear.

"Yes, yes, yes!" Randall half screamed and half sobbed.

Hart went still, his gun still jammed inside the man's ear. And Francesca knew he was ready to kill him.

"He is telling us what he knows," she cried. "He is telling us the truth! Hart, stop!"

"You don't deserve a trial," Hart began coldly.

Randall sneered, tears streaming.

Bragg seized Hart's shoulder. "He doesn't know where the portrait is. And if he does, killing him won't help us find it."

Panting, Hart slowly looked up at Bragg. Then he flung the gun viciously across the room. He leaped up and strode out, not even glancing at her. His face was dark with rage.

A terrible silence fell.

The chief broke it. "Boss?" Farr asked pleasantly.

And she was even sicker. Farr had just learned the truth about her portrait. Francesca was rooted to the spot. And Bill did not know where it was....

"Let him go. No one saw anything that just happened." He looked at Randall. "There were five witnesses to your confession, Randall." Francesca realized he would pretend that Hart hadn't ever been in the room. "Newman will take your confession." He glanced at Farr. "Chief, I'll see Mary again. I think we can break her now."

Randall did not get up. He was crying like a child.

The chief grinned, already crossing the room. He glanced at Francesca. "Hope you find your portrait soon, Miz Cahill."

Their gazes met. His eyes were filled with mockery and laughter. She inhaled as he left.

Her mind raced, but her thoughts were uselessly jumbled. Farr hadn't batted an eye when he'd heard that her portrait was a nude, but then, he was a master at playing poker.... Had he known for some time? Or had he known since Saturday night? He had been racing them to be the first to discover it, hadn't he?

Her mind sped. Rose had lied when she had first asked her about the portrait, which made no sense—why not admit that she knew of it? Hart hadn't told Daisy about the portrait. And Rose had once entertained Chief Farr. For all she knew, she had been lying when she had said she no longer did.... And she had lied again when she had made her odd confession to Francesca about knowing there was a portrait all along, while never revealing if she knew it was a nude. Hadn't she said something about Francesca not deserving to be hurt?

Why would she say that, unless she had known the painting was a nude?

Lovers talked. Farr had been her lover last spring. He'd known the portrait was compromising—Sarah had told him. And Rose was a big, strong woman, capable of removing an oversize painting from the wall, all by herself....

"Bragg!" she cried.

CHAPTER TWENTY

Thursday, July 3, 1902
Noon

ROSE LET HERSELF into the beautiful old Georgian mansion that Hart had bought for Daisy last winter. She was tense as she entered the spacious, parquet-floored foyer. The moment she closed the front door, she became aware of the haunting silence in the house. A tear fell. She glanced at the stairs, feeling Daisy acutely, almost expecting her to appear.

But she'd never walk down the stairs again, because she was dead. Even though Hart hadn't murdered her, he had killed their love. She hated him!

She started for the gracious staircase, looking for the fresh white lilies on the pedestal table in the entry hall. Then she realized the table was vacant. But Daisy had always kept a vase of lilies there. They had been her favorite flower, her favorite scent.

She started up the stairs, sick with the heavy sense of loss. She glanced behind her, almost expecting Brendan Farr to enter the house. He was a sick pig, and he still liked meeting her there. He liked to fuck in Daisy's bedroom.

She had never refused him. How could she? She was a whore, he was a cop. He'd toss her in jail, then throw away the key and simply leave her there to rot and die. He'd been shoving himself at her when he'd told her that....

Filled with bile now—she could not understand how she continued to survive sexual relations with him—she increased her pace. She hated Chief Farr more than she hated Hart, and that said everything. One day, she meant to somehow turn the tables on him. One day, she meant to somehow screw him over. But then she'd probably wind up dead.

He was a scary, dangerous man—and he had it in for Francesca.

She couldn't imagine what Francesca had done to arouse his hatred.

She glanced downstairs again. The hall was empty, the front door closed. She reminded herself that Farr was busy today—he wouldn't bother her until late that evening.

To stop her disturbing thoughts, she focused on Daisy. She imagined being in her arms, laughing. She imagined strolling the Ladies' Mile together, browsing the storefronts, as they used to do. She imagined riding the carousel at Coney Island with her—they had only talked about it, but they had meant to go. She reached her bedroom door, smiling a little now and trying not to cry. She knew she would never get over Daisy's death. She had loved her that much.

Rose walked into the beautiful gold bedroom. The other day, she had wanted to tell Francesca the truth. Francesca was a kind person. Francesca had helped her and she had helped Daisy more than once. But she hadn't dared. And she had hated lying to her! Now, she slowly closed the bedroom door.

Biting her lip, she faced Francesca's portrait, which was propped up against one wall.

BRAGG PUSHED THE FRONT door open. "It isn't locked," he said.

They were about to enter the stately Georgian home

where Daisy had lived; Hart had bought the house for her when he had made her his mistress. Even though that affair had been short-lived, due to their sudden engagement, Hart had let Daisy continue to live there. She had been murdered in the study in the back.

Once, Hart had thought Rose vengeful enough to be their thief—and he had thought she would hide the portrait in Daisy's house. But Francesca knew that Rose hadn't known about the portrait until after its theft in late April. Daisy couldn't have told her; Daisy wouldn't have known. No, Rose had only learned about the nude portrait from Chief Farr, once he had begun to investigate its theft. Lovers talked. Of course they did. The only thing she didn't know was how Farr had learned of its existence—and theft—in the first place. But he despised her and he had been butting into her affairs and investigations for months now. She assumed he'd been snooping.

Francesca knew in her bones that Rose was involved. And if Rose had stolen the portrait from Gallery Moore, which is what she believed, what better place to hide it? Daisy's house was less than ten minutes away on foot. Of course, Rose couldn't have carried the portrait for ten entire minutes. But she could have hailed a cab.

But why was the front door open? "Are we alone?" she asked softly.

"Are you expecting company?" His smile was brief, but he pulled his pistol from his shoulder holster

Francesca had been very surprised to see him arm himself before leaving headquarters. Bragg almost never carried arms of any kind, but then, he could summon a police detail to accompany him anywhere, if necessary. Bragg meant to protect her, of course. No one else must see the portrait.

Before she could admit that she did not know what to expect, a floorboard creaked. The sound came from the staircase. She and Bragg froze, still on the threshold, the front door open, staring at the staircase, which faced them.

A moment later Rose appeared on the stairs. She saw them and stumbled, one hand on the railing, her expression shocked.

The shock turned to fear.

Francesca thought she would try to flee. "Rose, wait!" she cried.

Rose glanced wildly around, as if trying to decide how to escape. Realizing that they barred her way out the front of the house, and that Bragg would obviously catch her if she tried to run out the back, she sagged against the banister. "Are you looking for me? I haven't done anything!"

Bragg strode to her. "We are looking for the portrait, Rose. But you already know that, don't you?"

Tears filled her eyes. She turned to look at Francesca. "I am sorry."

She had been right? "You took it?"

Rose inhaled. She looked back and forth between them, her visage pale. "Where is Farr?" she asked hoarsely.

It took Francesca one second to realize what she meant. "Farr took it?" she cried in disbelief. The anger began, and it was fierce.

Fear followed. What had he meant to do with it?

Rose began to cry. "He will kill me."

"He won't hurt you, Rose," Bragg said firmly. "Did you take the portrait from Gallery Moore on Saturday?"

"No," she whispered. Then she looked at Francesca. "I'm sorry. I lied. Daisy didn't tell me about it…Farr did. He showed me the portrait on Tuesday when…when we met. I lied about that, too. I still see him. He was gloating…he was so pleased…so smug.… He hates you!"

She had been mistaken. Rose hadn't known about the

portrait until last Tuesday. Farr had taken the portrait on Saturday, somehow, without the police knowing—unless they were all as terrified of him as Rose was.

Had he sent her the blackmail note? she wondered. Francesca asked hoarsely, sickened, "Where is it?"

"Upstairs." Then she cried, "Does he have to know that I told you? Can't you claim you found it by yourself? Please!"

Francesca looked at Bragg. "We need to protect her."

"I agree."

Francesca was surprised. How could he press charges against Farr without Rose's statement?

"You can't protect me! Even if you lock him up, he will get to me!" Tears fell. "I will have to leave the city!"

She was probably right, Francesca thought. Francesca exchanged a grim glance with Bragg. She imagined Farr capable of violence, especially against a prostitute. "If you decide to leave the city, I will help you," Francesca said.

Rose seemed ready to faint with relief. "How can you still be kind to me?"

"It is her nature," Bragg said. "I am going to need a statement from you, Rose, but it will be unofficial, for my eyes only." When she nodded, he gestured at the stairs. "Please, go up."

Rose turned and led them up the stairs. Francesca followed, Bragg behind her. Her heart began to pound. Rose paused on the second floor, her expression taut. "It's in there."

But Francesca didn't need Rose's comment to know that. The door to a beautiful gold bedroom was wide open. A canopied bed faced the hall. Her portrait was propped up on one wall, clearly visible from the hall and even the top of the stairs.

She felt sick as she went forward. It was as if someone had punched her in the abdomen. Farr had seen it.

Behind her, she heard Bragg make a harsh, surprised sound.

And suddenly she realized that he had never seen the portrait.

She had been in his arms, long ago, with half her clothing gone, but this was entirely different. She was provocatively posed on that canvas, and her expression had been meant for Hart, and Hart alone.

Her cheeks flamed. She faltered, not knowing where to go.

"It is beautiful," Rose said, breaking the awkward silence.

Francesca bit her lip, daring to turn and glance at him.

Bragg immediately jerked his gaze from the canvas. He avoided her eyes. She watched him as he walked over to the bed, ripped the covers off and draped a gold sheet over the painting. Finally, Francesca breathed.

He slowly turned.

She wondered what he was thinking. He was undoubtedly in disbelief that she had ever posed in such a manner. She cleared her throat. "What will you do about Farr?"

He finally looked at her. "Francesca, we need to keep this quiet. I can't press charges, unless you wish for me to confiscate your portrait as evidence. It will wind up in court. I can't open an internal investigation—not without keeping that portrait in my custody and allowing the investigators to see it."

The portrait somehow loomed between them, even now, when it was covered and behind Bragg. It was a moment before she could respond. "What about his men? They obviously know he took a painting. Is it possible no one else saw it?"

He shifted, still uncomfortable. "I imagine they are afraid of him. They knew what he did, but mean to keep silent. Farr would never let anyone glimpse something so potentially useful to him."

"Can you fire the chief?" But even as she spoke, she knew he could not. Farr could spread the rumor that a nude portrait of Francesca existed. That gossip would shock her mother and scandalize society—even if no one ever saw her portrait, even if the rumor was not confirmed. "We are being held hostage by that man," Francesca whispered.

"Yes, we are," Bragg agreed. "But there is something to be said for the adage, keep your friends close, and your enemies closer."

She stared. He stared back. His color remained high. She knew hers did, too. "Are you going to ask me why I did it?"

"No." He was final.

And for once in her life, Francesca did not pursue a subject.

THE HOUSE WAS VACANT. He had let all the staff off for the evening.

Hart clutched his whiskey and stared at the Matisse hanging over the fireplace in his library. But he did not see the spires of Notre-Dame. Francesca's golden image haunted him, her blue eyes filled with worry. Then he saw his half brother, sneering at him just before he'd pulled the trigger of the gun.

He had wanted to murder his own half brother. He truly wouldn't have cared if there had been a bullet in that chamber.

Hart! Don't!

But Francesca would have cared. Because she admired him, because she thought him noble, because she did not believe him capable of cold-blooded murder. Francesca—the best thing that had ever happened to him.

Their estrangement was for the best, he thought savagely. And the glass shattered in his hand.

He glanced down at his hand, unperturbed by the broken glass he held or the scotch streaming over his skin. It burned. He welcomed the sensation. It might distract him from the burning in his chest.

Francesca was good and golden, he was dark and without morals. Her conscience was pure, his was littered with the unspeakable actions of his past. She deserved Rick—he believed it! What she did not deserve was a lifetime shackled to him, with the monsters of his past always arising to haunt them.

Hart released his fist and let the broken glass fall to the rug at his feet. Were Francesca and Rick even now hot on the trail of the goddamn portrait? Had they already recovered it? Were they joyously together, thrilled with the recovery? Were they in one another's arms?

Have supper with me this weekend.

He heard his brother's voice so clearly in his mind, and he recalled Francesca's surprised silence—and the fact that she hadn't refused him. He imagined them dining in a private room at the Plaza, Francesca in her daring red gown, Rick in his tuxedo, a white-coated waiter hovering over them, pouring the finest wine.

They were perfect for one another!

And he cursed. Because he was a selfish bastard to the very core…

"Hart?"

He had been expecting her. Of course he had. Her tone was strained with worry. Feeling very predatory now, he turned. He did not smile.

She was very worried. "You let the staff go."

He felt his mouth curl. "Yes, I did."

She started forward. "Are you all right?"

"Why wouldn't I be fine?" he asked very calmly, when he wasn't calm at all. He felt like smashing something—preferably Rick's nose. And then he realized it wasn't Rick he wished to beat up; he wished to beat himself up.

"What happened?" she cried, rushing forward and taking his wet, cut hand.

"I broke a glass."

She looked into his eyes, her gaze filled with moisture. "Why are you torturing yourself? We have the portrait, Hart. It is over."

"I take it you didn't notice that I wished to murder my brother? And that I almost did so."

She paled. "But you didn't, Hart. You would never murder anyone in a fit of fury. I am certain."

He took her hands and removed them from his wrist, but he clasped them firmly. "Then you do not know me at all."

"No. I know you better than you know yourself!" she cried.

He felt something in him soften. But he did not want to soften. "Where is the portrait?"

She tensed. "It is in the front hall."

He debated how he would destroy it—perhaps with a knife.

"Stop blaming yourself. Please! We have the portrait. This crisis is over. Farr stole it from the gallery on Saturday night, intending one day to use it against Bragg or myself. For the sake of secrecy, we can't lay charges against him."

"We." It wasn't a question.

"You are the one I love, Calder."

"Perhaps. Or perhaps you will think about the fact that I held a gun to Randall's head today, not knowing which chamber the bullet was in, and that I pulled that trigger two times."

"I think you need me tonight."

He caught her chin. "Are you dining with Rick this weekend?"

She inhaled. "I haven't even thought about it!"

The jealousy, always simmering, burst into an inferno. "You are selfless," he said, "and I am a selfish bastard— who cannot give you up."

She cried out.

"Elope with me, Francesca...tonight."

THE MOMENT BRAGG walked through the door of his home, he saw Leigh Anne. Their luggage was lined up by the door and she sat in her wheeled chair in the front hall, dressed for travel. Her face was tight with tension and disapproval. It was almost four in the afternoon, and their train left at five. "We will miss the train, Rick," she said, her tone terribly calm. "You must rush."

He closed the door and became still, staring at her. His chest had been aching all day; it ached even more now. The comprehension he had had earlier was even more searing. His marriage had been over before it had even begun. He would provide for her and the girls until the end of his days. But there would never be a warm, loving relationship with Leigh Anne; he would never have a warm, loving family; and he would never be free to pursue a real relationship with the woman he truly loved.

But the one thing he would not do was go to Sag Harbor with her now. It would be hell and they both knew it. His decision was made. She could take the girls herself, with Peter and Mrs. Flowers. He would stay in the city and work. There was so much paperwork to take care of; he had Randall in custody and charges were pending.

"I am sorry to have held you up, but we must have a private discussion."

"Now?" She was incredulous.

"I am afraid so."

"We will miss the train and it is the last one today!"

Did she know that he wouldn't go with her and the girls? He wondered if he would always feel this acute sense of loss, which was so odd, as he hadn't ever had anything genuine to lose.

Before he could answer her, Katie came rushing down the stairs, Dot stumbling after her. She smiled at him anxiously. "Are we leaving?"

"Not yet—I need a word with your mother." It even hurt to utter those two words. He reached past her to catch Dot, swinging her into his arms before she fell. Then he slid his arm around Katie. "You were sleeping this morning when I came in," he told her.

"That's all right. Are we going? Will we miss our train?" Her dark eyes were huge with trepidation and excitement.

"Sag, Sag!" Dot shouted gleefully.

Bragg held her harder and kissed her; she squealed. At least one member of the household was genuinely happy, he thought.

He had to do what was right for everyone. Katie looked back and forth between them even more anxiously. He smiled at her as he set Dot down. "Can you take Dot into the kitchen for a last glass of milk?" When she and her sister were gone, he looked at his wife.

Her expression was deadpan. "What is this about, Rick?"

He hesitated. "I think you know as well as I do that it would be impossible for us to share a small cottage together for an entire weekend."

She sat up straighter. She finally said, "It would be difficult."

His heart pained him again. "Can we have one honest conversation?"

She nodded.

"I don't think it fair to the girls to see us in such a state of discord. I obviously make you unhappy. It is better if I stay here in the city. I always have work to attend."

Relief flickered in her eyes. "Katie hates the tension, Rick. You're right, it isn't fair to them—or us." She gripped the arms of her chair tightly.

"So you agree it is best if you go alone with the girls."

"Yes."

That one word spoke volumes. She was desperate to get away from him, but he felt the same way now. Relief warred with sorrow and regret. "I will take you to the station."

"Peter can take us—"

"No, I will take you. I wish to say goodbye to the girls. I will miss them, and I want to reassure them that nothing will change when they return—I will be here, waiting for them."

She nodded. "The girls adore you. They will miss you, too. Yes, you must reassure them."

It was truly over, he thought. Somehow, without ever saying so, they had both agreed to that. "How can we possibly navigate such a marriage, Leigh Anne?"

"I don't know," she said, finally looking him in the eye. "Maybe you should consider a divorce—or perhaps a separation."

Suddenly there was hope. He detested their living arrangements. They had been separated before. He could still take care of them, but he wouldn't be an intruder in his own home. "I would never give you a divorce. It would be morally reprehensible," he said slowly.

She looked aside. "But you will think about a separation—with separate residences?"

He inhaled. What she wanted was so painfully clear. But perhaps this was the only viable solution. "Yes, I will think about it."

She trembled. "I have an idea. It is not a permanent solution, but one that might suit for now. Will you let me and the girls spend the summer in the Sag Harbor cottage? They will love the beach and the bay—the city is stifling in the summer—and we will not be in your way. There will be no discord for poor Katie to witness, and I will not be an albatross hanging about your neck." She added, "It is only two months. Many couples vacation separately in the summer, and that will give you time to consider a separation."

He was shocked by the suggestion, yet his mind came to life. Many couples did spend the summers apart—married couples like him and Leigh Anne, who had no desire to be together except in name. And it would give them both a sorely needed respite from the divisiveness that had afflicted their lives. He began to realize that he liked the idea, even if his life loomed before him, dark and gray, like an endless, shadowy tunnel.

"Rick?"

He focused with an effort. He did have light in his life, even if he had to remind himself of it. He had his profession, his ambition, the many causes of reform and his dear friend Francesca. "I will arrange it," he said.

INSTEAD OF ALLOWING HER to descend from his coach, he swept her into his arms. "What are you doing?" Francesca cried.

"I am carrying you across the threshold of our house,"

Hart said calmly. But his eyes were gleaming and the barest smile was on his handsome face.

She met his dark, intense gaze and her heart soared. They were man and wife.

Do you, Francesca Cahill, take this man to be your husband? In sickness and in health, for better or for worse, till death do you part?

I do.

Still dressed in her navy blue suit, which she had worn all day, she had been trembling so badly that Hart had caught her arm to steady her. It was as if Judge O'Brien and his wife did not exist. Only the two of them stood there in his small parlor. She had seen such heat in his eyes.... But she had also seen love, and it had been fierce.

Do you, Calder Hart, take this woman to be your wife? In sickness and in health, for better or for worse, till death do you part?

I do.

Francesca could not look away from Hart now. The judge was prompting Calder for a ring. She had a moment of sheer, insane, irrational terror—they didn't have a ring! Would their ceremony become null and void without one? But then Hart had pulled her wedding ring from his breast pocket, and she had watched him sliding the gold band onto her finger, afraid she was dreaming....

"By the powers vested in me by the state of New York, I now pronounce you man and wife. You may kiss the bride."

And Hart had pulled her close and they had kissed deeply. When she looked at him afterward, she knew he was as stunned as she was....

"You don't have to carry me over the threshold," Francesca cried now, baldly lying. "That is such a silly tradition!"

"Spoken like a true bohemian," Hart murmured, striding up the front steps of the house. He somehow maneuvered the door open without dropping her. "I am carrying you over our threshold, Francesca."

Their gazes locked as he stepped inside. Francesca clung to his strong shoulders, absolutely breathless now. "We are married."

"We most certainly are." His gaze began a thorough inventory of her features, and her body tightened impossibly. She could barely speak. Dear God, they had eloped!

The fact that it was their wedding night raced through her head. "Julia will murder us both as soon as she hears of this!" she managed to say.

He began to smile, striding swiftly across the entrance hall past her portrait, which was propped up against one wall, its back facing out. The gold sheet still covered it. "She will undoubtedly be shocked, but angry? She will begin to plan our reception within two minutes. Care to wager?"

She laughed as he bounded up the stairs. Hart was right. Julia would be thrilled, once the surprise wore off. She would hold a huge reception in the fall. Then she sobered. Andrew was another matter. But he could not reverse something that was a fait accompli, and she would worry about cajoling and consoling him later.

Her heart skipped several beats as Hart reached the next landing. She had been waiting forever for this moment. She slipped her fingers into the V of his shirt, over his velvety skin. He smiled slowly at her. Her heart lurched wildly. There was no mistaking the promise in his eyes.

The intensity of her desire for him made her feel faint. "Hart."

He wasn't smiling now as he entered the master suite,

crossed the sitting room and approached his massive, canopied bed. "I am in complete agreement." His tone was thick.

He laid her down, sitting beside her. Instead of reaching for the buttons on her blouse, his palm cupped her cheek. His eyes shimmered. "I want to make you happy, Francesca."

She knew he did not refer to their lovemaking now. She went still, and then her heart exploded with joy and desire. She loved him so much! "You will."

"Will I?"

She lifted herself on her elbows and kissed his mouth, not once but several times, softly. "We are human. There will be good times and bad times, but our love will endure."

He took her shoulders and pushed her back onto the pillows. "You are a hopeless romantic, and I am a complete cynic. We are quite the couple." He began unbuttoning her blouse. "Have I ever told you that you light up my dreary life?" He pulled open her shirt.

"Yes," she managed to say as he ripped her chemise in two. "Another one?"

He did not answer, pulling her corset down and feathering her nipples with his tongue. Then he lifted his face and stared.

She touched his rough cheek, realizing she was starting to cry. "I will always brighten your life, Hart, even when you insist it is a black hole."

"Yes, Francesca, and only you are capable of such a feat," he said.

She inhaled. His words meant everything to her.

He stood, ripping off his jacket and then his shirt, tossing both aside. Francesca felt her heart lurch with dizzying force. He reached for his trousers and quickly divested himself of the rest of his clothes. She could not breathe. Hart was the most magnificent man she had ever seen; he was six feet of packed male muscle, and just then, he was entirely aroused. "You are so beautiful," she said.

"No, Francesca, you are the beautiful one, inside and out." He sat as she lifted her hair, shifting her back toward him. He began unlacing her corset. As he did so, his mouth strayed over her shoulders, her arms, the sides of her breasts. It became harder and harder to breathe. His hands moved to the buttons on the waistband of her skirt. As the fabric pooled around her hips and thighs, he slid her drawers lower. From behind, she felt him nuzzle her right hip. He rained soft kisses across the swell of her buttocks. She finally cried out. "Hart, I am going to die."

There was amusement in his tone as his hands closed possessively over each hip. "Yes, you will, and many times, I believe."

She was about to demand that he stop his seduction— she was ready now!—when he turned her around, laid her down and pulled her skirt down her legs. He tossed it aside and gave her a searing look. But there was more, and she did not know why he paused, staring as if embattled.

"Hart?" She inhaled, reaching for him.

He shook his head abruptly, his face odd, and suddenly he moved over her. "I am going to make love to you, Francesca." He kissed her throat. "I have never made love to anyone before."

She cried out and their mouths met. His hard thighs moved hers apart. She touched him everywhere as he ran his strong hands up and down her body. His mouth found her waist. His hands moved between her legs. She caressed his slick, long length, whimpering. His breathing was heavy—so was hers.

Then his powerful arms went around her and he settled against her and she choked against his collarbone. "Hart, please."

"I love you," he said, looking at her.

Tears blurred her vision, but she saw the strain on his face, and then his massive length was moving slowly inside her. The pleasure was shocking. The love was so strong that it hurt. Hart was hers now, she somehow thought, hers now and forever.

Not taking his gaze from hers, they became entirely joined. Francesca gasped helplessly, holding on to him, hard. And Hart said, finally, "You are my beacon, Francesca—always."

He began to move, and she wept.

FRANCESCA AWOKE deliciously. Her entire body throbbed sensually and pleasantly, everywhere. Then she became aware of Hart behind her, in a rather manly state, his arms around her. He kissed her ear. "It's the middle of the night, darling."

Her heart turned over, hard, as complete recollection came. She turned to face him, grinning. "We are married, Calder! You are my husband, and no one can do anything about it."

He smiled affectionately at her. "You looked very pleased, Francesca. Hmm...I wonder why."

Ha, she thought, thinking about the several times Hart had made love to her. She wasn't a virgin now—and his lovemaking had been worth waiting for. She slid her nails over his hard chest and watched him inhale. She grinned again. "I am very pleased, Hart. I believe I learned a trick or two last night."

His gaze was smoldering as he watched her toy with his chest. "I do believe I once promised you an education."

"You most certainly did," she murmured, kissing one very erect nipple. "Oh, Calder, impossibly, I want you again."

"I have created a monster," he said, but within moments, he was sliding deeply into her, and soon they were both riding that wonderful wave of ecstasy again.

Afterward, Francesca took him into her arms.

"What are you doing?" he demanded.

"I am holding you, silly man."

He gave her an odd look. "I am hardly a child, Francesca."

"As if I would ever think that!" She kissed the top of his head, then saw the portrait, propped up against the wall. The gold sheet Bragg had used to cover it with remained partially across the canvas. She sat up. "You brought it upstairs."

He sat, as well. "After you fell asleep, I went and retrieved it. I realized we might be very busy in the morning when the staff returns." He hesitated, his gaze on the painting. "It is very beautiful. Sarah caught your likeness exactly."

He did not want to destroy it, she thought. She suddenly tossed the covers aside and got up.

"What are you doing?"

Francesca smiled at him and walked across the bedroom, not bothering to take the sheet with her.

"Oh, I do like this," Hart said. "A modest wife!"

She laughed, whipping the rest of the sheet from the painting, aware of how appreciative his gaze was—and it was not on the portrait now. "Do I really look like that when we are together and about to make love?"

"Yes, you do," he said rather roughly. "But you are even more beautiful and desirable in the flesh."

Francesca trembled at his thick tone. She turned and saw him stand, but he went to the other side of the room and donned a silk dressing gown, casually belting it. She shivered, aware of being cold. "Are you being a gentleman, Hart?"

"Yes, I am—and I want to fetch us a bottle of champagne. I am not in the habit of racing around this house without my clothes. And, Francesca, I know you are very immodest and I may have created a monster, but you are not racing about in a state of dishabille, either. Rourke remains in residence."

She smiled as he returned to her and placed a paisley smoking jacket over her shoulders. She slipped her arms into the sleeves and saw his eyes darken. She instantly understood why. The jacket just reached her thighs.

"Sara should paint you like this," he said harshly.

"Hart!" she cried, but she liked the idea, oh, yes!

"I was in jest." He pulled her close and held her, just for a moment, hard. Francesca was surprised by the open display of hungry affection. Then he let her go, smiling, and as one, they both glanced at the portrait.

"It doesn't have to be destroyed," Francesca said.

He lifted a brow.

"I know you don't want to destroy it." She took his hand.

He sighed. "Do you already know me so well? No, I hate the idea of destroying it. One day, when I am old and gray, I will admire that portrait—recalling how we met and how we somehow managed, in spite of it all."

"You are a romantic, Hart!" she cried, smiling.

He squeezed her hand. "That is nonsense and you know it." He turned to gaze at her portrait again, and so did she.

"If we do not destroy it, I will have to keep it in my private gallery, under lock and key." Then he turned seriously to her. "I will do whatever you want, Francesca."

She didn't hesitate. She moved into the circle of his arms. "I want you to look at the portrait one day, when we are both old and gray, and reminisce about this time in our lives. And you will think about how we first met, and the crimes we solved, and how I jilted you at the altar! You will recall the night that we eloped. And you will remember the good times and the bad, and how our love grew stronger and stronger each and every day. And as you do so, Calder, our grandchildren will be racing about these halls, which will be filled with love and laughter, not demons from the past!" She smiled up at him. "I am your beacon, remember? I do not want the portrait destroyed."

His gaze had become moist. He blinked and it was a moment before he spoke. "Only you, Francesca."

She kissed his silk-clad chest. "Only me, Calder. Only me."

* * * * *

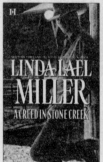 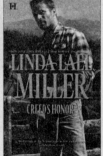 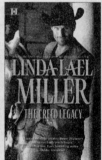

PRESENTING...THE SEVENTH ANNUAL
MORE THAN WORDS™ ANTHOLOGY

Five bestselling authors
Five real-life heroines

This year's Harlequin
More Than Words award
recipients have changed lives,
one good deed at a time. To
celebrate these real-life heroines,
some of Harlequin's most
acclaimed authors have honored
the winners by writing stories
inspired by these dedicated
women. Within the pages
of *More Than Words Volume 7*,
you will find novellas written
by Carly Phillips, Donna Hill
and Jill Shalvis—and online at
www.HarlequinMoreThanWords.com
you can also access stories by
Pamela Morsi and Meryl Sawyer.

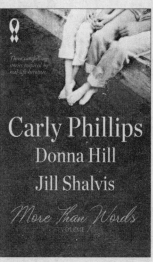

Coming soon in print and online!

Visit
www.HarlequinMoreThanWords.com
to access your FREE ebooks and to nominate
a real-life heroine in your community.

Proceeds from the sale of this book will be
reinvested in Harlequin's charitable initiatives.

REQUEST YOUR FREE BOOKS!

2 FREE NOVELS
FROM THE SUSPENSE COLLECTION
PLUS 2 FREE GIFTS!

YES! Please send me 2 FREE novels from the Suspense Collection and my 2 FREE gifts (gifts are worth about $10). After receiving them, if I don't wish to receive any more books, I can return the shipping statement marked "cancel." If I don't cancel, I will receive 4 brand-new novels every month and be billed just $5.74 per book in the U.S. or $6.24 per book in Canada. That's a saving of at least 28% off the cover price. It's quite a bargain! Shipping and handling is just 50¢ per book in the U.S. and 75¢ per book in Canada.* I understand that accepting the 2 free books and gifts places me under no obligation to buy anything. I can always return a shipment and cancel at any time. Even if I never buy another book, the two free books and gifts are mine to keep forever.

191/391 MDN FDDH

Name _____ (PLEASE PRINT) _____

Address _____ Apt. # _____

City _____ State/Prov. _____ Zip/Postal Code _____

Signature (if under 18, a parent or guardian must sign)

Mail to the **Reader Service:**
IN U.S.A.: P.O. Box 1867, Buffalo, NY 14240-1867
IN CANADA: P.O. Box 609, Fort Erie, Ontario L2A 5X3

Not valid for current subscribers to the Suspense Collection
or the Romance/Suspense Collection.

Want to try two free books from another line?
Call 1-800-873-8635 or visit www.ReaderService.com.

* Terms and prices subject to change without notice. Prices do not include applicable taxes. Sales tax applicable in N.Y. Canadian residents will be charged applicable taxes. Offer not valid in Quebec. This offer is limited to one order per household. All orders subject to credit approval. Credit or debit balances in a customer's account(s) may be offset by any other outstanding balance owed by or to the customer. Please allow 4 to 6 weeks for delivery. Offer available while quantities last.

Your Privacy---The Reader Service is committed to protecting your privacy. Our Privacy Policy is available online at www.ReaderService.com or upon request from the Reader Service.

We make a portion of our mailing list available to reputable third parties that offer products we believe may interest you. If you prefer that we not exchange your name with third parties, or if you wish to clarify or modify your communication preferences, please visit us at www.ReaderService.com/consumerschoice or write to us at Reader Service Preference Service, P.O. Box 9062, Buffalo, NY 14269. Include your complete name and address.

MSUS11

BRENDA JOYCE

77547	DEADLY KISSES	___ $7.99 U.S.	___ $9.99 CAN.
77541	DEADLY ILLUSIONS	___ $7.99 U.S.	___ $9.99 CAN.
77507	THE MASQUERADE	___ $7.99 U.S.	___ $9.99 CAN.
77460	AN IMPOSSIBLE ATTRACTION	___ $7.99 U.S.	___ $9.99 CAN.
77442	THE PROMISE	___ $7.99 U.S.	___ $9.99 CAN.
77275	A DANGEROUS LOVE	___ $7.99 U.S.	___ $7.99 CAN.
77244	THE PERFECT BRIDE	___ $7.99 U.S.	___ $9.50 CAN.

(limited quantities available)

TOTAL AMOUNT	$ _____
POSTAGE & HANDLING	$ _____
($1.00 FOR 1 BOOK, 50¢ for each additional)	
APPLICABLE TAXES*	$ _____
TOTAL PAYABLE	$ _____

(check or money order—please do not send cash)

To order, complete this form and send it, along with a check or money order for the total above, payable to HQN Books, to: **In the U.S.:** 3010 Walden Avenue, P.O. Box 9077, Buffalo, NY 14269-9077; **In Canada:** P.O. Box 636, Fort Erie, Ontario, L2A 5X3.

Name: _____
Address: _____ City: _____
State/Prov.: _____ Zip/Postal Code: _____
Account Number (if applicable): _____

075 CSAS

*New York residents remit applicable sales taxes.
*Canadian residents remit applicable GST and provincial taxes.

✦HQN™

We *are* romance™

www.HQNBooks.com

PHBJ0311BL